Joseph F. Hess

**Out of Darkness into Light. An Autobiography of Joseph F. Hess**

The Converted Prize-Fighter and Saloon-Keeper

Joseph F. Hess

**Out of Darkness into Light. An Autobiography of Joseph F. Hess**
*The Converted Prize-Fighter and Saloon-Keeper*

ISBN/EAN: 9783337136642

Printed in Europe, USA, Canada, Australia, Japan

Cover: Foto ©Raphael Reischuk / pixelio.de

More available books at **www.hansebooks.com**

# OUT OF DARKNESS INTO LIGHT.

## An Autobiography

OF

# JOSEPH F. HESS,

## THE CONVERTED PRIZE-FIGHTER AND SALOON-KEEPER.

---

### INTRODUCTION

BY

## P. A. BURDICK, EVANGELIST,

AT WHOSE MEETINGS, IN THE CITY OF ROCHESTER, N. Y., HESS WAS
TOUCHED BY THE SPIRIT OF THE LORD.

---

*Before his conversion, Hess travelled in nearly all parts of the world, and the story
of these travels and the life he led are more thrilling than the page of
fiction. The story of his conversion, nearly five years since, and
the narration of his work for the Master since that date,
prove an epoch in the history of evangelistic
action and literature.*

---

## ILLUSTRATED.

Toronto:
THE PEOPLE'S PUBLISHING CO., YONGE ST. ARCADE.
1890.

THIS BOOK

IS LOVINGLY DEDICATED

TO MY DEAR WIFE AND CHILDREN,

WHO WERE FOR SO MANY YEARS DEPRIVED OF THE LOVE AND PROTECTION

THAT SHOULD HAVE BEEN GIVEN BY HUSBAND

AND FATHER.

*To-day all made happy in the love of Christ, who forgives every sin.*

# INTRODUCTION.

IN September, 1885, I had the pleasure of conducting a series of Gospel Temperance Meetings in the city of Rochester, N. Y. under the auspices of the W. C. T. U. of that city. The meetings, after the first week, were held in the Fitzhugh Skating Rink. One evening, the last week in September, I noticed four men enter the rink very much under the influence of liquor, and take seats near the door. While speaking it was noticeable they were quite uneasy, one of them undertaking to arise several times, but being restrained by his companions. At the close of the address they arose and went out, no one dreaming, as they walked out of the rink, that the spirit of the Lord had troubled one soul. Just one week from that night I noticed standing by the door a powerfully-built man, with his arms folded across his breast, and earnestly listening to the address. After I had closed my address he walked up to the platform and said, " When can I see you alone ?' My reply was, " Call at the Lister House to-morrow morning at 9 o'clock." He called the next morning and he made known to me the fact that he was Joe Hess the prize-fighter. During the hour's interview I was impressed with his honesty, in the desire to lead a better life.

He realized the absolute necessity of leaving his old companions. As he expressed it, " I never knew until I heard you talk I could be anything but a brute.  I want to be a man, I can never do that and keep with the gang of men I have always been with."  He seemed ready to do any kind of work to earn money for himself and family. During our conversation I said, " Mr Hess, what can you do ?" " What can 1 do," he replied, with tears in his eyes, " nothing that is honorable, but if you can get me a job of sweeping mud from the side walks I will gladly accept it."  From that moment I believed in him, never for a moment doubting his honesty of purpose.  That night he took the pledge, and within the week he found for-giveness for sins past, and promises for future blessings. With the light of God, and love for Christ in his heart, came the desire to undo the wrong he had done.  Un-learned in books, ignorant of social customs, he deter-mined to prepare himself for temperance work and tell the story of what Christ had done for him.

Under discouragements that would have caused many strong hearts to give up, he pushed his way.  He believed God would bless him and Christ would give him the victory.  Who can doubt this after nearly five years of labor for humanity and God ? His work has been most abundantly blessed.  Manhood lost has been restored. Homes, made hells by drink, have been made ante-rooms to heaven by his influence.  Hopeless and despairing souls have been made happy in the power of Christ to save, he pointing to them the way of life.  May God ever keep and bless him in his work of love and salvation.

P. A. BURDICK.

# PREFACE.

I SHALL attempt in this volume to tell the story of my life, which from boyhood days up to five years since was one of much sinning. I do not do so prompted by feelings of egotism, but from a prayerful and earnest belief that some who are now in sin and darkness, who are slaves to appetite and passion, may profit by my sad and bitter experience, and thereby be led to acknowledge Christ, and ever look to Him as the one who is abundantly able and who is ever willing to save for time and eternity.

I also hope that many young men who have not yet taken their first downward step, may take warning from this story of what was for many years a ruined, but which is now by the Grace of God, a redeemed life.

My feelings are those of humiliation and remorse, as I refer to my past life. I feel that God has forgiven my sins, but I know I have much to do by way of reparation; and now that I am clothed in my right mind, my daily prayer is, that the remainder of my life may be entirely consecrated to God's service, and that my evil deeds may be blotted out by good works.

Very truly yours,

J. F. HESS.

# LIFE

## OF

# JOE HESS.

## CHAPTER I.

Birth—Parents—Schooldays—At work—First use of tobacco—
Running away from home—Return Home—Father's advice—
Evil companions—First glass of liquor—Losing employer's con-
fidence—Shipwrecked—Learns the manly art—In Prison—
Delirium Tremens.

ON the sixteenth day of July, eighteen hundred and fifty-
one, I was born at Buffalo, N. Y., being the fourth
of a family of twelve children, composed of six boys and
six girls. My parents came to the United States from
Bavaria, in the year eighteen hundred and forty-seven,
locating upon what is now Pine-street, in the City of
Buffalo. Father, being a tailor by trade, and a good
workman, was not long without receiving employment,
also being a musician he secured the position of second
violinist in St. Mary's Church, a small brick building, at
the corner of Pine and Batavia (now Broadway) street.
As a result of integrity and industry, my father prospered and was soon able to purchase a lot on Adams-
street, upon which he built a small house. It was in
this house that I first saw the light, and entered upon a
life which, I think, my reader, you will agree with me,
has been in many ways a most remarkable one.

My parents, who were Roman Catholics, compelled me to attend a German Roman Catholic School, for a short period ; my education is therefore limited, and is from observation and experience rather than the study of books. Having been blessed with a good constitution and an almost unlimited amount of physical strength, I was able when quite a young boy to earn good wages. My first experience at hiring out was in the year eighteen hundred and sixty-two, when I engaged to work at Smith's brick yard, then situated on Clinton-street, in Buffalo, receiving one dollar and a quarter per day—good wages for a lad only eleven years of age. It was while employed here that I first learned to chew tobacco, believing, as many boys do to-day, that this filthy habit is an atribute of manhood. It is unnecessary for me to relate the consequences resulting from this first attempt ; all those who have *been there* understand them only too well, and those who have had good sense and decency enough to abstain from this disgusting habit would not be edified by a description of them ; suffice it to say, if one can imagine the very worst sensations of all other sicknesses combined in one, then but a faint idea of my first experience with tobaaco is obtained.

During this same year I left home for the purpose of learning the blacksmithing trade, but was finally persuaded by my father to return, as he was about to go to farming and would consequently need my assistance. The first winter I was employed in hauling wood to the city, and always having been blessed with a good appetite, I discovered one day where I could procure some sweet buns that were just to my taste, so much so, in fact, that I found my limited capital insufficient to furnish a supply equal to the demand ; consequently I opened a running account for buns in father's name, making him not only a silent but an innocent partner in the transaction. Finnally. however, when the account was rendered, the silent partner became the most active, in fact, so active did he become that I deemed it advisable to dissolve the partnership by leaving home, which I did without consulting with, or securing the consent of anyone. I came to Buffalo and shipped as a deck-hand on the propellor Burlington; upon our arrival at Detroit I came to the conclusion that I was not suited to "a life on the lake wave," consequently I induced my *chum* to join me in *jumping* the boat. We did so, remaining all night, and the greater part of the next day under a sidewalk, waiting for the Burlington to leave the city. During our concealment the minutes were hours, and my imprisonment became doubly hard, as I became hungry and my thoughts reverted to the *buns* which were so delicious, and yet the primary and principal cause of my being where I then was. At length the boat had gone and we felt safe in coming out of our hiding-place, our first thought being of something to eat. Upon taking stock we found our finances to be as follows : subscribed capital, thousands of dollars, according to our feelings; capital paid up, forty-nine cents; reserve fund, any amount of hard labor, accompanied by an unlimited amount of abuse. Our paid-up capital was soon exhausted, *a call* was made, but met with no response; consequently we were obliged to draw upon the reserve, which proved to be the only means by which we were enabled to ward off starvation.

By working and riding a little, and begging and tramping a good deal, we finally got as far south as Nashville, Tenn., but finding the air heavily laden with the fumes of powder, prompted by the first law of nature, we retraced our steps, and after many hardships we reached Buffalo again, much the worse for wear and tear but overjoyed to get home. Let me here say a word to boys who talk about leaving home whenever things don't go exactly to suit them. Take the advice of one who tried it, and banish all such thoughts from your mind. You will find little or no comfort in being thrown upon the cold charity of the world, without friends, money or influence, subject only to the kicks and curses of, in most cases, heartless and tyrannical employers. Boys, *do not* be in a hurry to leave the old home until you know what you are going to do.

I was now satisfied to remain at home and work on the farm, for awhile at least, but was soon seized with a spirit of unrest and dissatisfaction. Upon discovering this, my father decided it would be best for me to learn a trade; consequently I was apprenticed at Mr. Pierce's stave yard in Buffalo, to learn the trade of a cooper.

Although my father was a moderate drinker, always keeping liquor in the house, he never would allow his children to touch it. I often wondered why it could be so dangerous, and such a terrible wrong for the children to do what the father was doing. Let me say to the fathers who are moderate drinkers, some such thoughts as those once entertained by me may be passing through the minds of your little ones, and when you have passed into the sear and yellow leaf of this life, if you are compelled to know that one of your much loved children has gone down to a drunkard's grave, your grief and shame will be doubly hard to bear when you think his father gave him the example.

As I was about to leave home for the purpose of apprenticing myself to Mr. Pierce, my father called me to him, and with tears in his eyes said: "Joe, my boy, now that you are about to leave home, I pray you take your father's advice; never touch, taste or handle strong drink of any kind; avoid all evil company, and you will prosper in life and be a happy man."

My reader, had I followed that good advice, how many years of suffering and disgrace I would have been spared! And as I now think that hundreds of young boys are leaving home every day with the prayers and good advice of father and mother, my prayer is, God grant that all such words of warning may be heeded; disobedience to parents is usually the first downward step in a boy's life.

FIRST DRINK.—FIFTEEN YEARS OF AGE.

I began to learn my trade under very favorable circumstances, being blessed with that greatest of all blessings, good health. It was not long until one part of my father's advice was left unheeded, for I soon got in with evil companions, and became one of that much-to-be despised class, street corner loafers, thinking it manly to first be a listener, then a participant in the disgusting and disgraceful conversation indulged in by these people. To-day, how many youths, young men, middle-aged men and even old men, are given up to this pernicious habit of street-loafing, using language that causes a blush of shame to rush to the cheek of innocence, as it is compelled to pass that way; and it is the exception when a woman passes one of these groups without having insulting or indecent remarks made concerning her. No good but much evil will come to any young man who will seek such company. It was from one of this class of young men that I received an invitation to attend a social party, and while at this gathering the other portion of my father's advice was disregarded, under the following circumstances: As is customary at these social parties, the wine was soon forthcoming, a glass being offered me by a young lady; at first I refused it, saying: "I had promised my parents that I would never drink strong drink of any kind." She at once began to accuse me of being tied to my mother's apron strings, saying also, "I was now old enough to take care of myself."

A pretty girl has a wonderful influence over a chicken-hearted lad; consequently I yielded to the tempter, and thus took my first glass of intoxicating liquor. Well do I remember the night, for as we were returning to our homes, the city was all excitement, the news having been received that President Lincoln had been assassinated; therefore, on the fourteenth day of April, eighteen hundred and sixty-five, just as the terrible battles of the war of the rebellion were ended, my battles with the demon alcohol began, and the first gun of misery, degradation

and sin was fired when that young lady persuaded me to
drink wine. I fear this is a custom far too prevalent
among our young women; in many instances they rather
encourage than denounce a young man's ability to drink,
and be *one of the boys.*

But let me say to any young lady who will tempt a
young man to take his first glass, if in after life you are
cursed with a drunken husband or sons, ask yourself
whether it may not be a just retribution, inasmuch as
you may have been the primary cause of some young
man starting on a downward career which finally resulted in his becoming a drunken husband or son, thereby
bringing untold misery and suffering upon an affectionate,
devoted wife or tender loving mother.

If our young women would frame a code of morals for
the guidance of the boys, and see that they conformed to
it before being able to secure their approving smiles, we
would have fewer young men to-day being dragged down
through the curse of rum. Girls, exact of the boys what
they do of you in the matter of good morals, and you will
make many young men behave who now think, and with
some reason, that it makes little difference how they live,
for you will have them any way. How frequently we
hear parents say, "I suppose he must sow his wild oats."
What a speech to come from a father or mother,—there
are no more certain words than these, "What a man soweth, that shall he also reap;" so if you sow wild seed,
you must expect a corresponding harvest. In few cases
is the worthless seed supplanted by the good, that shall
bring forth good fruit. Abolish forever the wild oats
theory and guard against the beginning. If the wrong
start is not made, the end need never be contemplated.

. Now that I had entirely neglected my father's good
advice, I became reckless, and rapidly gave up to a life
of dissipation, spending the day in toil, and the night in
vain and empty pleasures, thus unfitting myself for the
day's labour. After a brief apprenticeship of scarcely

four months, my employers called me into the office one morning and addressed me as follows : " Punctuality and sobriety are among the foremost of our business laws, and we have decided that no young man who is carousing and drinking all night is needed in our employ." I was paid off and discharged.

Here is a warning for all young men who are starting in life with high hopes and aspirations. Here you have the case of one who, although not quite fifteen years of age, had lost the confidence of his employers as a result of drinking strong drink.

Having been discharged as I have stated, I did not dare to go home, consequently I shipped again on a lake steamer. As we were passing up the Detroit River a collision occurred, in consequence of which our boat sank and we were obliged to swim for our lives. The task was made doubly hard from the fact that the river was covered with a sheet of ice, it being the month of November. My great physical strength and wonderful powers of endurance enabled me to reach the shore. I landed at a place called Malton, in Canada, was taken to Detroit where I received forty dollars from the owners of the steamer. I purchased some new clothes, and started for Toledo, Ohio. I earnestly resolved that I would not drink any more, but on my arrival, the first building I beheld after leaving the depot was a saloon, and I went in, never leaving it until drunk. When I awoke next morning I found myself in the lock-up, minus my new suit of clothes. In great centres of large population men go into dark alleys to lay down when drunk. It was in such a state I was found by some unknown individual, who politely helped himself, in Yankee fashion, and in place of my new suit, simply dressed me in his old and ragged one I was brought before the magistrate to answer the charge, " drunk and disorderly." Ten dollars or sixty days was the sound that greeted my ears. Young men of fashion, stop; don't touch it again, and you will never become so degraded.

It is humiliating in the extreme for me to relate these disgraceful occurrences, but by so doing I am able to show how rapidly, and to what depths, a young man may fall through this terrible curse of rum.

When my sentence expired, I worked for some time on the levee in Toledo; it was here I first began to learn the *manly art.* I soon left Toledo, wandering aimlessly about the country, my time given up to drinking and fighting, eventually turning up in New York. One afternoon I entered one of the lowest and most disreputable dives on the Bowery, introducing myself as a fighter. A match was arranged for the same evening, but I soon discovered that something more than brute force was necessary in a contest of this kind, for I had scarcely stepped into the ring when I was sent rolling under the ropes, and failed to come to the scratch for a repetition.

From the time I was discharged by Mr. Pierce for two years I led a life of dissipation and debauchery, my parents never knowing my whereabouts or condition until one day they received word that I had been brought to one of the Buffalo hospitals in a state of delirium tremens.

My reader, pause a moment and think of it. A youth, scarcely seventeen years of age, after being for two years an outcast, brought down with that most terrible of all diseases, *delirium tremens.* Young man, take warning. The same is in store for you if you become a slave to your appetite for rum. You may say I can drink without making a beast of myself, but remember thousands are saying the same thing every year, who are finally ruined for this life and the life which is to come. *" No drunkard shall enter the Kingdom of Heaven."*

# CHAPTER II.

Marriage—Housekeeping—Sixty days in jail—A free fight— A father—A Contractor—Mobbed—Attempted suicide—Refused admission to see my family—On the Mississippi—Gambling room—A Perilous position—A sailor—Meeting my family— Locates at St. Catharines—Next Hamilton—Residence in Toronto—Working for Gurney & Co.—Brakeman, Toronto to Belleville—First prize-fight—Father's death.

WHEN my health was again restored, I promised my father and mother that I would never drink another drop of intoxicating liquor, and so faithfully did I keep my promise, that the people were again beginning to have confidence in me.

One day my parents called me to them and said, Joe, we think it would be advisable for you to get married, settle down, and you will yet become an industrsous, sober and prosperous young man. I thought their advice good, consequently started out in search of a wife. In December, eighteen hundred and sixty-nine I was rewarded by meeting a young lady at a funeral, rather solemn circumstances under which to enter upon a courtship, but such it proved, and on the twenty-second day of the following February, I led this young woman to the altar of the Roman Catholic Church, and we were made man and wife after the very brief courtship of less than three months. A joyous wedding it was; I often think the Germans are the only people who really know how to celebrate an affair of this kind, the only thing that is wrong with the celebration is the strong drink. The freezing of my ears on the way home from the church was the only mishap that occurred. They were soon thawed out in the jollification that ensued, and which lasted almost without interruption for three days.

After the wedding-feast had ended, I began to realize that I had assumed a great responsibility; and I began to reflect. I am afraid this is the custom of too many young people to-day regarding the marriage question; they take the step and then reflect thereon, when it should be *vice versa.* Here let me say to the young men, never marry if you are a slave to rum. You do not know the suffering and misery you will cause the very one you promise to cherish and protect. 'Twere better for her that she be disappointed in her early years than live a blasted life with a broken heart.

We began keeping house in the same building in which my parents first lived on their arrival in this country, namely on Pine-st., Buffalo. I secured a position as driver on a horse car, and for awhile got along well, but being constantly thrown among men who were drinkers, the appetite again took hold of me and I went down again and again, finally losing my situation—going so low that my father-in-law took his daughter home with him. I then left Buffalo, going to Franklin, Pa., where I met John Steele, better known as "Coal oil Johnny." I soon gained a reputation in the oil regions as a wrestler and rough and tumble fighter, or, in other words, an *all-round tough.*

I remember on one occasion, while in company with a number of others, I took a revolver from my pocket to show it to the fellow beside me. Murders and shootings were of such frequent occurence in that country that the fellow thought I intended to shoot him, and gave the alarm. I was immediately pursued by a mob and compelled to run for my life, taking refuge in an empty house; the mob followed me in, took the revolver from me and *fired* me through a window, some twenty feet from the ground. The fracas culminated in my arrest, conviction and sentence to sixty days. When my sentence had expired, I returned to Buffalo, secured work, and for some time led a sober life. In January, eighteen hundred and seventy-one, while not yet quite twenty years of age, I became the father of a fine baby boy. Thus responsibilities were on the increase; and I was becoming more and more incapable of assuming them. The advent of our boy seemed to bring me to my senses, and every morning I could have been seen starting for the woods with an axe on my shoulder singing, "Aint I the style for a family man."

I found the wages of a wood-chopper to be inadequate for my requirements, consequently looked for other employment. I moved my family to the stone quarries, where I received steady work at good wages, but was not able to stand prosperity. One Sunday, a party of eleven young men from the quarries, myself one of the number, went to Gardenville, and after drinking freely, proceeded to *clean out* the town, and so nearly did we accomplish our object, that the citizens sent for the Priest that he might use his influence in quelling the disturbance. He had scarcely appeared on the scene when one of the boys gave him a left-hander, making it necessary for him to retire from the field of action. The next day warrants were out for our arrest. Upon hearing this I sold my household furniture to my next neighbour for seven dollars (an extensive sale), and took the night train out of the city, arriving at Dunkirk about three o'clock in the morning.

My earthly possessions consisted of a wife and baby, and three dollars and sixty cents in cash. A fine predicament for a boy not yet twenty-one years of age to be placed in. My wife got work in an hotel, thus paying our board until I could find employment of some kind. I soon found work as a stonemason, working on the Silver Creek bridge. One church holiday there was an excursion to Niagara Falls. I decided to go, but as a result of leaving my work at a very busy time, I was discharged, and therefore obliged to look for a new field of labor. At Forestville I secured a contract to build a sewer and lay pipe to conduct water to the fish pond. In order to complete the job, I was obliged to hire labourers and got a number of Italians from Dunkirk. As soon as I succeeded in getting my men at work, I returned to the village to celebrate my good fortune; the celebration consisted of drinking, pool playing, etc., during the entire day. Being desirous of getting the work done at the end of the third day, I promised the men a keg of beer if they would finish as I desired. As soon as the beer arrived, they left the work and it was soon finished, not the work, but the beer; and they finally began to finish each other with picks and shovels. The next day, however, the work was completed. I sent the men back to Dunkirk, promising to meet them in a certain saloon kept by one of their nationality, and there pay them off, drawing one hundred and sixteen dollars for the purpose. The same night I got in a game of poker and lost nearly all the money, consequently did not go to Dunkirk for two or three days. When I did go I found my house surrounded by these foreigners who were fiercely demanding their money of my wife, who was unable to understand anything they said, therefore almost frightened to death, not knowing what they wanted. Upon my arrival I invited them all to a saloon, treating freely to beer and making up a story to the effect that I had been robbed: and was thus able to settle with them by giving each one dollar, which they accepted as payment in full for three days' work.

Again, finding myself without work, money, friends or influence, I became despondent, feeling that my appetite for strong drink had become a disease and there would be no possibility of my ever being able to overcome it. While laboring under a terrible fit of despondency, I made an unsuccessful attempt on my life, and to-day my blood runs cold when I think that had not God in His infinite mercy spared me, I would now be among the lost. Oh! how my heart goes out in gratitude to Almighty

God, when I think how He spared my life during many years which were given up to sinning against Him.

I now decided to take my family to the home of my father-in-law at Buffalo, where they would be cared for, and I would go, I knew, or cared not, where. Hearing of a cock-fight which was to take place in Rochester, N.Y., I decided to witness it, my passion for gambling and sporting being only second to that for drink. I remained in Rochester some time, working occasionally and drinking frequently, but finally returned to Buffalo to see my family. Imagine my feelings when admission to the house was refused me; knowing this to be my just desert, I started for the west, firmly declaring that none of my people should ever see or hear of me again. I was unworthy of their recognition, to say nothing of respect.

I succeeded in getting as far as St. Louis, Mo., and, what is most wonderful, arrived in a sober condition. I cannot approximately describe the forsaken feeling that came over me during my first night in that great city. Alone, friendless, homeless, abandoned by my own people, and one thing the cause of all this misery and suffering, brought on not only myself, but upon all connected with me, and that one thing *drink*.

My reader, do not here begin to denounce me as a miserable, heartless, drunken wretch, unworthy of the sympathy of any, for you cannot begin to understand the terrible tenacity of the drink habit when it is once deeply rooted. In my sober moments, few though they were, when I would think of my home, my wife and child, I would experience feelings of remorse for which death seemed to be the only relief. Truly has it been said, "The pillow of remorse is filled with thorns." You may say, Why did you not reform? That is easily said, but I firmly believe there is a stage which, if reached in this terrible habit, nothing but the grace of God is sufficient to free a man. At this time I had never thought of a God; of a Saviour who is always ready and willing

to receive the vilest sinner who, in true repentance, will
come to him.   No; I did not look to the blessed Jesus
for solace and relief, but terrible as it was, I sought a
deliverance from my feelings of abandonment in the
very thing that had caused all my suffering.

I had not been long in St. Louis when I shipped as a
roustabout on a Mississippi river steamboat, going as far
south as Cairo, where I was to engage in a prize-fight,
taking one of the worst thrashings a man ever got, and
all I received therefor was five dollars.   I now decided
to return to St. Louis, my main object being to witness
the Tom Allen and Mike McCool fight, which was soon
to take place in that city.   What little money I earned,
together with the five dollars made at my own fight, enabled me to bet on McCool, and fortunately for me he was
the winning man.   With the money won in this way I
improved my personal appearance in the matter of dress
and again started down the Mississippi, not as a roustabout, but as a full-fledged passenger, going as far as
Memphis, Tenn.   On these boats it was always an easy
matter in those days to find many opportunities for gambling by means of card-playing.   During this trip I
made enough money in this way to enable me to open a
gambling room at Columbus, S.C., in which I made money
fast, but spent it faster in riotous living.   I finally gave
up the gambling room business by request of the sheriff.
With what money I had, I decided to go to Sumpter,
where I lost my money, the second night after my arrival,
in a game of poker.   Laying in a supply of crackers and
cheese, I started to count the ties to Wilmington.   I
shall never forget the experience of one dark night during this tramp, when I was overtaken by a railway train
while in the centre of a long piece of trestle work.   I
could not make my escape from either end of the bridge,
so was obliged to slip between the ties and hang by my
hands until the train passed over.

My reader, you may in a manner appreciate my feelings as I hung there, expecting every moment to be

obliged to drop a hundred feet into the ravine below. Of course the fireman found it necessary to do some stoking while the engine was passing over me, in consequence of which I received a shower-bath of hot ashes. That seemed to me to be the longest and slowest train of cars that ever passed over a railway, but it did get over at last, and I scrambled on top again and resumed my journey. When I arrived at Wilmington, I began once more to think of my family, and decided to again see them if possible. With this object in view, I engaged as a sailor on an ocean-sailing vessel bound for New York.

Although perfectly ignorant of the duties or requirements of a Jack Tar, I represented myself to be an experienced sailor.

One day I received orders to go aloft to perform some duty, the nature of which I would have as well understood had the order been given in Greek. However, up I went, and assisted by the shouting and cursing of the Captain, I succeeded in loosening and fastening several ropes. At last, loosening a wrong one, down came the top-sail and up came the Captain to throw me into the sea, which trouble I saved him by climbing down the opposite side. I was never afraid of any one man on a solid footing, but did not care to fight an experienced sailor in the rigging of a ship. When we arrived in New York, the Captain threatened to hand me over to the police authorities, but after asking me a few questions, he discovered in me an almost exact counterpart of his own early life, his sympathies being aroused to such a degree that he handed me a twenty dollar gold piece and bade me good bye.

With shame I confess that this money went for drink until I had barely enough to take me on my way home as far as Batavia, N.Y., where I decided to remain a few days that I might get straightened up and meet my family in my sober senses. I was successful in my endeavors, and found employment at Kenyon Bros.' grocery.

In a few days I had a German friend write a letter to my father, asking him to bring my family to Batavia, as I had rented a house, and hoped to settle down as a sober, industrious man and enjoy once more the comforts of a home.   My father did as I requested, and greatly to my delight I found my family consisted not only of my wife and boy, but also of a little girl, seven months old.   We lived happily at Batavia for some time, but I was constantly meeting old associates from Buffalo; this so threatened another downfall that I decided to get away from them by going to Canada.   In less time than it takes to tell it I sold out and started, locating at St. Catharines, Ontario, fortified with all the good resolutions possible.   My first work in Her Majesty's dominion was carrying a hod; this was a means of getting up in the world in one sense at least.   I was soon fortunate enough to get steady employment at McKindley & Co.'s wheel works, where I remained several months.   Just here I would say a word to young men.   I can trace nearly all my downfalls after having formed good resolutions to the influence of evil company.   "Show me your friends and I'll tell you what you are," is a true saying, therefore form the acquaintance of those who will have a tendency to elevate and improve your moral character rather than those who will degrade and destroy it.

Satan again led my steps in the way of impure and unholy influences, and it was not long until my good resolutions were broken, and I became a slave to the *demon* that binds his victims so firmly with the chain of appetite that it is almost impossible for the poor slave to burst the fetters and free himself; but thanks be to God, He is ever ready to set the wine-chained captive free whenever he will call upon Him.   At this time I had never thought of a saviour, but was relying solely upon my own strength, which in so many instances had proved insufficient to withstand the temptations that surrounded me.

Again I decided to flee from evil associations and started for Hamilton, arriving in a large city in a strange land, with a wife and two young children and only seven cents in my pocket. After procuring a boarding-place for the family, I started to look for work, luckily meeting an old friend of my father's, from whom I borrowed one dollar, my capital being now increased to one hundred and seven —— cents. Going to a packing house, I purchased some cuttings, and began to manufacture sausage. I have heard it said that were an American to be shipwrecked and cast on one of the Cannibal Islands, he would immediately begin to sell maps of the country to the natives; I believe a Dutchman would make sausages.

As soon as I had sausage enough to make a respectable show in a basket, I started to peddle it from house to house, my entire stock being disposed of very quickly at large profit. Each successive attempt was attended with such good results that I soon rented a room and established a sausage manufacturing business. I soon discovered, however, that this business, although a profitable one, would not do for me, as the greater number of my customers were saloon-keepers, and through this damaging system of treating, I was becoming as full of beer as my sausage was of meat.

To use an expression more forcible than elegant, it seemed as if the devil were after me in the form of rum, chasing me from place to place, for I now went to Toronto, in which city I secured work in Gurney & Co.'s foundry, but as the dull season came on, I, with many others, was laid off. My next employment was on the Grand Trunk Railway as a brakeman running from Toronto to Belleville, on a freight train. On one trip our whole crew got drunk, an accident occurred, resulting in the destruction of a number of cars and our discharge. You may rest assured we received no letters of recommendation.

I continued the spree, returning to Toronto, going from there to Buffalo, where I saw my father for the last time.

B

I can even now hear his words as he greeted me thus, "Oh, Joe! Are you drinking yet? Will you never reform?" I now believed myself to be past reform, and in a fit of desperation started for the west, fetching up in Columbus, O., where I fought my first genuine prize-fight, for one hundred and fifty dollars a side.

I won the battle, and with my winnings started for Chicago, where I kept up a continuous spree. One day, while drunk, I attempted to *clean out* a saloon, which feat I accomplished pretty effectually, but for my pains received ninety days in the Bridewell, then under the supervision of Captain Mack, who is now a resident of Rochester, N. Y. While confined in this prison, my father died. Just think of it, my reader,—A few years before, I left home for the purpose of learning a trade and becoming a useful and industrious man, but when a young man once starts on a downward career, the descent is steep, the rate of travel extremely rapid, and the chances of arrest in this terrible downward flight very few, and so true did this all prove in my case that in a few short years I had been the means of bringing my old father down in sorrow to the grave; a grave prematurely reached on account of the sins of a wayward son, for whom he had once cherished such fond hopes and ambitions. Had I never taken that first glass of wine at the social party, I would not now have to think with a heart filled with sorrow and shame that my father died while his son was in prison,—in prison through the curse of rum.

In every life the first step to sin presents itself sooner or later, and when once taken, succeeding ones come thick and fast. Young man, guard against the first step in a downward career; if the start is not made, the end need not be contemplated.

# CHAPTER III.

Lost in the Michigan forests—Prize-fight—Returns to Toronto—
    Sad condition of the family—Becomes coachman to Robert
    Walker—Drunken spree and smash-up—Goes to Whitby—
    Works as a farmer—Forsakes his family—Life as bartender
    and gambler—Assumes the name of John Brooks—A bartender
    —Meeting Frances E. Willard—Inebriate asylum—The far
    West—Salt Lake City—City of Tents—A stage trip through
    Utah Valley—Black Rock canon—Great Sand Desert—Silver
    Reef—Tender feet—Row in a dance hall.

WHILE confined in the Chicago prison, I firmly decided,
after many hours of meditation, to get away from
temptations by going to the lumber regions of Michigan.
My time expired and off I started for the Wolverine State.
The first Sunday morning I was there a large deer crossed
in front of the camp.   A Frenchman, one of the members
of the camp, said to me, let us follow his trail, so
taking our rifles we started.   After a long and rough
tramp we finally saw the object of our search, and succeeded
in dropping him, but upon discovering that we
had no knife, my mate set out for the camp to get one.
After he had been gone about two hours, I saw him
returning from the opposite direction, not having found
the camp.   We now became painfully aware of the fact
that we were lost—lost in the great forest.   Starting
several times in search of the camp, after wandering
around for several hours we invariably brought up at
the place from which we had started, namely, where the
deer was killed.   I then remembered what I had heard
about the moss growing upon the north side of the trees.
Taking this as a guide we started north, supposing the
camp to be in that direction.   We tramped around till
night overtook us, and knowing how plentiful the wolves

were, we knew it would be necessary to kindle a fire as a protection against them. What was our state of mind upon discovering that we had no matches. I had always proved to be a pretty good planner, but it seemed as if I was to be baffled on this occasion. However, when we had almost exhausted our mental resources, I struck on a scheme. Breaking some small sticks and taking some dry leaves, I dug a hole in the ground in which I placed them, covering them over with powder; going a short distance away, I fired my rifle into the sticks and leaves, the powder ignited from the discharge of the gun, the sticks and leaves taking fire at the same time, and thus we were able to have a fire which proved not only a protection against the wolves, but also against the weather, as it was the month of December and very cold. We slept and watched alternately, and thus the night passed.

In the morning we continued our search for some sign of deliverance. We had not gone far when we beheld a clearing and began to take courage. What was our great disappointment upon discovering the clearing to be a swamp. The second night came and was spent much as the first, our search being resumed early in the morning. My reader, if you have never been lost in a forest, you are utterly unable to appreciate the feelings of one who is placed in that terrible position. Just about dark on the third day of fruitless search, we came to a roadway. This gave evidence that at some time, if not then, human beings had passed that way. We took fresh courage, and had not gone far on the road when a light met our gaze, and a welcome sight it was, for we dreaded the third night, thinking we would be too weak the next morning to resume our journey. The light, although seemingly near, proved to be a long distance away. We finally reached the cabin from whence it came, and knocked at the door; a voice from within asked what was wanted. I at once perceived that he used the German accent; taking advantage of this I replied in *Dutch.*

Immediately the door was opened and we were extended a very hearty welcome.

Our host informed us that we were eighty miles from the camp, and that to walk was our only means of getting back. After resting a couple of days we were well equipped with provisions and ammunition, and started on a comparatively straight road for the camp, the only adventure on the return trip worthy of note being the killing of a monster black bear.

In due time we reached our comrades, who were overjoyed to see us, so much so that a general jubilee was entered into by all.

I worked at lumbering until January, getting not only my own wages but the greater part of the other boys' as well, by means of card-playing, at which I had now become quite a professional.

In January I left the lumber regions, going direct to Oskosh, Wis., where I was matched to fight a local champion of that place. I succeeded in winning the fight, also sixty-seven dollars, and decided to use this money in going to Toronto, Canada, where I had left my family, to see if they were still alive. To-day, as I think of the great suffering that family endured, and which was occasioned by my being a victim to drunkenness, a feeling of shame comes over me that is almost unbearable, my wife being compelled to wear out her young life at the wash-tub, in order to support the children of a drunken husband. Great as the disgrace is, am I to bear it alone? Are there not hundreds, yes, thousands of husbands throughout the land doing the same thing to-day? To those who are thus giving themselves up to a life of debauchery and degradation, let me say: Consider what you are doing, and if your appetite has become master of your mind, and you are unable to control it, I beseech you, look to Him who is ever saying: "Come unto me all ye that labor and are heavy laden and I will give you rest."

Upon my arrival in Toronto, it was some time before I could learn the whereabouts of my family, but after a

diligent search found they were living on Stanley-street.
I had not the courage to go direct to the house and there
face that wife I had neglected so sadly for nearly two
years, consequently I had a man write a note, which I
sent by a small boy, telling Mrs. Hess that a man wished
to see her on important business at the street corner below.  She very properly refused to comply with the request, but at the same time was overcome by that natural
instinct, *a woman's curiosity*, and came out in the yard
to learn, if possible, who had sent the strange note.
Her efforts were successful, for she discovered it to be her
truant husband, waiting anxiously for some token of a
welcome home.  I was beckoned to the house, and eagerly
accepted the invitation, although I had proved so unde-
serving of the respect or even the recognition of my
family.

I was greatly pleased to find a second little girl already
a year and a half old.  My joy, however, was soon turned
to sorrow, for the little boy and girl I had left two years
before remembered their father, but only to shrink from
him as he came near them.  Oh! the terrible thought
that came to me.  Have I fallen so low that my children,
my own flesh and blood, refuse to recognize me?  Such
was the case, and it was not for some time that I could
get them near me.

I at once set out to look for work, and succeeded in
getting a situation as coachman for Mr. Robert Walker, of
the celebrated Golden Lion dry goods house—presenting
a fine appearance, perched up behind a spanking pair of
bays, and in full livery attire.  Mr. Walker and family
soon went to their summer residence, leaving me in sole
charge of the house, horses, grounds, etc.  One morning,
when down in the city, I happened to meet one of my
old chums, who had worked with me in Gurney's foundry.
I told him what I was engaged in, and that I was proprietor *pro tem.*  He premised to call and see me that
afternoon, no doubt imagining an excellent opportunity
presented itself for a good time.

We had not been chatting long over old times when he produced a bottle, inviting me to drink. I shall never forget the terrible sensation that came over me at that moment, how the devil did hiss in my ear, *take it, take it,* until finally I yielded, and the fire was started. That afternoon we took the fine horses and beautiful carriage and started for a drive around the city. Imagine, if you can, two drunken men *doing* a city under such circumstances. The whole affair resulted in our smashing things up generally; when we had taken what was left of the carriage to the driving house, we started out as pedestrians, leaving the horses in the stable, without removing the harness. It was not until the following afternoon that I came back to look after my duties; the horses, having remained all night with the harness on, presented a fine appearance, other things in proportion. It was very necessary that the hot-house, in which were growing some very tender plants, should have been uncovered every morning, so that the sun's heat, intensified by glass, should not destroy its contents. I was horrified to find all the plants completely killed by the excessive heat. Knowing there was no alternative for me but to leave the place, as my tenure of office had proved too disastrous to permit of my holding it longer, I tried to light on some plan by which to raise funds for a trip. This presented itself in the nature of a glove contest with a local sport named Thomas. The time appointed for the match arrived, and you would be surprised to know what class of people comprised the greater part of the audience. Suffice it to say, they were the very men who, above all others, should have been instrumental in putting down such inhuman exhibitions. We were uninterrupted, and the fight (a hard one) was won by the *ex-coachman;* this provided me with funds, and a new idea came to me, I thought that were I to go on a farm, I could become a sober man, as I would be away from evil associates and the temptations of the city. Hearing of a farm that was advertised for rent in Whitby, I started at once to see about it, and was not long in making all arrangements for the moving of my family to that place in October. My expectations and hopes were realized, for not one drop of intoxicating liquor crossed my lips during that fall or winter.

In the following June I saw an advertisement calling for a quantity of stone, and as there was considerable of the kind wanted upon my farm, I went to Whitby to see about it.

The business was transacted in the hotel, to which was attached a bar-room; after all arrangements had been completed, the usual and customary *curse* of treating was indulged in. At first I took cigars, but one of my friends (?) was constantly persuading me to take something invigorating ; the temptation at last becoming too great, I fell. I sometimes think those men who are ever ready and do tempt men, knowing at the same time their weakness, will have much to answer for. Here was the beginning of a terrible spree. I was ashamed to go home, to a home that had become a comparatively happy one as a result of my having lived a sober life for five or six months.

In a drunken condition I started for Toronto, in which city I remained for a few days, finally taking a steamer for Lewiston, *en route* for Buffalo; here, not knowing how, when or where, I purchased a ticket for Chicago, also securing a berth in a sleeper, and upon reaching which I was very soon fast asleep, nor did I awake until the car porter informed me that I had arrived safely in Chicago. I was greatly surprised upon receiving this information, as I was unable to remember that I had left Buffalo. When I asked the porter if I had any baggage, he brought me an empty collar box by way of a joke. Some of my readers at least can imagine how I felt about this time, and how badly I wanted something to quiet my nerves. I left the car and started up Madison-

street in search of a saloon and while strolling up the
street, the thought came to me that I had better investigate the state of my finances. Doing so, I discovered that
my capital amounted to only twenty cents. It now became necessary for me to kill two birds with one stone,
by visiting a saloon where a free lunch had been provided
during the night. I had been in Chicago sometime before this and remembered that during that visit I had
made a friend who was engaged in the saloon business on
West Randolph-street, consequently I set out in that direction and soon discovered the place ; finding my old
friend Charley behind the bar. The saloon was crowded with that class of people known as night hawks.
I walked to the bar, took some whiskey, and then
proceeded to devour what was left of a very fine
lunch ; it was not long until I was recognised by my old
friend who came from behind the bar and gave me a
hearty welcome, insisting that I should go to work for
him at once, as he was in need of a man. I told him
that I was not suitably rigged out for a Chicago bartender ; he then gave me twenty dollars with which I was
to get a new suit of clothes and become a respectable (?)
whiskey vendor. I now began to think of the lemon
sours, gin slings and whiskey cocktails that I would be
able to treat myself to. Fortune, if such it may be
called, smiled upon me, inasmuch as I had secured a good
situation of the kind. The very kind above all others
that I should have avoided. My boss was obliged to be
away for three days and on his return I handed him two
hundred and ten dollars, this being the receipts for
drinks sold during the very short time of three days and
three nights. As a reward .or the faithful performance
of my duties, I received a ten dollar note. I now started
for a faro room, and on entering placed my ten dollars
on the ace and won ; my luck was so good that in two
hours I left the room with three hundred and eleven dollars. Going to a large clothing store at the corner of

Madison and Clinton-streets, I proceeded to equip myself
in the costume of a professional sporting man.  When I
returned to my post at the saloon, Charley's suspicions
were somewhat aroused, for he knew I had not received
money enough to go into such extravagances.  I had expected this would be the result, so at once asked him to
take a walk with me.  We went to the gambling room
and I soon satisfied him that the money with which I
purchased my new clothes did not belong to him.  I now
decided to remain with my friend Charley and improve
all my opportunities for gambling.  In the short time of
three months I had saved seventeen hundred dollars, and
now my sporting life began in earnest, my passion for
this kind of a life having grown into a mania.  I assumed the name of John Brooks, and it is by this name that
I am best know in the sporting world.  One day, while
enjoying a short vacation in the form of a spree, I was
met by a man whom I had formerly known as a well-
known gambler and sport.  He began to talk to me concerning my bad habits, I informed him that I was well
posted on that subject and not at present in need of any
enlightenment. He finally asked me to come with him for
a walk and having no very urgent business just at that
time I consented.  We walked a short distance down
South Clark-street, and turning, went through an Arcade
entered a door at the right, passing into a large room in
which were many people gathered.  I was led nearly to
the front seat, and pretty soon they all began to sing.
After singing two or three songs, a lady took the platform and began to speak on temperance; upon inquiry I
found out that the speaker was none other than that
great temperance woman, Frances Willard, whose real
worth was just at this time beginning to be known.  As
soon as the meeting had ended, I was greatly surprised
to see Miss Willard coming straight for me, and knowing
my condition, I felt like making my escape, but found
the means cut off by my friend who had brought me to
the meeting and who now stood just behind me.

I was asked to sign the pledge, but replied, as so many young men do to me at the present time, " I can drink or let it alone," knowing at the same time that only the first half of my assertion was true. I was now besieged on all sides by Christian men and women who urged me to sign the pledge. In order to get away I made this promise : " Let me go this time and I will come back to-morrow." I can scarcely tell how it came, but strange to say, I did as I promised. On this occasion I had a long talk with Miss Willard, who gave me advice, which had I then taken and lived up to, I would not now be obliged to look back over a dark and sinful past life. How is it that men are willing to accept all advice that is calculated to advance their temporal welfare, but that which pertains to spiritual welfare and which is of far greater importance is in nearly every instance rejected. Although I could not be prevailed upon to sign a pledge, I firmly resolved to make a determined effort to conquer the drink habit. Acting upon the advice of Miss Willard, I went to the Washington Home for Inebriates and during the time I was there, this good and kind woman wrote one letter for me to my family, but no answer was ever received; this made me feel as if I was looked upon by them as an outcast. After being about three weeks at the home, I asked permission to go down to the city one afternoon, believing that I could now withstand the temptation which presented itself on almost every corner, but my strength was not sufficient and again I went down.

Now just a word regarding the inmates of this asylum. They were of many classes, not alone the degraded and depraved specimens of humanity that one might expect to find, but professional men ; merchants, teachers, and just at this particular time a Roman Catholic priest was one of these unfortunates—men were there who, according to ability, should, and under different circumstances might have been found in high places of authority.

I had not been long away from Washington Home when one day I met Miss Willard who told me that no

word had ever been received from my family; I now felt
sure that they no longer cared what became of me, and
while in this frame of mind I purchased a ticket via the
Union Pacific Railway to Ogden, where I changed cars
and started for Salt Lake City, Utah.　Upon arriving, I
put up at Walker Bros' Hotel, one of the leading houses
of the city.　In all my travels I have never been in a
more uniform, or a prettier, cleaner city than Salt Lake.
The streets are beautifully graded and down either side
thereof flows a stream of beautiful spring water from the
mountain, thus the gutters are always kept perfectly
clean.　The great Mormon temple being built at a cost of
three million dollars, is the first noteworthy object that
meets the gaze of the tourist as he approaches the city.
Looking two miles and a half towards the mountain and
to the left of the city may be seen Camp Douglas, from
which floats the stars and stripes.

Twelve miles down the valley on the east side, we find
Little Cottonwood Canon which is also the location of
the famous Emma mine.　Still further down the valley
is big Cottonwood Canon, the scene of so many terrible
avalanches.　Ten miles further in the same direction is
Spanish Forks; then American Forks, directly across the
valley from the last named place in Binghamton.　All
these places are rich in gold and silver mines.　This beautiful and wonderful valley is forty miles wide by three
hundred and forty long, and for fertility and productive-
ness of soil is unsurpassed in our land.　One hundred and
twenty-two miles down the valley we come to what was
then (in 1877) the terminus of the Utah Southern Railway, at which place was situated the town of York, but
which I shall name the " City of the Tents " as there was
only only one frame house in the place, but more than
five hundred tents, so placed that regular streets were
formed similar to those of our towns of to-day.　Our
journey from York was by stage.

Our party consisted of fourteen men and three women,
all compelled to remain in the same tent at night.　When

ON THE PLAINS—A COWBOY.

a short distance from Corn Creek, we came into the Alkali Country, where rain is almost unknown, the farms being watered by means of irrigation.  After travelling in this manner for three days and two nights, we arrived at Belleville, a place at that time of about two thousand inhabitants, having a large woolen mill, some smaller factories, and ten saloons wherein gambling could be seen at any hour of the day or night.  The following day we left Belleville, passing through the most romantic country I ever saw, stopping wherever night overtook us.  At last we came to the foot of Black Rock Canon, and in the ascent of the mountain the passengers were obliged to walk behind, holding on a long rope which was fastened to the stage, and which answered as a help in climbing the mountain.  The stage at times ran so close to the edge of the Canon that we were able to look into the great abyss, but so great was the depth that it was impossible to see the bottom.  We started the ascent at two p.m., arriving at the top about five, occupying three hours in going two miles.

On top of the mountain, much to our delight, we found a beautiful grove in which we could rest and cool off. The next morning our driver imparted to us the very cheering intelligence that we were to cross the great sand desert six miles wide, and nothing but sand, without the least sign of vegetation.  When we arrived at the place, orders were given for all the men to walk, as the stage sank from one to two feet in the sand.  As the sun was extremely hot you can somewhat understand what we were obliged to suffer in going those six miles.  We eventually reached the other side and made a stop for dinner; from this point we could see Silver Reef, which was our destination; and a welcome sight it was after a week of journeying such as we had passed through.

The road to Silver Reef was good and we were soon rolling up Main-street, and when we came to a stop were at once surrounded by an eager crowd, anxious to learn

who the new tender feet (a term applied to eastern
people) were, each one hoping to find some one from the
same section of country they had left many years ago.

Silver Reef was at this time one of the hardest and
most wicked places in the far west; its people were of all
classes, colors and nationalities. There were numerous
stores and business places, but saloons, gambling dens,
dancing halls, etc., were in the majority. The first night
in the town I found my way to one of the last named
places. Here could be seen drunken cow-boys, miners,
and some of the roughest specimens of humanity imaginable. I selected a partner, and after we had finished
the dance, I asked her to go to the bar and have a drink;
had I neglected this invitation I would at once have been
looked upon as having no manners. While standing at
the bar I had a dispute with the bar tender, suspecting
that I was being imposed upon. He ordered me out; I
refused to go. He proceeded to execute his orders, but
found he had reckoned without his host, for my first blow
succeeded in knocking out the notorious desperado, James
Trevelyn. I at once started for my hotel, fearing Judge
Lynch. I was not disturbed, however, and thus did I
spend my first night in Silver Reef.

# CHAPTER IV.

Roaring Thunderbolt—Among the Cowboys—Catches the Arizona
mining fever—Some exciting experiences—Meeting a hermit
—A roll down the mountain side—The mountain meadow massacre—Stage robbers—Sevier river—Bubbling springs—*Pete
Nolan*—A fight for a whiskey bottle—Prize fight with Nolan—
Ninety-nine rounds with Trevelyn—Takes passage for Australia—Returns from Europe—A varied experience as saloon-
keeper—Fight in a gambling-room—Champion walker of Nebraska—Sparring *Billy* Madden—Forming a sparring troupe.

THE morning following the night of the dance, I came
to myself, as it were, and began to think what I had
done. The first thing I realised was that all my good
resolutions were again things of the past, for the experience at the dance-house would most likely be followed
up by fighting, drinking and other crimes. As I was
thus reflecting, that terrible sensation of abandonment
again came over me, and I cared very little whether I
lived or died; consequently, putting on my belt containing my revolvers, I set out for the dance-hall saloon to
see what was to be the outcome of my first visit there.
The place was yet filled with cowboys, etc., who had not
gone away since the dance. After treating the crowd, I
called one of them aside to inquire the price of drinks in
that country, so that I would know whether or not I had
been imposed upon the previous evening. My new
friends informed me that ordinarily the price was twenty-
five cents a drink, but on the occasion of a dance *fifty
cents* was the regular price, therefore I found out that I
had been to blame and decided to make an apology to
the man I had struck. I had not been long in the place
until I heard several remark, "Here comes Jim," and
looking towards the door I recognised my man. He came
straight for me, placing his hand on his revolver; notic-

ing this performance, I did likewise, thinking to myself, if I have to go I will try and take you with me; but what was my surprise when he called all hands to the bar and began to address me as follows:—" Wal, old pard, shake hands with Roaring Thunderbolt of Black Rock Canon; you're the fust clapping lion that ever shut my mouth with one poke of a mud hook; now let's be pards, but you must let old Thunderbolt have a chance to show his skill with his crapping tongs."

I promised to do so and we now became fast friends. Thus after twenty-four hours at Silver Reef I had become the *pard* of the most desperate character in the west, one who thought no more of shooting a man than a dog.

My new friend now undertook to show me the town; we went down the street but a short distance when we entered another saloon.  As my *pard* looked around the room, he saw a very fine photograph of a celebrated prize-fighter hanging on the wall; turning to me he said, watch me knock him out in the first round, and suiting his actions to his words, drew his revolver and blazed away, and I tell you *everything went,* as the saying is. He threw down a five dollar note to pay all damage and off we started for fresh fields to conquer. The whole day was spent in this manner and resulted in our finishing up the dance hall in the evening.  Early in the evening *Thunderbolt* left the hall and I never knew where he went.  I only knew that he did not turn up for a week.

That evening at the dance hall I was very heartily congratulated upon my narrow escape, for it was looked upon by nearly all that country as almost certain death to have a quarrel with *Roaring Thunderbolt.* Everyone was very anxious to treat *Clapping Lion,* as I was now called, consequently I got laid out completely before morning.  I kept this spree up for the whole week, when my money began to give out, which made it necessary for me to think of some plan for raising more.  One afternoon while sitting in *Thunderbolt's* saloon, meditat-

ing as to what course I should pursue, who should appear
but the proprietor. I told him what was troubling me,
and he came at once to my relief by making me his bartender; thus the very man I had knocked down a few
evenings before, was now my best friend and also my employer. At the expiration of three weeks the great Blue
Ridge Mountain excitement sprung up and I decided to
go to Arizona ; I notified my boss to this effect, and although he was sorry to see me leave, he paid me up in
full and I proceeded to look for a pack-mule, a bronco,
and then for two small barrels of whiskey, knowing that
if I could succeed in getting it to the Blue Ridge I could
readily dispose of my whole stock in trade at a good
price. I had only been about five weeks at Silver Reef,
but already I was master of the language (slang), and
was therefore qualified to start out for myself. A person
from the east might almost as well go to a foreign country as the mining districts of that time. He would certainly understand the language as easily.

A party numbering forty or fifty people had made all
preparations and now set out for Blue Ridge Mountains,
Arizona. I was probably the most conspicuous person in
the company, as I had my *Jack* loaded with the precious
*spirit lifter*, which being translated means whiskey.
After four days of hardships of every description, we
reached the mountains, where there were already located
three or four hundred people. Leading my pack-mule,
upon which the whisky was loaded, to a prominent position, I realized that my time had arrived to open a saloon,
which I did, using *Jack* as a bar. At first I was at a loss
to know what to charge for a drink, but knowing that I
could drop easier than rise in price, I decided to start high
enough, which was one dollar per drink. I had no idea
my customers would stand this, but to my surprise not
one word was said regarding it. In four hours from the
time I landed on the mountain, I had disposed of every
drop of whiskey and had four hundred and sixty-five

C

dollars in my pocket. The excitement which brought us to the mountains proved to be a hoax, and vengeance was sworn against the man who had raised it, but could not be found. Messrs. Walker Bros., of Salt Lake City were the heaviest losers by the swindle, so I have heard it rumored.

I returned to Silver Reef, sold my Jack and bronco, and started for Babylon, a small town, three miles from the Reef, on the Virgin river. Here I went to work in the twenty stamp mill, taking charge of the vats at five dollars per night. While at work here, I was taken sick and obliged to give up my job. My next move was to St. George, about thirty miles down the river. This is rather a peculiar trip to make. As one starts out they first travel through a very fertile and beautiful tract of country, where everything is in bloom, but gradually ascending higher and higher, we come to snow, when sleds are brought into use for eight or ten miles, then a descent begins, bringing us again into the fertile valley. As we looked far down in the valley from the snow capped mountain, we saw small objects which we discovered afterwards to be Mormon homes in the town of St. George, a very beautiful place, somewhat resembling Salt Lake City, only much smaller. It possesses a very fine Temple, presided over by Bishop Gardner, who had over thirty wives, which accounts for the fact that nearly every other person I met was a Gardner.

I remained but a few days in St. George, when I started for Pine Valley, which lay about forty miles northwest of St. George. This is the only timber district in that section of country, hence its name. This place was founded some years before by Bishop Gardner, and I also found many who bore his name in the littie town of Pine Valley. I engaged to work for a man who was operating a sawmill, and was sent into the mountain to fell trees and send them down the slide leading to the mill. This was 14,000 feet above sea level, and we had plenty of good fresh air. After working as a bushwhacker for two months, I procured a partner. We each bought a saddle horse and a pack horse to do us both. I learned that we were not far from that memorable spot where the terrible Mountain Meadow massacre took place. I was very anxious to see the place, as I had heard so much about the dreadful affair which took place there.

The following morning we started, our intention being to go to the head of Sevier river, where we would put in a couple of months' hard work as prospectors. We finally reached Iron City, so named in consequence of the iron ore found there.

The journey so far had been a somewhat remarkable one, as part of the time we were passing over snow from forty to fifty feet deep and the remaining part through beautiful, warm and fertile valleys. We remained at Iron City several days, doing a good deal of prospecting, but with no success. One day while far up the mountain, I chanced to step on a large boulder which immediately started down the mountain side, and I after it, with no means of coming to a stop until I came in contact with a large rock; the collision shook me up considerably; otherwise I was uninjured.

Let me here give you a description of my friend. Frank Carrico was the only survivor of the terrible massacre to which I have already referred, and was living the life of a hermit. He presented a strange appearance with his long shaggy hair; but the most wonderful thing about him was the great length of his beard. I noticed he kept it inside his blue flannel shirt; one day I asked him why he did so; he replied :—" So that I can keep it from getting tangled up in my feet." Of course, I thought this a joke and a stale one at that. He noticed that I did not believe him, so began to pull his beard from its hiding place, and to my astonishment it actually reached to his knees. Carrico was a Lower Canada Frenchman. His parents started for California at the time of the gold excitement in eighteen hundred and forty-nine, but, as already stated, were among the victims of the Mountain Meadow massacre. His description of this terrible affair was heart-rending in the extreme, and was somewhat as follows :

I well remember, he said, the morning of the night we camped at the meadow; we were just preparing to make a start when the cry of " Indians coming " was raised, and soon the bloody work began by which about two hundred innocent people lost their lives. I received a bullet in my shoulder and fell fainting to the ground, when another man was shot through the head and fell on top of me. After the terrible slaughter was finished, the Indians went over the ground to make sure that all were dead, and upon finding any that were not, a bullet was immediately put into them to complete the job. As I lay, expecting my turn to come every minute, the suspense was something fearful; fortunately for me, however, I was overlooked and as I lay weak and spent through loss of blood, I could hear the red men driving away our horses and cattle, and what was still worse, I discovered that the lives of the young women had been spared ; but that worse than death awaited them, as they also were to be carried away to the mountains where they would be subject to treatment too awful to describe, and as I had sisters in the camp, I knew they would be among the captured ones, and I, powerless to do anything to prevent it. All day I lay where I had fallen, fearing to move for fear some Indian might be watching me ; but towards evening, feeling that it would be perfectly safe for me to do so, I crawled from under the corpse that had been lying on me, and oh ! what a sight met my gaze. Among all those people who had comprised the camp there was now not a sign of life, and yet, with the exception of the young women, they were all there. I began to search for my father and mother, and at last found them lying near each other, having bullet wounds that must have proved instantly fatal ; from that moment I swore eternal vengeance against the red men of the forest, and seizing a rifle and pistols, set out in search of my sisters, but up to the present my search has proved a fruitless one.

This was the story told by my strange friend, and although, as far as external appearances were concerned, he was hardened by the terrible experience through which he had passed, and by his wild and solitary life, still, in that rugged breast there beat a warm and sympathetic heart, which was sworn to revenge the death of parents and the outrage of sisters. Let us return to the scene of my fall down the mountain side.

Carrico at once came to my rescue, expecting to find me if not quite dead at least nearly so ; but as I have already said, I was comparatively uninjured, and we began to investigate the place to which this accident had brought us. We had not done so long when a cave, or an old, unworked mine was discovered ; as we entered the doorway, my friend gave a shout that made the mountains ring, for in the centre of the cave or mine he saw a pile of human bones, and at once believed them to be those of the young women who had been captured by the Indians years ago. He fell on his knees and muttered something to himself, then left the cave. He would not enter it again, nor would he allow me to speak of our discovery.

We now ascended the mountain to where we had left our horses, and then proceeded on our journey to the Sevier river. After seven days' travel through a wonderful country of mountains, valleys, lava beds, etc., we came to the river ; going down this beautiful stream a short distance, we came to what is called Circle Valley, which contains an area of about ten thousand acres.

In this valley we found a Mormon sect who had adopted the socialistic method of living, as everything was controlled by the leaders of the sect, who in turn provided all necessaries of life. Numerous sleeping houses were furnished, but the whole number ate in one large building; thus did they live very contentedly and to all appearances enjoyed life very much.

We went still further down the river to Mary's Veil, where we remained but a few days, when we retraced our steps and proceeded to make our way to the source of the river, which we reached in about one week. Here we remained prospecting for several weeks, with no success, and finally decided to return to Iron City, which place we reached after a difficult and very tedious journey.

Carrico and I now dissolved partnership, and I sold out my interest in the pack horse to him, retaining my little white pony that had proved so faithful during our trip to the Sevier. I now decided to go to the great mining town of Pioche in Nevada, and in order to do so was compelled to cross Big Horse desert, forty-five miles in width. During the journey across this immense tract of sand, not one drop of water could be found, so you can imagine my pony and I were ready for a drink of nice cold water, when we reached the other side, where we happened to arrive at the camp of *Bold Bentaskey*, the notorious desperado and stage robber. I was bidden a warm welcome and invited to remain a few days with this robber and his queer subjects. Towards evening on the second day of my sojourn among these thieves and robbers, I looked out on the desert and saw a great dust cloud, but soon discovered that it was caused by a drove of horses that some of Bentaskey's men had stolen and were bringing to the camp. When these people arrived with their horses, I began to feel uneasy, fearing that they might take me for a spy and put me out of the way.

Having this idea, I concluded to make my escape as soon as possible. There were two roads from this point, —one leading to Pioche, the other to Frisco. I felt sure that when they would miss me, they would start on these roads to find me, so decided to again cross the desert. Knowing I would be discovered if I were to undertake to get my pony, I was obliged to leave it and start on foot ; this was something very few had ever attempted to do before, namely, walk across this great desert. I suffered very much from the heat and also from thirst, but finally succeeded in reaching the other side, abandoning, for the present at least, my trip to Pioche, deciding instead to make a tour of investigation of this phenomenal Sevier river, having had my curiosity greatly excited from descriptions given of it. I found it as described, namely, alternately above and below the earth's surface. One will travel for miles beside a beautiful and very rapid body of water, when suddenly it will disappear from sight, sink into its underground channel and remain there for a long distance, when it again boils up like a great volcano and continues its course overland. While thus travelling all alone on my sight-seeing tour, I fortunately met a waggon train and was invited to complete the journey with those comprising it; and very glad I was to do so, especially as they were to pass by all the principal points of interest connected with this wonderful river. The second day's travel brought us to "Bubbling Springs," away on the mountain top. These springs are formed by the Sevier, being a point where it emerges from its underground channel.

I am unable to give the number of these wonderful springs, nor can I fitly describe their beauty, especially as they appear in a beautiful moonlight night. They must be seen to be appreciated.

At this point I decided to leave the train and start again for Pioche, and after two days' travel reached this celebrated mining town, where I soon began to partake of refreshments, both liquid and solid. On my way to Pioche, I passed through Mountain Meadow, where the massacre of which I have already spoken took place, and where to this day there stands a large pile of stones to mark the spot.  Just a word here concerning a strange tradition that exists in that country.  The settlers of to-day will tell you that previous to the massacre this was one of the most beautiful and fertile valleys of the west, but since that time, in fact the same year, it became perfectly barren, presenting the appearance of a cement floor.  I cannot vouch for the previous fertility, etc., but I can for its perfect barrenness at present.

From Pioche I went to Frisco, in which place I had somewhat the same experience as that of my first night in Silver Reef.  I attended a dance, and while there had my pocket picked, which resulted in a row, making it necessary for the best preservation of my health that I leave town as soon as possible.  Consequently I started that night, and arrived at Hot Springs, eleven miles distant, about four o'clock in the mornine.  I did not remain long in this place, but, after having refreshed myself, again set out on my tramp.  I now began to feel lonely, being in a strange land without a friend, and what is still more, fearing to make any, for fear they would prove to be treacherous.  I had not gone far on my tramp from Hot Springs when I sat on a large stump to rest and lay out some definite plans for the future; while sitting here, I saw a fellow coming towards me with a little bundle tied up in a red handkerchief.  I thought to myself here is a chance to pass away a little time talking to this tramp.  As he came up to me he began to address me thus: " Wal, pard, what yer doin ? " I replied that just then I was doing nothing.  He said, " What *do* you do when you do suthin' " ?  I informed him that I *walked*, and asked what might be his occupation to which he replied " I fight."

After a little more conversation similar to the above, we shook hands and started on the road as friends and partners.  We had not proceeded far when my partner took a bottle of whiskey from his pocket, took a drink replacing it as before.  I looked at him for some minutes

and then said—*pard, let's have some o' that.* He couldn't
see it in that light, saying that he got that bottle before
the partnership began. See here, I said, you're a fighter ; if that's so, the best man will have the bottle. I felt
pretty sure I could get it in this way, so we threw off
our miners' jackets, and alone in the woods, with no
other reason save that you have already heard, we began
what proved to be a desperate fight. I cannot tell how
long the encounter lasted, but we were both exhausted
finally, and sat down about ten feet apart, and there
stared at each other like two game cocks.

At last we decided to call it a draw, and shook hands;
whereupon my partner fished the bottle out of his pocket,
saying to me, " You're welcome to half the *spirit lifter*
for you have given Pete Nolan, the champion prize-
fighter of the west, one of the hardest *bouts* he has ever
had." I then told him prize-fighting had been my business, so we now became the best of friends, and began to
dress each other's wounds. In a few days, we were able
to put in a half respectable appearance, and decided to go
to " Little Sandy," where we would appear to be strang-
ers, and endeavor to bleed some of the *suckers* of the
town.

Pete got a job in a mine, and I as a bartender, and as
it happened for the very man we wanted. This saloon
man, Baker by name, had a deadly enemy in Little
Sandy, who was the recognized *bully* of the place. One
night *bully* Ned, as he was called, came in the saloon, and
at once began to abuse the landlord, and every one connected with him. I now saw a good opportunity to gain
a reputation, so coming out from behind the bar, ordered
him out of the saloon. Of course he refused, and immediately threw off his coat which was just the performance
I wanted to see. At it we went, I discovered he was a
good *rough and tumble* fighter, so decided to make him
keep his distance, which I was able to do by my superior science. I allowed the fight to proceed long enough

for a crowd to gather, and then thought I would bring it
to a close by giving my bold fellow one from the shoulder, which resulted in doubling him up in a corner. The
news spread like wild fire, to the effect that the new bartender at Baker's saloon had *licked bully* Ned, and my
reputation as a fighter was thus very quickly established.
It so happened that Pete had got into a row already at
the mine, and gained a reputation which if anything sur-
passed mine. As soon as *bully* Ned heard that there was
a *good* man at the mines, he went at once to get him to
whip the bartender, and thus everything was working
around just as we had hoped for.

A fight for one hundred dollars a side was quickly arranged between *Pete the miner* and *Brooks the bartender*.
My reader, you will remember that I had assumed the
name, *John Brooks*, before leaving Chicago for the west.

It was arranged between Pete and me, that I should
win the fight after we had each received slight punishment ; but the most amusing part of the whole affair was,
that with the punishment came a spirit to *go in and win*,
and notwithstanding all arrangements to the contrary, it
became a fight, which was fought on its merits, and a
desperate one it was, consisting of fifty-seven rounds.
Pete failing to come to the scratch for the fifty-eighth,
and I was consequently declared the winner, and only on
account of my ability to win the match. I gave half the
purse to Pete, and, as soon as our wounds got well, we
set out in search of new fields to conquer.

The next place we reached was Park City, where I met
the man I had knocked down in the dance house at Silver
Reef, whose name was Jas. Trevelyn, a desperate prize-
fighter. We had not been long in this place until we met
one evening in a saloon.

"Jim" and I began discussing our little fracas. He
claimed he was drunk at the time, or I would not have
been able to knock him out. As a result of this conversation we arranged there and then to fight to a finish the
following morning at five o'clock.

Seconds were chosen and all arrangements were made for what proved to be one of the most desperate fights ever known. We entered the ring without having trained, so neither had the advantage in that respect. I will not undertake to give my readers a detailed account of the brutal exhibition, but will only say, that I had my nose broken, and in the ninety-ninth round I succeeded in getting a terrific blow on Jim's jaw, breaking it badly, making it impossible for him to come to time for the next round.

Thus, after ninety-nine desperately fought rounds I was declared the winner.

I now went direct to San Francisco for *repairs*, and, as soon as I could put in a half decent appearance, I took passage for Australia and remained in foreign lands from the year eighteen hundred and seventy-seven to eighteen hundred and seventy-nine inclusive.

On my return from Europe, I landed in Baltimore, and opened a fine saloon, which I ran in connection with a school for boxing, etc., doing well financially, but was soon seized with the spirit of unrest and a desire for the west, enjoying the rough and perilous life among the miners to a life in the more cultured, and I may say, civilized part of the country.

I went from Baltimore to Leadville, and upon the first night of my arrival I went to a Faro room to *buck the tiger.* While there, I was overcome with the effects of whiskey and a long journey and fell asleep, waking just in time to see a great big fellow with a broad-rimmed hat on stealing some of my "*chips.*" Scarcely realizing where I was, I sprang to my feet, striking him a terrible blow in the face, knocking him to the floor. In an instant, I was set upon by his comrades, who assailed me with chairs, pistols and knives; words are inadequate to describe the scene, but just at the commencement of the fracas, the chandelier was knocked down, leaving us in total darkness. I shall not attempt a description of the affair, the terrible cursing and swearing, which took place. By some miraculous means, I escaped from the place with any amount of bruises, a terrible gash in my shoulder made by a bowie knife, also a bullet wound in my neck.

After the above occurrence, I came to the conclusion that I would not feel very comfortable in Leadville, so decided to go to Denver, where I opened up a fine saloon ; but, becoming its most frequent patron myself, and never paying for my drinks, I was soon obliged to give up the business.

From Denver I went to Lincoln, Nebraska, where there was to be a grand fifty-hour-go-as-you-please walking match for the championship of the State, a gold medal and a purse. I succeeded in taking first money with a score of two hundred and fifty-eight miles, thus winning considerable money, a gold medal and the State championship.

In a short time, however, the money was spent, the championship lost, and the medal in a pawn-shop.

I now came east, as far as Burlington, Iowa, where I again started a saloon and boxing school. Let me here state the qualifications necessary to enable a man to start a saloon in any city in the United States other than prohibition States. Any man who has been, or is, a prize-fighter, gambler or black-leg of any kind, which will enable him to draw custom, after he has secured several respectable and influential citizens to certify to his *moral character*, can get almost any breweryman to start him in business by agreeing to sell none other than the beer manufactured by *his* and the *people's benefactor*.

I had only run the saloon for a short time when I secured a lease of the Valley-street House. Finding the life of an hotel proprietor too dull, I gave it up, and started for New York to enter the O'Leary International Walking Match ; but, as a result of being drugged, I was obliged to withdraw from the contest when I had completed one hundred and ten miles.

I next appeared with the Madden-Sullivan sparring troupe at Chicago, where J. L. Sullivan made his first public appearance. The same evening I engaged in an exhibition sparring match with "Billy" Madden, and by it gained many admirers in the prairie city. It was now a very easy matter for me to arrange fights, glove contests, etc., and secure any amount of backing.

As I look back upon that kind of a life, now that I have *come to myself*, I wonder how it is possible for a man to become so lost to everything pertaining to decency as to bring himself below the level of the brute creation. Dumb animals fight from passion, but the men to whom I have referred have not even this excuse, going into the ring as friends, and then begin to mutilate, disfigure, and it may be kill each other, until they come from the ring nothing more or less than libels on God's creatures— beings created in His own image, thus degrading themselves by these inhuman exhibitions which (with shame I say it) are patronized by the very men who make the laws for their prevention, and by others who are elected to offices that they may enforce such laws. I found three others who had no more respect for themselves than I, and we formed ourselves into the "Brooks Celebrated Troupe of Sparrers," travelling through the State of Minnesota. This enterprise proved successful financially, but otherwise disastrous, for it only furnished more time and money for dissipation.

It was not long until we arrived in Milwaukee, where we disbanded.

I cannot close this chapter without a word of advice to young men, who may think the life I have been describing is a pleasant one. Far from it; it is not living, but merely *existing*, with no aim or purpose in life, without a thought, or even a hope for the future, when we shall be called to give an account of the deeds done in the body. I beseech you men, young and old,

**"Prepare to meet thy God."**

# CHAPTER V.

Arrival in Milwaukee—Opens a Sporting Saloon—A Chapter of
Fights—Ryan & Sullivan's first appearance—Spar with Ryan
—Fight with Zowsta—Fight with Ward—Meeting "Jim" El-
liott—Wrestle with Primrose, Champion of Michigan—Dis-
covered to be *Joe Hess*—Returns to his Family at Buffalo—
Opens the East Buffalo Gymnasium—Again comes to Canada.

IN the month of November, in the year eighteen hun·
dred and eighty-one, I arrived at Milwaukee, and, as
soon as I had secured a hotel, I proceeded to view the
sights of the *lager beer* city. After going a short distance
on East Water-street, I decided to sample some of the
beer, entering a very fine saloon for the purpose; in a
little back room three men were enjoying a game of seven
up for twenty-five cents a corner. I was invited to join
in the game, and was only too anxious to do so; we played
nearly three hours, and I arose from the table thirteen
dollars ahead. Returning to my hotel, 1 paid a week's
board in advance, and after supper started to see the city
by gaslight. I entered many saloons, and nearly all of
them had music going all the evening. I began to think
that Milwaukee would be a grand place to start a saloon
with a stage attached, where a couple of *bums* might give
a sparring exhibition each evening. With this idea in
my mind, I resolved to go through the city and see whether there was any such place already established. After
making a thorough search and finding none, I decided
that I had struck on a good *scheme*, but the next thing to
be considered was, how could it be done when I only possessed the very limited capital of seven dollars, which, as
I continued my investigations, grew gradually less until
1 found myself in the morning with only thirteen cents,

It now became necessary, in order to carry out my purpose, that I set about getting more money.

With the anticipation of getting some kind of work, I got a friend to read the advertisements in the morning paper to me. I found one just to my fancy; it was for a man to work on a farm. I thought this would be the best way for me to make money and *save it*, as I would have none of the temptations of the city to contend with. Consequently I started to see the man who had advertised for a farm hand, and found him in the person of Doctor Williams. The doctor looked me over as a man would a horse, and finally concluded that if I was *willing* to work, I would certainly be a good man for the place.

I had not been very long in Doctor Williams' employ, when one day he began to ask me questions concerning myself, and when I told him I could use the gloves pretty well, he seemed delighted, and the next day when he came out to the farm, he had another man with him. I at once imagined he had brought some prize-fighter from the city that he might have some fun at my expense, but to my astonishment the man was put in my place, and I was promoted to the position of overseer with an increase of pay. I could now begin to see myself standing behind my own bar.

In a few days after receiving my promotion the Doctor asked me if I would rather not be in some other business. At once I opened fire on him, giving a detailed description of my pet scheme, and greatly to my surprise and delight he was quite taken with my idea of a saloon and sparring room in connection, so much so in fact that he told me to look for a suitable place, and he would help me get it. While passing along Chestnut street, I saw a sign in a window of a neat little saloon, which read as follows :—" For sale cheap, on easy terms." This notice seemed to me to have been placed there for my especial benefit.

On going in, I learned the price to be two hundred and fifty dollars,—fifty down and the balance payable on time to the Brewing Co., which held a chattel mortgage on the fixtures to secure two hundred dollars. I now went directly to Doctor Williams, who gave me fifty dollars with which to make the first payment. and by five o'clock that afternoon I was the owner of the saloon. The receipts of the first night were nine dollars at the bar, and fifteen dollars I won in gambling with the man I bought out, this enabled me to lay in a good stock of beer in the morning, when the wagon from the brewery came around.

I now began to study up something for the afternoon paper by way of advertising my new business. Just as I had about decided what I would put in, a Dutchman called for a glass of beer. We soon got into a conversation and I told him I wanted to get a piece in the paper, but would have to get some one to write it for me. He said he was just the man as he was a good writer and scholar ; of course I was obliged to take his word for it as I was not capable of judging. However, I began to dictate and he to write and this is the notice that appeared in the afternoon paper of that day given *verbatim et literatim.*

" Hey their lovers of fun in the art of self-defence take notice that I, the undersigned, have obent a frist glass sporting hous at No. 15 Chestnut street, where I will serve all with a fine cigare and a fresh glass of Schlitzer Celebrated lager beer, and aney one desireing a leson in the art of self-defense free. grand American obening tonight, by calling you Greatly obligt.

Your obediant servent,<br>
Јонн Вкоокѕ,<br>
Midell waite Campion of Callifornia."

My " *obening* " was a grand success and out of it I realized sufficient to repay my friend, the Doctor, and still have a small amount left. This was just about the time of the first excitement between Ryan and Sullivan, con-

AT ST. LOUIS — SILK HAT.

sequently I fortunately had a good string to pull on, and after continuing in this way for six weeks, I decided to launch out on a larger scale. At No. 312 Third Avenue I opened a saloon with Concert Hall attached, where exhibitions in sparring would also be given, adding the still greater attraction of girl *beer slingers*.

As the seventh of February, eighteen hundred and eighty-two, the date fixed for the Ryan-Sullivan fight drew near, my place became headquarters for sporting men generally, and those who were pugilistically inclined particularly, and from whom I reaped quite a harvest. I bet five hundred dollars on Ryan, and of course lost. This was quite a blow to me for I had about twenty people at work for me, and needed the money.

The day of the battle I made arrangements to receive particulars by wire at my saloon, sending out circulars to this effect, so that evening my place was crowded by an excited lot of men, all more or less under the influence of drink and spending money freely. The news at last arrived that Ryan had been whipped at Mississippi City. Then began the drinking, singing and shouting. The friends of Ryan were drinking for disappointment's sake, and those of Sullivan for joy's sake. I belonged to the former class as my five hundred dollars had gone.

A few days later word went the rounds of the sporting population of Milwaukee that Paddy Ryan was in the city, and would give a sparring exhibition ; provided he could get any one to stand before him for four three-minute rounds. One afternoon a couple of hacks containing some Chicago and Milwaukee's leading sports stopped at my saloon. Among the number was Paddy Ryan. A gay time was had for an hour or so, when the subject of Paddy's visit to Milwaukee came up, and before they left the place, all arrangements for a match between Ryan and me were made. The affair to take place on March the tenth, and was to be four rounds as already stated, for points. The place selected for the exhibition was the

D

Academy of Music, it being the largest hall in the city. The appointed time at last arrived, and with it a scene not soon to be forgotten. For blocks the street was packed with people making their way to the *Academy.* Tickets at first sold for one dollar, but were soon raised to one dollar and a half, and yet hundreds were unable to get admission.

As is customary on such occasions the first part of the evening was occupied by local sparrers, and it was twenty minutes after ten when Ryan and I were called out. As we came on the stage deafening cheers arose from the audience and were kept up at intervals during the performance.

At the expiration of the fourth round, when the referee stepped to the foot-lights and declared the match a draw, cheer after cheer went up for " Brooks," and the audience would not be satisfied until we came out for another round. I knew it would not count as the contest had ended, but wished to show the people that I had the *sand* to appear for a fifth round, so at it we went again.

When I got to my saloon I found it filled with an eager crowd, anxiously waiting to congratulate me upon my success. The receipts of my house on that night amounted to nearly five hundred dollars. My reputation was now established, and I soon began to receive challenges to fight from all over the country, finally accepting one from Martin Zowsta, who was called the champion tough of the city. The match was to be eight rounds; Marquis of Queensbury rules to govern. We selected the old base ball grounds and on the day appointed about fifteen hundred people found their way to the place.

At ten minutes to five I came on the battle ground, and went through the customary proceeding of throwing my cap in the ring, my opponent quickly following me. In the first round Zowsta led and I cross-countered with my right, bringing him to his knees; from this time I could not get him to leave the ropes, his object being to claim a foul, for, were I to strike him when touching the ropes, he would have won the fight on a foul. I had the best of the fight all through, but to my great surprise and disgust, when the eighth round was finished, the referee decided the contest *a draw.* Numerous howls of disapproval went up from the disappointed crowd, which realized that a very rank and prejudiced decision had been given. I took a hack and started for my place of business, finding it crowded to the doors when I arrived. Now came the time for congratulations, many of them being similar to those extended to a successful political candidate, the literal translation of which is " *Set 'em up.*"

It was not long after my fight with Zowsta until I received a challenge from John Ward, a big six-footer and the terror of the city. When we had carried on the necessary amount of newspaper controvery, we met and arranged to fight to a finish within ten miles of Milwaukee and for two hundred and fifty dollars a side. The principal topic for conversation among the sporting fraternity now was the Brooks and Ward fight for the championship of Wisconsin.

On the afternoon of the sixth of August, eighteen hundred and eighty-two, thousands of men, women, and children could have been seen making their way towards the Milwaukee Driving Park, which was to be the scene of one of those most brutal exhibitions, a prize-fight. The-ring was pitched just in front of the grand stand, which was filled with the respectable ?) portion of the audience, but gathered around the ring could be seen the most depraved, worthless, and hideous specimens of humanity ever allowed to exist, cursing, swearing and fighting for the most favorable positions in order to obtain a good view of the battle.

Time was at last called, and as we stepped into the ring I could easily notice by the applause of the people that Ward had their sympathy, and therefore I would have an up-hill struggle to win.

The first round was terrific. Ward got the first lead and landed just over my left eye, splitting it wide open, causing the blood to flow freely (I bear the scar of the blow to this day). " Kill the Dutchman," now came from Ward's friends, but before the round closed, I succeeded in getting in a fearful blow on Ward's under lip, splitting it half way down his chin. Thus, when the round closed, we presented a sorrowful sight, bruised, cut, and covered with blood.

In the second round with a swinging right-hander I knocked my man over the ropes, but scarcely a cheer was heard. At my side and a little behind me I chanced to see one of Ward's admirers raise a bottle with which to strike me; involuntarily I glanced around, when Ward took advantage of the no doubt pre-arranged plan and sent me off my feet.

When time was called for the next round, I decided to give up the fight, for I saw there was no chance for me to win, for not only were the spectators against me, but even my trainer and second had sided with the audience. I made my escape as best I could, secured a hack and went to my saloon. After washing the blood from my face and breast I looked in the glass, and must confess I hardly knew my own face, one side of which was swollen to twice its natural size. As soon as I could make my appearance, I went to the office of the Wisconsin *Evening News*, publishing a challenge to fight Ward again in two weeks for one thousand dollars and within five hundred miles of Milwaukee. The challenge was not accepted, for he knew that were I to receive fair play his chances of winning would be very small indeed.

Disgusted with the treatment I had received from the sports of Milwaukee, I sold out my saloon and took passage on a steamer for Grand Rapids, Michigan, where I soon made a match with Thomas Kanear, beating him in four rounds. I did not remain long in Michigan, but found my way to Chicago, where I learned that the notorious "Jim" Elliott was offering fifty dollars to any man who would face him for three rounds. I undertook to do so and received a *big head* for my pains.

This was about the time Charley Mitchell was matched to fight the *Maori*, Herbert Slade, and which was creating so much newspaper talk. Perhaps some of my readers may remember Mitchell's standing offer of five hundred dollars to any man who would be able to stand before him during four rounds. As soon as I learned of this offer, I started for Kansas City, Mo., where Mitchell and Madden then were, my object being to secure the five hundred if possible. Having met Madden before, I called at his hotel, but only to learn that the police refused to allow any such exhibition to take place, thus I had come all the distance for nothing. I had only been a few days in Kansas City, when I received a challenge from Merve Thompson, of Cleveland, Ohio, to spar me at one of the theatres in that city, points to count. The appointed time arrived and in the first round I sprained my right wrist which compelled me to retire from the contest.

I again started west, going as far as Terre Haute, Indiana, where I entered into an agreement to wrestle Primrose, the champion collar and elbow wrestler of Michigan. The stakes were five hundred dollars a side. I secured backers and the date was fixed for January the sixth, eighteen hundred and eighty-four. The struggle lasted for over two hours, when I was declared the winner, having won three falls in five. I became highly elated over my success, and as it is customary on such occasions, we all repaired to the bar to *congratulate* each other. While standing at the bar, a man tapped me on the shoulder, saying, "Isn't your name Hess, and are you not from Buffalo?" This quite startled me, for I had so long assumed the name of Brooks that I had almost forgotten that I had ever been known as "Hess." I soon learned from my new acquaintance that all my family were living

in Buffalo, and were anxious to hear from me, so I resolved to go to the home I had left about eight years
before. In a few days I arrived in Buffalo, and as I
neared the old home, where I knew my mother lived, I
began to wonder if she would know her prodigal son ; at
last I reached the house and who should meet me at the
door but my old mother, not the woman I knew eight
years before so full of life and spirits, but a silvery-haired
old lady, bent over and scarcely able to walk. As I stood
looking at her for a moment, I could hardly realize that
even seven years could make such a change. I did not
think of the great suffering of both body and mind she
had experienced during those years. With tears stream-
ing from her eyes my dear old mother received me with
outstretched arms. I asked where my own family was
living, when my brother opened a door leading into
another room, and in which was my wife with the three
children. What a carewon expression had taken possession of that face that was so bright a few years ago. We
all indulged in a good cry, and then began to tell all our
past experience, which conversation was alternately interrupted by tears of joy and sorrow.

The morning following my return to Buffalo, the very
best resolutions possible were formed by me, and I opened
a concern known as Joe Hess' East Buffalo Gymnasium,
but no liquor was to be sold in the rooms, which were to
be used solely for athletic purposes. I secured a large
class of young men, and everything went well for about
two months, when I decided to go to Lancaster, take my
class and give an athletic exhibition, which proved to be
a grand success. When we returned to Buffalo after our
performance we all went to a certain saloon, where drinking was freely indulged in until all present became more
or less intoxicated, which resulted in there being a general free fight and also a general arrest. Fortunately for
me I had taken no part in the row beyond making an
endeavor to quell it, and in order to do so I was obliged

to thrash the whole party. My ability as a peacemaker was so highly thought of by the police magistrate that he used his influence and immediately secured for me a position as policeman; but it was not long before I became more fit for a prisoner than a preserver of the peace, and soon received my discharge. Becoming again discouraged, I decided to go to Canada and advertise to fight any man in that country for the championship of the Dominion. The challenge was not accepted, and after roaming about London, Ontario, for some time, I returned to Buffalo and entered into a contract to train " Billy " Baker for his fight with " Pat " Slattery of Rochester.

# CHAPTER VI.

Training "Billy" Baker—The process of training—The Baker-Slattery prize-fight—The spectators—Arrest of the principals —Bailed out—Description of the fight—Arrested as a participator—Taken to Rochester—Out on bail—At work on Bartholomay's brewery—Sending for my family—Starting a gambling and boxing room—Roping in a *Sucker*—My last glass—At P. A. Burdick's Temperance meeting—Convicted — Resolve to drink no more—First tempter, NO SIR—O God ! help me—At church—Signing the pledge.

IN the latter part of July, eighteen hundred and eighty-five, I received a note from one Haley, requesting me to call at his saloon, on Mohawk-street, in the city of Buffalo. I complied with the request, and, after a few introductory drinks, was made acquainted with his object in sending for me, and found that I was wanted to enter into an agreement to train " Billy" Baker for his prize-fight with " Pat" Slattery. Everything being satisfactorily arranged, I inquired the whereabouts of my *ward*, and learned that he was in Rochester, but would soon be be in Buffalo, when we would go to Canada and commence the necessary work of preparation for the great contest, or in other words, bring a man to the very best state of health, that he may be able to enter a prize-ring, and there, in a very few minutes, perhaps become maimed for life. But conscience is not allowed a part in affairs of this kind. In a short time Baker arrived in Buffalo, and we left at once for Fort Erie, Canada ; the party comprising Baker, his trainer, and several of his backers and admirers. Baker is a short, stout man, with rather a kind face, when free from that glare of hell given it by rum. He is a very powerful man, and when in *condition*, presents a very finely proportioned physique. His eyes are hazel and have a pleasant, but

most determined expression. "Billy's" age at the time
of the above training, was twenty-three years; so you
see we have here a young man, scarcely out of his *teens*,
preparing to enter into that most disgraceful and sinful
of all exhibitions, namely a prize-fight.

The first night we spent on Canadian soil was a very
pleasant one, as we soon got rid of those who came over
with us, and retired early for a good night's rest, so that
we might awaken in the morning fully rested, and ready
for the first day of training, the programme of which
was as follows, and might be profitably adopted by some
who do not desire to enter the P. R., but simply as a
promoter and preserver of good health. About half
past six we would arise, and the first thing for me to do
was to give " Billy" a good hand rubbing; this for the
purpose of equalizing the circulation of the blood. After
the rubbing process a brisk walk of one mile was taken,
or which was just as good, a fifteen minutes' exercise with
Indian clubs, this to bring on a slight perspiration. The
next step was a sponge bath in cold water, containing
sufficient salt to make a brine, then a good rubbing with
a coarse towel until the skin is all aglow, and now the
*patient* is ready for and can eat a good breakfast, consisting of plain, nourishing, but unstimulating food.
Between one and two hours is allowed after breakfast
for the purpose of digestion, when a fifteen mile walk is
taken, and, if the person has been a drinking man, heavy
clothing is placed upon him, in order that the whiskey,
etc., may be sweated out of his system. After the walk
a fifteen mile run is taken, followed by a shower bath
and plenty of good rubbing, also a half hour lie down
for rest, then comes the dinner hour. After dining the
time necessary for digestion is allowed, when another
fifteen mile run is indulged in, and precisely at ten
o'clock preparations are made for retiring. All this is
repeated daily, for six or twelve weeks, according to circumstances. There is no man who would not rather
fight ten battles than train for one.

During the training not one drop of liquor of any description is to be used; then why is it that saloon keepers and their supporters will argue that liquor is beneficial in toning a man up?   But when it comes to a true test, not one saloon man, or any other sporting man, will wager one dollar on a man if he drinks strong drink. The time came when it should be decided between Baker and Slattery who should receive the one thousand dollars. Oak Orchard, in Orleans county, on the shore of Lake Ontario, was selected as the battle ground, and the time fixed for August 25th, 1885; consequently we left Buffalo for Rochester on the morning of the 24th, and on the afternoon of that same day there could have been seen on State-street, in the city of Rochester, small groups of men standing closely together, talking in a very confidential manner, and evidently in a state of great excitement. That evening these same men might have been seen boarding the Lake avenue street cars, going to the terminus of the street railway.   Upon leaving the cars, they made their way down a dark and winding road leading to the elevator which was to carry them to the glen; when they reached *terra firma*, the first move was towards the bar to procure some *courage*, or rather, that damnable stuff that gives men courage to do any evil deed, and without which their better nature would rebel against the act.   Every moment there were fresh arrivals, until the whole company was completed.   We then began to size each other up to see if we were *all of a kind*, and such we were willing to be considered at this particular time, while some who were present would have decidedly refused to recognise many of the others under different circumstances.   Nor is this to be wondered at, when I tell you that the company consisted of the following distinguished personages:—One justice of the peace; several lawyers; a gentleman who has since been appointed to the office of city sealer of Rochester; policemen in citizens' clothes; representatives of several lead-

ing newspapers, including one prominent Sunday journal;
church members; business men; gamblers; saloon keepers; drunkards and roughs; toughs, and bums generally,
all starting out to witness a prize-fight to take place
between "Billy" Baker and "Pat" Slattery.

Doubtless many of my readers are laboring under the
impression that such brutal affairs are only attended by
the most degraded class of humanity, and your first exclamation upon reading the list of spectators just given
will probably be: "Is it possible!"   I can assure you it
is; all these people were there, and how I come to know
it is because I was there myself; in what particular class
I came it matters not, for on this eventful occasion there
was a distinction but no difference.

The boat soon arrived that was to carry us to Oak
Orchard, the place selected for the battle ground, and as
we steamed out upon the waters of Lake Ontario we
could breathe more freely, knowing that, for a while at
least, we were free from the clutches of the law.  The
trip was occupied in betting, drinking and cursing;
some were sleeping, others singing, until about two o'clock
in the morning, when heavy rain set in, when we were
all obliged to huddle closely together in order to keep
from getting drenched.  Presently every tongue was
silenced by the alarm being raised that the Sheriff's boat
was after us.  When our captain realized this fact he
taxed his engine to its utmost capacity, but the Sheriff
had the swifter boat, and arrived at Oak Orchard one
mile in advance, but upon landing he discovered that the
principals whom he imagined to be in our boat, had landed some time previously, and had already been arrested
by the Sheriff of Orleans County, and were then securely
lodged in the jail at Albion.  The Sheriff, who had hoped
to capture Baker and Slattery on our boat, at once returned to Rochester, little satisfied and *less* gratified, as
he had arrived too late to secure the honor of such an important arrest.  A few minutes after the officers' boat

had left the wharf ours arrived, and we could at once tell
from the mournful expression on the countenances of
those who had already come upon the ground, that a
great disappointment was in store for us.   A company of
Baker's admirers had arrived from Buffalo, and was composed of very much the same class of people as I have
already said were in the Rochester party.

It was now decided that some of the leading Buffalo
and Rochester sports should go to Albion for the purpose
of bailing the prisoners.   This was successfully accomplished, and about three o'clock in the afternoon of August the 25th Baker and Slattery appeared, and everyone was at once in a great state of excitement.   A
council of war was held, and an agreement entered into
that we should go to Troutburg, pitch the ring and have
our battle.  Everyone was pleased with this arrangement
for they now began to feel that they were to be repaid
for their trouble and annoyance of waiting in the rain
for some eighteen or twenty hours.   All who were able
to do so got aboard the boat, the others forming a procession and going by an overland route.   While we were
proceeding by boat a second council of war was held, presided over by Coroner Daniel Sharp, of Rochester, who,
after hearing arguments *pro and con*, decided the fight
should take place.   Not wishing to deprive anyone connected with this *glorious* affair of any *honor*, I, therefore,
in justice to Mr. Sharp, state that he held the responsible
and *respectable* (?) position of referee of the fight.   The
above decision being final, we made preparations, when
off Troutburg, to land; and what was more remarkable,
we were assisted in doing so by a Deputy Sheriff who
had heard nothing of the previous day's arrests, and inno-
cently supposed us to be a picnic party.   The stakes were
driven, and the ring pitched just three hundred feet from
the Orleans County line, and in the County of Monroe.

Everything being now in readiness a call was made for
the principals.  The first to put in an appearance was

Baker, of Buffalo, accompanied by his second, *Joe Hess.*
The customary act, at such affairs, of throwing the cap
into the ring by the fighters, to signify that they were
not afraid to go in and bring it out, was done first by
Baker, amid the deafening cheers of his many admirers.
Slattery soon followed, in company with the veteran Jack
Turner, and his performance of the *cap act* was even more
enthusiastically received than Baker's. The men went to
their respective corners, Slattery in the southeast and
Baker in the northwest, these positions, of course, having
been tossed for by the seconds. It now became necessary
to select an *honourable* man to act as timekeeper, rather
a difficult task to perform you will say, but we succeeded,
after considerable discussion, in appointing Thomas
Mahoney, of Rochester, to the exalted position. Can it
be said we made a mistake in our estimate of an honest
man, when the same person has since been appointed to
the responsible position of City Sealer of Rochester? Thus
was Slattery's timekeeper selected. Baker secured Her-
man Burk art, of Buffalo, also an *honest* man ; *honesty* as
I have already said, being the necessary qualification for
this important office. All preliminaries being arranged,
the blankets were removed from the shoulders of the
principals, when a general exclamation of approval as to
looks, condition, etc., went up from the spectators. Principals and seconds now stepped to the centre of the ring to
do the customary handshaking, which signified that all
were friends. Just think, my reader, here were two young
men who had carefully brought themselves into an almost
perfect state of health, and who were now about to mutilate and, perhaps, injure each other for life. Time was
called, and both men advanced to the centre of the ring
with a determined and fiendish expression on their faces,
which suggested to the crowd that the fight would be on
its merits, and a desperate one.

"Billy" landed his left squarely on "Pat's" cheek,
who immediately returned the compliment by a terrible

right-hander planted on Billy's ribs.   Each man was now
aware that his opponent meant business, and that a fearful encounter would be the result of the meeting.

In the second round " Billy " had a slight advantage,
finishing in the best condition, although but little difference was perceptible.   From the beginning of the third
round " Pat " forced the fighting, and by a terrific blow
succeeded in laying " Billy's " eye open ; contrary to expectations, this seemed to bring " Billy " to his senses,
and he soon got in one on " Pat's " stomach that sent him
to the ropes.   A cry of foul was at once raised but not
allowed ; the fighting now became something terrible to
witness, many blows being struck, which were sufficient
in force to fell an ox.   A clinch was made, and I began
to think my man was done for, which I fear would have
been the result had not time been called, just at that
moment.

When the fourth round was called, " Billy " ran to the
centre.   I knew by this that he had recovered (in sporting parlance) his *second wind*, and that if he avoided
making a foul would certainly be victorious.   As " Pat "
approached the scratch he presented a careworn, nevertheless a determined expression.   Billy was quick to discover the condition of his antagonist, taking advantage of
it by rushing at him more like a mad bull than a human
being, thus driving poor Pat mercilessly around the ring
until time was called.   As the men came up for the fifth
round, it was a noticable fact that Pat's courage was on
the wane.   A frightful blow on the neck sent Pat to the
ropes, Billy quickly following up his advantage by plant-
ing another on Pat's breast.   At this point some of Pat's
friends pulled up a stake, bringing the ropes close to his
back, making it appear that if another blow were struck,
while this position was held a foul would be the result.
The blow was struck, a foul claimed, and Pat was dragged
from the ring.   When time was called for the sixth round,
Pat failed to appear, consequently I rushed to Daniel

Sharp, the referee, claiming the fight for Baker, he replied, "Yes, Baker wins." As the majority of the spectators were Slattery's sympathizers, a tremendous howl of disappointment, disgust and disapproval, went up as the above decision was made known. Being satisfied that my man had won the fight, I now went to look after him, and in some degree if possible relieve him of his sufferings. We had not gone very far in the direction of the boat, when we heard the crowd talking in a very boisterous and excited manner, and upon looking back saw the referee surrounded by a mob who demanded the fight for Slattery on a foul. The former decision was now reversed, and the fight given to Pat. Everything was now excitement, of a kind which it is difficult to describe, and the referee, fearing that he would be mobbed, jumped into a buggy and in company with Jack Turner, Slattery's second, started for Rochester. Just before leaving, however, he again gave the fight to Baker. During the fight, Slattery made a good defence, and fought bravely; but it could easily be seen that he was not in as good condition as Baker, as he had not entirely given up the use of liquor during his training.

In all my experience with athletes and sporting men, I will say that I never found one who was more conscientious in his contests, doing his best on all occasions, and winning if possible, than Billy Baker. Let us return to Troutburg, and see how the great crowd that had gathered there, dispersed. In every direction one could see wagons carts, drays and pedestrians, moving rapidly along the road; congratulations were freely given that no arrests had been made. Slattery started for the nearest depot, in one direction, and Baker for a similar object, in an opposite way, the latter taking the Rome, Watertown and Ogdensburg Railroad, for Niagara Falls, with the further intention of going to Canada. As I have already stated, the referee came by horse and buggy to Rochester, the remainder of Rochester's celebrities taking the boat. As we sailed from the dock, I noticed that with the exception of the Elmira *Telegram* representative, I was the only non-resident of Rochester on the boat. At half-past eleven in the evening we arrived at the Genessee landing, and took street cars into the city, many of us going to Jack Turner's saloon, which was the recognised headquarters of those interested in the fight that had just taken place. Upon my arrival, I learned that referee Sharpe had sent a written statement to the *Police Gazette*, giving the battle to Slattery. I knew this was final, as no verbal decision is binding in such matters. The jubilant feelings that I had experienced on the homeward trip were now those of disappointment, for I had been promised a large proportion of the stakes if Baker won, but would now receive nothing. While thus musing over ill luck, and cursing the fates, I fortunately ran across Ed. Mullen, who was one of Baker's principal supporters, and who very kindly gave me two dollars to get a ticket for Buffalo. It was some time before the train would leave, and I scarcely knew how to put in the time, having no money to get any refreshments, either liquid or solid. Fortune once more smiled upon me when I met Frank Lang, Slattery's trainer; of course, Frank was now greatly elated over the success of his man, and nothing would do, but that I should go and have a bottle of *extra dry*, and other refreshments in keeping. In a very short time, under the influence of such a banquet, I had forgotten that there had ever been a prize fight. It is needless to say the time was very happily spent till my train left for Buffalo, at three o'clock in the morning. I got on the train, fell asleep and knew nothing until five o'clock, when I was awakened by the brakeman calling out " Buffalo." My first thought was of a saloon, for I felt tough in the extreme. While walking up Exchange-street, I felt in my pockets for the price of an eye-opener, and what was my delight, upon finding a ten-cent piece, and also a two-dol-

lar note; how this bill came in my possession, I cannot explain, but there it was, and at that particular time most
ceptable.  I had not gone far when I saw a man washing the windows of his saloon ;  I entered the place, and
the first words the man said to me were. " Well, did you
have a good time at the fight ? "  I pretended to be
ignorant of anything of this kind, but he said Baker had
just been there and told him all about it; believing
Baker to be in Canada, I said " *yov're a liar,*" when he
picked up a glass and threw it at me ; I dodged, and out
it went into the street, right through the window he had
been washing, I quickly followed it for I was very much
afraid of being arrested, knowing that if I should be the
history of our Troutburg *picnic* would probably leak out
and result in our being sent up for some time, as the
penalty for prize-fighting is a heavy one.

I now started to find Baker, and where did I go to
search for him ?  In some respectable hotel or quiet
boarding-house ?  No ; but in the most degraded part of
the city, namely, in the vicinity of Canal-street.  I knew
if he had remained in Buffalo I would find him in a disreputable place of some description.  While continuing
my search in a half-drunken condition, the Captain of
No. 1 Station informed me that if I did not go home he
would *run me in.*  I obeyed his orders and at once started homeward, where I indulged in a good sound sleep.

Sometime during the day my little girl awoke me by
saying " there are two big policemen here for you."  Of
course, I knew what this meant, for I had been guilty of
an offence against the law of the State of New York.
The *bracelets* were placed on me, and from my own
house, and in presence of my children, I was led away
in shackles to the police station, where I was locked up.
It was not long before I saw my *pal*, "Billy" Baker, who
presented a terrible appearance from the effects of the
previous day's battle.  We entered into a conversation,
in the course of which I said to Billy, "Oh! for a drink of

E

the old *stuff."*    The reply to this exclamation came, not
in the form of words, but a very significant wink, which
I interpreted as meaning "wait a bit."    And sure enough
my *pal*, after a few minutes' absence, returned with a
bottle of old rye, which proved, just at this particular
time, to be a *life preserver*, as the stimulating effects of
the whiskey I had been drinking had almost completely
died out, and in consequence thereof I felt *broken up* generally.    Perhaps some of my readers can appreciate this
feeling.

News soon came to me that the Deputy Sheriff of
Monroe County had arrived, and was waiting to escort
me to the *Flour City.*    The bracelets were again placed
on my wrists and I was led to the depot, where we
boarded a train for Rochester, in which city I received
the very best of care, in fact so anxious were they concerning my safety, that the room I occupied at my *hotel*
was protected by iron bars across the windows, and even
the *porter* took especial care to lock my door from the
outside.    I began to meditate upon my chances for liberty, or imprisonment, and must confess that I fully expected to get, at least, two years in the Penitentiary, for
I felt the case would be a clear and strong one, remembering the fact that several of Rochester's policemen
were at the prize fight at Troutburg, and it began to
dawn upon me that they were probably sent as spies.    I
have since found out, however, that such was not the
case.    They were there of their own free will.    Do not
be afraid, boys, I will not give you away, although your
names are well known to me now.    Early next morning
Thomas Mahoney and Daniel Sharpe called, assuring me
they would secure bail and have me released.    I felt such
a thing would be impossible, but my benefactors proved
equal to the occasion, and soon returned with a prominent saloon-keeper and a professional gambler, who expressed their willingness to go on my bonds; and everything being satisfactory I was once more allowed to

breathe the free air until such time as I should be called
to give an account of my connection with Baker-Slattery
prize-fight.

Upon being liberated from prison I decided to seek
some legitimate employment and give up my sporting
career. This fact I made known to Thomas Mahoney,
who kindly offered to assist me in my efforts to get
something to do. For this purpose we hired a hack.
Think of it, seeking employment under these circumstances. A prize-fighter, a saloon-keeper and two prominent city officials driving about the city in search of
work for the *fighter*. After calling at several saloons
without any success beyond a few drinks, we started for
the Bartholomay brewery; here, after a few moments
of parleying, I was engaged to come to work the following morning.

On Friday morning, August 29th, about five o'clock, a
man could have been seen walking up North St. Paul-
street, in the City of Rochester, clothed in blue overalls,
and presenting every appearance of a "son of toil."
This man was *Joe Hess* on his way to the brewery, where
he expected to settle down, earn an honest living and become a sober man, and, my reader, I think you will
agree with me when I say, under very discouraging circumstances; for the first thing upon my arrival at the
place a glass of beer was presented, and every hour
throughout the day a bell is rung and every employee
takes his quart can, proceeds to the *dispensing* room and
has it filled with beer. I thought my will was sufficiently strong to withstand this temptation, so I sent a few
lines to my wife in Buffalo, requesting her to bring the
children and come to Rochester, where I had secured
honorable employment, and would provide a comfortable
home for them. It was about two weeks before my
family came, and in the meantime I had fallen a victim
to that *hourly* tempter, but still hoped to sober up and
remain so when they arrived.

The second Sunday morning after I had entered the brewery, my wife and three children came to Rochester, and I met them at the depot, but am ashamed to say, not in my sober senses. As we were proceeding up North St. Paul-street, to the three little rooms I had rented, I chanced to look over my shoulder, and saw my wife in tears, and I tell you, my reader, our procession was a silent one, for the remainder of the distance. When we reached our destination, I left my family and did not return for three days, but when I did my wife implored me to leave the brewery, and do something else, even go back to my sporting life, which would be preferable and safer than working in that *drunkard factory.* I secured the assistance of a saloon keeper, and procured a room on Main-street, which I fixed up as a poker and gambling room, with a wrestling and boxing school connected. I was successful in obtaining several scholars, and prosperity (of the kind) stared me in the face. I had three *pals* whose names I will withhold, who assisted me in *roping in suckers.* One day we chanced to see a farmer who was flourishing his money about in a very careless manner, and of course *spotted* him as our victim, and set to work planning a trap for him. We were successful beyond our expectations, for by three o'clock the next morning we had beaten him out of six hundred dollars, by means of card playing.

Let me here say a word to those who imagine themselves beyond the reach of gamblers and confidence men. Even our senators, our shrewdest lawyers, have been ensnared by these men, and when this class of men are made victims of, what chance is there for the rest. I will give you the only sure way to keep from being victimized; strictly avoid having anything to do with these thieves, this is your only sure plan of safety. The means used to swindle the unwary, are manifold, their name is legion. I will not undertake here to describe any of them, for by so doing I would be educating the rogues, as well as warning the innocent, and thereby more evil than good might be done. I will simply say, however, when a stranger comes to you with a plausible story concerning some scheme which is to be of so great a value to you, and he is to receive nothing from it, ask yourself this question: Why does this stranger take so much interest in me? Is it human nature, that he should give me everything and keep nothing himself? Then act upon a common sense basis, and have nothing to do with him.

With the money we won from the Monroe county farmer, we started on a spree; by we, I mean myself and my three pals. Securing a hack we visited nearly every saloon in the city during the day, and of course by evening became considerably under the influence of liquor. This terrible debauch lasted for three weeks, when one evening we had met in a saloon on State-street, where drinks were ordered. I shall never forget the occasion; for as I raised my glass I imagined there was pepper and salt in the liquor, and I replaced the glass on the bar; as I looked at it the second time, I saw worms swimming about, I went through the same operation of putting it back on the bar, waiting for some time before raising the glass for the third time, but when I did there were thousands of small black heads bobbing up and down. I now said to the bartender, "Charley, why don't you keep your glasses clean?" and began to describe to him, what I had seen. He replied, you are going to have the "snakes," and my reader so I was, on the very verge of *delerium tremens*. I drank the liquor as a preventive from this terrible disease, and as God is my judge, I can truthfully say it was the last glass of intoxicating liquor that ever touched my lips, and with His help it ever shall be.

We went out to our hack and the question was asked, what shall be done? I proposed that we go to the Fitz-hugh-street rink, to hear that temperance *bloak*," meaning P. A. Burdick. The proposition was accepted, and off we started for the rink, entering by the left hand door and taking seats far back in the audience. We had entered this place from no other motive than that of having fun, but Burdick soon got his eyes on us, and oh how he did open fire, every word he spoke only went to convince me what a degraded and sinful man I had become. I began to feel very uneasy under this terrific volley of words, and said to my partner who was sitting beside me, "this man has been up at my house and found out all about me, and now stands up here and tells all these people what a heartless wretch I am. I am going to get up and ask him what business he had there." I was just about to get up, when my *pal* caught me by the coat saying, "sit still you fool, he has been at my house too." I now became so thoroughly convinced of my wickedness, that I could stand the burning words no longer, and started out of the rink, followed by my three companions, As I was going out, I felt something hot on my cheek, and found it to be a tear, a thing that had not been there for many a long year, When we arrived on the outside I said to the boys, "boys, I drink no more." This raised a laugh, and brought out words like these : don't be a fool because you heard that temperance man. I repeated my assertion, and demanded to be driven to my home, if I may call it a home. When I arrived at the foot of the stairs that led to my furniture-less, comfortless rooms, I saw my wife standing at the top, holding a tallow candle in her hand, crying as if her heart would break, and as only a drunkard's wife can cry. As I came to the top of the stairs she said, "oh Joe, if I can ever see the day when you will be a sober man, I will be ready to die."

The following conversation then took place :—Jennie, forgive me this time ; it will be the last ; never again shall I drink a glass of strong drink.

Joe, don't tell me another lie, you have already told me so many, that I cannot believe you ; I know you want

to, but you never will.  I again expressed my determination to lead a sober life, and we went into the rooms.
As I sat gazing into the careworn face of my wife, my
thoughts reverted to the day when I had led her a happy
light-hearted girl to the altar where she became the wife
of one who had so cruelly neglected her for so many
years.  I entered the room where my two little girls were
calmly sleeping, and as I looked into their sweet, but
pale and wan faces, the words spoken by Burdick at the
rink came back to me, bringing conviction more forcibly
than ever.  I went to look at my boy, my only son, and
did I see in that face the evidence of a light, gay, and
happy heart, as there should have been?  No; the face
was pinched, the eyes sunken, and the form wasted by
hunger.  I began to realize what I had done, and took a
solemn oath that 1 would never again drink a drop of
intoxicating liquor.

My reader will remember that at this time I was not a
believer in God, and was relying entirely upon my own
will power to keep me firm in my new resolution.

The next morning I started down to the city, and had
reached the corner, where I was accosted by a man who
asked me to come and *take something.*  I said, " No, sir,"
and must have said it with a great deal of force, for many
of the bystanders stared at me, no doubt imagining that
an escaped lunatic had suddenly put in an appearance.
Just here, let me say to my young friends, is where I
achieved a victory by refusing the tempter at the very
outset.

I went to my gambling room, and the very first thing
I did was to throw my playing cards out of the window,
sending the poker chips after them.  I now locked myself
in the room and decided never to leave it till I should
get perfectly sober, and furthermore, overcome my appetite for drink.  Now my sufferings began in earnest, for
three days was 1 tortured as few men have ever been
before.  In my terrible agony I actually tore the hair

from my head, and shudder to think of the fearful oaths and curses I used, but at last I surrendered. About four o'clock of the afternoon of the third day, I fell upon my knees, crying, "Oh, God, if there is a God in heaven, prove it to me now, take away this desire for drink. Oh, God help me, I want to become a father and a husband; oh, God help me!" This was the first prayer I ever uttered, and is given *verbatim*. When I had thus prayed I fell to the floor and must have remained there for some time, for when I came to myself again it was dark, although all around me seemed bright, for God had heard my cry, and verily did He create a clean heart within me. I found that my clothes were wet from the perspiration, and I felt and knew that a great and miraculous change had taken place in me, for I had no longer that terrible temptation to drink. My first thought was now of my family, consequently I went home and enjoyed a peaceful night's rest. The following morning being Sunday, I said to my wife, "Jennie, let us go to church." She looked at me in perfect amazement, saying, "Joe, I have only this calico dress; you would not go with me."

I said, "Jennie, am I good enough for you? If so, you are for me," and off we started for Asbury Church, after which I remained at home all the rest of the day, spending the time with my family, and this was the first Sunday I had spent with my family as a sober man during the sixteen years of my wedded life. Monday morning I went down to my room on Main street, and as each of my old associates would ask me to drink, as regularly would I refuse them, always saying, "I drink no more." Of course this brought sneers, laughs, etc., from them, but I cared not for that; my mind was thoroughly made up to reform. This same evening I went to hear Mr. Burdick, and by his words I was fully convinced of my wrongs and determined more than ever to become a better man. I attended the meetings regularly, and at the conclusion of his address one evening Mr.

Burdick requested anyone who might be in trouble to come forward and have a talk with him. I accepted this invitation, but did not have sufficient courage to stand before the large audience and converse with a Christian man, so asked if I could see him at his hotel the following morning. I was given a very hearty invitation to call at the Litster House, and then left the rink with a light heart.

The next morning I started very early for my appointment, but found I would be obliged to wait some time for my turn, as quite a number were already waiting to receive a word of encouragement from the great kindhearted man.

When I was permitted to go to Mr. Burdick's rooms, he met me at the door and gave me a warm welcome, even calling me by name. I was surprised that he should know who I was, but he said, I know all about you. After a conversation lasting some time, and from which I received a great deal of encouragement, I was asked to come to the rink in the evening to sign the pledge. I promised to do so. That evening, in company with my little girl, I went to the rink. I did not hear much that was said, however, for I was contemplating the signing of the pledge. I realized the fact that I was about to enter into a very solemn obligation, for with me the making of this vow was no light affair.

The time for signers to come forward at last arrived, my little girl jumped up saying, " Come, papa, come and sign the pledge." I went slowly to the front, but it was a frightful struggle, for I was not sure that I would be able to keep the pledge, and so greatly did this thought weigh upon me that when I reached the table I said, " I can't do it." At this my little girl began to cry, Burdick picked up a pledge card and read it to me, then this thought came to me : I will sign it, not because Burdick asks me to, not because my little girl is begging me to, not because two thousand people are watching me, but because it reads, " God helping me," and ever since I signed that little card I have looked to God for strength, and he has kept me.

If all who sign the pledge would do so, not relying upon their own strength, but trusting in the saving and keeping power of the Lord Jesus Christ, temptations would lose their power, and all would remain firm to the end.

# CHAPTER VII.

" Now I love Papa "—Joe Hess the temperance man—Let us pray
—An errand boy—A book agent—Two,baskets of provisions—
My children at school—Brother Hess—On the avenue—I will
trust him—Moving—Wife, this is our new home—A dinner
party—Because I am a temperance man.


IMMEDIATELY after signing the pledge, my little girl
took me firmly by the hand, saying, " Now I love
papa." These were the first words of encouragement I
received, and coming from my own child, the child—that
up to a very short time before had refused to even call
me papa—conveyed more joy and happiness to me than
any other words could have done. I did not remain long
in the rink after signing my pledge card, for I wanted to
hasten home and show my wife what I had done, for she
had imagined that when it came to the test I would fail
to take the stand for right. As we neared home my little
girl ran on ahead, to be first in telling the good news, so
by the time I reached the stairway my wife was standing
at the top, but not as she had stood but a short time before, with tears in her eyes and a wretched careworn
expression on her face ; no, she was now ready and waiting to greet me with smiles and words of encouragement,
and hope for a brighter future, for she realized that the
step I had taken meant something.

From this time forth I began to find out that life was
worth living; my evenings were spent at the Fitzhugh-
street rink in company with my family, and on Sundays
we could all be seen at some church. What a change
had come over me. The very hours that I had hereto-
fore spent in saloons, amid corrupt and unholy influences,
were now enjoyed in a perfectly opposite way. I would
that some word of mine here spoken could convince every

drinking man who is giving himself up to a life of degradation, that the name "reformer" is sweet when compared with that of drunkard. For nearly twenty-one years that accursed name was applied to me, and I thank God to-day that it no longer shall be. I fancy some young man may say, I have sufficient self-respect to keep me from making a beast of myself; but let me say, stop and consider how many are saying the same thing every year; what positive proof have you that your fate may not be similar to that of so many, even of our brightest and greatest men. I say you have no proof, but on the contrary there is abundant, and I hope convincing evidence, that sooner or later strong drink will make a slave of nearly every one who uses it; and furthermore, it makes no particular choice, but fastens its fangs upon the high and low, the rich and poor, the educated and ignorant, the old and young; therefore I say, beware of the beginning. The first glass is the beginning of the end, and that end a ruined life, a dishonored name, a lonely grave, a handful of turf forever covering from sight the drunkard's or suicide's face.

The morning following the signing of the pledge I began to reflect upon my past life, and as I thought of all I had passed through, the dangers I had escaped, I could but exclaim, Surely, God has been merciful to me, a sinner!

After breakfast I started for the Litster House to see my new found and best of earthly friends, Mr. Burdick. While I waiting in the hotel office for an audience with him, a little man with a full beard stepped up to me, saying, "I believe this is Joe Hess, the prize-fighter." I replied, No! Joe Hess the *temperance* man. Our conversation was interrupted at this point by Mr. Burdick calling me to his rooms. After a short interview, during which I received many encouraging words, I took my departure, going to my old room on Main-street. Here I was sitting with my heels on the poker table, meditating and laying plans for the future. I had no trade, no education, could scarcely read or write, and with all these discouragements surrounding me, I had a wife and children at home, who were actually in want of the necessaries of life. I began to feel somewhat disheartened, when I suddenly heard somebody coming up the stairs. I wondered who it could be, for my old associates had already forsaken me. The door slowly opened, and who should enter but the *little man* who had spoken to me in the hotel office a few hours before. As he entered, he looked around the room, asking different questions; finally coming up to the poker table, he wished to know the object of the small hole in the centre of it. I now thought this man was trying to play me for a *chump*, so replied: "That is where we used to rob such suckers as you." He did not get the least offended at this, but kept right on asking more questions, when he dropped on his knees, saying, "*let us pray.*" At first I did not know whether the man was a *Christian* or a *lunatic*, but as I was slowly compelled to come to my knees and again ask God to forgive me for my past sin, and to help me in the new life, I became fully convinced that the *little man* was one of the first named, and to-day I thank God that this man, who was none other than Mr. P. H. Carver, of North Bergen, ever came to see me, for his kind and encouraging words greatly cheered me when I was feeling almost discouraged. As Mr. Carver took my hand to bid me God-speed, he left a twenty-five cent piece in it, and immediately left the room. I looked at the money and thought of the man, then thought of the man and looked at the money; then said to myself: "Well, this is my first *temperance* money, and it will buy three loaves of bread." So off I started for a bakery, that I should not go back to my family empty-handed. Before going home, however, I went once more to see my counsellor at the Litster House; he asked me what I intended to do, if I had a trade, etc. I said I had no trade, but was willing to do anything, even to sweep the street crossings, so that I could get out of the gambling and boxing room, with which were connected so many evil associations. As we were conversing, there came a rap at the door, and a Mr. Cobb, of Fairport, entered. Mr. Burdick said to him, "Joe is in somewhat straightened circumstances, is anxious to get out of his old business, and I propose to help him." Upon hearing this, Mr. Cobb replied, "So do I," at the same time bringing out his pocket-book and taking therefrom a crisp bank note ; Mr. Burdick duplicated the amount, and with ten dollars in my pocket, I started out to pay up my room rent and close it up *forever.*

As soon as I was alone, I began to think of the great kindness my new friends had done me, also of the faith they had in me ; then the thought came to me, who among my old associates would have thus helped me ? In times of prosperity saloon keepers are always ready to help in cases of temporary need, but in times of adversity, never.

The first thing I did by way of earning an honest living, was to run errands for Mr. Burdick, who, as many of you are aware, suffers from lameness. Although merely a message boy, I felt highly elated over my new position. After I had worked in this capacity for a few days, I spelled out an advertisement in the *Democrat and Chronicle,* to the effect that any man of temperate habits and willing to work, could find remunerative employment at No. 97 State-street. *Of temperate habits and willing to work ;* this so hit me now, that I decided to investigate further, never for a moment thinking of my inexperience in legitimate business, or my lack of education, but started for No. 97. As I entered the office, I inquired if that was the place they wanted a sober man to work. The man seated in a large arm chair before the desk, replied in the affirmative, adding this question, "Have you ever been a book agent ?" to which I replied, "No, sir" ; then came the words, "We don't want you." At this my face became greatly elongated, and I felt very much discouraged, for I was so anxious to secure some honorable employment, and now, almost my first attempt to do so was apparently to be unsuccessful. I walked across the room, and stood looking out of the window, when the tears began to roll down my cheeks, but I soon thought of those words, "If at first you don't succeed, try, try again." So gaining fresh courage, I turned to the manager saying, "Won't you give a fellow a chance?" He asked me a few questions, and finally prepared for me an outfit, for which I settled, and started out as a "B.A." (book agent), but did not even know of what my outfit consisted, that is, to any intelligent degree.

I now began to study upon the correct plan of work; whether to go to front or back doors, to the grand or poorer class of houses, and after thinking the matter over in all its different phases, as presented to me, I decided to begin at the front doors of the best looking houses; consequently set out for Tremont-street, and the first aristocratic looking dwelling I came to was to be my starting point. I had not proceeded far when I came before a large red brick house, and up to this time I had not thought of what I had to sell, consequently when I reached the steps I became painfully aware of the fact that I did not even know what to tell the people I had, and it was now too late for me to stop and open my box and study up, but, as my reader will soon learn, it made little or no difference on this occasion, whether I was posted or not. I rang the door-bell, and after waiting a reasonable time, there appeared before me the figure of a woman, with hair that very strikingly resembled the bricks in the house, and oh! what eyes; I honestly believe if she were to look into a powder magazine the whole affair would go up by spontaneous combustion. As soon as I mentioned the name "books," the great door was slammed in my face, and nothing was left me but to vacate. I met this same reception at the majority of the places. One lady informed me that she had done nothing but answer the door for us *tramps* all the morning, and hoped I would be the last. It is needless to say I made a memorandum of the number of that house, so that I might omit it if ever I came that way in the future. With this kind of luck, my first day as a book-agent ended. The next day I worked hard all day, but did not effect a sale; I knew, however, that others had succeeded in selling, and I determined to learn the secret, if possible. The third day the thought came to me that perhaps my *ability* as a salesman was not sufficiently appreciated by the *bon ton* of the city. I therefore decided to try some who were *fortunate* enough to be classed among those in the more humble walks of life. I soon found myself on Troop-street, and entered a gate which led to a small frame house; going to the back door, I saw a small, old man in the garden at work; I informed him I had some books to sell. "Books, is it? Will ye git out o' this, or I'll set me bull dog at ye," and I *got*. Meeting with this reception at the very first place I called after adopting my new plan, I became very much discouraged; in fact so much so, that I decided to go to my chief adviser, at the Litster House, namely P. A. Burdick. When I arrived at his apartments, he was out, but Mrs. Burdick gave me a hearty welcome, bidding me sit down and wait for Mr. B., who would return shortly. After inquiring after my health, both physical and spiritual, she asked what I was doing. I replied: "Selling books." "What kind?" was asked; and then I was compelled to refer her to the box, for I really did not know the names of them. Just as the books were brought from the box Mr. Burdick entered, his wife at once directing his attention to them, asking at the same time money to the extent of their value, that she might procure them. This made me all attention, for at last I was to be fortunate enough to make a sale, and, with the money, I at once started for the office on State-street, in order to secure another supply.

With my second lot of books I started up North Avenue, and upon seeing a doctor's sign I thought to myself, surely doctors ought to buy books; so I started for the door; but before I had gone half way up the walk the office door opened, and that grand man, Doctor Hulbert, gave me a very hearty welcome. I did not know him then, but have since learned something of this great, good man's true worth. When I had entered the office, the usual formal questions were asked, of course, including, "What are you doing now, Joe?" I replied, on this occasion, that I was traveling as a book agent. I thought *travelling* sounded pretty well; but when I was obliged to confess that I did not know the name of my books, the Doctor was greatly amused and proceeded to enlighten me on the subject, and before I left his office I not only knew what I had been trying to sell, but had made another sale. Now success seemed assured, and I again went to State-street for a fresh stock, and after securing them, started up Main-street until I came to the residence of Mrs. Holmes. I was greatly surprised, and also very much pleased, with the treatment I received as I went to the door. This time I was able to tell what I had for sale; so, as soon as the door was opened, I said that I was selling Graves's series of Home Libraries, containing such books as the Life of Washington, and other great men. I also went on speaking of the many good qualities of these men, and the advantages to be gained by having such books in the house, and in fact every argument that I could think of, when finally Mrs. Holmes asked me to come in, and I *now* believe, took the books, prompted by a desire to assist a man who was striving to make an honest living rather than from any particular craving she had for that style of literature.

Two sales in one day! This so delighted me that I started for home; but on the way I decided not to return empty-handed, consequently purchased two large market baskets and set out for a grocery store. Marketing in this direction was entirely foreign to me, so much so that I did not know what to buy after I had entered the store; but there I was with two baskets, and something had to be done. Saleratus was the first thing that came to my mind; after this, tea, coffee, sugar, soap, etc., until one of the baskets was completely filled. I now set out in search of a meat market, and there succeeded in filling the second basket.

If ever a man was proud in this world over his achievements I was that man, as I walked up North St. Paul-street, with a basket on each arm and both of them filled with the necessaries of life, and all these obtained as the result of honest labor.

When I arrived home, my wife met me at the head of the stairs, not with tears, as she had often done in by-gone days, but with a face radiant with smiles. I entered the House and began to unpack the baskets, and we had a very jolly time, laughing over my purchases. However, I had brought nothing home but what was of use. Just as we had finished unloading, my little girl, aged thirteen years, came in from her daily labor, at the tobacco factory, exclaiming, "Papa, I'm so hungry!" I said, "Daughter, there is plenty and to spare; eat and be merry." My reader, you will here observe that I was already becoming versed in scriptural parlance. After we had partaken of our evening meal, the evening was very pleasantly spent in discussing our plans for the future, and I decided, God helping me, that I would provide for my family, so that my little girls might go to school. When I told my little girl, who had for two years been working in order to help her mother, that she should go to the factory in the morning, draw her pay and return home, in order to make preparations to start for school on the following morning, a happier child never lived. My boy had up to this time, been working in a saloon. I also told him to draw his pay and forever get out of the influences connected with one of those places.

The second morning after this arrangement for our future, the two little girls began school, and I was able to secure a position for my boy in a leading carpet store. Thus did the good Lord open up the way for me and mine.

After I had been working as a book agent for about six weeks, I was one morning crossing the street at the *Four Corners*, when a voice called after me, "Hello! brother Hess." This quite startled me, for I wondered who was willing to, or would, call me *brother* Hess, right out loud on the street; but on turning around, I saw a man who is connected with one of the leading daily journals of the city of Rochester, and who gave me a hearty hand-shake. We engaged in conversation, concerning matters in general and myself in particular. This good man said : " Mr. Hess, you are not living in a very desirable locality ; the influences surrounding you on North St. Paul-street are not calculated to strengthen you in your endeavors to reform, you had better move into my part of the city." I asked him where that was. He replied on "*Jones-avenue.*" Avenue! AVENUE ! Just fancy, my reader, hardly two months a temperance man, and already contemplating a residence on the avenue. Our conversation terminated by my receiving an invitation to dine at the house of my new friend, and as I was anxious to know how affairs were conducted in the house of a Christian man, I gladly accepted the invitation. As we were walking along Jones-avenue, my friend said to me, "Do you see that little cottage over there ? Go over and see if it will suit you." I said that will suit ; why of course it would suit ; why not ?—from three little rooms in a garret on North St. Paul-street to a neat little cottage on the *avenue.* After dinner I went and looked at the place, and from there went to the real estate agent who had the leasing of it, where I learned the weekly rental was three dollars and fifty cents. I now began to think it would not suit quite so well. However, I reasoned like this : I have been spending

more than that amount for beer and whiskey; now why
can't I invest it in paying for a comfortable home for my
family, that they might once more enjoy life and feel
that they had risen above living in a hovel, or a drunkard's home?  How many men to-day are compelling
their families to live in wretched and comfortless homes,
without even the bare necessities of life, while the head
of the family, the bread-winner, is squandering his
money for that which does no good, but verily much
harm.  While I was thus meditating, the thought came
to me, supposing I rent the cottage, what have I to put
in it; and with this thought came the apparant downfall of all my bright plans, and I decided to go to my
friend, who had so interested himself in my welfare, and
make this humiliating confession. In doing so I found
relief, for this kind, Christian man said, " I will go your
security for a bill of furniture.  Come to the store of
Mr. Carter, on State-street, and we will make everything satisfactory."  When we reached the furniture
store on State-street, Mr. Carter would not accept my
friend as security; not because he was irresponsible, but
he said, " I want to show Mr. Hess that I have confidence
in his reformation, and will trust him all the furniture
he wishes for his new home."  This was a complete surprise to me, for I had never known this man before.  I
said to myself, can it be possible that Christianity will
do all this?  And the tears began to course down my
cheeks as I thought of the kindness that was being
shown to me, and I only reformed so short a time.

I set about making my selections and it was not long
until I had secured everything necessary for the comfortable fitting up of my little home.  Everything I had ordered was to be at the house by eleven o'clock the following morning, which was Saturday, and sure enough
when I went to Jones-avenue the next morning all was
in readiness, even the carpets were laid.  I then went to
the Transfer Co. to secure a waggon for early Monday
morning, that I might move.  Up to this time I had not

said a word to my wife about our new home, wishing to give her what she had very rarely experienced during her married life, namely, a pleasant surprise.

I could not canvass for books on Saturday, for my thoughts were entirely fixed upon what had been going on during those two memorable days, and even while at church, on Sunday, I must confess my thoughts were not *riveted* to the services.  On Sunday afternoon I went out for a walk, and before I knew it, found myself entering the little home.  I shall never forget the visit I made that beautiful Sabbath afternoon.  As I entered the house, it presented every appearance of neatness and comfort, such as my home had only experienced during a few short months when I first began married life, but for sixteen long years had been deprived of.  As I looked around me, tears came to my eyes.  They were tears of sorrow and joy combined ; of sorrow, over a wretched and disgraceful past life, and of joy, over the prospects of a bright future and a happy home.

Monday morning came, and I arose very early, waking everybody else in the house.  My wife wanted to know what was the matter with me.  I said, " Get up; we are going to move.  " Move ! what have we to move ? "  " It makes no difference," I said; " you get up, and take the children with you to the neighbours', and I will see to the moving."  Hardly had they left when the dray was backed up to the door, and we at once loaded on the furniture (?), which, however, was not a very tedious undertaking.  As soon as the load was completed, I sent for my family and proceeded to put them on the dray, and off we started, the driver and I being the only ones who knew our destination.  When we had drawn up in front of the cottage, I told Mrs. Hess that someone wanted to see her in there.  Of course she wondered who it could be that wished to see her, and even if she had been disposed not to come in, her woman's curiosity would have been sufficient to have compelled her to do so; consequently we walked right in, and as we did so, my wife said, " No one lives here." I said, " Jennie are you not some one ? Wife, this is our new home." She could scarcely believe the words I had spoken ; but when I began to bring in what little furniture there was on the dray, then she began to realize that it must be as I had said. After settling up the house, my wife set about preparing dinner, and a happy one it was. There we were, comfortably situated, and although not an abundance, yet plenty of everything that was necessary ·to make home pleasant and comfortable. Before partaking of our first meal in the new home we established the family altar, and returned thanks to Almighty God for all His mercies and blessings, and asked Him to keep us strong and to bless and guide us in the future, and abundantly has He done so.

Some of my new friends decided that I should give a dinner party on the following Thursday, and it was to partake of the nature of a surprise party, all but the *surprise*, for I was given to understand that everything would be provided by the guests, and so it was. The day came and with it the guests, numbering in all about thirty, including, of course, my best of friends, P. A. Burdick and his family. We talked, laughed and cried alternately, and the affair made an impression upon the tablets of my memory that will never be erased.

By way of encouragement to all who have signed the pledge, and as an inducement for others to do so, I want to say that my bill for the equipment of my new home was two hundred and twenty-seven dollars, contracted on Friday, November the 15th, 1885, and as I now write, namely, on the twenty-sixth day of August, 1886, I can say every dollar of it is paid. This is not the result of my having made a large amount of money, but simply because I have been a temperance man, and instead of spending my money for strong drink, I put it to better use ; and the same may be the experience of any man who is now squandering ·his money in drink, if he will only forsake his cups, and the path of sin.

# CHAPTER VIII.

First attempt at speech-making—A failure—Rehearsing—A call
—An audience of five people—Large audiences—Persecutions—Killed on the railway—"I signed the pledge"—"A
member of the M. E. church"—Curious introductions—
Fifty-seven cents.

IN this chapter I will endeavor to describe the means
through which I became an active temperance worker.

After I had signed the pledge, and during the remaining time of the meetings at the Rink, I was a regular
attendant, not only at the evening meetings, but also at
the afternoon prayer-meetings; these last named gather-
ings were a source of great strength to me and I thoroughly enjoyed them.

One afternoon when I arrived at the Rink I found
several hundred children there, patiently awaiting the
coming of Mr. Burdick, who was to address them. Word
was soon received, however, that Mr. B. could not pos-
sibly be present, and in consequence of this great disappointment the ladies who had charge of the meeting
were in a dilemma, and thinking to get out of it they
requested me to take Mr. Burdick's place. I plead for
my life as I had never done before, but all to no avail,
for speak I must. This was my first appearance before
an audience as a temperance and Christian man. I decided to tell a little of my past experience, as a warning
to the young, but I had scarcely commenced describing
the scenes of my childhood to these pure, innocent children when the thought came to me—Can it be possible
that my face once smiled as these before me in the
sweetness of purity and innocence, but since that time
has so often scowled in drunken rage? That my voice
once prattled the pretty language of childhood, but for

many years after that happy period had been used in cursing and swearing? As I gazed into those sweet, pure, upturned faces I said, " Oh, God! will it ever be that one of these shall lead a life similar to the one I have so recently forsaken?" This thought was too much for me, and the flood-gates of nature's fountain opened wide, preventing me from making any further remarks. I was greatly embarrassed, and I took my seat wondered what the people would think of me for making such a fool of myself. They did not seem to consider the matter in that light, but gave me many kind and encouraging words.

I continued to attend the meetings as usual, when one Sunday evening I was again surprised by Mr. Burdick calling on me to address that great audience of two thousand people. He had said nothing to me, therefore I had no chance to refuse, and I do not know that it would have been any use for me to have done so. Just here I will make a little confession. After I had made a failure in attempting to address the children, I determined that if I were ever called on again I would be better prepared; consequently, with this end in view I began to study up a grand temperance address, one that I thought would last a half hour or more. During the preparation of this grand piece of oratory, which was to be so great a *feast of reason and flow of soul* for all who should be *fortunate* enough to hear it, I could have been seen standing before a mirror laying it off both right and left, for I wanted my gestures to be as graceful as my speech. I had rehearsed my talk until I imagined I had it perfectly, and was only waiting an opportunity to electrify an audience, and this opportunity was presented on the Sunday evening above referred to, I was introduced by Mr. Burdick and stepped to the front of the platform, confidently expecting to redeem the failure of a few days before, but as I came forward and saw four thousand eyes intently fixed upon me every

TWO WEEKS AFTER REFORMATION.

word of my *great* speech was knocked out of me, and I
stood before the people without having the first word to
say; however, as I gazed over this sea of faces, I discovered some of my former partners in the old life, and
this gave me material to work upon, so I opened fire on
them, which lasted about twenty-five minutes. I do not
know what I said, but Mr. Burdick afterwards told me it
was the truth. This both pleased and satisfied me. Before I left the rink I promised to attend Mr. Woodward's
Gospel Temperance Mission on South St. Paul-street, and
speak to the people there on the following Sunday evening, on which occasion I took for my subject matter the
sad death of Robert Kane, who, in a fit of despondency
brought on through gambling and drink, took his own
life. Poor "Bob" was the man who sat beside me the
evening we first visited the Rink, and who said to me:
"He has been at my house too." Perhaps many of my
readers will remember the terrible affair to which I have
just alluded, and also the last words of Robert Kane,
which were so full of warnings to our young men.

After filling several other engagements in Rochester, I
was informed one morning by Mr. Burdick that I had
received a *call*, and what a *call* was I did not know;
however, it was explained to me that I was to go to the
village of West Henrietta and conduct a series of temperance meetings during four consecutive evenings.
Now, if my *call* had been for one evening, I would have
perhaps felt that I might entertain an audience by relat-
ing some of my experience, but when it came to *four*
evenings my courage failed. But I took it to the Lord
in prayer, remembering those words, "Strength for thy
labor the Lord will provide." I decided to go.

The first evening my audience consisted of the pastor
of the church, Deacon S. and wife, their son and his wife.
Nevertheless, we went through with the services as if
the house had been filled to the doors. The second evening there was a marked increase both in numbers and

interest, which continued until the fourth and last evening, on which occasion the church was not large enough to accommodate the people. The Lord blessed our labors abundantly, and many signed the pledge who are still living up to it in every particular.

The next call I received was from the Woman's Christian Temperance Union of Brockport. I felt somewhat timid about accepting this call on account of the size of the place, but again I remembered the words of our blessed Master, "Lo, I am with you always!" I said I will take Christ with me, will ask his blessing upon the work and it will certainly prosper in the right way.

The first meeting was held in the room belonging to the W. C. T. U., and was not very largely attended. The next afternoon I spoke in the Republic Hall, which was well filled. At this meeting the pastor of the M. E. Church came to me tendering his church for the evening meeting, it was accepted and every available space, both sitting and standing, was taken, making the meetings very successful, and thus did God bless my labors at Brockport.

Upon my return to Rochester a letter was waiting me from my friend Mr. Carver, of North Bergen, to the effect that he had made a three weeks' engagement for me in his, and the neighboring towns; our meetings were to be held in churches, school-houses, and in fact wherever we could find shelter. Mr. Carver placed himself, and his horse and cutter at my disposal, and was very kind in conveying me to and from my meetings and giving me a very comfortable and pleasant home at his own house. I shall ever feel deeply grateful to this good and kind-hearted man, not alone for his generous hospitality, but for the many helpful and encouraging words he has from time to time given me, and which have proved such a great source of strength and comfort to me during many persecutions and adverse criticisms. The meetings I held under Mr. Carver's management were very successful, and notwithstanding the fact that on many evenings the weather was extremely cold and stormy, still we were always at our post and always had congregations to address.

Calls came in from different sections of the country, and from that time forward I have always been able to keep at work for the Master and the great cause of temperance. My reader, do not for one moment imagine that all has been sailing in smooth waters; far from it. Many and manifold have been the unkind and discouraging words spoken by those to whom I had looked for the greatest encouragement on account of their church relationship. We reformed men do not expect to gain the confidence of the Christian people except by building up a good moral character, but what we do expect is that those who make a profession of religion will become absolutely certain that any reports that may reach their ears concerning us are true before adding fuel to the fire which is so calculated to destroy us. In other words, if nothing good can be said, say nothing, especially not without a full investigation of the matter. It is not in a spirit of fault-finding that these remarks are made. God forbid that I should say one word against the church, or Christian people, for it is to these I owe my reformation, and much of my success since that time, but it is very discouraging to reformed men to be unjustly denounced by ministers of the Gospel.

Since the first day of December, eighteen hundred and eighty-five, to the present date, August the sixteenth, eighteen hundred and eighty-six, I have addressed two hundred and ninety-six audiences of all sizes and composed of all sorts and every description of people from the minister of Christ to the keeper of the saloon and brothel. During the few months above referred to, over ten thousand have signed the total abstinence pledge, for which I heartily thank God, and ascribe all the honor, praise and glory to Him who hath redeemed and saved me; to Him who taketh away the sins of the world.

I will relate a few incidents that have occurred during my labors, and which I hope will be a warning to those who are yet in their sins and who are inclined to keep putting off that all-important matter of making their peace with God until perhaps it will be "*too late.*"

While at North Byron, in Genessee county, I asked a man to sign the pledge. He refused. I then asked if he was prepared to meet his God, to which he replied: "I have plenty of time to prepare for that after the busy season." The following morning, while this same man was engaged in shipping some farm produce at the West Shore depot, he was struck by the through express and instantly killed. There are those who will read this little book who are still putting this great question off for a more convenient time, but let me say to you, although you may be in the best of spirits and health, yet you know not the day nor the hour when you shall be called to give an account of your every act, thought and word, and are you ready *now?* Let me refer you to II Cor., V. chap., 10 verse.

I will speak of one other incident that occurred at Fairport, N.Y. One Sunday afternoon, at three o'clock, I held a very large and enthusiastic meeting, and among many others I had asked to sign the pledge and take the start for God and right, were two brothers, from whom I received evasive answers, to the effect that they still had plenty of time to attend to such matters ; but, my reader, before the sun had set on that beautiful Sabbath day the soul of one of those brothers was in eternity, and upon the following Tuesday morning it was joined by that of the other brother who lingered till that time, after the terrible accident of Sunday evening, an accident somewhat similar to the one referred to as having occurred at North Byron. These are no manufactured stories, but occurrences that actually happened just as related, and Oh! my readers, are they not sufficient to warn you against making that, perhaps, *fatal* delay ?

Besides many discouragements, and such sad experiences as those to which I have referred, many things have happened that gave me courage and a fresh determination to continue, with God's help, the work of Gospel Temperance.

Not very long ago a young man came to me while I was holding meetings near the place of his residence. asking if I remembred him. I had a slight recollection of having seen him, but on account of seeing so many I was unable to definitely recall to my mind this particular young man. However, he went on with his story saying : "I signed the pledge at your meetings when you were laboring at a certain village, and to-day I am living very happily with my wife, am foreman in the shop where I work, and everything looks bright for the future."

While I was standing in the Arcade in the City of Rochester, a young man took me by the hand saying : "Mr. Hess, the story of your life, as related by you at Cllfton Springs, some time ago, brought conviction to my heart, I signed the pledge, and with God's help have kept it ever since ; what is more, I hold a responsible position in my village, and best of all, 1 am happy in the religion of Christ and am a member of the M. E. Church.

I have also received many letters from old and young expressing experiences similar to those I have related, describing where men who were once brutes in human form have become tender and affectionate fathers and husbands, providing, and in every way caring for their families. I do not relate these things in a spirit of boastfulness, for God forbid that I should boast save in the cross of our Lord Jesus Christ ; I simply tell them that some who are in sin and wretchedness may be induced to forsake their sinful ways, believe on Christ and live. See St. John, iii: 16.

As well as the two kinds of experiences above referred to I have also had others that partake very much of the ludicrous.  These are principally the different ways in which I have been introduced to audiences.  In a small town not many miles from Rochester, the pastor of the church in which I was to speak made the following introductory remarks: "In this great work of reform we need many different presentations of the terrible evil of strong drink, and each man on the platform presents it in his own way.  To-night we shall have it brought before us by a man who has for many years been a slave to it; this man is none other than the great double-fisted, double-jointed, broad-shouldered and strong-armed Joe Hess.  Ladies and gentlemen, the converted prize-fighter will now address us."  Another introduction I received was what might be called *multum in parvo*, as follows: "Joe Hess of Rochester will speak to us this evening; many here know what kind of a *bum* he was a short time ago."  After I had made my address, this singular chairman arose and announced a collection for my benefit in these words: "We will now pass the hat, and any of you who want to can put something in it."  When the hat came in, fifty-seven cents was handed to me by the chairman, who said: "They have given you nearly twice as much as we generally get on Sunday, so you ought to be satisfied."

We often hear a cry raised by some jealous-minded person that temperance workers make too much money. In my own case I will say, I am not making one quarter as much in my new work as I did in the old, and yet I am able to provide a comfortable home for my family; and why is this? simply because I am not trying to support the families of ten or a dozen saloon-keepers.

# CHAPTER IX.

"Taking up my pen "—Early lecture experiences—Story of a
tobacco pouch--A copper collection—Speech at P. A. Burdick's
meeting—Attempt to murder Hess—Street Insults—"Shoot
the orator"—Reformation of Drunkard "Bill"—Opens a mission
on Water street—Some lively incidents.

*" I will guide thee with mine eye."*

AS I make the attempt this 17th day of March, 1890,
to take up the thread of my life where I left off
Aug. 25, 1886, I feel that I need some spiritual power to
guide me, that I may give as near a correct account of
my experience since that time as it is possible. When
I left off writing my autobiography I was seated in a
little town called Two Bridges, situated in the north-
western part of Orleans County, State of New York,
and to-day while taking up the line of thought I am
seated in the pleasant town of Bowmanville, Canada, in
the home of Mrs. Mason, a christian lady.

As it is nearly four years since I laid down my pen, it
will be quite a task for me to give an exact account of
all the incidents that have occurred during that time.
But trusting to God that by His grace my memory will
be strengthened, I will give to the reader such of my
travels since my Christian life as will elevate human kind.
Though my life has been a very pleasant one since my
conversion, yet I cannot help thinking of the truth that
God spoke to Ananias in the 9th chapter of Acts, 15-16
verses : " But the Lord said unto him : go thy way for
he is a chosen vessel unto me, to bear my name before
the Gentiles, and kings, and the children of Israel ; for I
will show him how great things he must suffer for my
name sake."

Like many of "God's" children, I have experienced the

hand of persecution.    But it is a great consolation to know that "Great shall be your reward in heaven, when men shall revile you, persecute you, and shall say all manner of evil of you, falsely for my sake."    But take note, dear reader, the accusation must be "falsely" brought against us.    In the year of 1885 I received a call from the town of " W— H—" to come and labor in the interest of humanity, to save them from a drunkard's gutter.    My labors were crowned with more success than I anticipated. These meetings were conducted in the Universalist Church, and presided over by Rev. Brother Fisher, the pastor.    On returning to Rochester Brother Fisher said " let us have our photos taken," to which I quickly gave my consent.    Just think !    One year prior to this I was associated with the lowest elements of humanity of the city, and now about to have my photo taken with a minister for my companion.    Was it not wonderful ?    I ventured to ask his reason for wanting the photos.    His answer was :    " Who can tell, this is the first opportunity and it may be the last, that we can do such a thing for in the morning one of us may be no more."    Is not this a serious thought ?    In the prime of life and health to-day, and to-morrow we may be lying in a casket.    May you be ready when the call comes.    I more readily complied with his wishes, as he offered to settle the bill.

After this performance was over I started for my neat little home on Jones Avenue, from which I had now been absent four days.    These four days seemed four years.    I found the family all at home, and now a scene commenced. Oh such hugging and kissing and patting.    I can never describe it.    After this affray had abated I pulled out a little leather pouch.    " This pouch has a history connected with it as a reformer ; ain't that funny ?"    The reform the pouch brought about was this :    a certain man who claimed to be a Christian, and who was one, said to me one day, " Joe, don't you smoke ?"    I answered, " No, nor chew."    " Well, I believe you mean it, and now J will promise you that I will never smoke nor chew again if you will take this pouch I have for my tobacco for a money pouch." I said, "That's a go." I had thought of buying a pouch, and here is one offered to me for a gift. I took it, and it saved me 50 cents. The pouch contained the collection of "Alexander the coppersmith." The amount was $16, nearly all in coppers. I thanked God even for the coppers, because a hundred coppers makes one dollar. I poured the contents on the floor, on the carpet, and I sat down on the sofa. "Say," drinking man, it seemed funny to take a seat on my own sofa, and you may imagine my delight at seeing my children scramble for the coppers.

Reflect for a moment. Three short months after renouncing rum and its power, sunshine came in where formerly dreariness reigned, because I had been converted to God. This same night I went to the Fitzhue rink, where P. A. Burdick was still conducting meetings. "Say," reader, I wish you had been an eye-witness to the sight. For ninety consecutive nights from 2,500 to 3,000 gathered nightly to hear this God-fearing man. Nine thousand signed the total abstinence pledge, and thank God I am one who is numbered amongst that nine thousand. Arriving at the meeting Burdick called on me to say a few words. I made no hesitation in coming forward. I sometimes think the reason why many go back to their cups is that they don't go to work. My experience has been that when I make an effort to save others I become stronger. One other reason why many return to their old way, is people have not charity enough for those who are striving to do better. When men give up these cups they do not only do that, but along with the cup goes the old boon companion of long years' acquaintance. Therefore they must needs have new friends and companions go the rounds with them, and extend the hand of true friendship to them. Were this more done in the church of God more would come to the altar.

G

When I arose to address the vast audience I was greeted with great cheering and waving of handkerchiefs. I told them of the success I had at " W. H." This news was received with great applause.

After the meeting I separated from my friends, little dreaming that I was so near passing over Jordan. I boarded a Lake-avenue car for home. Walking up Jones-avenue with my hands in my pockets, and thinking over the word "blood" that was connected with the liquor traffic, I decided to make that a subject. Looking up I beheld two men coming toward me, and stepping to one side to let them pass by, one of the two stepped in front of me; at the same moment I was struck on the head with a brick by a third man and knocked down. This blow was just hard enough to deaden my faculties of arm and speech. As I arose I was again knocked down. After being knocked down three times my speech came back, and I shouted with what seemed to me a great voice, "Murder." This cry was enough to arouse both my son and neighbor Williams, and as they were coming to my assistance the would-be murderers took flight. I say murderers, for I am fully convinced that but for the timely arrival of my friends there would have been a murder committed that night, and Joe Hess the victim. I was assisted to my home by my son Henry, who was one of the first to arrive at the place of conflict. This was the first persecution that I received from the "Rummey fellers."

The secular press had it the next morning that I was killed, but praise to the Lord, some of the secular press, brewers, and saloonists, have long since learned I was a live corpse, one that can kick and hit back with equal force. At another time I was walking on Lyle-avenue with a large Bible case in one hand and a box of books in the other. Coming to a certain point in the street near the canal I saw seven men standing outside of a saloon, all more or less under the influence of strong drink ,and seeing me, it seemed to raise the hatred within them, and they shouted, "Here he comes." I knewthat I was in for it. I could not turn back, as my destination lay on the other side of the canal. Putting on a bold front I walked up to them and I was surrounded by these whisky-bloated faces. Something had to be done and that quickly. The thought suggested itself that the Bible had knocked out the devil many times, why could it not now knock out some of the old fellow's children. At that I let fly the Bible case and three men were smitten to the ground, at the same time I let go the box that contained George Washington and Daniel Webster. I do not mean the live men, but simply their great power put into book form. This act laid out two more, and one of the remaining two had the misfortune to run against the fist of my right arm, and down he went ; the other and last one of the seven took " leg-bail." After a moment's pause, looking over the battle field, and seeing myself the conquering hero, I said, " praise God ?"

The next morning the press had it, "Joe Hess at his old trade, knocking 'em out on the street." Some of the people that had four eyes said, " It was too bad that Joe was drunk again." Others said, " I told you so, he will never stand." But praise be to His Holy name, 1 am still standing in His power.

One day while walking down State-street, I beheld quite a number of my old companions standing outside of a saloon. Like all manufactories, when they have completed an article, it is a rule to place the same on the outside as a sample, and the manufactories of drunkards turn out their samples. As 1 neared these samples they commenced to shout, " Hello, Rev. Sir," " Shoot the orator," " Ain't he a nice parson." " Come in and have a drink." During this time old cigar stumps and old quids of tobacoo were freely hurled at me. One hit me in the back of the neck. I confess that I needed all of the grace that God gave me to keep down the devil temper, so as not to turn on my persecutors, but like Jesus I cried, " Father forgive them; they know not what they do."

I kept right on in spite of all obstacles that were placed in my way. Night before New Year's of 1886, I went down with my wife and son to buy a suit; my coat had to be a Prince Albert. You see I was becoming quite well known as an " *Orator*." New Year's day was a happy one, as I rose from bed, into which I had entered for the first time on that anniversary in many years, a sober man. On this New Year's morning my head did not pain me. After dinner we all started for the W.C.T.U. hall, where I was to make a speech. On our way down we found that the winter clothing that we had on kept us warm. It was a bitter cold day. I had to pass the place where two months previously I was assaulted with cigar stumps and vile names. Some of the same men were there with their hands in their pockets, their teeth chattering, their necks pulled in between their shoulders and no overcoats on their backs. When they saw me come along with my family they lifted their hats and one of them stepped out and said, " Joe, forgive me for the insult I heaped on you that day when I threw my tobacco cud at you." I told him that he had been forgiven long ago. I said, ". Bill, what have you to show for the money that you spent since that time. You haven't even the necessary clothing to protect the temple of God." He looked up and said, "What's that you say, temple of God, say Joe, this is the temple of the devil." Well then, " Bill, come with me to the meeting, sign the pledge, give your heart to God, and by that act make it the temple of the Lord." During this conversation, tears rolled down his face. My wife spoke kindly to him, and the result was " Bill " came with us to the meeting, gave his heart to God, and to-day that same " Bill " is one of Rochester's bright business men, and a pillar in one of the leading churches.

Dear reader, have you not started on the right road, then come and do it now, remember the royal invitation, "Come unto me, all ye that labor and are heavy laden, and I will give you rest." You must enjoy that rest before you can tell of it. Your time may be nearly up, be sure you are ready.

In the month of Jan., 1886, I was walking on Water-street, one of the hardest streets in the city. I saw a family moving out, and on going over I saw it was a saloon they were leaving. As the man took down the sign the thought flashed upon me why cannot another sign be put up there instead of for the devil, for God. I enquired as to who had the letting of the place; receiving the information, I started to find the owner. I had not gone far when for the first time I realised that I had no money, but having knowledge of the fact that the Lord sent out His disciples without any money, and yet they prospered. I said, I am a disciple of Jesus, and started. Finding the owner at his office, I laid my plan before him; he listened with all patience, and then said, " Joe, I am glad to see you stick, when I saw you come into the office, I was under the impression that you wanted the place for a saloon. You have no money." "No," said I, " not a red." " But you have something which is better than money, you have a four months' character that is good, I will let you have the place," and at that he gave me the key, the rent of this room was $40.00 per month.

After receiving the key I was happy, for the fondest hopes of my heart were about to be realized, to start a mission in Rochester where the boys could congregate nightly. Though I had the key I was yet far from having the room fitted up. There were seats to be gotten, lamps, platform, organ, stove ; all these things I had to get, and no money to get them. But again the precious words rang in my ear, " I will guide thee with mine eye." It was now 10 a.m., and I wished to open for God at night. Going

to the door I met a Salvation Army captain, I asked him
if he knew of seats. He said there were some over at the
barracks that I could have, so I sent an express driver
after them. In the meantime I looked for a stove, this
makes me think of what we read in the Bible, "seek and
ye shall find." I found a stove, then I went to a coal
yard and after telling what I intended doing, I received
the promise of coal. Again true, "ask and ye shall receive." Returning from this expedition I found the seats
had arrived. When they were unloaded I told the man
I had no money, and he flew into a rage. Said he, "Why
did you not tell me before I had unloaded." I knew he
would not load them up again and I needed the seats. I
consoled myself by thinking of the passage we read in
the word of God, "As wise as serpents as harml ss as
doves." During the time that this man gave vent to his
devilish feelings, a gentleman arrived, and said to me,
"What's the matter Joe ?" I told him I owed the fellow
50cents for express charges and had no money to pay him.
Said he to me, "What do you intend to do ?" My answer
was to start a mission. He looked at me in blank astonishment (he was an infidel). After a moment's reflection he gave me ten dollars. I thanked him and, strange
as it may seem, I did not hesitate in taking the amount.
After paying the driver, I proceeded to get the seats in,
then I thought it would be a nice thing to have a platform. I knew a lumber merchant on State-street. I
went to him, told him my plan, but said I have no
money. He promised to send the lumber, then another
thought came that he might send a carpenter with the
lumber and some nails. Osborne looked at me and said,
with a smile, "Anything else ?" yes, said I with a grin, if
you want to come down you can drop a $5 bill into the
collection box.

About an hour after a wagon drew up in front of my
Mission room loaded with lumber, carpenter, nails and
tools. Showing him where to erect the platform

I started for lamps and found a good man, who donated them to me. I had him prepare them with wicks and oil ready for use, then I started for curtains. Water-street had many low dives, and their fashionable curtain was a red cloth across the window. So I wished to get some of the same to catch the poor misguided victims. Fitz-simons contributed the curtains. As I was leaving the store, I was greeted with a "How do you do, Mr. Hess," by a Christian lady, to whom I related what I had done. She rejoiced when she saw the seats and platform. I told her the next thing I needed was an organ. She promised to have one sent, and the organ came. In the meantime stove and coal arrived, fire started, then I proceeded to put up the curtains. Door opens, in enters lamps. Lamps put up. (Perspiration rolls down my face.) It was now 5 p.m. I had forgotten I had nothing to eat all day. Going to the door I met one of the old boys, a painter by trade. Said he, "Hello Joe, old boy, what are you doing down here," I told him I was opening a saloon for Christ. He seemed to enjoy the idea. I said, John, you're a painter, haven't you a large black board?" to which he replied "yes." "Well, let me have it to put up on the corner of Maine-street, and you put on it, 'This way for Joe Hess' Mission.'" He did so.

At this moment a lady came along. She said, "Bro. Joe, what are you doing down here in such a low locality as this?" I was going to ask her the same question. I said to her, "I shall have a grand opening to-night in my new saloon." She looked horrified. This was too good to let pass without having a little fun at her expense, so I said come in and have a drink. As I was turning to go in she grabbed my arm and pled that I should not go in, but at this moment the organ arrived. When she saw the instrument the truth flashed across her mind. I showed her the inside and she praised God. I told her I had no player, when she volunteered. Everything being now ready to do business, I knelt down and thanked Him on High.

After reviewing the work once more I discovered that
I had no hymn books. I went to E. F. Carter, told him
what I had done, he gave me an order for 50 copies of
Moody and Sankey hymns. After having lit the lamps,
it made my heart rejoice at my day's work, and I could
not refrain from repeating the words, " I will guide thee
with mine eye." Soon several good brethren came in and
we sang "Praise God from whom all blessings flow." During this time people came in and by 8 p.m. the room was
packed, when the request was given that if there were
any seekers for prayer. God blessed our first request
with 33 souls. At 10 p.m. we closed, and thus there was
the first Mission established in that part of the city, the
change of the place from a saloon at 9 a.m. in the morning, to a soul saving saloon at 10 p.m. at night, was certainly a most wonderful change  This will show what
can be done by the  Christian who is willing to work in
the vineyard of our  Lord  and Saviour  Jesus Christ.
" Amen."

# CHAPTER X.

Dissensions among the workers—Break up of the Water-st. Mission
—Difficulties in the pathway—Out of work—An overruling
Providence—God takes care of His own—A remarkable experience—Some soul-stirring incidents in the work—Influences that
work against Temperance—What one sa'oon did—A newspaper
criticised.

"Create in me a clean heart, oh God, and renew a right spirit
within me. Then will I go forth and teach transgressors thy way,
and sinners shall be converted unto thee."—Psalm 51, 10,13.

THE mission on Water-street became my nightly resort,
and as my delight used to be great when a number
of us frequented this same room singing when it was
given up to the devil's work, I even rejoiced more now,
because in this same room I sang praises to the most high
God. I soon went forth to labor in toher fields; it was
therefore necessary that the mission should be presided
over by some one. Bro. Morly and Bro. Vorheen were
the chosen ones. Soon strife came amongst the brethren,
which finally resulted in breaking the mission up, and as
I returned one day I saw the sign was taken down—the
mission was no more. The brewery men, saloon keepers
and gamblers have a motto, which I wish our church
people would adopt, and that motto is, "In unity is
strength, united we stand and divided we fall." If this
were adopted in the church of Christ, more sinners would
be willing to come to the altar.

I have been made sad at heart because in some places
where I lectured I found the church divided; and when
this is the case, what example is set before those who are
out of Christ? Let every Christian read 5th Math., 14th
verse: "Ye are the light of the world" (16th verse),
"Let your light so shine before men that they may see

your good works, and glorify your father which is in heaven." Then by our works we bring others to the knowledge of Christ.

During the first three months of 1886, I met with much persecution. Many times churches were refused because I was an uneducated man, and few ministers I could get to assist me. At one place, when I arrived I found the minister of the church, and after looking me over, he thought it best not to allow me the use of the church, but consented to have me go into a small room in the basement, without stove. Of course I had no meeting that night. School houses were also closed. People said the great "grammarian" will speak in this town; all this was ridicule. I faced it all and bore up under it, until I came to a certain town where I had the hall from one who was no believer in Christ. As the people assembled, and the time had arrived for the opening services, I learned of a minister present. I asked him to pray; he replied that if I could not pray myself, I should not run round the country posing as a speaker. This refusal was a severe blow to me. I asked the people to join with me in the Lord's Prayer. Then I spoke, and dismissed the people without even taking a collection. As I neared the door an old, gray man shook me by the hand, and said, "God bless you; keep right on." And with these remarks he passed out, but left a big silver dollar in the palm of my hand. I said nothing, and walking I did not care where, I found myself finally at the station, and the 10 p.m. train just steaming out, I jumped aboard, and went home to Rochester. Having rung the bell, wife came to the door. Learning who it was on the outside, the door opened quickly. I entered. Wife looked in astonishment; said she, "Why, Joe, I thought you were out at ———," naming the place where I had left my valise. Said I with a smile, "Well, I guess I am here now," and said I, "Jennie, I have come to the conclusion to give up this work; people are right,

I have no education, and I have no business to run round and hold meetings." Yet at each meeting the Lord blessed me wonderfully. I told Jennie that I was going to get work in the city—"I have many friends and there will be no trouble to get work." But like what many hundreds more have done, and still do, "I counted my chickens before they were hatched."

I went down in the morning to the place where I was confident I would get work as a porter. As I entered the store, Mr. A——— came forward to greet me with glee. After I told him what I had done, I asked him for employment. He said, " Well, I am very sorry that that is the case," for he could do nothing for me. At this moment the door opened, and a man came in and enquired whether they had advertised for a porter, to which Mr. A——— answered "Yes." Taking and reading the reference papers that the applicant tendered to him to read, A——— turned and called the name "George," to whom he gave instructions to show the new porter to his place. I could not speak. I had asked for the position, and he, telling me he could do nothing for me, then turned and engaged the other man. I went away with the tears in my eyes. I tried for three weeks without success.

One morning wife said : " Joe, the last pound of flour is in the pan, and there is only one bucket of coal in the house." And said she, " You owe $10.50 for rent, and the lady from whom we rented has demanded the rent, and declared that if she did not have it by a certain date she would put us out." Sitting by the table, I was thinking what to do, and the devil came up and said, " What are you fooling away your time for ? Take your gloves and go down and make some money." At once I acted upon the suggestion. I brought forth the gloves that I had used before my conversion, and started for the door by the back way, so as wife should not see me. I got as far as the woodshed door, and for my life I could not go farther; I went back. After another spell of sitting I arose in a great haste, took my gloves and ran for the back door, but this time, like the first attempt, I failed. I tried it the third time and failed again. I now was satisfied that some higher power than mine was acting upon me. Going back into the room, I said, "Jennie, come, let us pray, and if it is God's will that I should be in this Gospel temperance line, may He send aid and calls, and I will promise that I will always work in His interest."

After prayer I started for down town. On my way I stopped at the post office and called for my name, and I received a letter. Breaking the seal, a $2 and a $5 bill dropped out. I hesitated to take it, but went to my friend Williams, and told him of the occurrence. He thought some friend had sent it, and I am sure it was a friend, as I have had no one yet call for it. Securing paper, I had my friend write a letter to a firm at Buffalo. Taking this to the post, I again enquired, and to my surprise, received another letter. This contained a money order for $25, and the other paper contained the following words, " Dear Bro. Hess—Enclosed find a post money order for $25. A friend from Boston who listened to you last fall at Clifton Springs, New York, left $15 for you; I add $10. May God bless and keep you right on in your good work.—REV. A. J. KENYON, Pastor M. E. Church."

Do you call this an answer to prayer? I should say yes. I ordered some groceries, also one ton of coal, then proceeded to pay my rent. Arriving at the landlady's house, she seemed to be very indignant, but when she had the money she cooled down wonderfully. I started for home. I was greeted with joy by the children and wife. After they told me about the nice things that came and the coal, I said, " And here is the receipt for the rent, it is paid." And now it was wife's time to surprise me. She held up three letters that came that day; Mamie opened all and read them. They were calls from different places where they wanted my services. We knelt right down and thanked God for this kindness.

The next morning, bright and early, I took the first train for the nearest one of the places, and labored a week, and when the No-license election came, it was made known to us that the town went dry, as the result of the labor of one week; this was really my first genuine victory as a laborer in the vineyard of the Master. I have ever since been in the field, harvesting humanity for God's Kingdom. This incident will prove to the public that God has opened the way for me. While laboring in the town of "B." an incident occurred during the time I was speaking. A man arose and blurted out, "Say, Joe, it is a long time between drinks, come let's have a drink." I must confess for a moment I was taken back, but in another moment I rallied, and replied, " Yes, it has been some time between my drinks, almost 7 months, but by the looks of your face, I am led to believe that the time between your drinks has been not over an hour, for which I am sorry, but, I said, if you are really in need of a drink, come right up here on the platform and I will treat you with a drink, fresh, cool, clean, a drink which has been provided by God, the drink that gives moisture, health and strength to the plants ; come, man, drink of the pure crystal water." At this he took his seat, and when the invitation was given for people to sign the pledge, he was among the first ones to come up. Thank God, to-day that same man is a happy Christian. Signing the pledge is what started him, years ago.

I invited at one time a gentleman to come and drink with me, to which he replied, when I will drink like an animal he would drink with me. I could not make out what he meant, but I now have a conviction, what he meant at that time—drink like an animal—they drink the clear water and nothing more.

During my labors in the town of "N.," where we had a great rousing meeting at the town hall, I was entertained at a temperance house. One day while sitting in my room reading the Bible, a knock came on the door; opening the door I found a young boy there with a parcel in his hand; he said that a gentleman sent it; I took it and laid it away to one side, resuming my seat to study my Bible lesson. A violent rap came at the door, and the same moment it swung open, and two men entered, shouting, " Ah, we caught you now, posing as a temperance man and here you are drinking all the time." For a moment I could not reply to such an accusation ; when I had collected myself, I said, " I do not understand what you mean." One of the gentlemen said, " It is reported on the street that you have beer by the bottle brought to your room."

At this I pointed these men to the parcel the boy had just brought, and which was unopened yet. At this they coloured up, and one of them commenced to undo the parcel, when two bottles of beer came to sight. I turned to the one that took the most active part in denouncing me, and said, " You are the man that sent the boy ; come, let us hunt up the boy." At this he took his bottles and left. This man owned property which he rented for a saloon, and he a member of one of the orthodox churches. Here, again, is the truth that we find in the Bible made manifest, " Fret not thyself because of evil doers; neither be thou envious against the workers of iniquity. For they shall soon be cut down like the grass, and wither as the green herb."

The meetings were the wonder of the people of that section of the country, as it is a great country for raising grape. It is said the wine is a temperance beverage, and a " high-toned " drink. The tone of the wine may be very high, but when men have well drunken, and they reel and stagger because they drank this wine of high tone, it is then I think that the proper name would be low tone wine. Conversing with some of the ministers of the place, which are four in number, I said to the

M. E. minister, " How many members have you in your church ?" He replied, 145. "How many male members?" He replied, 15. Next was the Baptist. He counted 98 members, with thirteen regular male members. The turn now came for the Presbyterian. He had 180 members. Said he, " My male membership is not quite so large as is my brethren's here. We had ten, but since John P. St John ran for president, some of my members took wings, and now I have but four live male members, whom I am holding down so they won't fly away." The fourth one in the place was a Roman Catholic, who was not present at the interview. This will show that the idea of wine being a temperance drink, is based upon false presumption. " Wine is a mocker, strong drink is raging, and whosoever is deceived thereby is not wise.' Prov. xx. 1.

I received an urgent call from the W.C.T.U. at " P," to come and labour in the interests of humanity. I finally consented to go. Successful meetings were the outcome, and many signed. In this place I met a man who held that a well-regulated tavern was right, and not only right but a necessity. A saloon was established, and a grand opening was given, and for the first time in many years the town was made boisterous during midnight hours, by the men that lost all reason. One morning the terrible news was spread in the community that a man was found insensible back of an outhouse. When the man was brought back to consciousness he told how himself and others were drinking, and walking home with one of the boys, he was struck down and robbed. Detectives were employed, and in two days the man who did the deed was caught. I hear you say, Who was he ? Well, he was the son of the man who was so sure that a well-regulated tavern was a necessity. When the news was brought to him, he said, " What, my boy the first victim of this well-regulated tavern!"

The trial came on, the son was found guilty, his sentence was pronounced, which was that he was to be confined at Auburn State prison for the period of seven years. The doors of the prison swung open to receive a young man of twenty-three years, as the result of a well regulated tavern. Will this crime end here? No! For when the young man has served his time, and comes forth from his seven years' abode, he will bring out with him the stain upon his character of an ex-convict. This well regulated tavern has since sent its scores to the jail.

Arriving at home I found my mail had accumulated, and amongst this was one call to speak at a camp-meeting for Rev. John A Copeland, who was conducting a temperance Camp at Rock Glen, and, as he had to take an admission fee of ten cents to defray expenses, a certain " Mrs. Blank," who acted as a reporter for one of the Warsaw secular papers, and who made claims as a Christian, was displeased with the idea of taking a fee at the gate on the Sabbath, and set her brain in motion, and riddled me full of hot shot. The article was so mean and contemptible that I will not reproduce it in print, but instead shall reprint an answer to the same by an unknown defender. May God always prosper him for his noble defence in my behalf. I will here give the article in full, as produced by my unknown friend:

### JOE HESS AND MRS. BLANK.

Mr. Editor,—In your last issue a Mrs. Blank ventilates her perturbed spirit very freely, and makes Joe Hess the scapegoat to carry the sins of a great many people. Mrs. B., we deeply sympathise with you in your very great desire to have all reform work done by very good people—people who have always acted with decorum, and have never been known to outrage decency. But, good Mrs. B., unfortunately for your theory of those who should do the reform work, God has seen fit to use others—men who were guilty of the grossest sins, men whose sins were as scarlet, to lead other sinners to repentance. Mrs. B., it often happens that the most pharisaical are the most strict in requiring others to do, or not to do. Think of Paul; he persecuted to the death such as he considered were departing or had departed from the faith, and he stood by consenting to the murder of Stephen when they were stoning him to death. But Saul, the persecutor and murderer, became the

apostle to the Gentiles. He told of his past life, and declared himself to be the chief of sinners. He often refers to the sinfulness of
his past life when writing his epistles. Did he not accomplish a
great work in the world? Some, when they went to hear him,
said, "What will this babbler say?" Remember John Bunyan.
Call to mind, Mrs. B., his life before his conversion to Christ.
Bunyan has told us of how he had been led, and has been the instrument of leading many to the fountain "opened for all unclean-
ness," where they washed and were made whole. What has been
done may be done again. God is able "to use the foolish things
of the world to confound the wise, and the weak things of the
world to confound the things that are mighty ; and base things of
the world, and things that are despised, hath God chosen—yea, and
things which are not, to bring to naught things that are." Let us
be careful, Mrs. B., how we judge others, lest we be judged. Let
us lay no stumbling block in the way of a converted sinner. If
Joe Hess is a converted man, and is doing work for God, don't let
you and I be found railing at him, or keep raking up his past life.
If he is earnestly seeking to live soberly, righteously and godly, let
us speak words of encouragement to him and seek to strengthen
his hands and encourage his heart. Mrs. B., were you ever tempted
"above that you were able to bear," and did you fall? You may
have done so, and the world never knew it ; but if you repented,
did not even the remembrance of your past sin make you shudder?
Think how you would feel if others knowing of your defection
should only meet you to shun you, or in speaking of you speak dis-
respectfully and slightingly. If God forgives sinners whose sins
were of the deepest dye, can we afford to condemn? Think—

> One short word in kindness spoken,
>   Costing scarce a moment's breath,
> May bind up a heart that's broken,
>   Save a sinking soul from death.

Mrs. Blank, we think were you to re-write your article, you would
deem it best to be a little more merciful. There has something
soured your feelings to an extent. We of course do not know
just what it is, but there is something. Let us surmise a few
things ; you need not tell if some is the root of your feeling. We
mean no offence. May be you are not in accord with the temperance sentiment of the day. Again, some one of your friends may
be engaged in the traffic, or you may be better in showing others
the way than you are in leading. Now, we will close with a sentiment that we think you will endorse: If Joe Hess is not what he
ought to be, may God make him what He would have him. We
would say to Joe: Joe, don't let yourself to any man or associa-

H

tion to speak in camp-meetings on the Sabbath, where a gate fee is received for admission to hear the truth.    It smells too much of filthy lucre to warrant you in giving it your countenance.    Avoid the very appearance of evil, and do all you can to save fallen brothers and sisters, and may God bless you and enable you to walk carefully, and speak fearlessly, and bear crosses patiently. "Hold that fast which thou hast, that no man take thy crown." Good-bye, Joe.                              Yours truly,

FRIEND.

Dear reader, is not this proof that God will take care of His own ?  "Trust in the Lord and do good," is a safe guide.

# CHAPTER XI.

Incidents of travel—Downfall of a promising young man—Hess'
politics—Slandered by a clergyman—A vigorous reply—"Making money out of temperance"—Some plain talk—A happy
Christmas and New Year—Buying coal by the ton, not bushel—
Confession of a drunkard.

" Let every soul be subject unto the higher powers, for there is
no power but of God ; the powers that be are ordained of God."—
Romans 13 : 1.

AS I travel from town to town, exhorting men to the
power of God, mighty to save, I have seen many
who neglected this power and trusted in their own
powers, and I am grieved to say that I fear many of the
same have resisted, to their damnation ; for many of
those who made light of my exhortation have travelled
the long, lone journey of death. Some overcome by
drink have taken their life with their own hand, others
have fallen from their wagons and the wagon passed over
them and crushed them to death. I have in my mind a
young man who attended my meetings in the town of "R."
He was a nice young man, but he drank a little ; he had a
lovely young wife and one child, a boy. When I asked
him to sign the pledge he became enraged at me, saying
he was not going to be on the roll with a lot of drunkards, that he could drink it and let it alone. He remained firm against all the arguments I could bring up, but
I did not feel that I could give him up. I then tried his
young and beautiful wife. As I came to her asking her
to sign so as to influence her husband she became indignant and left the hall. It was about two months from the
time she left the hall, when I read in the papers of Rochester a very sad account of a young and industrious farmer who came to the town of "R." After making his

sale he repaired to a saloon, and in the company of others, drank very freely and became very drunk. On his way home he fell from his spring seat, and was found by his wife lying dead in the box of his wagon, his neck being broken. The verdict of the coronor's jury was death caused from a fall from the seat breaking his neck, fall caused by an overdose of strong drink. Had this young man signed the pledge he might to-day be with his now heart-broken wife and child.

While laboring in the town of Newfane, speaking to crowded houses every night, at the commencement of the meetings I said I did not go round as a politician, but a Mrs. C. H. St. John came to occupy the platform one night during the service. After making her eloquent address, she said, " Now we will learn where Bro. Joe Hess stands." I then and there declared that I was a member of the Third Party, at which the Rev. J. R. Stratton took high offence, and took Joe Hess for his text on the Sunday following, declaring that he saw me drunk. The following is an abstract of his discourse as it appeared in one of the Lockport journals, which was republished by the Buffalo *Sunday Express*, and recopied by the 16th Amendment Journal. Here is what the report had :

" The redoubtable Joe Hess was lecturing in Newfane recently, when he heard that the Rev. J. R. Stratton was slandering him by stating that he was intoxicated half the time. As the ex sporting lecturer was there under the auspices of the W.C.T.U. of Niagara county, it was rather a bad imputation. Complaint papers were drawn up and left in the hands of the president of the society to serve within twenty-four hours if the Rev. Mr. Stratton did not retract, and the papers have not been served."

" The foregoing appeared in the Lockport correspondence of the Buffalo *Sunday Express*, and we reproduce it to state emphatically that we do not believe the statement. If Joe Hess were to get drunk just once we should all hear of it, and if Joe Hess got drunk he would have taken the elder in chancery instead of proceeding in the manner alleged. It is due to the cause that facts shall be stated, and we trust Mr. Stratton will at once made public his proofs if he has any."—Editor 16th Amendment.

I will here make a clean statement as to what the papers were that were drawn up. When I had learned of the base slander coming from a minister of God, I felt very much grieved. After thinking the matter over I decided to put my defence in writing. I therefore drew out a paper in which I denied the charge and stated most emphatically that unless the Rev. Stratton withdrew the base slander within twenty-four hours I would publicly denounce him as a most vile and base slanderer, along with it a most contemptible liar and false accuser in the eyes of the public. This paper was placed in the hands of the president of the W.C.T.U., and as he (Rev. Stratton) has not retracted he still stands branded as above stated.

While laboring in the town of Willson, Niagara Co., N. Y., in the year 1886, a great work was done in that town. The cry was raised again that I was in the work for money, and strange as it may seem, this cry is never raised by the saloon-keeper, or brewery man or wholesale dealer, neither is it raised by the distillery men. On the contrary, it comes from the so called moral respectable men who take their drink behind the door or get drunk at night in their own cellars. Let any common man with common sense reason for a moment that the only " biz." wherein money can be made is the liquor " biz."

Should I want to make money only and do injury to my fellowmen, I would not be talking temperance, but instead go into the town, work up the editor of a secular paper and promise him a good " whack " out of a sparring exhibition. Let his paper puff me indirectly on one page, then come out in an editorial and denounce the idea. In this wise it would stir both sides of the community, and even those who were loud against such a proceeding would yet be the ones who in the secret of their hearts would wish the thing to take place. After a certain length of time the fighters would come on, and the town band would play in front of the hall, and where men would not give one red cent for a temperance speech, they would come down with their dollar for a sparring match. Yet men run round and shout that men advocating temperance are only doing it for the money that they get out of it. Can money pay for the value of one home made happy, because a father was influenced to become a total abstainer?

I have in my mind many such a home that to-day is happy because the bread-winner has given up his cup, while God has used me as the instrument in His hand to lead these men to the blessed idea of sobriety. Think of the faces that are made happy throughout the country because of the spread of this most happy disease, total abstinence. Then on the other hand, glance in the past, then in the present, then in the future, and see the terrible suffering and the devastation of humanity both young and old, all caused by the spread of this hideous and odious disease, intemperance. Come to the rescue, my brother and sister, to raise the fallen, to cheer the blind, to lift the weak, weary and heavy laden, and with a united effort let us drive the monster Alcohol from our fair land.

In this town of W. a wonderful work was accomplished, many men who had been given up as hopeless cases were again redeemed, and to-day are living monuments of the power of God and the pledge against strong drink. Some reason that God has given us the grain to do with it as we liked. That is wrong; God gave us and gives us grain that we should use it for food to give strength to the body, and not to turn it into soul-robbing drink. As we are nearing the month of December of

1886, and when all hearts look forward with glee for the great day on which we celebrate the birth of our Saviour, so this is the day when all should be happy. But I am sorry to say that I knew a family in Rochester that would not be rejoicing, the reason is this : When I came back I had learned with sadness of heart that my friend and brother William Demeing, who was taken into the church the same time as I had been, one who was a hard drinker but had given his heart to God had again fallen. This is the way he fell : He was constantly walking among his former companions, making his boast that he was strong and could resist the temptation, but alas ! he, like many others who have tried the same thing, soon fell a victim to his old enemy. To-day, poor " Bill " is I know not where. His family is broken up, his wife heart-broken and he an outcast. Surely his Christmas was not a happy one.

Well, the happy day came, and I was permitted to spend it in company with my family, and, dear reader, we gathered around a well provided board filled with good things, along with it a great turkey. As I stuck the fork into it and then drew the knife over it, thoughts came that in my former life, the money I spent for liquor went to buy turkeys for the grog seller, and while they used to eat, I and mine would have to lick our fingers. I think of the turkey since that time on every Christmas day. We had a turkey; this was not all. We all, five in number, came out rigged in new suits of clothes, and I tell you we did look nice, now wasn't that funny ? The cellar was provided with coal, also twelve bushels potatoes; you see when I was drinking I used to buy the coal by the bushel and potatoes by the ounce, but that thing was changed about four weeks after my signing the pledge, and ever since I have been buying coal by the ton and 'tatoes by the bushel. I remember well when I used to buy neck beef, because the saloon-keeper had to have the best part of the creature. Now we buy meat by the quarter, all because of temperance. When New Year's day came there came into the house (well, you see, when I was given up body and soul to the devil, then my children used to say when they heard music in other homes as they passed by on the street—often I listened to their talk—how nice it would be if they could have so and so)—well, on this Christmas day I had to keep a secret from them. Then the day before New Year there came a ring at the door, and I found it was the man with a beautiful $300 piano. The joy of the children knew no bounds, and there was happiness in that home, 21 Jones-avenue.

While there was happiness in that home there wandered upon the streets of the Flower City the cry of many a poor victim. The following will show how a beautiful boy came to love liquor. In his own language I will give you his tale of sorrow, and, reader, may you ponder over his bitter experience as he related it:

"I have heard my dear mother say that when I was a little baby she thought me her finest child. I was the pet of the family. I was caressed and pampered by my fond but too indulgent parents. Before I could well walk I was treated with sweets from the bottom of my father's glass. When I was a little older I was fond of sitting on his knee, and he would frequently give me a little of the liquor from his glass in a spoon. My dear mother would gently chide him with ' Don't, John, it will do him harm,' to this he would smilingly reply, ' This little sup won't hurt him, bless him.' When I became a school-boy I was at times unwell, and my affectionate mother would pour for me a glass of wine from the decanter. At first I did not like it, but as I was told it would make me strong, I got to like it. When I left school and home to go out as an apprentice, my pious mother wept over me, and amongst other good advice urged me never to go into the public house or theatre. For a long time I could not be prevailed upon to act contrary to her wishes, but alas! the love for liquor had been implanted within me. Some of my shopmates at length overcame my scruples and I crossed the fatal threshold. I reasoned thus: My parents taught me that these drinks were good, I cannot get them here except at the public house. Surely it cannot be wrong then to go and purchase them. From the public house to the theatre was an easy passage. Step by step I fell. Little did my fond mother think when she rocked me in my little cot, that her child would find a home in a prison-cell. Little did my indulgent father dream when he placed the first drop of sweetened poison to my childish lips that he was sowing the seed of my ruin. My days are now nearly ended, my wicked career is nearly closed. I have grown up to manhood, but the curse of intemperance has added sin upon sin. Hope for the future I have not. I shall soon die a poor drunken outcast and disgraced."

Oh, reader, what a tale of sorrow! O, rum, rum, thy tender mercies are cruel, but thou shalt stand indicted as the great crime creator, and warfare shall be against thee until the last, or thy agencies shall be no more! "Wine is a mocker, strong drink is raging, and whosoever is deceived thereby is not wise." With this chapter closes the year of 1886, and a memorial year it will be in my days to come. One solid year of peace and happiness was ours. The children kept on in the school instead of working in the tobacco factory, while the wife was happy in her bright little home, the roses that had left her cheeks now came back and the lilies left her, and instead of the lily sitting on her cheeks and the rose upon my nose, the rose took its seat upon her cheeks while the lily came and hopped on the end of my nose. May it with the help of God always rest on that end.

Praise His name!

# CHAPTER XII.

A Three years' blank—A happy New Year's Day—Other New Years—Cider and politics—No blood money for Joe—The jealousy of singers—Joe and the school-teacher—Comes out head—Encouraging words—Not all smooth sailing—The Christian's prayer.

"Ye are the light of the world. A city that is set on an hill cannot be hid."

SO with the text I will make a feeble attempt to bring before my readers the twelfth chapter which really ought to be the thirteenth chapter, as I have left untold about three years of my life, which have been so reckless, covering my travels in foreign lands, that I have not one item to dwell upon with profit. That chapter shall go into eternity, and shall only then be revealed by Him, the Ruler of rulers; and now I will proceed to throw some light upon the twelfth chapter of my life.

The New Year of 1887 was begun in this wise. I watched the old year out amidst the brilliant stars, as the bells tolled forth the hour of 12 o'clock, bringing with it a chorus of happy voices: "Wish you a happy New Year, papa and mamma;" and truly it was a happy morning. There I sat in my sober manhood, at one end of the table, while my better half was at the other end, talking over the many New Years that brought no joy and happiness to our home, when we contrasted the past with the present. As I now look back to that early morning of the first day in the year, everything so changed, and take a peep at the happy children, and compare my situation with that of the New Year of 1885, when there was a drunken, staggering form entering the house, I cannot but offer a silent prayer to my God that He raised up a W.C.T.U., and an I.O.G.T. association, and last, but not least, that by His grace He redeemed such a noble fighter as P. A. Burdick, whom God has endowed with talents to reach all hearts. After we had offered up a thanksgiving to God, we all went to bed, as it was now one o'clock in the morning. After breakfast we talked the matter over how we would spend New Year's Day. It was decided that we go out for a sleigh drive, then to the Knights of Temperance concert in the afternoon. In the evening we all went to Mr. Lee's house. Brother Lee had been a hard drinker, and had neglected his family; but he came forward one night while I was holding meetings in the Lake Ave. Baptist Church, signed the pledge, gave his heart to God, and to this day he is a good standing member in the church. The next morning or, rather, about noon, the post brought me a letter, and the following lines were written on the paper : " Mr. Hess,—I would wish to give you many words of encouragement, and to say, God bless you and keep you. I would like to give more substantial aid if my means were not so limited, and my bodily strength so little. May you and yours always be blessed for what you have done for my dear husband and his family. Yours in the cause. E."

I knew at once who it was that had been made happy. Though often times came when everything looked dark, yet such an encouraging letter would give me renewed strength to go on.

On January 6th, 1887, I started for Rushville, N.Y. This is a beautiful town, it lays in among the mountains to the south of Canadaigua about 10 miles. There is a beautiful drive here in the summer season. Rushville has a High School, a Congregational church, over which Rev. Mr. Fry was pastor, and it has a grand M.E. church, over which the Rev. Mr. Young was pastor, and a fearless defender of right was Brother Young. The meetings were held in the opera house, which was packed nightly, and wonderful work was done. One of the principal

features of the meetings was the Bible readings every
noon.   Though it was 25 to 30° below zero yet the hall
was packed.  On Sunday night I spoke on "Cider," which
caused a great commotion.   People are always willing
that we talk about some one else, but just as soon as you
talk about the things they like to do, they are up in arms.
Well, one of the features of this night's meeting was
that the hotel keeper's wife came forward and signed
the pledge.   This stirred up everybody, and in all corners
you could hear them talk about the meetings.   On Jan.
12th I discussed the barley question which seemed to
rouse the people that had not been roused.   This was
brought about in the following manner : Having sent out
my envelopes for people to place therein their contribu-
tion, on opening one of these, I found a 25 cent piece,
with these words written on a slip of paper :  " Mr. Hess,
you said last night that money coming from the brewery
is blood money.   Well, I received this blood money from
the brewery to-day, and I enclose it to you."   I took this
and went to the hall, and  held  up the money and read
the paper, which had no name signed to it.   I said, " If
the man is in the hall who sent it he can get it back ; if
not I will cast it from me, as I don't want blood money."
I threw the money into the audience.  Bro. Young rose
from his seat, and said, " I wish to define my position
right here.   Know all members of my church that you
need not bring me any of your money for which you sold
barley."  This created consternation in the Methodist
camp, and then the fun did begin.  Satan got many a
hard punch, which I richly enjoyed.

On January 12th Bro. Fry made a stirring speech, in
which he declared on what side he was politically ; and
as this was not to be a political meeting I rose and
declared my position.  This so enraged the elder that he
got up and ran away, forgetting to take his hat and over-
coat.   Next day I received a call from Bro. Smith, who
said that after to-night the meetings would close as far

as he and Bro. Fry were concerned. They would not be responsible any longer for the rent. My first engagement was for ten days, but at the end of seven days these men became sulky, like a horse that at first is all fire if he can have his own way, but put the check on him and he is all "boggie." After the interview with Bro. Smith I was satisfied that I must bring the matter before the people. In the evening I made a statement of the case. The whole audience arose and voted that I should stay five days more. I had to make another statement that about $30 were required for my hall and rent. This was brought forth in ten minutes, and the meetings continued. The next day nine rose for prayers at the Bible reading. January 16th the meetings closed, and Rushville had such a stirring on temperance as it never had before.

During the time that I was at Rushville I received a call from Rev. K. B. Nettleton, the pastor of the M. E. Church, of Nunday, N.Y. Nothing unusual took place in this town, only that our efforts were crowned with success. Here is where George Ackerman became my leader of the singing with his cornet. He was a small man, but when he brought the cornet to his mouth you would think a 200 pounder was back of it. Then, again, the notes were brought forth sweet and mild and clear. Many hard drinkers signed in this place.

My next place was at Hamlin, N.Y., where we had splendid success, but here, like many other places, we found that some people had the big head among the singers. I am satisfied that there is a great deal of jealousy amongst preachers and public speakers, but they cannot hold a candle against the singers and musicians. Even in this small town there was fighting amongst the singers.

The next event was when I went to Pittsford. Here a great work was done, in spite of the opposition which came from the Rev. Mr. Close. He said he did not believe in the way Joe worked, yet he was there nightly. "He would have the people think;" in one word, he threw cold water on the work, trying hard to freeze it out, but he failed to do it. While opposition came from that side, I found a friend and true Christian in the principal merchant of the place, James T. Wiltsie. This God-fearing man was converted from a path of sin, and became an earnest worker in the vineyard of the Lord, and is to-day one of my warmest friends on earth. May God always bless him.

The work went on—during my stay in the town the teachers had a convention, and I having never been at such a convention, thought it a good thing to go, and I went. While there the Professor called on a certain number of teachers to form a class to be instructed by him. After calling fifteen he thought he would like his class to consist of sixteen, and he called on me. I had no idea what was going to happen, so I went up and took my seat. Giving each a little pad to figure on, he gave the problem as he termed it, then he called 10, 14, 16 to step out and put it on the blackboard the quickest and most original way. To be sure this was quite a task, yet I did go to the blackboard and with eighteen figures I placed the whole problem on the board, then walked to my seat amidst the cheers and applause. One of the others was next finished, the third man I pitied him. I had to leave the hall, and he may be figuring yet for all I know. The teacher thought to make me a laughing-stock for his school, but he had to take the medicine he had bottled up for me. Generally when a man tries to dig a hole for some one else to fall in, he, as a rule, falls therein himself.

February 21st, 1887, I was attending an auction in Rochester, when two buffalo robes were put up for sale. These were robes that had covered my knees on many a drunk, but you ask why were they put up on auction. The same explanation applies to many other cases. The owner of these robes was a splendid fellow, but had one failing, " he could drink or let it alone," but there came a time when the appetite had fastened itself upon him so that he could not let it alone. As a result of that we see two splendid gray horses, a carriage that cost $1,500 in hard cash, a sett of harness almost new, along with many other things up for auction to satisfy creditors. I bid on the robes and they were knocked down to me at $15.00 the two. I took them home and put them on the beds of my children for warmth. I wish that all men who drink and go out driving when the " buffalo " is spread over the knee, would just think about their little families at home.

During or at the close of my meetings I have received various tokens of kindness which have stimulated me many times in the hour of trial and temptation. Such words of regard as the following will cheer most any one. Here is a short letter sent to me while at Pittsford and Lima, N.Y :

LIMA, N. Y., Sept. 16th, 1886.

MR. HESS, DEAR BROTHER IN CHRIST,—God bless you in the work you have undertaken for Him. I feel that He has set His seal upon it, and he that endureth unto the end has the promise of eternal life. Trust Him day by day to keep you; trust Him for all needed good. He sometimes leads us into paths which the flesh shrinks from, but He knows the end from the beginning and nothing can come to a child of His without He permits it. When trials and persecutions come, as come they will, remember that is just what the Master has told us we should have in this world, but in Me ye shall have peace, that is our comfort and joy, the peace of God which passeth all understanding is more to a child of God than all else. How it rejoices my heart that Jesus said just before leaving this earth, " Lo, I am with you always, even unto the end." If God be for us who can be against us, and surely He is for us in the temperance work and we shall yet see a mighty deliverance.  He will make bare His arm and overthrow this great curse.  I am in sympathy with you and bid you God speed.  Yours in Him.                                        MRS. M. E. MILLER.

This letter makes me think of what I read in the book of Daniel, xii, 3.  "And they that be wise shall shine as the brightness of the firmaments; and they that turn many to righteousness as the stars for ever and ever."  Here is another token of encouragement:

DEAR FRIEND IN CHRIST,—Please accept this trifle; I would gladly give more.  I sincerely trust you will be greatly blessed in your work and at last receive the crown of life promised to the faithful.  Your friend,
                    AN INTERESTED LADY LISTENER.

That is just what I am fighting for, the crown of life, but I wish that many shall be crowned in the same manner on the same day and hour.  One day while having the blues the mails brought me a letter, and I give the wording of the same:

"MR. HESS, BROTHER IN CHRIST,—Enclosed find one dollar.  This is the Lord's money and I know you will be blessed in its use.  May the Lord keep you from all temptations and lead you on in your good work.  "I will instruct thee and teach thee in the way which thou shall go, I will guide thee with thine eye."—Psalm xxxii, 8.
                        ROSE A. PILLSBURY.

Truly can I say the Lord is a good instructor, and a fearless leader, and one who is ever watchful over his own.

One day I was laboring in the town of " B.," which was cursed with strong drink—and this caused me to work harder than ever, but no results had I seen, and it seemed that demons had conspired against me—when the mail again came to my rescue in the shape of a letter, which read as follows: "Mr. Hess, I thank God that His great and wonderful love saved and sent you here to help not only me but others in the good way; God has blessed your labors; I realize this as I meet one and another, and learn of the many hearts that have been reached. May our Heavenly Father bless the words spoken more and more, and as you leave ' B.' I hope the good work commenced may continue until many may be brought to Christ. Pray for me and one other, that he may become a Christian. God be with you. Yours in Christ." Such words as the above inspire me with renewed courage to fight on.

While in the town of Mendon I was called to come and hold a meeting in the Friends' Meeting House, which I considered a big honor, because I was the first man outside of their own denomination who ever spoke in their church. In this way the Lord opened the doors of places where I least dreamed of.

In one of the western towns of New York State, where I was called to hold meetings for a no-license campaign, it seemed that the minister of the place opposed my coming with all his might; but woman is woman the world over; when she wills she wills, and when wont she wont, and you might as well try to turn a horse that wants to go the other way, as try to turn a woman from her way of thinking. So the Woman's Christian Temperance Union had me come. On the way from the station, the committee informed me that they could not procure a church, as the minister was not agreeable, consequently we must go to the small school-house. One of the very first callers I had was from a tall, well-formed man, in middle life. In introducing himself, I was astonished to know that this was the very same man who so strongly opposed my coming to the place. After the usual greetings from one stranger to the other, he at once stated that the school-house was too small, therefore he would tender me his church, and, said he, at the same time pulling out his purse, " 1 wish to give $2 towards your support, as they always

I

forget to pass the collection box on the platform." I was amused at this, for I saw through his little game with one eye shut. This tendering me his church and his great benevolent heart was brought into action because the old fellow feared that I would get wind of his opposing my coming, and he took this method of squaring himself in my eye. I took the proffered things, thanked him, at the same time I said to myself, " Old fellov, this wont save you, for you must feel how it hurts when some one is talking about you." I took the platform, and I gave him (not personally) a regular trouncing that night. He said he was very sorry that he could not attend my meetings, as he had to go away; he was very sad to think he had to leave now, when he would have such a treat in listening to me. Oh, that all mankind would know that their faces are the great mirrors of what is going on in their hearts. It is impossible to hide from the face the inward feelings. Let it be joy, the face will show it; let it be earnestness, the face will tell it to the world; let it be deceitfulness, the face brings it to the light; let it be sorrow, it will bear the tidings to the world. So in all things that come up in daily life the face is the transparency that makes it known. How do I know this? For my life long I have made a complete study of the human face, as a sport and gambler this was the most essential part of my work. While I am now engaged in public life again as an Evangelist it is my work to study humanity, but it is not faces so much I now make a study, but deeds of the body, and I can tell a Christian from the works the body does. If a man is a Christian you will find him not only one on Sunday but Monday and on Tuesday, and so on all through the week until Sunday comes again. A Christian will pray the following prayer and live up to the same. Each morning I give myself into my Master's hands for the day, saying, "Take me to-day, Lord, and use me as Thou wilt. Let me be about my Master's business.

Whatever work Thou hast for me to do give it into my hands, and give me grace to do it. If there are those whom Thou wouldst have me help in any way send them to me, or take me to them. Take my time and use it as Thou wilt. Let me be a vessel emptied of self and sin, washed in Jesus' blood and filled with His Spirit, close to Thy hand and meet for Thy service, to be employed only for Thee and for ministering to others in Thy name and for Thy sake."

If this prayer were offered up by every so-called Christian man and woman, and their religion were based upon such an idea, the world would be taken for Christ in a week. "He that knoweth the Son knoweth the Father, and he that knoweth the Father knoweth the Son."

# CHAPTER XIII.

An important point in Hess' history—Buys a home—The pleasantries of house-moving—Description of the new home—Speaks for P. A. Burdick at Syracuse, N.Y.—Downfall of a prosperous business man—Work among the children—A telling story of one man's reformation—The saloon in poetry.

"All things work together for good to them that love the Lord."

'AS this will be a most interesting chapter for me to write, I have selected the above heading from choice, because it so plainly speaks of my new life. Though the struggle for manhood in the first year and six months was hard, yet with the help of God I was able to overcome all obstacles in my way, and you will see by reading this chapter how the Lord takes care of those who are willing.

My whole career up to this chapter has been one of almost unmitigated woe ; with the exception of my childhood, and some three months of my new life, my whole life has been one of unceasing, perpetual struggle, and not until the time when I began life in that part of the year when the things occurred that I shall describe in this chapter did the bright aspect of the real life dawn upon me. When we put all trust in God we will succeed. In Psalm xci., 4, we read : "He shall cover thee with his feathers, and under his wings shalt thou trust : his truth shall be thy shield and buckler." Truly can I say that he had covered us as a family up to the beginning of this chapter, and had caused our "cup to run over with good."

January 24th, 1887, was a mild day. Closing my campaign at Nunda, I arrived at Rochester at 10.20 a.m., and after consulting with my faithful partner in life, we decided to take the 2.25 p.m. train for Holly, New York, and look for a home that we might buy, and settle down in it for life.    After considerable looking about, and not finding what we were looking for, we conceived the idea of getting a livery team, and drive over to see our friends, Mr. and Mrs. Carver, who lived about seven miles from Holly.    On our way over we had to pass the romantic little village named Clarendon.    Clarendon has about 450 population, has two churches, one the M. E. Church, and the other a Universalist.    It has a grand school, also several stores, also a flouring mill, saw mill, and planing mill.    Just the kind of country place where one can receive the fresh air which is pure.    Clarendon has, besides these different places named, a grand temperance camp meeting for ten days every August.    This camp is under the able management of Herbert S. Copeland, a son of the pioneer, George M. Copeland.    Stopping on our way at the store, we thought we should like to live here.    This plan was heartily entered into by Herbert Copeland, who at once accompanied us to several places that were for sale, but none were to our liking, until we came to a beautiful little home on Town-Hall-street.    This place had five large cherry trees along the front on the street, with some other fruit.    No sooner did we see the place when, as with one breath, both wife and myself said this is the place for us.    On entering we were received with a hearty good-day by the lady, who was introduced to us as Mrs. Jonas Shaw.    Mr. Shaw coming in, we made our object known to him.    He said yes, it was for sale.    Having learned the price, I at once, without any further hesitation, handed him $20 to bind the bargain, he to vacate the place so that I could take possession of the same by the 1st of April, he to receive $180 more on that date.    Both agreed to forfeit $100 if one or the other failed to comply with the above.    Now we started for friend Carver.    Next day we went back to Rochester; the children seemed to go wild over the idea that they were to have a home from which they would not be driven. When I handed the $20 to Mr. Shaw, I felt that it was much better for me to do this

than to pay $20 to some one for whiskey.  Why I grew
six inches taller, but since then I have settled back to
my former height.  Now all was anticipation, and the
time from the 24th of January seemed a long way off for
the children, but to me it came soon enough.  I had not
figured what it would cost until we were settled in the
permanent home.  As the time came I found I needed
more money than I possessed, and where to get it from I
did not know, but here the words, "All things work
together for good to them that love the Lord," were proven,
for a friend named James Wiltsie came to my rescue and
helped me.  The first time we moved we were able to
pack things together in a very short time, but since then
things had accumulated, and now it took a man six
nights to box and pack them so that they would be safe
for shipping by rail, and the house was "turned upside
down."  These are trying times for men—the days of
house-moving.  But the Ruler of all things above came
again to my rescue and I was called away to lecture
while the packing, moving and unpacking was going on.
So I left home in Rochester and went to Clarendon and
was there greeted with a welcome by my family that was
a royal one, and truly all were happy.  This moving and
packing had to be accomplished under the supervision of
Mrs. Hess, and she did it well.  Well, the next thing we
had to have was a horse and a buggy.  One day going
to Holly I bought a democrat—I don't mean a political
democrat—and yet during my life, at one time or another,
I have bought many a Democrat to vote as I dictated.
This was a democrat waggon, or, in other words, it was a
canopy top waggon, perhaps you will better understand
me when I call it a light spring waggon.  The next work
was to stretch the Brussels carpets.  Just think—a fine
Brussels carpet on the floor of my parlor and gold paper
on the walls and on the ceiling, with some extra fixing
round called border, then a crown in the centre from
which a hanging lamp is suspended to give light to all

who are in the house. All this was new to us. Wife
often complains that I tramp so heavy as I walk across
the floor, yet when it came to carpet-stretching I became
a useful article. Stretch the carpet! why if I put my
little tiny feet on that carpet it commenced to stretch
like a rubber strap. That's what you get for being heavy.
After the carpet had been laid the room looked very nice,
then we moved the piano. Say, drinking-man, there was
a time when I used to buy those playthings for the saloon-
keeper's home, and mine was without one, now when I
get home I sit myself down while my little daughter
softly glides over them dar, shiney keys they calls them,
and oh how she makes them fingers fly just like there
was no bone in dat hand, and she goes tra la la, tra la la la,
and den dat makes mine feet go so funny, and den I pulls
mine mouth so and so, and I feels just like I was in
heaven. Now, when I was drinking, I could plainly hear
the piano send forth its sweetest tunes from the parlors
of the homes of the men who sell liquor to their fellow-
men ; but things have changed, and soft and melodious
sounds come from the parlor window of my home.
" Home, Sweet Home," how pleasant it sounds. One of
the amusing features of my present home life is, that the
saloon-keeper sometimes drives out and we meet each
other. He drives a fine horse, *so do I.* One morning the
mail brought me a letter; breaking the seal I saw it
came from Syracuse, from my kind and noble benefactor,
P. A. Burdick. I went to that city to speak for him.
Had the Alhambra rink jammed with people. On my return from Syracuse I bought a set of fine parlor furniture
from Mr. Wippel, then went to Clarendon. Up to this
time I had been a member, with my family, of the Baptist Church ; no such denomination existing in our town
we concluded we would all become members of the M. E.
Church, therefore on the 24th day of April we joined the
church in Clarendon. I praise His name that all my
children have given their hearts to God. Being spring-

time I now worked in the garden, which needed a cleaning up ; how pleasant it is when you can go to the garden and get your greens and have them nice and fresh.

While lecturing in the town of P., in Western New York, an incident occurred which I think should be given here.  Usually when you go into a town you will hear some simple minded person say: "What is lecturing? that's no work."  While in the town of P., such a simpleton threw out that he could do just as well as Joe Hess, if he had only a chance he would show that he was right.  The next day this man called on me and made his wishes known to me.  I agreed to give him thirty minutes of my time next evening.  This I made known from the pulpit that Mr. —— would speak on the morrow evening.  We had an increase of audience. After introducing the man he jumped up, but when he faced the audience he was speechless ; his speech had entirely left him.  As he stood there amidst the roars of laughter I took pity and told him to sit down, he not only sat down but grabbed his hat and left the hall by the rear door, and for two days we did not see him; on the third day he returned. Said he to me, " Let me say just a few words," but I could not induce him to get up on the platform.  As he arose he brought forth a scrap of paper on which were written these words, "Good friends,—I was bitterly opposed to our Brother Hess on his arrival ; I had been satisfied that I could do the same as he, and made my claim that he is too lazy to work. Mr. Hess gave me an opportunity to speak.  I was confident that I could do it without any trouble, but I failed.  I now am satisfied that Bro. Hess is working hard, and I, with the help of God, shall help him to work, therefore I subscribe my name to his pledge." He signed it, became a useful member of society once again, and is to-day a worker in the vineyard of the Master.  It is wonderful how the Lord works.  Surely His way is a mysterious one.

Monday, May 16th, 1887, I took out an insurance policy

in the Good Templars' Insurance. On the same day I went to Mr. Mose Goodman and bought a lady's watch for my wife, as a present, which she appreciated much. Say, drinking man, how much better for me to buy a watch for my wife than to help to pay for one that the saloon-keeper bought for his wife.

While holding meetings in the town of Livonia, a man came to me one day wrapt in tears. This man was a prosperous business man at one time. He also was a first-class boot and shoe maker. Said he to me : " Mr. Hess, I have listened to you last night and this morning ; something, whatever it is, compels me to come and show a living witness of the power of whiskey to destroy the body, not only that, but the soul also. Here you have two powerful illustrations. You represent the power of the Gospel to save men from their evil ways, while I represent the power of the liquor traffic to-take men of purity and drag them down to ruin ; God help us. With this he roared aloud ; his roar was that of a maniac. In due time I talked to him, and he became more easy ; he promised he would come to the hall and sign the pledge. The hall being crowded, I looked in vain for the man. Not being able to discover him, I gave it up and was feeling sad, when my ears were greeted with, " I am here, Mr. Hess." Looking to the right of the hall I beheld the man, and now I was satisfied. At the close of the meeting this man was the first to sign, and the last I heard from him he was safe and happy with his family. Oftentimes I am asked what is the most pitiful sight I ever saw. Why the people ask me that, I don't know, and why people like to listen to sorrowful tales I cannot understand. The most pitiful sight that comes to my eyes is the child of a drunkard, and I can best answer this question in the language taken from John B. Gough's history. After being asked this same question, he answered: " The most pitiful sight he has seen was ' An old child,' a child with wrinkles in its face, that is not yet in its teens, a child

made old by hard usage, whose brow is furrowed by the
ploughshare of sorrow ; that," said John B. Gough, " was
one of the most pitiful sights on earth." To this I say
Amen. Most people underrate the capacity of a child to
suffer, as they do often their ability to understand. Many
a little one has wept hot, scalding tears at the knowledge
of being the child of a drunkard. To show this is so, I
will here reproduce an incident from John B. Gough's
book. " One time while he, Gough, was driven from
Hartford to a village where he was to lecture, the man
who came to bring him had a-fine span of horses, and
quite a stylish vehicle. ' Ah !' said he to me when we
had fairly started on the road, ' Ah ! if you had seen me
eight years ago, when I was carted out of Wellington,
you'd have thought I was a hard case. Everything I possessed in the world on a one-horse cart—wife and children, furniture—what there was of it on a one-horse cart.
A man lent me the team to get me out of the place, and
such a horse ! you couldn't see his head move more than
half the time ; I knew he had a head 'cause when I'd pull
the rein he'd kind of come round, and so slow, why the only
effect of leathering him was to make him go sideways,
but not a bit faster. Now I am driving you to my native
town with a span of horses. They're mine, I own this
team ; that off-horse is a good traveller (g'lang !—I'm in
a hurry). Why eight years ago I was carted out, and
now I'm driving you there with my own team, for a temperance lecture (get up ! g'lang). My father lives there
yet, and my old mother that has prayed for me so many
years (get up ! g'lang ! I'm in a hurry). It is the hap-
piest day of my life. My wife's people live there too. They
never spoke to me for years before I signed the pledge,
and I have a letter in my pocket inviting me to bring
you to their house. G'lang !' he shouted, and we span
along the road at the rate of twelve miles an hour. Slack-
ening the speed, he turned to me and said : ' I look like
a brute ; everybody said I was a brute ; but I am not a

brute.' No, certainly not, I replied. 'Well, I'm not a brute; and yet—well I'll tell you. I came home one day irritated with drink, ready to vent my anger on anything. My boy, about ten years old, came to the door, and as ·soon as he saw me he darted off, Dick, come here, come here. When he came his face was bloody and bruised, his lip cut, and one eye swollen. What have you been doing, Dick? I've been fighting. I had no objection to the boys fighting; but I asked: What have you been fighting for? He said: don't ask me, father; I don't want to tell you. Tell me what you have been fighting for. I don't want to. Full of rage, I caught him by the collar of his little jacket, and roared out: now, tell me what you have been fighting for, or I will cut the life out of you. Oh, father! he cried out, piteously, don't beat me, father, don't beat me. Tell me what you've been fighting for, then. Oh! I don't want to; I struck him with my fist on the side of the head. Now, tell me what you've been fighting for. Oh! father, father, don't beat me. I will tell you. Well, then, be quick. Wiping the blood and tears from his poor, swelled face with the back of his hand, he said: There was a boy out there told me my father was a poor old drunkard, and I licked him, and if he tells me that again, I will lick him again. Oh! Mr. Gough, what could I say. My boy, ten years of age, fighting for his father's reputation. I tell you that liked to kill me. How I loved that boy, that noble boy. I could almost have worshipped him. But oh, oh, the drink, the cursed drink —my love for that was stronger than my love for my child.' "

This proves how even the little ones suffer. May God help these little ones, and inspire friends of humanity to reach out a helping hand to these despairing, but innocent victims of this horrible vice of drunkenness.

As I go from place to place, I am more impressed with the importance of the work of training children in the principles of temperance. If we neglect the teaching of

the children, we will lose the hold on the general public
mind.  Every night's rest advances the little ones towards manhood or blooming womanhood, and it is these
then that will rule or govern society.  The power for good
or evil is yearly increasing.  What must be done is to
start the little ones right, and no man of mind will say
total abstinence is not right.  Total abstinence is a safe
tl ing, while drinking strong drink is a risk of all good
qualities that men possess.  Is this a fact? then come
and extend a hand to the children, make them strong
that they may in their homes influence their parents t
take a bold stand.  Talk about the children not knowing
what they do when they sign.  I can speak from experi
ence, that about seventy per cent. of the young people who
have signed the pledge some four years ago have kept it,
and may keep it all their days.  You take a boy who will
sign to himself the freedom that this country assures him
when he is fifteen years and keep it, by the time he becomes a citizen, the community will have before them,
not the production of the grog shop, but of the temperance room.  Take two young men, placed alongside of
each other, of the same age, of the same temperament,
and it will be shown which will be the best positive
evidence as to the power of the promotion of mankind by these separate institutions; the young man
coming from the saloon will show the marks of dissipation in his face, in his walk, and his speech.  Look at the
bleared eyes, the bloated face, the shivering form dressed
in ragged attire, his pockets empty; see him looking at a
free lodging room, see him stretched out on the hard
boards, this is the production of the saloon.  Now turn
and look up at the young man who came from the
temperancee room, how different these young men.  The
temperance boy has a bright and intelligent eye, his flesh
is clean, he stands erect, his clothes are of the best material,
of the latest cut, his attire is that of true manhood, his pockets
contain money honestly earned with which he will pay his

way. Which of the two do you think, reader, would be the most valuable to the country, to which one would you give the hand of your only child, a daughter? You would hand her to the sober young man. You investigate, and you will find young boys who had joined the army of temperance boys fifteen years ago are to-day steadfast and holding to their principles. One day while a cart was driving up one of the principal streets loaded with whiskey-barrels, one rolled out and a bystander cried aloud, "what a pity that that liquor is spilled." "Oh," shouted a little boy, "it's no pity, it had better be on God's earth than in God's image."

While I was laboring at Bath, N.Y, to which I was called by Rev. Brother Bell, the Pastor of the M. E. Church—a regular war-horse is Brother Bell; I wish we had more ministers like a Bell that would keep on tolling the year round, and make the church welcome the sinner. While there, a lady came to me and told me her sad tale. It was the old story, the bread-winner of that family was behind the prison gates, in jail. I learned from her story, which was delivered to me in broken sentences, the tears trickling slowly but surely down her pale cheeks, that he was a kind husband and a loving father when not in liquor. The charge preferred against him was drunk and disorderly, fine $15.00. I went to the clerk and found that his sentence would expire in two weeks. I paid the fine and went to the jail and demanded the prisoner; he was delivered into my hands, and then, when on the street, I told him who I was. He seemed so overcome with joy that he could not find words to express himself. I took him to his family, and oh, such a sight, really it did my heart good to see how happy they were. "Surely it is more blessed to give than to receive." I gave the mother of this home not money, but gave her back the husband who had been detained from her side by force— through, the agent of drink. This man came to the meetings, and by last account, he is steadfast. God bless him more abundantly.

The works of the saloon can best be shown by the
following words in rhyme :

His house from others you can tell,
Its doors are wide—the gates of hell ;
A cask, red curtains, all are shown
As signals of the work that's done.

Now enter in,—oh, horrible !
The fire, the smoke, the sulphur smell,
The barrels, bottles, glasses too,
Brimful of hell's black mountain dew.

Men, boys, black, white do mingle there,
They sing, they fight, they howl, they swear.
Some sit, some lie, some stupid stand,
They reel and toss on every hand.

Some few in frantic madness roar,
Some loud beneath the tables snore ;
Most strange to some these things have seemed,
But 'tis the effect of being "steamed."

What are prisons, poorhouses, orphan and insane asylums but storehouses for the drunkard makers' manufactured goods ?   Some years ago a Mr. A. Champion and a
person still living paid Mr. S. Chipman, $1,200 for one
year's labor in visiting those institutions in the different
counties in the State of New York, getting certificates
from each, showing that from two-thirds to three-fourths
of the county taxes were caused by intoxicants. God give
us courage to battle this foe and wipe it from the face
of the earth that little ones shall have sunshine and
happiness.

# CHAPTER XIV.

Half-hearted Christians—An interesting campaign in Lockport—
Talking temperance for money—First and last experience as
an orator—Syracuse by gas-light—Experience as a camp manager—Telling incidents—Hess' secret of success—First appearance at Grand Lodge I. O. G. T.—The high-license agitation
in New York State.

" We then, as workers together with him, beseech you also that
ye receive not the grace of God in vain."—II Corinthians vi., 1.

HOW I wish that all who profess to be workers would
adopt this text, and have unity in their ranks. The
cause of Christ would receive a great impetus. The
Christian who dare not take a bold front on the side of
sobriety ought to read the 16th verse of the above chapter every day, wherein is asked the question, "And
what agreement hath the temple of God with idols ? for
ye are the temple of the living God ; as God hath said, I
will dwell in them, and walk in them, and I will be their
God, and they shall be my people."

This, then, is the answer to the Christians who are
afraid to identify themselves with this branch of work.
If God would dwell in them, they would not be full of
man-fear. If God were in them, they would be filled
with the spirit, and they would be up and doing the
Master's work. They would become the people of the
Lord. Their light would shine before men ; by this act
they would glorify their Father who is in heaven. The
Father's command to His children is written in the II.
Corinthians, vi., 17, which reads as follows : " Wherefore
come out from among them, and be ye separate, saith the
Lord, and touch not the unclean thing : and I will receive
you." How I wish I could write on these pages, white
and fair, that there is not one of God's children on earth

who would be guilty of touching the unclean thing of intoxicants. What a change there would be in a short time, what a reform would be brought about; but as long as eight-tenths of the people who are members of churches are using the dark beverages of hell in a moderate way, so long we will have to battle this mighty foe.

June 1st, 1887.—I was called to speak for ten days in one of the western cities of New York State. This city was Lockport, a driving place; it is well known for the many "canal locks" it possesses. Upper Lockport is the most intellectual, while the lower part of the city is composed largely of the laboring class. This city is cursed with strong drink. The first of the series of meetings was held in the lower part of the city; the audience was a small one, but what it lacked in quantity it made up in quality. Lockport has many noble defenders of the temperance cause. Of many I might write. I will here refer to one only, John Crampton, a man with one arm, a true knight of the cause. Brother Crampton is a loyal Good Templar, and a man who is not afraid what the public will say, because the principle he advocates is a God-given principle. In this city I also met for the first time Rev. C. H. St. John and wife, from Kansas, both devoted Christian temperance workers. When I said I met these people for the first time, I mean personally, for I had seen them both in Denver when I was keeping saloon, and they were opposed to my business, consequently I was opposed to their method of work. So far only was I in sympathy with them. As long as they would try and convert the drunken vagabond, who so often, to use the language of one of the presidents of the Brewery-men's Congress of the United States, " Proves a pest to the well-regulated tavern." But how different was our meeting now in the city, both working on the same side of the fence. These good people held forth under the tent, while I had the large rink. The rink was crowded nightly, so was the tent, during my stay in the city.

June 4th, the Sunday school of that district had a convention at Rogers' Grove. Short addresses were delivered by Rev. St. John, Mrs. Stout, Rev. Ferbish and your humble servant. As I faced this grand audience composed mostly of the rising generation, I scarcely found my speech as these little ones were all dressed in white, and trimmed with red and blue. I thought of the millions who were yet without the necessary clothing to come to such feasts, because the father spent his earnings for drink. At this place, after I had done speaking, a gentleman grasped me by the hand, saying, " Well Joe, you did well ;" for a moment I could not place him, after a moment of reflection I knew him. He was one of the " Tenbrook " boys who kept a saloon a little over a year prior to this occurrence. I drank at his bar. He said " Stick to it, Joe, it was the best act you ever did in your life." Much good was accomplished, many hard drinkers signed during the time, while I am very sorry to say that many have violated their obligation ; yet I can count about fifty of the old soakers that have kept steadfast, and to-day are respectable members of society.

Many times I hear the statement that I do the work for money ; for argument's sake I will say, I do make speeches for money. Take into consideration how much is a man's soul valued at—$1.00 or $1,000, or can a soul be bought with money ? There is only one price for which a soul can be bought, or has been bought. That price Jesus paid on the tree. Let us compare the temperance question as a matter of business. Then let me ask the question, does any man work without getting pay ? Does any man sell goods simply for the glory ? No man preaches the great Gospel truth without getting money for it ? The manufacturer of the Devil's strong drink does it for money. Why ? Because we need the money to produce the necessaries of life. We don't seem to mind when we lay down 50c., 75c., or $1, for a theatrical entertainment which does not seek to elevate men.

J

On the contrary, it only brings about a desire in the mind of inexperienced youth to become a theatrical man. Yet these same people will not pay 5c. towards sustaining temperance meetings. For instance, during my life of nearly five years' lecturing I can distinctly recall two weeks of hard work, afternoon and evening, when at the closing meeting, which was a big success, as well as other meetings, a collection was taken up for the speakers. When the plates were returned I was handed the astounding sum of $8.76 for two weeks' hard work, yet I have to meet all these accusations, "You are talking temperance for the money there is in it."

As we live not far from the banks of Ontario's lake, and every one seems to know me in that section, I can draw a great crowd at any time. With this knowledge the proprietors of the hotels at Troutburg were possessed. Arrangements were made that they would celebrate the fourth of the month with a jubilee, and I was expected to make the grand oration. My ideas as to what an oration should be were lofty and high. I could see visions of all sorts, and when I beheld the great flaming posters of the great celebration that was to take place at Troutburg, on the same grounds where a year previous the Baker and Slattery prize-fight occurred, and Joe Hess, the converted fighter, was to be the orator of the day, I grew an inch every time. I used to walk away from the places where I thought I might find or see the bill posted. My reason for this was, I was afraid I would grow too tall. The height of my vanity was reached and complete when I received a card by mail on which the word "orator" occurred. Having an idea of what an orator ought to be, I asked my wife to sit on the sofa and listen. This she did three times, then she thought she had all she wanted. The day came, when in company of my friend and Bro. R. H. Carver, we drove to the place. Thousands of people had gathered, and the hour having arrived, I was introduced and received with a hearty cheer. All the people before me knew how hard I was struggling for my manhood. I began, when the applause ceased, by speaking some words that I had read somewhere, which ran as follows : " One hundred years ago the ground upon which I stand was a howling wilderness," but I could not go farther.

"One hundred years ago this very ground upon which I stand was a howling wilderness." Stop again.

"One hundred years ago this ground upon which I stand was a howling wilderness," but I stop again, saying, I wish to God it was yet.

At this timely moment the Lord sent down the rain, and the audience dispersed, and I thanked God. After this great masterpiece of oratorical powers, I had no time to stay any longer, and started for home. In the evening we had a splendid time. Surrounded by many of my new-found friends, we gave a small display of fireworks, which was enjoyed by all. After that we sat down to ice-cream and lemonade, and cake. In this wise we spent the fourth of July, the birthday of American liberty. While in years previous I was drunken, and the family suffering, we now all enjoyed each other's company, and I went to bed sober.

July 21st.—Received a call from Syracuse ; found on my arrival Bro. F. Blake, who conducted me to his home ; spoke at the Alhambra Rink in the evening to a large gathering. After the meeting the committee desired that I should show them some of the holes in the city. My companions were the Rev. Bruce, Prof. Meads, Mr. Greg, and Bro. Blake. The gentlemen were astonished at the doings carried on inside these licensed places. Some of these places had rear doors, where could be found young girls not over fourteen or fifteen years old, with the marks of dissipation stamped upon every line of their features. Yet these men know that they violate the law by tolerating such a thing. At the same time they know that they are a power in politics, therefore they will not be prosecuted by the law-makers and the law-protectors. At another place was seen the disgraceful sight of drunken women and men dancing, as they call it, to the tune of a three-string fiddle. Many other things they learned that night that they never knew before. The next day being Sabbath, the Alhambra was packed to suffocation. Many signed the pledge. The next day, July 24th, there could be seen multitudes of people going to the Lakeside to take part in the celebration of the Leiderkranz Society  On the morning of the 25th, the Syracuse *Standard* had the following as a heading in one of their columns, which I here reproduce :—

## SCENES ON THE LAKESIDE.

### THOUSANDS SPENT THE DAY WITH THE LIEDERKRANZ SOCIETY.

*Joe Hess, the Temperance Orator, distributes tracts.*

"The Liederkranz Society went to the pleasant beach in two boats, leaving at 9.30 and 10 o'clock in the morning, and the throngs followed them all day. Col. E. S. Jenney was there, and so was Poundmaster Abe. Lincoln. Prof. Joe Hess, the temperance lecturer and ex-pugilist, was there, in company with Prof. C. P. Meads, the writing-master. Many in the crowd were talked to by the couple, and invitations were distributed to attend the temperance lecture, at the Alhambra, in the evening."

The above was meant to hurt my influence and cast a slur upon me. When, at the time these disgraceful scenes were being perpetrated at the Lakeside, I was talking to 2,000 people at the Alhambra; many a good man has had his influence for good destroyed by the secular press publishing a slander and untruth.

Tuesday, July 26th.—I started to join the Stuben County Prohibition Tent, which was in the hands of Wellford S. Bailey, another reformed man. On my way

I had to pass through Addison, on the Erie road, where I met James Baldwin, a great prohibitionist. He was a banker in Addison and spent much money to have the town grant no license which, to the surprise of all, gained the victory. And now the fall election coming on, he was the prime mover in the tent campaign. Bailey having to go home, I was to take his place in speaking. Baldwin sent me on to Canistota on the same train, there I took the stage for Rexville. On my arrival I was greeted by Brother Mumford, a small man. The evening audience was a good one, but in this case it was a Catholic element and all Irish at that, and the priest being absent and no Protestant living there, the rabble had full sway. The place contained three rum holes; you could easily see how hard it would be to talk prohibition. The next afternoon's meeting was a good one, but for an unwise expression of Brother Mumford. It seems the barkeeper of one of the saloons was in the meeting, when he arose and started out, Mumford seeing this said, " You need not go out if the load is too heavy. If you wait till I finish I will help you to carry it out." It seems this message was brought to the ears of the man, and he came over and asked me who was the man that spoke last. I pointed to Mumford, and the first thing I knew, these two had a battle of words which were very unpleasant to my ears. Mumford finally appealed to me. I simply told the man that I did not come here to fight any man's battle, but if he, the barkeeper, would lay hands on the man before him I would certainly have to interfere. He was quieted down and went away. Mumford not being satisfied had to go over to the corner and begin the same thing. During this time the cook went to the store to buy butter, and after having paid for it, the keeper of the store said, " I hope it will stink before you bring it to the camp." He then went to the butcher; after paying for the meat he, the butcher, said, "I wish the meat would be rotten before you cook it." Night came and the people were stopped on the road to the tent by the mob that had gathered, consequently our meeting was a slim one. During the time of speaking they threw stones into the camp, destroying the meeting. I saw that we were in for it, consequently I ordered the canvas to be tied up all round so that I would be able to see, but this the boys thought would be an unwise thing. All of a sudden, bunches of fire-crackers were fired into the tent, and revolvers were freely used. On looking for my boys, I found they had fled and left me in charge. I was able to quiet the mob, and after peace had set in I looked for the boys, when I found them in a hay-loft. I said, " Now Mumford, you started this racket, you are the boss, what are you going to do?" He said, " We will move to the next place." So at 4 a.m. we left Rexville. Walking ahead of the teams was Brother Mumford with a white plug hat, and his coat-collar standing up, a big stick in his hand, and along with him was the leader of the singing He was a great man, he played six instruments at one time, but only one thing he lacked in them all, that was cord and tune. So while they were walking ahead I could not help remembering what I had read in the Bible where Moses led the children of Israel out of the wilderness. Said I to the driver, " What do these men put you in mind of?" He said he did not know, so I said, " Moses and Aaron." He laughed and said, that was so. Our next move was to Greenwood, N.Y. We soon had the tent pitched, thinking we might have a day's rest, but this was not to be our luck, for in the evening they commenced to pile into the tent, and I was compelled to get up and go at them, which I did in grand style. Next afternoon Brother Bailey arrived, and he gave me a cordial shake of the hand. On Sunday morning the Methodist pastor gave up his service and we all united in the tent and had a wonderful time, the love feast was indeed a feast. At 11 o'clock your humble servant talked from the 20th chapter of Proverbs 1st verse. In the afternoon

James Baldwin, the banker from Addison, arrived. This
was one of the grandest days for the Lord Greenwood
ever had. Some little disturbance during the day, but
all was quieted down.

August 2nd, 1887.—I was asked to speak at Oakfield
Temperance Camp Meeting. I had a good time; fair-sized
audience. I spoke the year prior on this same platform,
and many came up after the meeting and told me how
much I had improved in the past year. This encouraged
me. I next held a campaign at Pultneyville. This place
is situated on the bank of the beautiful Lake Ontario. It
has within three miles south a fine bed of iron ore, and a
great fertile soil for farming. Farmers raise as a principle crop blackberries and raspberries, and apples. Some
excellent people live there. I was made right welcome
by a noble defender of right against wrong; his name is
E. D. Stoddard, and is one of, in fact is the leading business man in the town, and is the owner of a sash and
blind factory, and planing mill combined. His son-in-law
is another fine man. The ladies of these two homes are
bright and intelligent, and know how to welcome a
stranger amongst them. The meetings were held in the
Grove, and large crowds gathered nightly; much good
was done in the place, and many signed the pledge. After
leaving this place I went to Rochester, and then to Clarendon, and people sometimes marvelled at the success
that crowned all my efforts.

Dear reader, allow me to take you with me into my
secret chamber, and if you will promise not to reveal, you
may become a sharer in my secret.

When I first started out I thought I must follow other
men of fame as speakers. In one word, I thought to be
a success I would have to copy their style, but frankly I
now tell you that it was not very long when I made a
wonderful discovery. When young people go before
the public they imagine that when they walk on the
street every one is watching them, and I was no excep-

tion to this delusion. The first discovery that I made was that all people were not observing me ; the second discovery was that trying to play a role to which I was not accustomed would not help me, for the world was not blind, and would estimate me at my just value. When I had made this discovery, I was perfectly cured, and by the help of God I decided that I must be natural, and let the world select my place in it. From this time on I became a success, As I grow older in the work, I look back to my first starting out, when I thought I would turn this world in a few years on the question of prohibition, and laugh that I was so wise,

August 8th, 1887.—Our great temperance camp meeting opened. The speakers of the day were Harry Gurney, Rev. C. H. St. John and wife, Prof. C. Price, of North Carolina, a Negro, but a very fine speaker ; the second day, Col. Richardson ; the third, the Gough of the West, as he is termed, Lou. J. Beauchamp, a very pleasant talker ; the fourth day, M. C. McConnell, from Ohio ; and the fifth day, a treat that will live in the minds of the people for many years to come, the Hon. John B. Finch. For logic I never heard his equal. This camp meeting was a rich treat to me. Here's where I met these leading speakers for the first time, and much encouragement did I receive from them to go on.

My next exploit was to take my family to Hemlock Lake, where I had undertaken to run a camp. I, like many more, have always thought that the managers of these temperance camps make lots of money. Those who speak so have never had any experience in camp meetings. The first thing, you have to lay out for printing large posters from $15 to $25, then from $5 to $10 in having them put up around the country. Next come the different helps, such as watchmen, hostlers, ticket sellers, speakers, musicians, and singers, and you know the woods are full of singers. But there is only one trouble with 'em, they are always on the " fly." Next comes the

JOSEPH F. HESS.

man from whom you rent. All these, I suppose, people think live on wind, but I know different; they all want their money. Again there are the speakers who come from a long distance. You know a prophet is best known out of his own camp or country. These men all cost from $25 to $30 each and expenses, and to collect these dollars by ten or fifteen cents admission is rather slow work. Count the rainy days that the manager must lose; when the speaker is on the ground, rain or shine, he has to have his pay. If it is not taken in at the door, the manager has to put his hand in his trowser pocket and pull out and settle. My camp meetings were a perfect success, to take out of my pocket $172 in eight days, but this was money well invested, as I never again said these men coin money.

August 24th, 1887.—I attended the Grand Lodge Session of the Independent Order of Good Templars, which was convened in the New Opera House, in Rochester. I was called on to speak, and introduced by my friend and brother, Mr. Martin Jones. This was my first attendance at the Grand Lodge, and to me it was a grand thing. I received renewed inspiration.

August 25th, 1887.—I was sent as a delegate for Monroe County, N.Y., to represent W. J. Osborne's seat at the Prohibition Convention at Syracuse, N.Y. This will always be a proud day in my life.

August 26th, 2 p.m.—All fell into line at the Empire House, and headed by the Prohibition band, composed of young men. I was chosen as captain, and with banners waving and mottoes, "The saloon has got to go." It was the proudest moment of my life, as this was the first time I had ever marched in the ranks of the Prohibitionists. Over 1,000 delegates were in line. Arriving at the Alhambra, and business resumed, the platform that the committee presented was discussed. The sixth plank was, that we stand as a party for Woman Suffrage. This caused a hot debate, and after being recognized by the chair, I moved that the sixth plank be adopted in full as written, which was seconded by a hundred voices, and being put to a vote it was carried amidst a thunder of applause. Mrs. Mary T. Lathrop was then called upon and addressed the convention in a neat speech, thanking them for the action they had taken. This was a day which will live in history.

September 8th, again a delegate to County Convention of Good Templars of Orleans county.

September 10th, I had a very pleasant talk with Mark Foster, the hotel-keeper, of our town, who said he would go out of the business if the storekeepers would give up selling tobacco and the temperance people give him a small fund. This, I thought, was easy to do, because the temperance people would comply at once with this request, but I figured wrong, therefore we retained the hotel.

The 11th September I started away and came home October 10th. Spoke every night while away.

October 31st, 1887, I gave my first of ten free services in behalf of the Prohibition party. My companion in this meeting was the nominee for Senator, Mr. Cook. The first meeting was held at Kenoville, next at Lyndenville, Barry Centre, and at each point we were greeted by large audiences.

Friday, Nov. 4th, the Academy at Auburn, N. Y., was crowded, both pit and gallery. I spoke of the feasibility of high license. While I was holding forth there Hon. Warner Miller was at the Rink talking. He said that high license was the right thing to deal with the liquor traffic; both meetings were a success. As this was a year of hot discussion on the worth of high license, all sorts of arguments were used in our State for the saloon.

It is not often that the liquor dealer can be got into the position of defending his business in the arena of public debate; the position is not an easy one, and the dispensers of ardent drink are not as a rule fitted by nature or training to the employment of even the ordinary weapons of logic, much less to the use of those subtle and crafty sophisms which become necessary in an attempt to defend an indefensible business. With "arguments" of a purely physical sort, the average grog-dealer is fully equipped, and in the use of these his skill and power are unsurpassed. No one can swing a club, or thrust a knife, or use a torch or a pistol more neatly and effectively than he when occasion requires. The case of Haddock, at Sioux City, and more recent events at Highland Falls, N.Y.; Ottawa, Canada; Cochranton, Pennsylvania, and Howland, Mich., may be cited as proof of this fact. When it comes to such fine work as poisoning a well, shooting a preacher, blowing up a church or a parsonage, cr burning a village, the grog-seller is at once on familiar ground. He can run a caucus, pack a convention, manage affairs at the polls, or even carry a bill through the legislature in the most approved fashion. In the arts of bribery and perjury he is an adept, and no one can excel him in getting off easy in a court of justice. In all such doings the grog-seller is the superior of any man. It is only when he condescends to speak for himself, on the public platform, to wrestle with logical and moral problems, that he cuts a slim figure, yet now and then emergencies arise which compel the representatives of the saloon to adopt the ordinary and milder forms of argument, and come out openly in defence of the business. Recent events in the State of New York have brought them to this embarrassing situation. Failing to defeat the high license bill by the usual methods during its passage through the legislature, they have been compelled to oppose it in the open field of public discussion. The friends of the temperance cause as well as those who are the friends of the liquor devil made their appearance before Governor Hill and argued the case.

The champions of the saloon were heard first. Three men appeared on the saloon side, and the substance of their arguments was as follows:

One said, " I represent the four associations of liquor dealers of Brooklyn.  Our opposition to the bill is that it is a local and special measure, and we say it has been put through the legislature in opposition to the wishes of the people affected.  Only three Assemblymen in New York voted for this bill.  There are at present 3,000 saloons in Brooklyn.  We calculated that only four out of five would be able to pay the $1,000 license fee.  One out of five would be forced out of business.  The owners of these saloons would have to sell their fixtures and good will.  We calculate the loss of these men would be $3,000,000; they would be thrown out of business without compensation from the State.  This bill strikes the hardest at the middle-class liquor dealers.  We say that drunkenness and disorder are as repulsive to liquor dealers as to any one else.  We claim that the middle class of liquor-dealers are the great conservators of order.  We claim that the principle of this bill is wrong, as it takes away from the poor man the right of the temperate use of alcoholic liquors.  The cheerlessness of their lives makes liquor peculiarly gratifying to poor men.  They are not more prone to drunkenness than rich men.  This tax will not be imposed upon the liquor dealers, but upon the men who buy liquor in the saloons; it will be felt onerously by the poor."

The next champion who appeared said he was a representative of the Maltsters' and Brewers' Association :

" We object to the bill because it is not needed, because it is unjust, and because it will not diminish liquor selling.  In the second place, the law will not reduce the number of saloons.  We deny also that it would reduce drunkenness.  Thirdly, the bill is unjust.  It would reduce the number of saloons indiscriminately, whether they were respectably conducted or not.  The conscientious liquor dealer will not evade the law; the disreputable will do so.  The law will drive out of the business the moral liquor dealers who are content with small profits and who will not seek to make large gains by getting men drunk."

It is not necessary for me to enter into any elaborate refutation of these objections to high license. All I need do is to set the reasoning of the second speaker over against the first, and they will demolish each other. The only point to which I wish to draw attention is the reasoning in behalf of the poor man. I was not permitted to be present when this liquor vendor made this pathetic appeal in behalf of the poor man. But I am sure the touching picture of the poor thirsty and saloonless man must have drawn tears from the eyes of many present, and the one most affected must have been the liquor seller. See how he pulls out his snow-white handkerchief to wipe away the glistening tear. Then to the remark made that liquor dealers are the great conservators of order. This point and the poor man were the only striking argument. The most crushing blow dealt the High License Bill was a circular sent out by the Wine and Liquor Association. I will give the language in full : " Friends engaged in our honest business ! The time now shows how necessary it is for us to join in organization, all for one, and one for all. Our enemies have shown in Albany what they mean to do. They drive the highest taxpayers out of business, and let you and your family starve. This makes it necessary for us to show front. If we don't, why before two years have passed you can leave twenty to fifty years of labour behind you, and be bound to starve. We must show our enemies our strength, and election day is not so far away, when we can go hand-in-hand with our friends of liberty, show our enemies the front, and show them that we demand what George Washington demanded one hundred years ago, when England was wiped out. We also want to wipe out these fanatic hypocrites, who are a danger to our country, our family, and our business. Again, friends, do not wait one minute longer to fight for our principle, liberty, and freedom, which we claim as American citizens. We have one friend left, and this is H. D. Hill, the Governor of our State. We must show him that if he is our friend, we will carry the banner with him next election."

It is evident that the more we have of such speakers and circulars, the better it will be for the cause of temperance. Just as soon as the liquor dealers go into argument, they lose ground. Why should they not, with their brain filled with poison. May God enlighten these people. Amen.

# CHAPTER XV.

" Consistency, thou art a jewel "—Injurious influences of inconsistent christians—Fighting for woman's ballot—A lively scene —Sad stories of those who have suffered—The Evangelist, the confidant of the sorrowing—Hess visits Auburn State Prison—" What I saw behind prison walls "—Various lecturing trips —An outline of the Brook's High License Law.

" Blessed are the merciful, for they shall obtain mercy."—MATT. v. 7.

THIS is a glorious truth.   If to-day the Christians would have more mercy with those who are trying to lead a better life, not nearly so many would go back to their old life.   But it is no wonder that many turn back, when we take into consideration the icebergs that surround the Church of God.   The first intimation I received from these icebergs was about three months after my conversion, when I began to see things that were not right in the church, and I, like a child, would stand upon the platform and tell the truth.   Some people want a man to fire at some one else, and they will pat you on the shoulder and tell you that is right.   But turn loose on some of their faults, then, " Oh, my ! " you will hear these goody-goody fellows commence to say—" Ah, I'm disgusted the way that fellow expresses himself."   Now ain't that a little funny ?

Monday, Nov. 7th, 1887, the ladies had a meeting at the M. E. Church.   At this meeting a resolution was passed that the next day, which was election day in the town, the ladies should make an attempt to vote.   This news spread like a prairie fire, and many were the comments pro and con that were passed upon the resolution.

. Tuesday, Nov. 8th, was a bright morning, and about eight in the morning the ladies gathered in my home, and by ten o'clock about thirty had come in, and after prayer and singing, I started to fall the ladies into line, and much trembling and fear was amongst them. But an encouraging word here and there was sufficient to make them feel at ease. All being ready, we marched from the house to the town hall. The weaker sex (men) were all standing round the door of the town hall. As I marched the ladies into the hall, a good temperance man said, "Shoot the captain of the calico brigade!" Soon it came my turn to vote, and I cast the first prohibition ballot in that box on that date. Next came Mrs. Hess, but here the proceedings of balloting stopped because of a challenge that came from one of the weaker sex (miserable man!) The question was put to her whether she was a male citizen. This was the argument that they used. I demanded that the voter's oath should be administered. This the inspector refused to do. Not having a right to stop the voting, we stepped away. This step to vote the ladies was taken so we might make a test case out of it. Before the election most of them promised—I mean the temperance men—that if they refused the votes of the ladies, that we would prosecute the inspector for not administering the oath. Next day after the election I went to these men and asked them to contribute the amount to proceed against the inspector, and to my surprise I found that nearly all had changed their minds, and said that they thought it was best not to go any farther in the matter. I was called the "Woman's Mayor of Clarendon." To this I did not object at all. I would sooner be called a woman's mayor than be named a whisky mayor and elected by the corrupt element of the town.

In these times in which we are living it requires a man to stand firm and strong on God-given principles. In these days of social impurity, political corruption, murdered justice, and rum rule, God must necessarily raise up men like David and the prophets of old, fearless and aggressive in this warfare of right against wrong. If then God sees fit to call upon me, and to fit me into one of the grooves, His will shall be done and not mine.

During the two years that I have taken a stand in the temperance work I have had occasion to be a witness many times to the distress and misery brought upon the innocent by the drunkenness of near relatives and friends.

This terrible vice of strong drink not only blasts the victim, but ruins in many cases those connected with him. It ruins man and brings misery to wives and children, parents, sisters, brothers. Take a tender-hearted man; let him drink, and in a short time he is made cruel. The generous are made selfish; those who would be noble are made mean; the high spirited become debased; the ambitious become hopeless; the proud become grovelling and degraded; beauty is blighted, purity defiled, all that is noble, glorious and God-like in a man is blasted and mildewed by the damning influence of drink. Could we lift the curtain that conceals from our view the secrets of the charnel-house, every eye would be dimmed by the hideous sight, every heart would swell with an indignant and fierce resolve to battle to the death any agency that could by any means or possibility produce such untold horrors.

Come, my friend, listen to the bitter cry of the suffering who suffer because of the curse, Rum. Hear it coming up from the depths, and listen to the moans of the dying drunkard and bottle up the tears of heart-broken mothers and starving children. Can these things be in this Christian and civilized country, and we be still? A mother writes me: "It would take months to tell you how I have suffered from a drunken son." Another writes: "I have listened to your story and how your wife suffered, yet none has ever suffered as I have." Once more the mail brings a letter which reads: "My head reels when I think how we suffered, as I look at my poor suffering father. Oh, my poor, poor father! My mother's heart is broken. My hand is unsteady, my eyes grow dim with tears. Think of it—when I was a tender

K

age I was compelled to leave school, father losing his reason as the effect of rum."

Listen to this mother's story : " O God, the staff of my old age is broken, my boy is a drunkard."　Here is a warning to young ladies :  " In the beginning of the war my father enlisted ; my eldest brother would not remain at home and followed him to the army ; my second brother served in the navy.　My mother, whose health was delicate, a younger brother, and two sisters, mere children, were left at home.　We suffered privation and hardships ; we bore all cheerfully, when the crushing intelligence came that father died in Virginia.　Still we bore up, when the news came that my brother in the navy was dead.　This was hard, but we did not despair.　But oh ! the heavens grew black as midnight and the load crushed us to the earth when my eldest brother came home a hopeless, confirmed drunkard.　Then mother's heart broke, and now with feeble health I am struggling on alone.　Perhaps this is presumption in me to tell you this.　Use it as you will, but do not let the writer's name be seen by others, as an unsympathising world should never know of my private troubles."

A heart-broken father comes to me and tells me : " My only son is a drunkard.　He has ruined me, and oh ! "— with his hand pressed on his forehead, he gasps forth— " he is bringing his mother to the early grave.　Oh, oh ! can you not reach my boy ?　Save him !　I will give my life to save his from a drunkard's grave.　Can you not show him his error ? "　Wringing his hands, he cries aloud, " Save my only boy, and God will reward you."

Dear reader, are not such tales enough to rouse men to action ?　My heart bleeds at such revelations.　Many more letters have I in my possession that come with a tale of woe brought on by this blighting curse.

Monday, Dec. 12th, at Auburn, N.Y., I held a mother's meeting.　After the meeting I received a call from a young lady, good looking, her manner that of a highly educated person, though her dress was that of one in poverty. Said she: "Mr. Hess, I have heard of you a great many times, and how people come to you and tell you of their suffering." Here she was overcome with emotion, and she rose to go, but I detained her and asked her to proceed, which she did. From her lips I learned the following story: Said she—"1 come to see you on account of my father, who is throwing himself away with drink. But do not condemn him. He is as kind and gentle as any father could be when sober, but in drink he is inhuman and he treats me so cruelly." Here again tears rushed to her eyes, and before I knew it she had gone. Though I did not learn the whole story, still I am able to draw what the conclusion was—another victim added to the many tens of thousands that had travelled the same road before.

Dec. 11th, 1887, I visited Auburn prison. Having had some acquaintance with the Rev. Chaplain Searles, it was not difficult to gain admission, especially it being Sabbath. We were given a place where we could have a good view of the poor prisoners as they came in. We had not long to wait when the turnkey came in with a big bunch of iron keys. In another moment we heard the clanking of the doors, and the prisoners came marching in dressed in their striped suits. It was something to behold; about eleven hundred were seated in front of the chaplain; on every side they were surrounded by great prison walls, yet with all this there were men paid by the government to stand over these men with loaded guns. Amongst this number there were about seventy-five men who had been sentenced for life: their crime was that of taking their fellow-men's lives when young men. Oh, dear reader, the sight of these now gray-haired men was a sad sight; to think that they were deprived of their liberty simply by the fiend of rum. After service I ventured to ask Rev. Mr. Searles what was the principal cause of these young men's crime. He answered that "seven-tenths are here for crimes committed while under the influence of strong drink." The ages ran from 18 to 33 years, more at that age than over. While sitting there listening to the chaplain, I discovered many of my old companions. I marked especially one who had refused to sign the pledge when asked to do so. He continued to drink, he committed a crime, and received seven years in the State Prison, and now while writing this he still lingers in prison. This young man was asked into the office, and this is the message he gave me to deliver: "Joe, go out and tell all the young men who allow themselves to be carried away by strong drink and evil associations, to beware lest they finish their course as I did in State Prison. Tell all fathers to use their influence to check this awful curse, that their sons and daughters may not enter such a dismal place." After a few parting words I shook his hand. While I passed out into the free air, he for whom this free air was made had to turn back and go down into his small cell, a prisoner deprived of his freedom. Yet young men say you wish to deprive them of their liberty when you ask them to sign a pledge.

Dec. 23rd, 1887, returned home and found all well and happy. After supper I took the children and we went to the Christmas tree, and we did enjoy the scene. This was the first Christmas tree that I had ever gone to, consequently it was a new thing to me. Next came the day of the birth of our Saviour. Wife and I went to Rochester. I addressed a meeting at the new Opera House; had a large audience. How different my Christmas was spent from former occasions! As I look back I see the miserable life that I led, and when I do look back I always see the sad picture of my wife and family—the home of poverty which might always have been a home of comfort but for the damning influence of strong drink. I see my poor old mother sit and weep bitter tears because of the reckless life of her eldest son. When I think it was I who caused the wrinkles to come upon her brow—when I behold the ringlets of gray hair—when I think of the great heart that beats in that noble temple of God, I can only cry out, "Oh, God, forgive," while mother, like all mothers, forgives and forgives. Compare the happiness of my family now—the comforts that they now enjoy—with that of old. What a change!

When I see the beams of delight upon my mother's face, when she sees me come, instead of the tears, I can only say, "Jesus did all for me, even me."

January 1st, 1888, I started for a tour in Southern New York, and the wind did howl and blow. Going over the mountains my journey was not the most pleasant one. In the work in which I am engaged a man has every opportunity to study human nature, as he comes in contact with a great many people. This New Year's day was not started as pleasantly as was the one the year previous. As men engaged in philanthropic work are constantly thrown amongst all classes of people, and they must often put up with a great deal, it has been my lot to fall into all kinds of homes, both rich and poor; but sometimes you come in contact with what is called a shiftless man, a sort of a lazy fellow. This was my luck on this New Year's day. When I awoke I found the snow on my covering and the wind howling through the room. I stuck my head out and quickly pulled it back again. Finally I braved the dancing wind and rose for breakfast, which consisted of—I do not know what. The host was a sight to behold. Though a temperance man, his hands were fit to plant 'tatoes on. His hair I do not think had seen a comb for the year. His clothes were one whole patch. His house floor was more holy than righteous. His window panes were those of old newspapers and rags. His doors were off from the hinges. His barns were dilapidated. He owned 250 acres, had 25 cows, 10 horses; but the cows and horses were so thin that if you would hold a candle light on one side of them, you could read on the opposite side. The stables had not been cleaned all winter. He said that in the spring he would back the wagon in, and in that way would clean his stables. I ventured to ask this strange being, who was so heartless to dumb animals, how many children he had. Said he, "Not one." I could not help from saying aloud, "Praise God from whom all blessings flow." Said he, "What is that you say?" I told him that I would pity the child who would have to call him father. This aroused him to a fury. I did not stay at this place. I soon found another place. After describing the man you will want to know something about the woman. Well, she was tall, raw-boned, coarse featured, but had a mild expression. She was a quiet, inoffensive woman, kept her house as well as she was able, as she had no means by which she might do better. She seldom spoke, but constantly was reading. She was clean in her own person, while her clothes were shabby. I considered her more punished than the wife of a drunkard.

January 14th, 1888, I met with some of Rochester's leading citizens to organize a limited stock company to publish the *Weekly News*, a Prohibition paper. On this day I was one of the five who signed their names to a petition to the Secretary of State to organize the stock company. This was one of my many mistakes in my reformed life, for the company only lived a year, then died a natural death.

January 15th, addressed a large audience at Holly, Rev. Mr. Pickard, pastor. Monday, 16th January, we were given a treat in the town hall by listening and watching a man talk with his hands and mouth at the same time. This celebrated personage was Rollo Kirk Bryan, the chalk-talker from Michigan. I was called upon to act as chairman.

January 17th I was in the company of the chairman of the National Prohibition party of the United States, Hon. Prof. Dickie, of Lansing, Mich. We met at Syracuse, N. Y.;-there listened to a very fine address. January 18th was the day set for the Executive Committee of the State Prohibition party to meet in conference at Utica, N. Y. The train leaving Syracuse on the morning of the 18th had on board the following well-known and staunch defenders of the party principle: Hon. Prof. Dickie, A. A. Cobb, from Fairport; Hon. W. Martin Jones, Rochester; R. McCargo, of Holly; Mr. Rumsy, of Geneseo, and the writer, from Clarendon; and a jolly party we were. Arriving at Utica we proceeded to Mechanics' Hall; found numbers already assembled; was given a hearty shake of the hand by Hon. Fred. Wheeler, the State Chairman of the Prohibition party, though a young man in years yet a fearless worker. I was called upon to address the conference. Here is where I used the words: "If I cannot speak grammatical, I can vote as grammatical as any man." These words have been reprinted a great many times. Had a general good time. Left Utica in company with Mr. Dickie, arriving at Rochester 10 p.m.

Jan. 25th I was coming from Kendall, on the Rome, Watertown road; had a collision at Sharlotte, big snow storm; leaving Rochester for home on the 5:05 train.

Jan. 26th, snow storm so bad that we had to pull the horse and cutter out of the banks. Jan. 27th, 1888, it blew a regular hurricane, snow piled up mountains high; was compelled to stay in Rochester as all roads were blocked. Being Sunday, I went at 2 p.m. to the gospel temperance meeting, at the new Opera House, where I was called upon to speak.

Jan. 31st, 1888, went to hear J. W. Walker, the converted prize-fighter. This was a blessed greeting, as we had known each other years ago, when both were serving the devil. Brother Johnny Walker drew his arms around me, while the congregation sang "'Tis the promise of God full salvation to give who on Jesus, his Son, will believe."

Feb. 2nd, 1888, I started with the family to hold a series of meetings, on behalf of the *Weekly News* of

Rochester. Among the many places that we visited was Weedsport. Arriving there on Feb. 6th, I was made welcome by H. E. Rheubottom, had a crowded house; brother H. E. Rheubottom is one of the firm of corset manufacturers, a staunch prohibitionist, and knows how to welcome any one. On this trip I introduced at every lecture Uncle Sam's elephant ; but he was a poor venture, and he has been stopped ever since. This was a trip of 10 days that will long live in my memory. One day we arrived at a place, and on going with the check to receive our goods, I found, to my dismay, that the baggage had not arrived there ; it was 7 p. m., and at 8 the curtain would rise, and all the children's music. Oh, my, what a time ! Nothing had arrived, but Uncle Sam's elephant was there all right, and on hand. Well I felt so "funny." Say, reader, did you ever have such kind of luck ? Well, if you did you know how funny a fellow feels. Such a time as that is the time when you feel like saying some very nice things.

You may say, what sort of an animal was Uncle Sam's elephant ? Well, he was full grown, but I had him in 7 different parts : on cartoon paper, representing the liquor traffic of the United States.

Feb. 11th, 1888, we arrived home, and found the good " wife," who was glad to welcome us home. After supper the children thought that there was not as much fun in travelling as there might be.

Feb. 12th I received a call from Prof. A. D. Lane, and after a conversation with him, I engaged him to lead my singing, and become my musical director. Prof. Lane is a large man, and is in possession of the strongest bass voice I ever listened to.

Feb. 13th I took the train at Rochester, N.Y., for Wallsboro'. Pa. The call came for help from the weak and oppressed, which was caused by the spreading of the greatest disease that ever befel a nation, I mean " Uncle Sam's elephant," the dominant liquor power in our land.

Hearing the drums beat and the cry of the vast army of starving, half-clad children, the ever tramping sound of once bright-eyed and sturdy frames of 53,000 men, who are robbed of the blessing of liberty, and are now incarcerated within stone walls by this man destroyer—strong drink. The field is large and the workers are few.

Just before leaving my home, I took one more good look into the faces of the sleeping children, resting at ease in their nice beds. I could not help thinking surely if temperance and prohibition can do this for one family, it can do the same for tens of thousands.

While we were going over the Erie road, a lively set of young men, seven in number, came aboard at one of the stations. They seemed to have entered on a discussion before entering the car ; as this was the year in which a president of the United States was to be elected. I soon became wide awake, and learning that they were talking as to who should be president, with a careless remark, said, "Boys, you are having a good time." "Yes," answered one, "We are going to have an election right now as to who is going to be the next president of the United States. Ballots were made and deposited in a hat. The votes were counted, when to the surprise of the seven men, there were five for General Fisk, one for Blaine, and one for Sherman of Ohio. Though neither of the men told for whom they had voted, yet by the light of their eyes it could easily be seen who were the Fisk, the Blaine and the Sherman boys. Well, after election, all these three candidates were elected, that is, to stay at home.

Arriving at Corning, the streets and corners were lined with men, and being a stranger in the place, I took up my place on the street corner like the rest. I was not long standing when the word, to the convention, greeted my ear. I started down Main-street, when a tall man came walking up Main-street. He was dressed in black, and a silk hat covered a manly head with bright eyes.

I said, "Ah, he must be one of the Lord's children." At once I accosted him with, "Beg your pardon, but are you not a minister?" To which he replied, "I am." "And a Third Party Prohibitionist?" to which he again said, "Yes."

I put the question as to what sort of a convention was to be held in town, to which he said, "I do not live here." Where do you live? I asked. He replied, at Cuba, N. Y. And your name, said I, is Rev. F. D. J. Bickley (now ain't that a long name for you). Questioning him as to the Prohibition Party in Cuba, he said, "We are going to put a full (not full of whiskey, but water,) ticket in the field." Just then a procession of men passing by, the question was again raised as to the convention, when he said, "It is a Democratic caucus." Thanking him for the information, we bid each other good-bye and God speed. I strolled on towards the Tallbrook Station, and having over an hour yet to wait, I thought it to be a good opportunity to continue the reading of the History of the Bible. The only person in the waiting-room was a little old man, who, hearing the drum beat, said the Democrats had a big time now, but this fall they will take a back seat. 1 became interested in this little old man, and a conversation was opened by my saying, "that's so," to which he answered, "I am delighted to hear you say so." I put the question as to where his home was, he answered, "I live in Harrison Valley, Pa." Asking him as to how whiskey was getting on, he said, "We are all Prohibitionists down there, and we have it too." At this it was my turn to be delighted, and I at once remarked that I was a Third Party man, thinking that he was one, from the statement he made, but I soon learned that he was not, for no sooner did he catch my words than he gave me a look that if a look could kill, I would not be amongst the living to record this. He grabbed his valise, and turning to me, said he didn't know what he had done that he should be haunted by the Third Partymen. Said he at the top of his voice, "You're the sixth man to-day," and he sailed out of the station. He may be sailing yet, if he has'nt stopped.

Five o'clock, "All aboard," shouted the conductor, and the iron horse commenced to spit and snarl and puff, and we rolled on towards Wellsboro', Pa., which was the end of my journey. On arriving I was grabbed by the hand, by the noble, whole-souled Brother Bristoll, who conducted me to his home, where we laid hold of something for the inner man, after which we adjourned to the I. O. G. T. Lodge room, and here I was welcomed by 118 members of the lodge. This was one of the most active lodges that it has been my pleasure to visit. A lodge of temperance of any order can be made a success, by unity and work. I was introduced to Brother Bullard; asking him how the political out-look was, he said the Republicans have control of the license question in Tioga Co., Wellsboro' being the county seat. Though this party claimed to be the temperance party, yet in spite of the remonstrance of the majority of the citizens, the Judge, whose name was Willson, and a Republican, has granted licenses to all who applied. Brother Bullard, who had been redeemed from a drunkard's gutter, said " Would every Christian vote as he did, the curse of rum would soon be a thing of the past."

Feb. 16th was the day set for the Republican County Convention, to appoint candidates for the spring election. The principal nomination was for Judge of Tioga County. This caused a great stir. Judge Williams, who had been Judge, had gone to the Supreme Court, and left his office open, to which Judge Willson was appointed. Wellsboro' being the home of ex-Senator Mitchell, his faction were trying hard to nominate him as the candidate. The Willson faction wanted him, as he had granted license to all. The day closed without any candidate being nominated, —the old proverb, " A house divided against itself will not stand."

Wellsboro' has Brooks High License Law, No. 53, Laws of 1887, which reads as follows :

An Act to restrain and regulate the sale of vinous and spirituous, malt or brewed liquors, or any mixture thereof.

Section 2.—Licenses for the sale of vinous, spirituous, malt or brewed liquors, at retail, in quantities not exceeding one quart, shall only be granted to citizens of the United States of temperate habits, and good moral character.

Section 3.—Such licenses may be granted only by the Court of the Quarter Sessions of the proper county, and shall be for one year from date fixed by rule or standing order of said court. The said court shall fix by rule or standing order a time at which application for said licenses shall be heard, at which time all persons applying or making objection to applications for licenses may be heard by evidence, petition, remonstrance, or counsel, provided that licenses under previous laws shall not be granted later than June 30th of this year.

Section 4.—It follows that all who apply for licenses must, three weeks before court, deposit $500 with the county clerk, who must publish each applicant's name three times.

Section 5.—Said petition shall contain :

First.—The name and present residence of applicant, and how long he has there resided.

Second.—The particular place for which a license is desired.

Third.—The place of abode of said applicant, and if a naturalized citizen where and when naturalized.

Fourth.—The name of the owner of premises.

Fifth.—That the place licensed is necessary for the accommodation of the public.

Sixth.—That none of the applicants are in any manner pecuniarily interested in the profits of the business conducted at any other place in said county, where any of said liquors are sold or kept for sale.

Seventh.—That the applicant is the only person in any manner pecuniarily interested in the business so asked to be licensed, and that no other person shall be in any manner pecuniarily interested therein during the continuance of the license.

Eighth.—Whether applicants, or any of them, has had a license for sale of liquors in this commonwealth during any portion of the year preceding this application, revoked.

Ninth.—The names of no less than two reputable freeholders of the ward or township where the liquor is to be sold, who shall be his, her, or their sureties on the bond which is required, and the statement that each of said sureties is a *bona fide* owner of real estate in the said county, worth over and above all incumbrances the sum of two thousand dollars, and that it would sell for that much at public sale, and that he is not engaged in the manufacture of spirituous, vinous, malt or brewed liquors.

Tenth.—This petition must be verified by affidavit of applicant made before the clerk of the court, a magistrate, notary public, or justice of the peace, and if any false statement is made in any part of said petition, the appli-- cant shall be deemed guilty of the crime of perjury, and upon indictment and conviction shall be subjected to its penalties.

Section 8.—That all persons licensed to sell or retail any vinous, spirituous or brewed liquors, or any admixture thereof, in any house or room or place, hotel, inn or tavern, shall be classified and required to pay, annually, for such privileges as follows :

Persons licensed to sell by retail, resident in cities of the first, second and third class, shall pay the sum of $500, those resident in all other cities shall pay $300, and those resident in townships $75, which sum shall be divided in portions as follows : In cities of the first-class, four-fifths shall be paid for the use of the city and county, and one-fifth for the use of the commonwealth.

Thus you see this Brook's High License was a strong law, and yet it is a failure. License laws in regard to the liquor traffic will always be a failure.

# CHAPTER XVI.

At Wellsboro', Pa.—Taken from the gutter—The Saloon Clock *vs.* The Home Clock—Campaign at Elbridge, N. Y.—Niagara Falls in winter—How the iceberg struck Joe Hess—Eight days' meeting at Mohawk—Delegates to the Prohibition Convention —Something about tent work.

" Wine is a mocker, strong drink is raging : and whosoever is deceived thereby is not wise."—Prov. 20th chap., 1st verse.

HOW I wish I had the power to make all men understand the above truths ; many would not then be cursed with the demon of rum that are to-day led astray. If wnic is a mocker, why then will humanity consume the same, and who is the one that does not know that it mocks the person that dares to tamper with it ?

That strong drink is raging all whoever beheld men overcome with the demon know that it fairly makes devils out of good, honest, loving, upright men.

. Tuesday, February 14th, 1888.—The sun came out in all his splendor and beauty as he peeped over the tops of the mountains that surround the grandly located town of Wellsboro', Pa.  It was one of the grandest sightsthat it was my good fortune to behold for many a day.

After breakfast I strolled down to Major Herrick's law office and secured the statute of law for the year 1887, wherein I found what the real import of the license law was.  Taking this book under my arm I strolled down Main-street towards Brother Bristoll's photograph gallery and had my photo. taken, with the book under my arm.  Surely this was high protection sure enough, when I was so surrounded by the law.  The court house was packed to suffocation in the evening ; many left the hall during the speaking. You ask what was the matter with

them ?  They were mad at what I said.  Truth is hard
to stand.

February 15th.—I was pleasantly entertained by Major
Merrick, a prominent politician.  In his office were
gathered with me ex-Senator Mitchell, of Pa., and several
other leading citizens of Wellsboro'.  The conversation
drifted to the amendment.  All agreed that it would be
adopted when it came to a vote.

Monday, February 20th.—I was ivited to take dinner
with the famous General R. Cox, of great military fame
in the late civil war.  The General is a resident of Wellsboro'.  I was surprised when he took me to his stables,
and pointing to a very fine chestnut horse, he informed
me that the horse was his companion all through the war.
Said I, how old is he ?  The General said the horse was
in his thirty-third year.

The Court House was again packed in the evening,
many came forward and signed, amongst them was a
ragged and forlorn-looking man ; his face showed plainly
what was the cause of his rags.  As he placed his name
with a trembling hand upon the roll, I read the name
Miles O'Connor.  His signature showed that he must
have had the advantage of school in his early days. After
a little inquiry I learned that Miles O'Connor was at one
time the leading citizen in the town, once owned the
largest hotel.  When he opened the hotel he was a temperance man, but soon began to drink, and in a few years
people commenced to say, O'Connor is going down the
road to the drunkard's grave.  He had a lovely wife, and
a family of three children who adored their father.  Soon
he lost his hotel ; then came separation of family ; soon
the wife was compelled to seek employment.  Miles was
sinking lower and lower every day, until he became so
low that his bed was taken up in the horse stables and
cow sheds and waggon beds of the town, and all this was
brought about through the curse of drink.  This was the
man who signed his name.  We then invited him into

the Good Templar Lodge, the writer paying for initiation. This was in the year 1888, and at the last accounts he is still a sober man. The ten days' work in this place wound up with over 750 who had signed the pledge, the majority of these were drinkers, more or less.

February 24th.—I arrived at home. What a pleasant thing it is to go home. When I was drinking I used to think the fingers on the saloon clock were going round so fast, and when they would point to the midnight hour I would have to go home, after all, at that hour of the night, for there is no other place for any one to go to but the home or the police station. How different now, the clock goes round so slow, and the time seems so long till I can return home, and then when I get home the time seems to go so fast, and ere I am aware the time has come when I again have to leave it.

Feb. 27th, 1888, I started for Rochester, registered at Jackson's hotel, 212 Main-street, attended a temperance meeting at the new Opera House in the evening, where I was called upon to speak, and seated on the platform were the following well-known lights and agitators in the temperance cause :—Rec. C. H. Mead, of Hornnesville, N.Y.; Prof. A. A. Hopkins, of Rochester, N.Y.; Prof. George Chambers, of Ackron, N.Y.; Prof. F. Lorenza, of Rochester, N.Y.; Rev. J. Tucker, of Perry, N.Y.; and the writer, of Clarendon, N.Y. The hall was packed, and all felt it was good to be there

Feb. 28th, 1888, was a cold, bright day; this date is a memorable day in our home, for this is the birthday of Mrs. Hess, and we always look forward to the day with delight now, as on this day I always try to make it extra pleasant for her who suffered so much because of the drink her husband drank. During the year I saved up a little money, and on this bright day I walked down to Goodman's jewelry store and bought a handsome silver water pitcher for a present for her birthday. I expressed it to her, and of the two I don't know who was the happier, she or I. Had I still been drinking I would not have sent it.

Feb. 29th, I opened meetings at Elbridge, New York. We had a grand time at this place; Elbridge is situated about 4 miles from any railroad, and has chair factories and glove shops; over 120 were initiated into the Good Templars in the seven nights that we were there. The last night we closed with a children's concert, and at the conclusion I was given a regular caning in the shape of a gold-headed cane. As I took it into my hand, it being accompanied with an eloquent speech by Bro. Charlie Morgan, I arose to reply, when some one shouted " Take it to the White House "; to which I replied that I will as I live in a white house. During these meetings many were stirred to action. I remember on Sunday night, March 4th, I addressed a large audience in the Presbyterian Church, with Rev. Rogers, and Rev. Rich in the pulpit. Subject: " Responsibility of the Church." At the conclusion a man arose quickly and said he had been silent on this temperance question, but henceforth he would be active, and not a stumbling block in the way of sinners; said he, " I will let my light shine." Thank God his light is still shining.

March 9th was a gala day for me. After my conversion, my mother, who is a devout Roman Catholic, would not recognize me, and even forbade me entering her door, nor did she allow my sisters to entertain me. I did not blame her for this; mother is a good christian woman, and if there is one christian that will go to heaven it is my mother. Well, on this 9th of March I made bold to enter her home, and after some talk a reconciliation was effected, and truly I was happy, and that evening we started for Washington, Pa. Arriving there we were conducted to Bro. John Bets' place to be entertained. Learning that Major Hilton was holding meetings, we went to his Bible meetings in the afternoon, also spoke briefly in the evening. The Opera House was crowded for the ten

L

nights that I remained.  One of the most earnest workers of this campaign was George McCaskey, "he was little, but oh my!"  At one of these meetings I asked Rev. B. B. to sign the pledge for influence.  He said he had no influence; he spoke the truth, for his church was empty; had but a few to preach to, and these were in a bad state of mind.  Think of it, a minister of the gospel not having any influence.  Over 1000 signed during these meetings.

From Washington we went for three days to Claysville, where many hard drinkers signed.  Then we stopped for one night at Mansfield, Pa.; great crowd.  Left the South for Niagara Falls.  First meeting Y. M. C. A., then the Baptist Church.  Sunday evening the Methodist Church was crowded.  Monday we commenced a week's work at the Suspension Bridge.  This was the month of March, and it was very cold.  The spray from the fall of the water had gathered a regular iceberg near the edge of the Falls.  I thought it would be a nice thing to take a view of the 'berg from the bottom, so we took the incline railroad.  When at the bottom on the edge of the river we were received by some of those men who are ever ready for a twenty-five cent piece to show all there is about the Falls.  One of these suggested that we put on creepers.  I don't mean life creepers, but simply iron ones on your feet to climb with.  After much climbing we reached the top.  We were informed by our guide that the week previous they had a man climb the iceberg on horse-back.  This seemed somewhat strange, but the guide made it clear, and we could understand how it could be done.  After taking a good view of the country we commenced our descent. If the ascent was an arduous undertaking, the descent was much more so.  None can form any idea, only those who try it.  This iceberg was sixty feet high, and was located at the foot of the ice-bridge over the falls.

Tuesday, March 27th.—We visited the famous whirlpool rapids.  As we stood on the banks the water seemed to roll down upon us, as it was twenty-five feet higher in the centre of the rapids than it was on the edge. While looking at the water rushing by, it makes one feel like jumping into the mad current.

Thursday, March 29th.—Mrs. Jennie Hess, wife of the writer, came to the Falls, and we had another grand time taking in the Falls, as this was wife's first visit. She enjoyed it immensely. Taking a hack, and driving over Goat Island, the wonder increased.

March 31st.—Wife and I went up to Buffalo, and when mother saw her, for the first time since my reformation, which had occurred two years and six months prior, she stood in amazement at the improved condition of my wife, both in health and looks, besides the great change in her clothing. When she last saw my wife she was a washerwoman. Why, because her husband was a drunkard. A rational man, in the language of O. Dewey, is described thus: "You are a man; you are a rational and religious being; you are an immortal creature. Yes, a glad and glorious existence is yours; your eye is opened to the lovely and majestic vision of nature; the paths of knowledge are around you, and they stretch onward to eternity; and, most of all, the glory of the infinite God, the all-perfect, all-wise, and all-beautiful, is unfolded to you." This rational man destroys all these beauties by drink. Oh, man, stop and think before it is too late. The meetings at the Bridge were a grand success.

April 1st, 1888.—I was at home. My sister Maggie and my little niece were at my home visiting. We had a very enjoyable time.

April 9th, 1888, I was called for an eight days' lecture course at Mohawk. We were entertained by Lowell, a reformed man. Had excellent meetings conducted under the auspices of the Good Templars. Next we went to D'olgeville for a week's campaign, the roads were something beyond the power of the pen to describe. D'olgeville is situated about 10 miles north-east of Little Falls, its population was about 1,700, mostly all Germans ; the town had its growth in less than three years, it had no side-walks at the time, only one small Methodist Church ; but did have 13 rum holes ; a large felt factory, which is owned by D'olge, from which the town derives its name. Sunday is not known in this town. Some English speaking people reside in this place.

On the 19th April I travelled over snow banks and ruts for a distance of 6 miles to a place called Salsbury, a small audience was present. After speaking for an hour a collection was taken up, and \$1.17 were gathered. Sometimes I think that collections are injured by the long prayers of the ministers. I have one place in my mind where the minister actually prayed for 17 minutes by the watch. I guess he had not prayed all week and took this opportunity to make up for lost time. In this town lives a noble family called Jennings, right royal people they are ; had good meetings, and much good was done.

April 24th, 25th, 26th, 27th, 28th, 29th, and 30th, were spent at Little Falls, N.Y., and Herkimer, where a lodge was established. Then we went to Utica for one night ; had a grand house there. May 3rd arrived home; a week's campaign was inaugurated in this town, and good results were the outcome.

May 13th I was asked to speak at the city hall, Syracuse. It was here I met for the first time for many years " Ben Hogan," the other converted prize-fighter, and we both enjoyed each other's company.

May 18th we went to Weedsport, N.Y.; we were made welcome by brother Rcheubottom. The hall was nicely decorated with flowers and the photo of John B. Finch, and many other prominent workers ; good work was done in this place. A man who had sold rum for over 30 years, came forward, signed the pledge, gave up his business, joined the Templars, and last accounts were that he is still faithful. Such is the work moral suasion has done.

May 28th.—E. H. Reheubottom accompanied me to Syracuse, where we met the New York delegates on their way to nominate General Clinton B. Fiske, as candidate on the Prohibition party ticket. The Convention was held at Indianapolis, Indiana, May 29-30. As the train arrived at the West Shore depot, everything was alive. The car was beautifully decorated on the outside with great portraits of Fiske and Brooks. Amongst the delegates from New York were John Lloyd Thomas, George R. Scott, Col. Chevies and Lady, and many other prominent men of the party. We returned in company of the delegates to Weedsport, and at the depot we were met by the boys of the town, and after three hearty cheers for the success of the ticket, the train pulled out. This was our closing meeting, and a big success it was. Brother E. H. Reheubottom presented the writer with a fine trycicle as a token of his esteem for my noble work. The trycicle arriving at home, Henry thought he would take a little drive himself. Starting off nicely, everything seemed to work like a charm, but no one knows what is in store for one the next moment. Henry turned a corner rather quick, and over went the carriage and Henry under, and the trycicle on top.

June 2nd, 1888, was a gala day for me and my home. For the first time in my life since my reformation, mother came to visit us at our home, which I call my own. As mother saw how everything was so nicely arranged by the hand of my true and noble wife, she admired it all. Mother came to stay but one week, but stayed over four weeks, and it was so pleasant to have her with us. Oh, reader, when once mother is passed away, then this world will seem a blank. I hope all young men will be kind to their mother and father. How happy I felt when I took wife and mother out for a drive in my own carriage. Had I been drinking, this home would not have been mine, neither would I have taken wife and mother for a drive.

June 6th, 1888.—The news was flashed to all parts of the United States that Grover Cleveland was re-nominated for President of the United States. Great was the jubilee in Rochester. Many predictions were made.

June 7th.—I commenced a series of meetings at Little Valley, N.Y., and found a great deal of opposition.

June 16th.—We started for New Millford, Pa., where we did some tent work. This tent was bought by the Third Party of that State, and was taken from town to town to hold political meetings. On arriving at New Millford we were made welcome by Prof. Replogell, who was the County Chairman of Tioga Co. of the Prohibition party. We had our first meeting at 2.30 p.m. Just as we were about to commence a terrific wind-storm came up and blew all the poles down, and after the wind a big rain-storm followed, but we had a good meeting after all. In the evening the ladies gave an ice cream social in the Court House lawn.

Sunday noon and evening the tent was crowded, and it was a great day for the temperance cause. The evening meeting was one of the largest of the series, excepting a few stones that were hurled on the top of the tent by some little boys. This concluded the tent services at New Millford, and the political campaign had been opened in earnest in Tioga Co., Pa., and a hot one it proved to be.

# CHAPTER XVII.

A chapter of tent work—Working for the Prohibition Party—Attempts to break up the meetings—The "Hoodlum" element of the old parties to the front—Letter of a Republican Prohibitionist—Delegate to the Prohibition Convention at Syracuse, N. Y.—An apt quotation from John Wesley—"Hess, Hess, Hess, come down quick"—Tent work in Pennsylvania.

*"Making request, if by any means now at length I might have a prosperous journey, by the will of God."*

MONDAY, June 18th, 1888, we started out upon a long journey to educate public sentiment upon the most vital political issue at that time and now still before the American people. Education is the chief corner-stone of the Republic, and popular education is the only safe and stable basis of liberty. So thought the fathers and founders of the great republic, and the principle of education is to be found interwoven in a thousand forms into the very thread and texture of political institutions. Remove education—religious, civil and political, which sounds forth its thunder from the pulpit, school and public platform—I say, remove these educators, and the country would soon tumble over.

It was to educate the people in the evils of strong drink and the ruin it causes, that the tent was procured, and manned by the following men: Joe Hess as speaker, Prof. A. D. Lane as musical director, Prof. Replogal as superintendent, and Brother Smith as property man. As the clock struck 10 a. m., the Prohibition wagon started for "Jackson," Pa. Passing through the town all started to sing, and the Prohibition banners were flying from the top of the wagon for Fiske and Brooks; the outfit consisted of a wagon with low wheels and a box twenty feet long, eight feet wide, and one foot deep. This wagon

191

served as a platform to speak from, when under the tent, by taking off the wheels.  Going from place to place, the organ was placed in the centre of the wagon on rubber and securely strapped.  We arrived at Jackson, 3 p. m. This was a no-license town.  Just as we began to raise the tent the rain came down in torrents.  By 6 p. m. everything was ready, and we had a splendid meeting. Rev. Skimerhorne led in prayer, and Prof. Replogel made the opening address, after which the writer spoke for one hour, and heads could be seen skaking whenever I touched the doings of one of the old parties.  We held three meetings in this town.  The next town visited was Thomson, Pa.  On our way we passed 3,000 Italians who worked on the new railroad.  The Republican party shouts "high protection" to the laboring man, and then has men in its ranks who import pauper labor, while the American laborer must stand back and starve, or be compelled to work for the same low wages as the "Italio." Low pauper labor and the saloon is what is cursing our fair land to.day.

Arriving at Thomson, the tent was pitched in front of the school house on top of a hill, alongside of the great liberty pole.  Soon a fight was on.  Replogel conceived the idea that it would be a nice thing for the American flag to fly above the Prohibition tent, but on making a demand for it, the Republican who had it in charge refused ; not only refused to let us have it, but also heaped such abuse and insulting language as I never heard man utter before.  The tent was packed in the evening.  On the second day we gained the victory, and the flag was swung to the American winds, and oh, how beautiful she did wave, as much as to say, " A little over a hundred years ago I first flew to the breeze in Philadelphia, Pa., declaring that this was now a government of the people, a government by the people, a government for the people, and now I wave for Prohibition."  In Thomson there were two brothers, Messenger by name, who were staunch men for our party.

At 3 p. m., Saturday, the 23rd of June, a great wind came up suddenly and, as if by magic, our tent was flat on the ground. Not five minutes before, about thirty children had been in the tent. Soon every Democrat in the town assisted to put the tent up again, and by 6 p.m. we were ready for another battle, and, at 7.30, the band came marching down the road. Here we organized a Prohibition club of twenty-three members, a gain of nineteen for our side. Sipier Lamonte was chosen president of the club, and G. Tallman, secretary. In Thomson there was a regular old bear of a Republican, who wrote following article for one of the newspapers :

" The advent of the ex-saloon keepers as apostles of Temperance is viewed with alarm by sensible Prohibitionists, and the gratifying fact that 20,000 saloon-keepers let loose in this State during the past year by the Republican legislation, are to a man crying 'Kill the Republican party', is not considered a sufficient offset to the expense likely to be incurred should the remaining 19,999 ex-saloon keepers catch on to the $3.00 a day-and-found racket, and start out as apostles of Temperance, and board around among the faithful, pocketing the contributions, and paying their board bills by holding forth on every street corner. St. John, our popular jeweller, has returned to the Republican ranks, convinced that Republican Prohibition is just as good as any other kind and less expensive. And John Mulvey, who was so deaf that he could not hear the arguments of "prize-fighter Hess", but chipped in a dollar on general principles, would do well to accept the Prohibition which within two years is sure to be effected by Republican legislation, and join with the other deaf man in rejoicing over a victory thus obtained."

Signed E. A. Foster.

THOMSON, JUNE 27th, 1888.

MONDAY, JUNE 25, '88. I started for Syracuse as a delegate-at-large (A large delegate), from the town of Clarendon and county of Orleans. On the train I met brother Baldwin from Elmira, with several others, also delegates to the Prohibition Convention. We registered at the Empire House, which has no "bar." Going into the dining room, I found Prof. A. A. Hopkins, from Rochester, N. Y.; also Fred. Wheeler, from Albany, he (Wheeler) being the state chairman of the Prohibition party of the State of New York. After supper we all adjourned to the Alhambra Rink, where a diamond medal contest was taking place. Many were the fine speeches delivered by the children. Were these same speeches delivered by adults, they would have been hooted, but the children sent them into the hearts of men. After the contest, there were in different rooms caucuses held, to settle on a choice for candidate for Governor of our State. Such well-known names as Demorest, from New York, Dr. Lawson and Hon. Powell, were mentioned. There were four secret Conferences that night in the Empire State. Next day the Conference was seated for business. Before the regular session, there was a prayer meeting, which was largely attended; and many earnest prayers went above the roof of the building. Brother Baldwin, from Elmira, was called to the chair *pro tem*. In the afternoon, W. Martin Jones was elected permanent chairman of the Convention. In the evening, the writer was called on to make a short address. Wednesday, June 27th, 1888.—After the Convention was seated again at 2 p.m., nominations were in order for Governor. The nominees were as follows: Mr. Demorest, of New York City; Hon. Dr. Lawson, of Jefferson County; Hon. W. Martin Jones, of Rochester, N.Y.; and one other candidate, from Niagara Co. When the first count came in, Demorest was in the lead with a little over four hundred votes, Dr. Lawson with over three hundred, Jones with over two hundred, and

the Niagara Co. man with about fifty. On the third
ballot, W. Martin Jones was elected by a large mjaority
This was the end of my work at the Convention, and I
returned to Pa. to take again my tent. On my way
down I passed through Binghampton and New Mil-
ford to Nicholson, then drove 13 miles to South
Gibson, where I found the tent with the boys.
All were delighted to see me again. Spoke at a
meeting in the evening. This is where I met the old
war horse, Mr. W. Searls. The next night we held
forth in the Methodist church. As it rained the night
on which the boys arrived, the hoodlums of the town
stole quietly up to our tent while the boys were sleeping, pulled up the stakes and let the tent fall upon them.
This was about the only disturbance we had at this
place.

June 30th.—We started over a mountainous road to
Hopbottom, Pa. After the tent was pitched, next to the
railway track, we were invited to take dinner at Mr.
Wright's, a prominent Republican. The Democrats controlled this town. While I was sitting at the window
above the store I heard some loud talking, and, being in
the campaign, I had my ears open for everything ;
listening, I heard the following conversation : A fellow
that was drunk commenced, "What has that Joe Hess
come here (sic) for ? he-he men-st to (sic) ki-kill the
Republican party (sic) ; Hess is free drade, (sic) I am for
higher protection, what will the laboring man do (sic)
when the Hess Free Drade party wins ? Hip (sic) hu-
ra-h for Harrison, high protection." On inquiry, I learned that this same man under Republican rule worked for
80 cents a day on a railroad. We had wonderful meetings here. After a stay of three days, a prohibition club
was organized of 45 voters, this was an increase of 41,
as the town had only four men who dared to vote the
ticket. D. W. Warren was chosen president of the club,
and Dr. Fawcet was made secretary.

July 3rd, 1888, was a hot morning, and this day was chosen to travel over a dusty mountainous road to the county seat, Montrose. On our way when we would meet farmers we would shout " Hurrah for the Fiske-Brook meeting." Finally we arrived at Montrose. After we had taken our dinner at the hotel, Mr. A. H. Gill took the writer to his home to be entertained. During the time the tent was being raised many threats were made about tearing it down. The tent was placed in front of the park ; in the front of the tent was the court house and jail ; on the other side was the church, and on the northeast was the school, and on the south side was a saloon. This was a contrast of educators, each one educating people in its own style ; the school to develop the intellect in the young minds, the church, God's nature, and preparing humanity for heaven. What is the education of the saloon ? not of the same kind as the preceding ones. It takes man's money and robs him of understanding ; it takes man's money and makes the loving husband and father a demon ; it takes man's money and educates him for jail and the gallows ; it takes the money and destroys man's chances for salvation ; it takes man's money when he ought to use it to buy nice clothing for his wife and children and put upon the table beefsteak and roast instead of liver with a bone in the middle. What luck can men have who deal in this infamous poison ? Listen to the voice of John Wesley ; hear what he thought of those who sold rum. He said : " Those who sell this poison murder His Majesty's subjects by wholesale, neither does their eye pity nor spare, they drive them to hell like sheep. And what is their gain ? Is it not the blood of these men. Who, then, would envy their large estates and sumptuous palaces. A curse is in the midst of them ; the curse of God cleaves to the stones, the timber, the furniture of them. The curse of God is in their gardens, their walks, their groves ; a fire that burns to the nethermost hell ! Blood !

blood! is there; the foundation, the floor, the wall, the roof are stained with blood. And canst thou hope, O, thou man of blood, though thou art clothed in scarlet and fine linen and farest sumptuously every day, canst thou hope to deliver down thy fields of blood to the third generation? Not so, for there is a God in heaven; therefore, thy name shall be rooted out, like as those whom thou hast destroyed body and soul, thy memorial shall perish with thee." Such was the plain language of a plain man, yet, educators like these men get a certificate of being men of a good moral character.

Night came, and being 3rd July, we feared some of the boys might get too much on board and become noisy; it was therefore thought best to have a night watch in the tent. Leaving the sides of the tent down, brothers Smith, Reynolds and Gilbert were constituted the police force. At 11 p. m. I went to bed. It was about 1 a. m. when some one shouted, " Hess, Hess, Hess, come down quick and help us; they are trying to kill us!" I quickly jumped into my old clothes, and by the time I came down stairs Mr. Gill was ready and we started for the circus. Sure enough, in front of the whiskey hotel was gathered a mob of fifty of all sorts, from the bummer in the gutter to the politician and church man. I gave a shout, jumped into their midst, and said, "If another man will fire a Roman candle into the tent, I would fill him full of holes, so that if he fell in the river he would sink." Brother Gill was in advance of me, and, at that moment, a big burly nigger picked up a stone to hurl at Gill. Just as the nigger was raising his arm I hit him under the jaw, which sent him to the earth as if he had been struck by lightning. At the other end they had old man Smith against a tree, shouting, "Burn the old cuss's whiskers. Hip, hip, hurrah for Harrison!" But I soon stopped that little fun, and quiet reigned. I told the boys to lay down and go to sleep, which they did. At 4 a. m. I went back to bed.

Fourth July morning we took a survey of the damage done, and found that thirty holes had been burned in the top of the tent. Many half-pound bombs that were thrown did not explode. We picked up one peck of these on the grounds. This will leave the reader to understand whether they meant it simply for fun. One of the town papers had the following report: "The series of Prohibition tent meetings were closed in this place on Friday evening last, upon which occasion Joe Hess gave a sketch of his career. It was the best address on temperance ever delivered in this town. The address won hearty encomiums from all who heard it. There were some occurrences in connection with the stay of the tent in town that, for the good name of the town, we wish had not happened. The attack upon the tent on the night preceding the 'Fourth,' was reprehensible in the highest degree, and unfortunate, because it had the appearance of a species of intolerance that is not becoming to a town composed of so intelligent a population. We do not think that the mischief makers on that night were acting by any special spite toward the Prohibitionists, but rather by a devilish desire to have what they call 'fun,' and the tent proved an inviting target for them. Of course, the members of the Prohibition party feel outraged, as well they might, but it is a mistake to undertake to transform what was in reality only the reckless, dare-devil pranks of a heedless crowd of fourth of July fun seekers into a political crime and as evincing a spirit of anarchy." This article had the desired effect. Those who denounced the attack who were in sympathy with the other political parties soon took the same view of the matter. I can only wish that the editor who wrote the above would have been in old man Smith's place, with a lot of hoodlums surrounding him, and throwing large bombs at his feet and firing rockets at him. I don't think he would have called it "fun."

A large club was organized, numbering about eighty.

July 7th, we started for Halstead, Pa., a railroad town. The tent was pitched upon Hon. Chase's grounds, in the rear of his residence. As we were told that this was such a hard place, we naturally looked for a general fight, but, to our surprise, the boys gave us a very agreeable reception. Just before the evening meeting the band came marching with flying banners down the street. At first we thought it would be an opposition meeting, but we were happily disappointed. As the band came to the entrance of the tent they turned and came in; this brought a great crowd of people, and we had a most pleasant meeting. Hon. S. Chase and Dr. Church occupied seats on the platform. Hon. S. Chase made the opening address and the writer followed. July 10th we had the closing meeting at Halstead. The following gentlemen assisted in the speaking, as the writer had a severe cold: Hon. S. B. Chase, Prof. Replogel, Mr. Ross, Mr. Tyler. A club of fifty-six was organized here, a gain of fifty voters.

Our next place was Susquehanna, Pa. This city is situated on the New York & Erie Railway, on the top of a mountain, and is well known for its great Irish Roman Catholic population, and for its many saloons. The tent was placed in front of the Congregational church, and a part of the tent was on the grounds of the Roman Catholic church. The priest was a very nice man; he tolerated the tent with more grace than the Protestant minister. Here we suffered a great deal of abuse, and the Republicans hired a band to play near the tent to draw off the crowd. Many times the writer was interrupted, the stones constantly rattling on the canvas. Though we had three watchmen, yet the ropes were cut. In this town I met the roughest crowd I had ever come in contact with in all my life. When we came into the town it had but one Prohibitionist. July 15th we packed the tent, and handed it over to the committee as our engagement was only for one month, and the month being up, we concluded our campaign. One of the dailies came out with an article headed, "The ex-prize fighter wheeled out cf town." Said this report, "He came in a carriage drawn by four white horses; he goes, but had his baggage wheeled to the depot with a wheel-barrow." All this was a falsehood, as I neither came in a carriage, neither was I wheeled out on a barrow.

July 15th.—In the evening I spoke in the M. E. Church at Great Bend to a large audience, and after meeting, Mr. C. T. Langley's man took me to Binghamton, 22 miles distant, to catch the early morning train for home, and all were much pleased to see me return in health. You can put yourself in my wife's place for a moment. She at home and I away, constantly the year round, she not knowing what moment the report might come that I was killed.

July 19th.—I received a telegram from New York city to come at once to that city to do temperance work. I started on the 20th, after a stay at home of only four days. I arrived in the city on the 21st, at 7.30 a.m., and was driven to 14th street. Finding the headquarters of John Lloyd Thomas closed, I strolled to the Dairy Kitchen for breakfast. After breakfast I visited the office of the *Voice*, the national prohibition organ. Next I visited the *Pioneer*, George R. Scott's paper, Mr. Scott becoming my escort to W. J. Wardville's office, who welcomed me royally. I was then piloted to Joseph Bogardus on West-street; he then piloted me to 284 Greenwich-street, the home-made restaurant. In the afternoon I had a visit from Rev. Daly, an ex-Roman Catholic priest, but oh! my, how seedy he did appear. Here the power of the digestive organs could be seen; before me sat a man who had been educated, honored, reared in refinment, but the power of appetite for strong drink made him tumble down from his position, to become an outcast, beggar and tramp, for such I learned from his own lips he was, prior to his connection with the Executive Committee of the Prohibition party of New York. Can this be a warning to the hundreds who allow themselves to be dragged down with drink? Oh, the bitter cup, the starvation cup, the cup that means death! Run, run, young man, from it ere it is too late! On Sunday I went over to Staten Island, to Richmond Park, to see Dr. W. Boole. This park is called Prohibition Park. Dr. Boole spoke in the afternoon, the writer being called upon for some remarks at the close. In the evening another large audience was addressed by Dr. Boole. God bless him.

# CHAPTER XVIII.

At Freemansburg, Pa.—Melodies of the Camp Ground.—Home
Once More.—Mamie a Silver Medalist.—A Great Address by
Hess.—Meets Col. R. S. Cheves and Sam Small.—Big Country
Meeting.—Taken Suddenly Ill.

"The wicked flee when no man pursueth, but the righteous are
bold as a lion."—Proverbs xxviii. 1.

WHAT glorious words are the above! I wish that
all who call upon His name would be bold as
lions, then the great evil of strong drink would soon be
a thing of the past.

July 23rd, 1888.—I left New York city for Freemansburg, Pa., where Hon. S. B. Chase was holding camp
meetings. I spoke briefly that evening. At 10 p.m. the
camp seemed all in slumber, except that occasionally
there could be heard some very intelligent language in
the tents, such as you would hear in your own house.
Some nights, oh! say, it is just too funny for anything
to sit in a camp ground in the midnight hour, surrounded
by those cotton houses, and listen to the different melodies of the songsters who sing by snoring.

July 24th was the day set down for Dr. D. H. Mann to
speak. The doctor is the Grand Chief Templar of the
I.O.G.T. of the State of New York, representing 35,000
Templars. This day was called Good Templars day.
Dr. Mann not feeling well in the morning, I was requested
to address the people. Many of the order came in from
all over the country. During my address I advanced
the idea that the man who voted for a political party
that was in favour of whiskey or alcoholic drink as a
beverage, was in league with the rum power. This was
a little ahead of the time, and, as of old, when men ad-

vanced new ideas they were sat upon. My idea stirred up a hornet's nest. After the meeting I was haunted on all sides by I. O. G. T. members, but I held that I was right, and I think so yet.

In the afternoon Dr. Mann gave us one of the finest addresses that I had ever listened to up to that time. The writer held the plank down at night, and discoursed on the " Old and New Home."

July 25th was one of the most lovely of days. The children assembled from all the country round, as this was children's day. Allow me to say right here that if we will root out the liquor fiend, it will have to be done by educating the children. In the evening of this date the writer spoke in German to a good audience.

July 26th the following well-known speakers occupied the platform: at 11 a. m., Mrs. Burt of New York, State President of the W.C.T.U.; in the afternoon, Miss Narcessie White, of Pennsylvania, and Hon. S. B. Chase; the writer again in the evening.

July 27th was a rainy day yet the camp ground was well filled with people hungry for the truth in regard to Prohibition. This subject was ably and grandly discussed by Frank C. Smith of New Jersey. The writer spoke again in the evening to a large audience.

July 28th I started for New York city to fill an appointment at Prohibition Park, on Staten Island. The tent was crowded. Great was the enthusiasm at the close. Dr. and Mrs. Boole entertained me most kindly while at the Park.

July 29th I left New York for home, arriving at Rochester the next day, 8 a.m. Found wife at Jackson's hotel. After doing some shopping we took the Falls road to Holly, which is our railroad station, from which Clarendon lays three miles south. Children were glad to see me. July 31st wife and I went to Buffalo to visit poor mother; had a very pleasant time.

August 1st Mrs. Hess and I went to Clarence, N. Y., to speak at a camp meeting. Returned to Buffalo the same night.

August 6th we had a golden day at Lockport, N.Y. Hon. W. Martin Jones, candidate for Governor of the State on the Prohibition ticket, was the principal speaker. Great torchlight processions were held that night; the writer was the first speaker of the evening.

August 9th, 1888, I was delighted to have my youngest child win a silver medal at the Clarendon Town Hall, for prize speaking on temperance.

August 10th I came to Rochester to be present at the Prohibition rally at the new opera house. The hall was crowded. The speakers of the evening were Rev. M. Mullen, from Albany; Ed. Carswell, of Oshawa, Ont. One of the secular papers of Rochester had the following heading:

### "JOE HESS SPEAKS."

" The last speaker at the Prohibition rally which was held at the new opera house last night was Joe Hess, the ex-pugilist, whose reformation was one of the principal incidents of the work of P. A. Burdick in this city in 1885. Since then Mr. Hess has been constantly engaged in the temperance work, and has met with more than marked success. He was received with loud applause. ' Joe' is not a polished orator, but his originality and enthusiasm make up for minor defects, and there are few more entertaining talkers than our ' Joe.' He began his remarks by expressing his gratitude that he could once more appear before his many friends. He briefly and modestly referred to his work since he had entered the ring for God and temperance. He then alluded to the beneficial effect the Gospel-temperance meetings had upon the people throughout the country. It would be a grand victory for the enemy of mankind (alcohol) if the temperance people would be silent He said that Christ would be a prohibitionist if He were now on earth, and that Christ's followers should, therefore, belong to the same party. He assured his Christian hearers that Christ watches them as closely when they go to the ballot-box to vote as when they are on their kness in church, or going about their daily business, and that He expects them to vote right, as well as to do right in other respects. He then quoted from the Constitution of the United States the following reasons for adoption of that instrument. (1). To form a more perfect union. (2). Establish justice. (3). Insure domestic tranquillity. (4). Provide for the common defence. (5). Promote the general welfare, and (6). Secure the blessing of liberty to ourselves and to our posterity.

" He held that the liquor traffic is opposed to all the ends sought by the founders of the nation, and that therefore all laws protecting the traffic are unconstitutional in spirit at least. He held that the Government would be rotten as long as it recognized the saloon vote and bid for it. He urged all conscientious and patriotic voters to join in the effort to do away with the greatest curse the nation had to contend with."

August 11th and 12th.—I spoke at Blood's Station at the temperance camp meeting. At 2 p. m. on the 11th, the enclosure contained over 3,000 people. My subject was " The Growth of the American Saloon." After the meeting the old Republicans did roar and cry vengeance against that ex-prize-fighter. I do believe that the knowledge of my former powers with my hands when doubled up (I don't mean doubled round a knife and fork) into a fist saved me from a pounding. They swore they would not return to hear me again. The 12th was Sunday; rain just came down with the greatest of ease; it did not seem to be any trouble whatever to wet all through those who had the good luck to be under it.

The rain ceased to pour, and by 11 o'clock the grounds were black with people. At 11.30 a.m. over 1,000 teams were upon the ground, and some 7,000 people had thronged into the enclosure. The front seats were occupied by the very men who had done the hardest denouncing the day previous. My text was Matt. xi. 28-30. During the speaking the handkerchiefs were doing active service. Men and women who had not shed tears since their childhood were now in the melting process ; and many were the " Amens " and " Hallelujahs " that were spoken from the throng.

The afternoon speakers were Miss Frances Varnum, a devout woman, and the famous Rolla Kirk Bryan, the chalk-talker. Rolla is small in stature, not greatly gifted with his tongue, but what he lacked in that line he more than makes up with his chalk in his fingers. Another great assembly had gathered at 2 p. m. to listen to these gifted people. This was a great day for the cause.

August 13th, 1888.—I travelled over the Erie road to Owego, N.Y., and from that point to Newark Valley. On the train I had the pleasure to meet Col. R. S. Cheves, from Kentucky, the Southern orator and a fearless worker in the cause. In his company was Sam. Small (he ought to be called Sam. Long), of Georgia, a reformed man, who is now devoted to spreading the truth. Many men have been induced by his logic to become prohibitionists.

After supper we went over to the tent which was to be our house for the next two months. Its seating capacity was about 1,000. The tent was packed, hundreds could not gain admission. This same night Warner Miller was holding forth at Owego, which is only a short distance. Miller, being the candidate for Governor on the Republican ticket, he stood out for high license.

Aug. 14. We started the campaign in Tioga county. Everything was put into shape this day, cooking utensils and oil stove were placed in our charge, also an extra tent to sleep in. The first meal was cooked by the cook; you

ask me what was the cook's name ?   Well, I don't know
that I had better tell tales out of school, but as I have
not begun before, it is not too late now, and I will tell
you who the cook was.   He was a good-natured and a
large-sized man, a German descendent, his name, if I
recollect now, was Joseph F. Hess, from Clarendon, N.Y.

Aug. 16th.  We started bright and early for Berk-
shire.  Found Bro. Mories Williams.   He showed us
where to pitch the tent.  We stayed at this place over
Sunday ; meetings were large ; many signed the voter's
pledge.

From here we went to Richford, N. Y.  Brother
Finch, a relative of the great John B. Finch, now deceased, made us welcome.  We had a hard time to secure a
place for the tent.  It was finally placed on the grounds
of Bro. Finch.  Brother Herrick, the county chairman,
was present in the evening ; good feeling prevailed, notwithstanding the Republicans made threats that they
would not allow the tent in town.

Aug. 21st. The rain prevented us from having a meeting, consequently we retired early.  The tent blew down
during the night, and the whole force was called out to
pull ropes and drive stakes, not a very pleasant thing,
with the rain coming down in sheets.  You may talk
about having a nice time in a tent, but I prefer a wood-
en house when the rain comes down as it did on that
night.

Aug. 23rd. We started for Gas Hill Corners, a distance of twenty-eight miles.  Brother Bateman came
after us and we enjoyed a very pleasant time.  This city
has a very large population, four houses and three barns
and one pig pen, a post office, a sort of a tri-weekly; you
put the mail in one week, and it will be sent in three
weeks.

I wondered where the people should come from, the
tent being pitched in a 50-acre lot.  When the time
came for this meeting, the place was made lively by

hundreds of people and teams. Where they came from I do not know, but I do know that some came twelve to fourteen miles. The tent was crowded. Brother Hochkins offered up a prayer. Mr. Oakly, of Owego, opened the meeting as chairman; then he called on Mr. Ball, of Minneapolis, Minn. Mr. Ball was a convert of seven days' birth, and like all new converts to any cause he turned loose, and tore things—people always tare things when they are away from their own town, but when at home they are as quiet as clams. The writer brought up the rear, and held the audience for three consecutive days.

Aug. 26th.—Sunday will be a day long remembered in that town. By ten a.m. fully three thousand people had gathered on the grounds. Rev. Deyer preached a fine sermon in the morning; then Brother Oakly held a Sunday-school. At two p.m. the tent was filled. The writer asked a young man to sign the pledge, but his father being present, said no.

This young man had begun a wild career. That afternoon he went with several others to a drinking house, where they became drunk. On his way home, he drove recklessly, and nearing a steep embankment, the horse and waggon coming too near, it rolled over the embankment, the horse being killed, the waggon smashed, the young men (three in number), one killed outright, the other died a week later, the young man whose father refused to let him sign the pledge, had both his legs broken, and one arm. Had the young man signed the pledge, this terrible calamity would have been prevented. Set a good example, fathers, for your boys.

On Sunday night the writer was overcome with sickness, congestion of the lungs, and had to cease speaking, and take to the lodging tent, and roll up in blankets. This caused great excitement. The meeting broke up, and a number of the ladies and gentlemen gathered around the saw-buck bed on which I was resting; and of all the remedies that were suggested, one said give him some hot whiskey; another would suggest hot bricks, not to swallow, but to put around me; another said St. Jacob's Oil, and a lady shouted, " I have it with me, I always have it, for I often get that way." Finally, after a council of war, it was resolved that to save the life of the speaker, he must be well rubbed, and accordingly, the blankets were partly removed, and a great big but good man rolled up his sleeve, and holding up the palm of his hand, he poured oil on it; and now he became like the good Samaritan. On bended knee he stretched forth his hand and began the invigorating process.

While he was rubbing, I wondered whether the hands of the Samaritan had such a fine touch. Every time he extended his hand to the full extent, he covered one side of my chest, and I imagined he had a rasping iron, or in other words, a gridiron. However, when he was tired out, the slimy grit on the inside let go, and I rested easier. During the time the people were invigorating me on the inside of the tent; others were anxiously waiting for the verdict on the outside. Because of the excellent treatment that I received at the hands of many willing friends, the verdict was, that I would turn out all right in the morning, which verdict was a correct one.

At this moment I look back to that night, and raise my head with a "God bless the noble farmers of that part of Tioga County." All partisan strife had been forgotten when the life of a man was in danger, which is usually the custom with American people. As I lay that night, I thought of the words that we read in the Bible — " Boast not thyself of to-morrow, for thou knowest not what a day may bring forth."—Prov. 27th chap., 1st verse.

# CHAPTER XIX.

A Continuation of Tent Campaign Work.—The Start made at
Apalachin, N.Y.—Chasing a Slander.—Attitude of the Party
Press.—A Great Meeting at Hickstown.—Some Appropriate
Quotations.—Big Success at Lockwood, N. Y.—A Notable
Letter from Hon. W. Martin Jones, of Rochester, N.Y.

"Therefore, if any man be in Christ, he is a new creature, old
things are passed away, behold all things are become new."—
II. Cor., v. 17.

HOW great a change this would bring amongst God's
people if these words were fully realized by those
who profess His name. These words should be compre-
hended by the man who defiles his mouth and body with
tobacco.

August 27th, 1888.—We started for Apalachin, N.Y.
To reach this place we passed through one of the most
fertile sections of Central New York. The tent was
pitched back of the M. E. Church. In the evening we
had a grand audience, barring a few stones that were
hurled on top of the canvas. After the meeting the
writer boarded the train for Albany, the capital of the
State, where the Grand Lodge of the Good Templars
were in session. The first man I met was Ed. Marvin,
from Albion, Orleans county. I was told to stop at the
American Hotel which was a strictly temperance house.
I was heartily greeted by W. Martin Jones, also the
Silver Lake Quartette and many others. Found Fred.
Wheeler; had a talk with him about the campaign.

At the evening mass meeting I was called on to make
a short address. The other speakers were Dr. D. H.
Mann, Grand Chief Templar of New York; W. Martin
Jones, of Rochester; J. N. Stearns, of New York, and
others, and a delightful meeting it was.

August 29th I returned to where I had left the tent with the boys. During my absence from the session, delegates were nominated to attend the Right Worthy Grand Lodge of the World, which was to be convened at Chicago in 1889. The writer received fifty-seven votes, which I consider was a compliment.

August 30th.—We started with the prohibition wagon for Owego. We pitched our tent near the Court House on a lot owned by Judge Clark, one of the leading men of the Republican party. All sorts of rumours were set afloat about the writer. Some had it that my wife was keeping a saloon in Rochester while I was out on the temperance platform. Now, the writer could put up with most any insult so far as he was concerned, but when the slanders touched the name of the one who suffered so intensely because of the drink drank by her husband it was too much. On hearing the base slanders I started out and traced them to their source. It was said that a certain druggist invented the base lie, but on interviewing the man he denied the story. It was then said a cigar store man was the author; he in turn said that it was a liquor man from Rochester told him. When the people learned that it was false they rejoiced.

Many insults were hurled at me during the stay. Several times I was threatened with a mob, but, thank God for the courage which was given to me in Christ. We had good meetings during our stay in the town. A club of fifty-eight voters was organized in this place, an increase of thirty-two.

The Owego *Times* inquired: "Why is the circus tent perambulating this county?" The Democratic organ made the following answer: "We are not good at answering conundrums, but in this case we would venture the reply that it is for the purpose of increasing the prohibition vote." Just before the arrival of the tent in town the Owego *Times* had the following item: "The Prohibitionist with his tent is out this presidental year. The purpose is to try and draw off from the Republican party all the votes he can.  Who is he working for ?  Evidently for the benefit of Grover Cleveland and the patron saint of the whiskey barrel, D. B. Hill.  He is not honest enough to confess his pious fraud, but it is the truth.  Farmers, you are generally sober men (taffy).  Don't be caught by chaff.  There is no religion in this game.  Many men who never touch liquor are the meanest men you know. Cleveland and his free trade needs votes badly and will pay for them.  The Prohibitionist is his decoy duck. Don't be taken in.  His net is spread in the sight of the bird."

This kind of stuff came from a Christian journal which puts party above God and principle.

September 3rd, we entered the town of Candor.  The prohibition tabernacle was erected on the grounds belonging to the M. E. Church.  At first people made fun of the circus, as they termed it, but about the fourth meeting, when the tent was packed, some of the Republican politicians set a fellow who was drunk to ring the fire bell to draw the people from the tent, but as soon as the bell struck a man in the audience arose to his feet and told the people that it was a trick, and that he had helped to plan it, but repented now and was sorry for it. He declared that prohibition was right, and that he would defend it.  The Republicans seeing their game foiled became enraged.  A club of sixty voters was organized.

September 6th, the chariot of truth rolled on its way to Spencer, N.Y., where we located on the fair grounds, occupying the building in which to hold our meetings. Arriving at Spencer we learned that Briggs and wife were at Hickstown, ten miles distant, with their tent. After consulting with the boys it was decided that we drive to Hickstown and surprise them.

Reaching Hickstown we found the road full of wagons. The tent looked gay with its flags waving for Fiske and Brooks.  When the hour for the meeting arrived, we entered and in a short time the place was packed. The writer, with his boys, took seats in the rear of the tent, but it was no use. The eagle eye of Brother Briggs soon spied us, and we had to go on the platform, which we did. Briggs made a strong plea for the cause. To my surprise a man arose and said that he sold whisky because of the money which he made from it. Too many, I fear, are doing this because of the money that they derive from it. Men should consider that it is not for ourselves alone that we work and strive. It is for others as well as for ourselves. There are moral laws, family ties, domestic affections, home government and guidance, which stand on a higher level and are based on nobler considerations than selfish pleasures or money payment. We must beware how we allow our views to centre in ourselves. "No one," said Epictetus, "who is a lover of riches, or a lover of pleasure, or a lover of glory, can at the same time be a lover of men." "To be a lover of men," said St. Anthony, "is in fact to live." Thus, then, love is the universal principle of good. Love is glorified in human intelligence. Love is the only remedy for the woes of the human race. "It is sweet in action, in learning, in manners, in legislation, in government." "What is temperance?" said a great divine. "Love which no pleasure seduceth. What is prudence, but love which no error enticeth? What is fortitude, but love which endureth adverse things with courage? What is justice, but love which composeth by a certain charm the inequalities of this life?"

Said Socrates: "Many fearful things took place through the empire, of necessity, but when this God was born, the God of love, all things arose to men." And now, let me say, that the man who sells rum for the money there is in it, and to get that money he knows that his business will cause heartaches, it will produce everything that is unlovely and never be conducive to love. There is more money by being thoughtful and kind, having consideration for the welfare of others, and being of such frame of mind will repay itself. We stayed at Spencer for four days. Much rain prevailed while we were in camp. A club was organized.

September 10th,—We proceeded to bombard the town of Lockwood. In this town we had much opposition and trouble; at every meeting it seemed that a fight would be the next thing; a club of 24 voters was organized in this town—an increase of 23 voters.

September 12.—We made war in Waverley, which I can best explain in the language of the *Gazette* of that town. "Waverley, September 18th.—The prohibition tent arrived here last Thursday morning from Lockwood, and was pitched on the vacant lot at the corner of Broad and Johnson-streets. As there was no meeting set down for that day, the manager, Joseph Hess and company, visited the Chemung county tent, at Chemung that evening, and Mr. Hess spoke there. On Friday afternoon the tent was opened with a fair sized audience. The meeting took the form of a fellowship meeting. At its close, Mr. Hess invited everybody interested in the homes and good government of America to come forward and join the prohibition ranks. Four new names were added to the list. In the evening the tent was packed by 7.30, and many people had to go away, they could not get near the tent. The meeting was opened by singing, prayer was offered by Mr. Hess; another song. Mr. Hess then spoke for one hour, subject, " Is liquor a crime-creator;" Mr. Hess proved that it was, and made his points very clear and strong; the subject was handled in a masterly manner. Saturday afternoon Mr. Hess addressed a large audience. Subject, " High License." He showed that high license does not decrease, but increases the consumption of liquor and beer. In the evening the town was alive with people, the cause of the stir was that Hon. Mr. Jones of Rochester, Prohibition candidate for Governor, had arrived during the afternoon, and was the guest of

O. B. Corwin, of Fulton-street. At 7 o'clock a great throng of prohibitionists from all over the country formed into a procession at the tent, and marched down Broad-street and up Fulton-st. to Mr. Corwin's residence, whence Mr. Jones was escorted in a carriage with Jos. Hess, Rev. D. H. Cooper and Mr. Herrick, Chairman of the County Committee, to the tent. There was a fine display of fireworks and Greek fire all along the line. It was the most respectable political parade of the season. At the tent the meeting was opened by singing, prayer being offered by Rev. Mr. Cooper, after which Mr. Hess spoke briefly. After the remarks of Mr. Hess, Mr. Jones was presented to the vast audience. Mr. Jones spoke for two hours, touching on high license, then upon the Maine election, showing that the prohibitionists had made gains all through the States as compared with the election of '84, the Presidential year. Mr. Jones was frequently applauded, his speech was clean, without slang or abuse. Mr. Hess again spoke Sunday. Hess is a good speaker, and makes his points very plain. he has won many friends in this place. Henry Hess, who accompanies his father, assists in the singing; he is a young man nearly 18 years old, and has never drank beer nor liquor nor used tobacco in any form. The meetings were a grand success."

September 17th, '88.—We landed in the town of Barton, Tioga County; tent was pitched next to the M. E. Church on a 100 acre lot. Rain poured, we therefore crawled into the M. E. Church, and built a fire in the stove. Things moved slowly, a club of ten however being organized. Next we went to Tioga Centre, had excellent meetings.

September 22nd I was called to speak in the city of Elmira, for the Prohibition Club. Had a splendid audience.

September 24th,—We started to wind up the campaign again at Newark Valley, where we began; the

tent was packed both afternoon and evening ; at the afternoon meeting the writer gave a report, of his six weeks
work, and reported 480 voters signed pledges, who had
never voted before on the prohibition ticket.  The report
was adopted, and all were pleased with it.

The evening meeting was addressed by the colored
orator, Rev. J. H. Hector of Cal.  The next day the Hon.
A. A. Hopkins, of Rochester, N.Y., spoke.  The writer
bid good bye to his friends on the 25th September, 1888,
and started for home for a much-needed rest.  During
the campaign I had written a letter of congratulation to
Hon. W. M. Jones on his nomination as candidate for
Governor of our State, to which he replied in following
words.

Mr. Joseph F. Hess, Clarendon, Orleans Co., N.Y.

My Dear Sir :—I have read your letter with more
than ordinary emotion.  It is true that it is lacking in
some unimportant particulars, that better opportunities
in your early life would have supplied, but it does not
lack anything to make it a substantial, generous outpour-
ing from your heart, and I accept it in the spirit in which
it is written.  I have many letters from all parts of the
State and from many other sections of the country, but
no letter has touched me more closely than the one I have
received from you.  I know that there is no word in that
letter that is not the honest, outspoken sentiment of a
noble-hearted man, and I assure you that I shall never
forget the generous words of congratulation that came
from your heart through the medium of this letter, and
I shall not forget the service that you rendered in the
canvass made at the Syracuse Convention.  To receive
such a nomination is certainly an honor, but it is coupled
with such responsibilities and sacrifices that I am con-
strained to hesitate in returning thanks for it.  Yet I am
bound to take the act for what it was intended, and in
that light I do return to you and my other friends in

convention my most sincere thanks. I need not tell you what you know so well that I neither expected nor sought the nomination, and I have felt not a little doubt of my duty in accepting it. In view of the fact, however, that I can never shrink from making such sacrifices as my principles exact from me, I am compelled to accept the nomination in the spirit that you and other noble friends have manifested in tendering it to me. So I take the standard where others have left it, and shall bear it forward in the van of the fight with sincere desire to promote the interests of the great cause for which we are both laboring, and eventually to win the fight and leave no saloon between the oceans. Thanking you again for your generous letter of congratulation,

I remain as ever,
Yours sincerely,
W. MARTIN JONES.

This letter shows plainly what a grand Christian gentleman our party had selected as their standard-bearer. I know of no man in the State of New York, who would have made a better candidate. Hon. W. M. Jones is an educated man, a lawyer by profession, a logical speaker, a close reasoner, one who is thoroughly acquainted with the history of legislation on the temperance question.

Elections were now on and I cast the first vote in our town, and it went into the box declaring that I was against the saloon and the drink traffic. The day before the election, a reporter interviewed me about the election. I gave him my opinion that it was sure that Grant would be elected as Mayor of the City of New York, while D. B. Hill would again become Governor, and that Cleveland, by a mere chance, may be elected. Cleveland was elected by the people, but he failed to get the states that had the most electoral votes. The year 1888 will long live in the memory of many of the United States voters; the party that had the largest boodle got there.

N

# CHAPTER XX.

The idol of to-day—Work in Jersey City—Some cheering results—
   Speaks in Chickering Hall, New York—Visits the old Washingtonian Home—Once an inmate himself—A graphic description of
   21 day's campaign in Evanston, Ill.—The home of Miss Willard,
   as seen by Hess.

"But take heed lest by any means this liberty of yours become
a stumbling block to them that are weak. For if any man see
thee which hast knowledge sit at meat in the idol's temple, shall
not the conscience of him which is weak be emboldened to eat those
things which are offered to idols. And through thy knowledge
shall the weak brother perish, for whom Christ died."—1 Cor. viii.
9-11.

THE idol of to-day is the liquor traffic; men uphold it—
even some who are in the church of God—because
of the revenue it brings to the State. These men are
stumbling blocks in the way of the drunkard; many a
drunkard has gone down to a drunkard's grave because
of the inconsistency of the members of a church.

February 6th, I arrived home for a few days. I found
my wife very sick, and the weather was very cold; the
children were all delighted to see me.

Saturday, Feb. 9th, I went to Holly for the purpose of
organizing a lodge of I. O, G. T. People said it was no
use : I could not do it. At 8 o'clock, the time for the
meeting to begin, the hall was packed. The writer
brought his project before the people, and at the close of
the meeting about 25 of Holly's best citizens signified
their desire to become members of the Order; John Bud-
ington was chosen secretary, the lodge was duly organized, and its power is felt to-day in that town and surrounding country. The membership is 120 at this writing, and the outlook is good for doubling these numbers
within a year.

February 12th, Started in company of my son Henry for Jersey City ; arrived there at 7.30 p.m. The next day we began a series of meetings in Pavonia-avenue rink. The evening meeting was attended by about 500 people ; the next night the audience was increased, and perhaps 800 were out, and many signed the pledge ; and, dear reader, it is in centres of large population where we can see the evils of drink. One man coming in shouted out it was too late to save him. He rushed from the hall, and when out cut his throat with a razor. The audiences at the rink kept increasing from night to night, until from 2,500 to 3,000 were gathered there nightly.

February 18th, I was requested by the president of the W. C. T. U., Mrs. Carnes, who was a very highly educated woman, and one who had the love of children at heart, to speak for her at the mission. Their rooms were located in one of the hardest parts in Jersey City. I found it filled with children, boys and girls. Upon their features could be seen the stamp of vice, despite their young years. Girls not yet in their teens used the language of harlots and street walkers. Should you ask how this comes about, I would answer, through the indifference of good people to temperance work. The liquor traffic has everything its own way, and the fathers of these young creatures are debauched, degraded, and debased, and they drag down with them their posterity. These children gave me their best attention, and good work I believe was done.

When I returned on Sunday night to the same place the hall was packed, and the children's faces looked bright, clean, and fresh. One little girl came up and said "How do you think I look in my new dress ? " Said I, where did you get it ? She said, " that she sold newspapers and blacked shoes, so that she could get money to buy the dress, for which she paid a dollar," and she said that she would always be a temperance girl. She was about 13 years of age ; the last letter I had from her she said : "Mr. Hess, I am all right; I go to the M. E. Church and to Sunday school." A kind word here, and a kind act there, has been the means of rescuing many a one from hell; it was a kind word that saved John B. Gough.

Feb. 19th we had a grand meeting. A man came forward to sign, and he did sign ; then he burst into tears : he cried aloud, for his past life had been one like the writer's. He said he knew not where his wife and child were; for five years he had not heard from them; he had accidentally strolled into the meeting. While crying, a woman was pushing her way through the crowds, and reaching the platform she gave one look upon the poor man, when she gave a gasp and cried "My John !" and fell on the neck of the poor husband, for such was he. The last time they were together was at the saloon, where she pleaded with him to come home. The dram shop had parted husband and wife, but the temperance meeting gave back the husband to the wife, and to-day there lives a happy family in that city, who praise God for the temperance cause. Yes, many are the happy families around the country who thank God for the temperance wave that sweeps from time to time over the country, which stays the steps of many a one from going down further to ruin.

February 20th, my voice gave out, but timely help came : Col. R. S. Cheves came over from New York and assisted.

Sunday, Feb. 24th, I spoke in Chickering Hall, New York City, to a crowded audience. The New York *Sun* gave the following account of the meeting: " Last Sunday, Chickering Hall, this city, was packed, and the musical programme which preceded the speakers was loudly applauded. The Rev. Dr. A. G. Lawson, of Boston, spoke and denounced purely political harangues on Sunday. He went on to say prohibitionists should leave woman suffrage out of their platform. He was followed by Joe Hess, a German ex-prize fighter, who said he used to believe in women suffering when he kept a saloon; but he did not any more. He said that when he died he wanted his wife, who was taxed, to be represented in the government that taxed her; and therefore he was in favor of giving women the ballot. Joe has a characteristic way of speaking that delighted the audience. Last Tuesday he opened a series of twenty meetings at Greenport, L.I., under the auspices of the Good Templars. He is well known throughout the State, both in his former and present character as a temperance worker." The same evening I again spoke at the Jersey Foundry Mission; and God blessed my efforts that night, as 44 rose for prayers. This finished my labor for a while in that part of the country, and I returned toward home; but on my way stopped over at Fort Plain, where I was billed to speak. From a report of the Fort Plain *Standard* I quote:

"Monday evening the greatest temperance orator of the age, Joseph F. Hess, addressed at least eight hundred people at Fricher Opera House; subject, "Success." Every recurring appearance of Mr. Hess here wins for him public esteem. and should he again visit Fort Plain with sufficient advance time of notice, we doubt if this village contains an auditorium of sufficient seating capacity to accommodate those eager to listen to him. There cannot be a doubt but in the person of Mr. Hess, the temperance people have one of the best, most earnest and conscientious laborers for the cause in the country. His name is becoming world-famed, if not already emblazoned far above all competitors in the same noble cause. His advice to the young ladies and gentlemen, particularly, Monday evening, cannot fail to be heeded."

Such notice of man's work would almost make any man's head swim with vanity, but thank God, my head only did swim once with pride, and it sunk.

Feb. 28th.—I again came to the city of Gloversville, and was made welcome for the second time by L.

Heacock, 44 Forest-street; all were rejoiced to see me return. We had crowded houses as on former occasions; Henry sang solos, which were warmly applauded. On Sunday we attended the Freemont M. E. Church, Rev. Mr. Brundage in the pulpit.

I again spoke in the Hall in the evening, subject: "Responsibility and Duty of Church Members."

I started for Chicago, and there I visited the old Washingtonian Home to see Prof. Wilkinson, who was there in 1875, when I was placed in the Home by Miss Frances E. Willard. The Professor was delighted to see me, after I had made myself known to him. The old Home when I was there was an old frame building, but now they have a magnificent Home erected of brick; it is an honor to the city of Chicago. At 12 a. m. I took the Milwaukee & St. Paul road to Evanston; at the depot I secured a cab and drove to Rest cottage, Miss Willard's home, where I received a thorough christian welcome.

During the evening I had numbers of callers, among them the Adams trio, three brothers, whom I have learned to love for their christian zeal in the cause of the Master. They are beautiful singers, and were my nightly assistants while in Evanston. The next day was Sunday, and in company of Miss Willard, I spoke in the M. E. church. Rev. Bro. Zimmerman was in the pulpit, and preached a very practical sermon. At this meeting my eyes were opened, and for the first time I realized what I had undertaken. Evanston is the place where the great north-west University is located. Talk about grammar, my! there is where you get it. I tried hard to bring a little piece with me when I came away, but I had no room in my trunk.

Evanston is one of the most delightful spots on earth, situated about 12 miles from the city, fronting on the shores of Lake Michigan, a beautiful sheet of water. It never had any saloons, and prohibition is a success in

that city.  This place was the home of one of the greatest platform speakers this country ever had, I make
reference to the late Hon. John B. Finch.  His widow
and only child, little Johnny Finch, still reside in the
place.

Sunday, at 3 p.m., the meetings were opened.  On the
platform were seated Mrs. L. Vane, the president of the
Evanston Union; Mrs. Buell, Mrs. Finch, Mrs. Riley,
and Miss Frances E. Willard.  The hall was packed,
many students being present, who came as I suspect to
criticise me.  I was given a hearty reception, but I did
not hear it, for I was suffering.  This was my first
appearance, and I knew of my deficiency in education.
But when I thought of the words " Lo ! I will be with
you always to the end," I took courage.  I spoke on the
subject, " Out of darkness into light," and won many
friends.

Tuesday, March 12th.—I received an invitation to dine
with the divinity students; about 30 were gathered
round the table at Mrs. Ball's home.  During the time
we were waiting for the second dinner to "top off," the
question was asked by the writer, " What are the boys
learning ?" Said one, " Theology." "What's that ?" "Why,
to find out what God is."  Then the writer was all attention, and asked the question, "Whether they have found
out yet," to which the answer was, "No."  Had a great
meeting that night, hall packed to suffocation.

Next day I paid a visit to the *Lever* office at Chicago,
also to the headquarters of the W. C. T. U.

Returned to Evanston and had a rousing meeting.
Many signed. During the time that I was in Evanston, I
was agreeably surprised to meet Dr. Tanner, the 40-day
faster, who gave us a very eloquent address on total
abstinence.

Friday, March 22nd, 1889,—I was more than surprised
to receive an invitation to go to the Memorial Hall to
address the students.  To say I trembled is putting it

very mild. Every bone was shaking. Especially did I tremble, because on my arrival one of the newspapers had said that the ladies of the Union had made a mistake in bringing a man to this place who uses bar-room phrases, and slang talk; to which another of the newspapers replied, "We think the ladies brought the right man to this place; the coming of Joe Hess to Evanston is resulting in the stirring up of the temperance forces, and Union Hall has been packed nightly to hear him. Sunday afternoon he was greeted with a crowded house, and the interest is increasing daily. Mr. Hess has good ideas, however crude they may be in expression; his hearers feel that his conversion is truly of heart, and that he is trying to make amends for a misspent life in the past. He makes good use of his pugilistic ability by fighting the liquor business straight from the shoulder. He is honest and earnest, straightforward and forcible, and reaches a class of people who might never be influenced by the more established and systematic methods of evangelization. All should hear him."

From 400 to 600 people were present in the hall, chiefly students. I took for my text 1st Timothy, 4th chap., 16th verse, "Take heed unto thyself, and unto thy doctrine. Continue in them, for in doing this thou shalt both save thyself, and them that hear thee."

I remember that as I took my place, the first thing that I said was that I did not expect ever to become a professor in a college of Theology; I consider that I am making progress, as I am to be the teacher, this audience before me then must be my class, and if they did not behave, I should be under the painful necessity to reprove.

March 23rd.—I was invited to take dinner with Rev. J. J. Maily, a student, who lived in Evanston with his family. This good brother in Christ was my main stand-by of the male sex while I was in the town. Brother Maily was touched by the hot coal from off the altar when he was but 19 years. Many years before he ran away when a boy from his parents, and has lost all traces of them ; he wandered out into the world, beginning to lead a reckless life, but his steps were stayed before he had gone too far, and to-day Illinois has no more powerful preacher than Maily. God bless him, he has been a friend to me.

March 24th.—I went to hear Rev. Dr. Thomas preach in McVicker's Opera House, on South Madison-street. In the afternoon of the same day, I went in company of Rev. J. J. Maily, and several members of the W. C. T. U. to the Chicago Bridwell, a prison in which I had occupied a cell for nine months, because of the licensed whiskey I had drunk. As I entered the same door where I had entered many years before, a queer feeling came over me. We were cordially greeted by the officials. We were invited to take dinner; when I was under the devil's management, I had to walk up and take my bowl of mush with black strap mollasses, but now when I came to the same place under God's direction, I was invited to sit at the table spread with God's good gifts. What a change! but the trying time came.

When after dinner I was permitted to see walking in Indian style, over 600 prisoners, mostly all young men and women, little boys not 10 years, a little girl just entered into her teens, as I arose to speak I was overcome with sympathy for these poor unfortunate ones who were deprived of their freedom because of the sin of strong drink. Quite a number of the grey heads I remember were there when I was one of them ; many recognized me. I pointed them to a loving Saviour ; what a change God had brought about in me, and he could do the same for them if they were willing. It was a sight to behold this audience of stony hearts, moved to tears, and as they passed out and I stood at the door, there came up many a "thank you." After the meeting we all went into the prisoners' quarters ; I took a look at the little room which I had made my home ; there was the same old furniture, the little room had not grown any longer, 8 feet by 6 was the size, the little iron bedstead stood on the identical spot, the head rest was the same, the sliding bolt for a lock was the same. It was while in this room, years before, my father appeared to me, dressed in white, resting over my head, bending his head up and down, as much as to say, "Has it come to this?"

This made me hurry from the place, and leaving the building on that side, the keeper said, "I will take you over and show you the new part, which cost many thousand dollars to erect." During the time we were passing through, I asked the question, "How it is that you must have more room? You have high license in Chicago." Said the keeper, "Mr. Hess, license, high or low, we have not room enough to store the products of the saloon. We have now a different grade of prisoners. There are more of the respectable young men, who think it manly to patronize an institution because it pays $500 per year for its existence."

After thanking the keeper for his kindness, we made our way back to Evanston. That evening I was permitted to preach in the Methodist church, which was packed to overflowing. This night I concluded my work in Evanston, where my first engagement was only for 10 days, but had been prolonged to 21 days. Much good had been done; over 900 had taken the pledge, many who were moderate drinkers. The I. O. G. T. lodge received a revival during these meetings by the untiring efforts of Mrs. Frances E. Finch. Many were the God speed you, and God keep you, at the close of the meeting. The ladies made me a present of $225.00 for the length of time I was there.

Monday, March 25th.—The following resolution was placed in my hands by the president of the Union, Mrs. L. P. Vane:

Resolution of endorsement of the W. C. T. U. of Evanston, Ill.:—Whereas Mr. Joseph F. Hess, of Clarendon, N.

Y., came to us, a stranger, except that Jesus Christ his Elder Brother was with him to introduce him.  This blessed friend abided with him, and the result of his stay amongst us has been happier homes, and many happy hearts.  Resolved, as a Union that we take great pleasure in commending Mr. Hess and his work, while our heartiest " God bless him" go with him everywhere. Resolved, That we heartily endorse Joseph F. Hess, of Clarendon, N. Y., as a successful temperance evangelist, and recommend that his name be placed on the list of the Woman's Lecture Bureau.

Mrs. B. F. Week,<br>
Rec. Sec. W. C. T. U., Evanston.

# CHAPTER XXI.

A Contrast—Joe "now" and "then"—Work in Peoria, Ill.—
Dick Corbett's fall—Hess and St. John—Voluntary and valu-
able testimony—Paying for the Home—In the Pennsylvania
Amendment Fight.

" Blessed are the meek : for they shall inherit the earth."—
Matthew v. 5.

WHILE walking in a Western town one day I was
observed by many, and the next paper that came
out had the following notice :—

### A GREAT CHANGE IN JOE HESS.

" I met Joe Hess on the street to night," said one of
our citizens on Friday evening, "and I could not help
thinking of the great change that has come to the man.
I thought of the time he came here, some years ago, as
one of the Baker and Slattery prize fight company.  He
was among toughs then.  Before his connection with that
Sunday row he was indicted and arraigned before Judge
Signor, but was allowed to go at liberty and remain free
so long as he behaved himself.  Joe signed the pledge in
Rochester, was afterwards converted, and joined a Baptist Church, and from that day to this there has been a
steady growth in true manhood.  His home, once a place
of poverty and misery in the city, is now a place of comfort and happiness in the town of Clarendon. His family
now welcome him, when before they often feared the
approach of his footsteps.  Without any education, he
has applied himself to study, often sticking to his books
until the small hours of the morning, and he has gained
a fair store of knowledge.  He has overcome his natural
German brogue to a great extent, and can now speak

connectedly and interestingly. He is in good demand for temperance addresses and is making and saving money. And what a change in his personal appearance. It does my heart good to look at such a man, and it sets me to wonder why other poor deluded whiskey-soaked creatures do not look at Joe Hess and learn from him the vast advantage there is in living a sober and useful life."

The above was clipped from the Albion papers and is correct, with the exception that where the writer said that I signed the pledge and then was converted, I was converted before I signed the pledge. I am working hard, but as to making money I don't know why I do receive such notice, simply because I have become meek, and trusted in the Lord; and then put my shoulder to the wheel and did some of the pushing.

At 10.30 a.m., March 25th, I left Chicago for Peoria, Ill. I was greeted there by Mr. Collins who conducted me to his house, where I was made to feel at home by the good housewife. In the afternoon the M. E. Pastor called on me and bade me welcome to the town. The meetings were held in his church, and by 7 p.m. the church was crowded. Brother Winslow, the pastor, was chairman, and after some rousing singing and prayer the writer was presented to this hungry crowd of people. After speaking for an hour the pledge was offered and 150 took it. Among these were some of the hardest drinkers, and the last I heard of them I learned they are on the rock.

Many a time we hear a man or woman say that they will not sign away their right to drink. Let me give you an incident. During my stay in Peoria, when the opportunity was given for the pledge, there could be seen a man coming forward clothed in rags, with swollen features and bleared eyes. As he approached nearer it seemed that I had seen this face but could not place it. He picked up the pen with a trembling hand and wrote the name, Dick Corbett. It was like a flash of lightning.

Memory came to my assistance and told me where I had seen the face. I jumped from the platform, and took him by the hand and said, " Dick Corbett, is that you ? " he answered " yes, all that's left of me," and now came a flood of tears. Three years before, this same man said to me, " I learn you have signed the pledge, well, I am glad you took a tumble." Said I, " Dick, you come and take a ' drop,' and sign the pledge." I received for my answer a sneer, with the remark, " I am not as weak as you." He then was nicely situated, had a good business and many admirers ; but little by little he drank more ; soon his business was neglected, and I saw no more of him until I saw him sign his name. I asked him to say a few words, which he did, and as near as I can remember I will give them to you :—He arose and said : " I rise to say to you that I came to this place looking for the policeman to give me a night's lodging. I learned that he might be found at the temperance meeting. I saw the lithographs in the window, and read the name of Joe Hess. Says I, that cannot be Joe Hess from Rochester ; I will go and see. I came and stood in that doorway, I saw it was the same Joe. I heard the men say he was a liar, that he never did go down as low as he said. I came to sign the pledge, and I did " (holding the card up). Said he, " Three years ago this same Joe asked me to sign it. I sneered at him and told him that I was not so weak ; when I see it is going to hurt me I will stop. I wish to God I had the weakness then that I have to-night ; then I had a good business and a good name. For the past three years Joe has been going up while I was going down. What is the difference to-day in our position? Just the reverse. Three years ago I was respected, honoured and admired by all, while they only talked of Joe with a sneer,—scarcely a kind word for him. To-day he is honoured, respected and admired, has a happy home while I am an outcast, degraded, debased, defrauded of my manhood by the Demon of Rum. I wish all young men

would come to-night and resolve never to touch it again.
While you go to your nice bed to-night I shall have to
abide with the boards of the station-house. Once my family
gave me the best bed in the house. I have signed the pledge,
I trust God will help me to keep it. As he stepped down,
I grasped his hand and said, " Dick, old boy, you will
not have to sleep in the jug to-night, nor to-morrow
night, not if Joe has a dollar." I gave him some money;
next morning he started for Chicago, I never heard of
him any more, he has left no trace behind him only his
words which I have treasured as near as I was able, and
have imparted them to you, reader ; may they be of some
value to you.

Friday, March 29th, I went to Chicago, to fill a call to
speak at the Y.M.C.A. at the business men's meeting at
12 p.m., which was crowded. At 3 p.m I addressed
the Young Men's Prohibition League. Returned to Peoria : as I alighted there was a mob of hoodlums at the
station who wanted me to get back on the train, but
they had figured without their host, for I did not understand that kind of language, and I did not go back, but
passed right through the bummers. That evening the
church was more crowded than any night yet. On Sunday Rev. J. J. Maily came out to help me and gave us
one of the best sermons I ever listened to, on the origin
of Christ's Kingdom.

Monday, April 1st, was the closing night, and by six
o'clock the church was packed. This night we had the
great pleasure to have with us Uriah Copp, jr. He is
the Grand Chief Templar of I. O. G. T. of Illinois, he
stayed over the next day and organized a lodge ; over
650 signed during the campaign. While there I learned
to know D. I. Christian who was mainly responsible for
my coming to Peoria. He is one of the great land
owners in that locality. At the last meeting at Peoria
the pastor handed the following document to me, which
reads :

" Bro. Joe Hess has spent the last week in this place lecturing upon temperance and drawing crowded houses each evening. His work has been very successful and we part with him with regret. It gives me great pleasure to recommend him as a christian gentleman and an earnest and successful worker in the temperance cause.

"G. W. WINSLOW,

" April 2nd, 1889.        Pastor M. E. Church, Peoria."

April 2nd I started for Chicago, put up at the Dearborn House on State-street, and found ex-Governor John P. St. John, who was glad to see me again. Said St. John, " Well, Joe, I see you are doing a good work," Handing me the *Lever* of Chicago, I read the following item :

### JOE HESS AT EVANSTON.

" 'The only and original' Joe Hess has been here. Joe is a marvel to all who hear him, to-day few men strike harder blows against the infamous liquor traffic. He holds important vantage ground from the fact that he was once a saloon-keeper and understands the inner workings of the business. Many thought that his coming to Evanston was a mistake, there are so many attractions here, and the ears of this people are so refined that it was feared he would not draw. But he has completely won the hearts of this people ; those who expected to find a rude ignoramus were agreeably surprised to find a man of good sense and native refinement. As a speaker he is graceful, eloquent and convincing. Besides being master of his subject, he possesses an unfailing fund of illustration and wit. Hundreds have signed the pledge, and many of the leading citizens gave their earnest support to the meetings, and even the churches were aroused."

After reading this I said—Thank God, if I can be the instrument in God's hand to arouse the church, for it is tenfold harder to arouse the church than the drinking man, but the drinking men will hold back until they see the churches take a stand. What shall the responsibility of the church be at the final judgment?

Here St. John said, " Joe, this is election day in Chicago, let us tramp round and see what the black-legs are doing." We started round to the polling places, and strange as it may seem, none of the ticket pillars asked us whether we came to vote. A trip round to the polling places on election day in the States will give you an idea how or who run elections; the lowest outcasts, cutthroats, thieves and prize-fighters, gamblers, rum-dealers, negroes of the most vicious kind, are the elements that peddle votes. Think of it! a good ministerial shepherd walking up to some thief and taking from his hand a ballot to represent his honest conviction as to what man is the best for the office. Is it any wonder that governments are beginning to run from the path of right when cancers and polls are controlled by such an element? Awake! christian knight, and demand that things shall be changed in the future.

April 3rd I opened the ball at Watseka, Ill., the county seat. I was received by Judge Whitehall. The ladies having a Fair in the hall that night gave me one night's rest, which was quite acceptable. The evening of April 4th the hall was well filled. The following night the hall again was well filled. The third day I learned that some of the union were sorry they had brought me. On learning this I went to their meeting at 3 p.m. and told them that I was no tramp, and that it would be impossible for Gabriel to come to Watseka and do anything as long as the union held back and found fault, and I told them that my engagement ended right there and then. The outcome was I stayed by their earnest solicitation, and that night the ice bursted and a work began that will be remembered as long as Watseka will stand. Watseka had seven saloons each paying $750 per year for license. The pastors commenced to take a hand in the fight, and now Rome did commence to howl, and the heathen did rage. Some little disturbance was threatened one night, and a policeman was to be called in, but none was to be found. Why are policemen called peelers? Because they peel out of the way when they are needed. This night I talked on personal liberty. What does it mean?

Poor fellow before the Judge: "Do you think the prisoner struck you with malice-pretense?"

Complainant: "No, Judge, he struck me with a mallet about six feet from de fence." Is it not remarkable the conception some people have of things.

April 10th.—I closed my meetings at Watseka: hundreds could not gain admission. The result of the week's work caused the seven saloons to be voted out, which makes the city of Watseka a prohibition town. The following are the papers that were handed to me at the close of the meetings:—

To whom it may concern: The bearer, Mr. Joe F. Hess has conducted a very successful temperance campaign in our city this spring. We cordially recommend him as an earnest, sincere Christian and practical worker. His ready wit holds the attention of his audience, while the pathos with which he relates his own experience often moves his audience to tears. We believe he is fitted to accomplish much good in the temperance reform, especially among those who are the victims of the drink habit, as he himself has been. Signed by the pastors of the city, E. P. More, Pastor Presbyterian Church; W. H. Kerr, Pastor Christian Church; C. F. Cullom, Pastor M. E. Church.

Along with this was also one handed to me from Judge Alex. L. Whitehall. To whom it may concern: Joseph F. Hess, the bearer, for one week has laboured in our city as an advocate of temperance, and I have been an interested listener, having been all my life a total abstainer, in the strictest sense, and I do not hesitate to say that

Mr. Hess has done a good work for us in this city, just on the eve of our city elections. He is a forcible talker, and readily wins the confidence and applause of the labouring men, and parties who most need labouring with, and because of his honest, earnest way of putting things, makes himself solid with every man or woman who has the love of humanity at heart. Very respectfully, Alex. L. Whitehall, Watseka, Ill.

How different is the feeling with the people when the work is done. I sometimes think the temperance people are like the omnibus man. When he is full of drink he thinks there is just room for one more. So with a man who at first arrives in town to talk temperance. When he is ready to go, then the people feel there is not one who could do more than he did. It puts me in mind of the little fellow wanting to know what the three balls hung outside of the store for.

Bobby—" Pa, what does the pawnbroker's sign of three balls mean ? "  Pa—" It means, Bobby, that it is two to one that the man never redeems his property."

So with public speakers ; you may use them as well as you can, but the impression you leave upon them on their arrival will stick, and when they go away, it is two to one they never return.

I took the midnight train for home, arriving there on April 12th, 6 p.m. ; found all as well as usual, and as I threw $256 on the table, all were delighted. This was paid on the home.

The 13th day of April, 1889, I was happy beyond expression. What was the cause of my happiness ? I took my bank book—say, drinker, have you a bank book ? if you have not, why not ?—and went to the bank : drew out $260 to pay the principal on my home, not on the saloon keeper's home, not to pay the principal on the brewery men's building, but my home ; how nice that sounds, " my home."

Sunday, April 14th, 1889, I spent at home, the first Sabbath for a long time. This day we had Pastor Milleman with us for dinner. I can remember when I would not allow a preacher in my house, much less to take dinner, and perhaps if he would have come he would be compelled to go away without anything to eat, because, may be, there would not be anything to put between his teeth, all because money went for whisky.

Monday, April 22nd.—I spoke in Rescue Mission, on Front-street, in the City of Rochester, and took the 11.50 night train for Waterbury, Conn. I arrived at Waterbury 4.50 p.m. Mr. E. G. Frazier and Mr. Thompson were at the station to greet me. Frazier was a reformed man. I held meetings here for eight days.

April 29th I made a pledge that I would draw nearer to God, and I did, and prosper better. The nearer we get to God the farther we come away from sin. During my stay in Waterbury I became acquainted with a family that drink separated. The husband signed. I tried all I knew how to bring this family together again, but all to no avail. Wives often drive their husbands to drink, and this one that I speak of was one of this kind. Many a woman drives the husband away because she has no kind word for him, not a smile, neither any sympathy.

May 2nd I arrived home at Clarendon, N.Y., and then proceeded to Mount Morris to speak for one day. The local press had the following notice next day:

"Joe F. Hess, of Rochester, delivered a temperance lecture in the Baptist Church, Saturday evening, and on Sunday afternoon and evening at Livingstone Hall. At the Sunday evening meeting the hall was filled, not even standing room to accommodate all, and many were unable to obtain admission. Subject: ' A saloon keeper's experience.' His address was eloquent, and will leave a lasting impression on his hearers."

While labouring at a place called Tuscarora, N.Y., the press gave the following account of the work :

"Joseph Hess, the Gospel Temperance evangelist, has been labouring in this town. Although the weather has been unfavourable, yet the Presbyterian Church has been filled and the greatest enthusiasm prevailed; nearly 350 have signed the pledge."

Returned home May 4th; then to Buffalo to see dear old mother; then returned to Clarendon and rested until the 8th day of May, when I started for the Amendment campaign, which was then the contest in the Key Stone State, Pennsylvania. I was to begin my labours under the auspices of the Tioga Amendment Committee, at Blossburg, where I had laboured the fall of 1888.

Into this Amendment Campaign I threw myself with all the energy I possessed, speaking nightly at many different points in the State. The result, so far as the voting is concerned, is to-day a matter of history; 150,-000 of a majority was recorded against the Amendment. How this majority was obtained was well understood by the friends of temperance at the time. All their impressions of the fraudulent means adopted have since been confirmed by the clever exposure in the New York *Voice*, in the working up of which my warm and able friend, Col. R. S. Cheves, took a leading part.

# CHAPTER XXII

An invitation to take Canada—Starts for London—Feeb'e hands and weak knees—Clifton and Nia ara Falls—A hod-carrier in St. Catharines—Work in London—Testimony for anti-Scott Act men—Chased home with boils and grippe—Miss Cleveland's eloquent reply to Dr. Howard Crosby.

"All hands shall be feeble. and all knees shall be weak as water."—Ezekiel, chap. vii. 17th verse.

THIS was the verse that we read for our scripture lesson at the family altar, on the morning of the first day of the New Year, one thousand eight hundred and ninety. While we were rejoicing and revering the year that had just passed into eternity, we beheld the many blessings that the Almighty had showered upon us as a family during that time, and a silent prayer went up on high.

The new year was entered into with a resolve to do even more for the Master's cause, in lifting up fallen humanity from the shame and degradation into which so many have fallen through strong drink and vices of the devil.

At 12 a.m. my son Henry brought the mail, and amongst fourteen letters I found one from Brother Thomas Lawless, Grand Secretary of the Grand Lodge of Good Templars of Canada. His letter informed me that I was to begin my labours in the interest of the Order at London, Ontario.

This agreement was entered into some months before, and now came the time when the work should begin. It was at this time that the above verse was applicable to me, for my hands began to feel very feeble, and my knees began to get weak. The reason was this: I had been known at one time in London as a fighter for the devil, and usually when we labour for his Master Satanic there is left a trail behind which is not of the purest kind, neither the most honest.

Satan whispered, "I would not go to London," and, like Eve, he nearly had me persuaded to obey him; but at this opportune moment God's voice rang within me: "Hearken not unto him, but go as I command thee," and I determined to go. But again the tempter came, and held up to me that now I had a reputation, why would I cast it from me? Said the devil, "There is plenty of work for you to do in your own land—why go to Canada?" and almost he had conquered; but a voice again rang out, "Lo, I will be with you always unto the end."

On the sixth of January, 1890, I started for London, Canada. I was obliged through a delay in the train to spend some time at Clifton, and was struck with the beauty of the place. Clifton is situated on the Canadian side of Niagara Falls, and directly opposite Suspension Bridge. About 500 yards down the river is the great American whirlpool. It was in these waters that Captain Webb lost his life, like many others who have been foolish and venturesome enough to undertake this perilous trip all for nothing else but notoriety. You may say: Have all who undertook this trip lost their life? I answer, No; the man with the barrel passed through the stream three times, twice by himself, and once a reckless young lady, who was seeking notoriety, accompanied him; but she did it only once. The barrel gave her some hard raps on the elbow, in other words called the funny bone; this bone was nearly knocked silly, if the young damsel was not. She said that all the money the United States was worth would not induce her to try it again.

On the other side of Clifton is to be seen what is known as Horseshoe Falls; this name is given because the rock is so worn off in the centre that it resembles the form of a horseshoe. Clifton also has some fine summer hotels, and many other attractions too numerous for me to mention.

We soon were rolling over towards London. The first stop was Thorold; this place has several mills, amongst them a large paper mill, in which the writer was employed some 17 years ago. He soon lost his situation, because of the cup of damning poison, strong drink. How many have passed through this same ordeal, losing their employment because of drunkenness.

Again we hear the whistle blow, and the brakeman sings out "St. Catharines!" This is a beautiful city, situated on the banks of the Welland canal. It was in this city that the writer labored as a hod-carrier, and also worked in a wheel factory, but the curse of rum robbed him also of this employment, and in the middle of winter, between the small hours of four and five a.m., 17 years ago, there could be seen a man toiling with several boxes which acted as trunks, dragging them toward the depot, followed by his wife and two small children, to take the early train for Hamilton, leaving behind a debt of $8.00 for rent.

How came this debt? The liquor man had to have his rent paid, consequently mine had to go unpaid, because my money went to pay the rent of the man who sold me damnation.

"All aboard!" shouts the voice of the conductor, and the train moves forward again, over a beautiful landscape. On our way we pass Grimsby Camp Ground, a pleasant summer resort. We finally reached Hamilton. There, like the rest of the places, queer recollections came to me. It was in this city that I had landed years before with two children and a wife, with about 60 cents in my pocket. In this city I bought one dollar's worth of cuttings and borrowed a grocer's sausage grinder, and I ground my meat fine, and the next day I started to peddle sausages. I prospered in this business, but soon beer, whiskey and politics got the upper hand.

These were my sad reflections. We again moved forward towards London, but were delayed on the road on account of the heavy snow-storm, arriving a little late at London. As I jumped from the train on to the depot platform a little man stepped up to me and said: "Is this Brother Hess?" To which I replied: "Yes." Said he: "My name is E. S. Cummer; I live in Toronto, but have travelled ahead of you for the past ten days, making arrangements for dates." He conducted me to the Grigg House. After partaking of refreshments, I was informed that I was to speak at the East London Methodist Church. At the church I found seven people. The storm raged in all its fury, and I was not surprised to find so few at the church. It was finally decided that we postpone the meeting, and go and hear the Evangelists Hunter and Crossley, which we did, at the Queen-street Methodist Church, which place was fairly well filled. The reason for this was not so much the storm, but the la grippe had everybody down; hundreds were called home to their last resting place by the grippe. I organized a lodge within six miles of London the next night, then spoke at several other appointments. At one of the places a man came up to me after the meeting. Said he: "Mr. Hess, I was one of those cowards that you spoke about, who worked for the repeal of the Scott Act. I thought that. if the town had a hotel it would be the making of the town. I was under the impression that property would go up in price, and I might sell my lots, so this right arm cast a ballot for the repeal. The law was repealed, the hotel was opened with great pomp, and thirteen kegs of beer were consumed that night; a part of this went into the stomach of my seventeen-year-old boy. In the morning the boy did not come down to breakfast. I went up to his room; at the door I halted, fears came over me when I heard his loud sleeping. Can it be that this my boy came home drunk? No, I could not believe it. Finally I turned the knob, again I halted for a moment.  At last, wild with fear, I pushed the door open, and, oh, what a sight," and here the old man had to stop, because of the tears that had rushed from his eyes, "there lay my boy, dressed as he came in at night, his legs on the bed, his head hanging over the other side of the bed, and, oh, what a sight was on the floor.  I called for help, and placed him on the bed. During this time he opened his eyes.  Calling him by name, I pointed to what he had done on the floor. 'Oh,' said he, with a demon's laugh, 'father, I did not do that.'  Said I, who did it, then?  Listen to the answer he gave me: 'Your vote did that, father.'  I rushed from the room ; this truth was the strongest lecture I received in my life. "Oh," said he, "this arm I could cut off; could I have the power to wipe out all the hells that entice and drag down the young boys by drink." Here the old man again wept. I ventured to inquire as to where his boy was. "God knows," said he, "This I know, he is not a sober man, nothing but a drunkard, my vote did it." What does his mother say ?  The old man again broke down, and pointing in a northerly direction, he said : "She lies over there, heart-broken.  My vote did it. all."

Dear reader, such distress as that is enough to move a heart of stone.  How many fathers are guilty of sending their boys down to a drunkard's grave by their vote; they did it.  How many mothers' hearts are made sad by the man's vote, who at the altar vowed that he would protect her, and do for her what he could to make her happy, and yet these same men have become hardened to the appeals of their wives, the mothers of their children. So hardened have they become, that sooner than let the party go, they will help to establish institutions that will drag down their boys.

I laboured just two weeks in London, when the devil sent me a lot of "Job's comforters," in the shape of boils. On my way home the grippe got me, and to say I was a sick man is expressing it very mild.

I reached home, and I had a very hard time of it.
Every time one of Job's partners would leave me, another
one would come and board with me for a week or ten
days. I had twenty-two of these fellows pay me a visit,
but at last the family died out, and I was pleased to see
the last one kick his last kick.

After this I gave several talks in my neighbourhood,
then turned loose upon my study for ten days, and by
hard work replenished my head with useful knowledge.
During this time I received many letters from mothers
who have suffered from the demon drink. Some of these
were most heartrending."

*    *    *    *    *    *

"I do not wonder that excellent women, whose husbands
or sons have become sots, should advocate total abstinence for every one. I have heard of a good woman
whose boy had cut his finger nearly off with a knife, wish
that there were no knives in the world, and if she could
have her way, she would have them all destroyed forth-
with. It is natural, and a woman's cry on such an occasion excites our tenderest sympathy. But who will consider that an argument."

The above paragraph from "A Calm View of Dr. Nel-
son," by Rev. Howard Crosby, D.D., in the *Evangelist* of
March 17, has most pertinaciously haunted me ever since
the perusal of the article last evening. "That this,
above any other paragraph, should most impress itself
upon the impressible mind of one emotional woman in
particular, or of woman as an emotional creature in general, will surprise no man. It is, as the doctor says, natural; and I am certain that multitudes of women besides
myself are to-day smarting under these 'calm' words,
against the imputation of which every fibre of the woman
nature rises up in revolt. The male animal is very fierce.
The female of all genera is comparatively and in general
non-combative. But the same science which tells us this
tells us also that the mother, among all beasts, in defence

of her young, is the fiercest of living creatures.  The
lioness, under ordinary circumstances, is easy of conquest;
but a lioness robbed of her whelps no man or beast cares
to encounter.  Both these phases of the female nature
are undoubtedly natural. 'They belong,' as Bishop Butler
said of certain so-called supernatural phenomena, 'to the
natural, of which there are two courses,' the one ordinary
the other not supernatural, still less superhuman, but ex-
traordinary.

"You see, Mrs. Foster, that this 'mad-dog' you talk
about is to be put, by a calm view of the thing as it is,
into the same category with cutlery.  You have no more
real right to 'cry' about this unloosed beast because it
may meet your children on the way to school, and may
bite one or two of them, than you have to cry out against
the manufacture and sale of knives, because your boy
cut himself once.  The perfectly clear thing is, if you only
had head enough to see it, that the manufacture (by fer-
mentation, not distillation), of the mad-dog (not very
mad, but only some mad) ought to go on, and that one
mad-dog (of this good kind) for every one thousand people ought to be protected by law from the bullets of hy-
drophobia-haters.

"This calm view of 'the evil' which—because of some,
in fact several, cases of hydrophobia among us, has come
to be called by unthinking people, 'a mad-dog,' is proven
by concurrent testimony of experience, science, scholar-
ship, sound philosophy, and, above all, rightly-read Scripture, to be a good creature of God. The calmly Christian
thing for you to do, 'on such an occasion' is not to go up
and down 'crying,' but to stay at home, and teach your
little boys and big boys how a little mad-dog's bite is
good for them, but a big mad-dog's bite is very bad for
them.

"You ought, if you would only do the thing you ought—
instead of the thing you like—to mix up a little wine
and water for your little boys at dinner, so that they may

early learn the difference between true temperance and this miserable parody on true temperance called 'total abstinence,' and may be prepared to make a manly protest against drunkenness when they shall be grown up. It is simply silly—yes, while we feel the tenderest sympathy for your sorrow, we must say it is silly for you to refuse to see that knives and mad-dogs are especially dangerous. It is as ridiculous for you to demand that all alcohol shall be banished from the beverages of mankind because this fiery liquor is burning out the manhood (in more ways than by its consumption, of the world) as it would be for you to demand that all the wells should be dried up because men lose their lives by drowning! Alcohol and water are so exactly analogous, if you could but see it, you foolish woman! Your cry is no argument; it were better you would stop your crying.

"Dr. Crosby, we cannot; try we ever so hard. We cannot defy or deny nature. God has made us a crying genus. We cannot understand why a mad-dog should not be killed. We cannot understand how knives and mad-dogs are just alike. We cannot help crying if only one to every one thousand human beings is let loose in our streets. These things are too high for us; we cannot find them out. It is not our blame, it is our nature, and we dare to say that through the pure and unsophisticated nature of the human mother God's argument against any use of alcohol, save as a medicine, is given to the world to-day.

"When the young Queen of Austria, pressed on every side, by the ruthless oppression of the great Prussian King, fled trembling into Hungary, and with her infant in her arms, her royal crown upon her head, appealed for the protection of her kingdom to her loyal subjects there, those stalwart Hungarian nobles rose in a mass, and laying their hands upon their swords at their sides, swore in a shout whose heroic ring echoes down the years:— '*Moriamur pro rege nostro*, Maria Theresa!' And how they did die all the world knows.

" It is not for rhetorical effect, still less for the excitation of 'tenderest sympathy' that I revert to this well-known historical incident. It is that I may call attention to the argument in the cry of those men—for I suppose a man's cry 'may be counted as an argument.' I wish to beg you to notice those words, *rege nostro*, that expression of those Hungarian nobles—our King Maria Theresa, instead of our Queen Maria Theresa, has been interpreted to represent an idea in their minds to suit the mind of the interpreter. 'Woman's Rights,' speakers have made them an acknowledgment on the part of those most masculine men, that here was a woman who was more man than any one of them, or altogether, *i.e.*, more able to command them, by having more that was kingly in her.

" Hence, *pro rege nostro*, than *pro rege regina nostro*. Chivalrous knights-errant of our day make this expression to indicate the most refined and splendid chivalry in those Hungarian nobles, as if they had said to this threatened and trembling mother, clasping the future king in her arms, 'Never mind, now! You shall be just as much sovereign as if you were a king yourself. We will die to make it so, *pro rege nostro*.'

" Now, I make this expression to mean neither of these things. I believe that these strong and straightforward warriors roared out these words as the simplest usage to express their most instant and impulsive expression for all that men as patriots should die for. I believe that this crowned mother stood to them as the representative of their nationality, their rights, their honour, summing up in her person, as did the ruling sovereign of those days, their country and their country's cause. They formulated in their expression, *rege nostro*, the sentiment which Louis XIV. taught in the words, *L'etat c'est moi !* They proved this, for they did fight, and many of them did die, and men do not deliberately die for a beautiful, weeping woman, though they love to swear to that effect some-

times, unless there be some worthier object to be gained
by their self-devotion. But whether my idea of this be
fanciful or not; whether it be calm and logical; whether
it be good criticism, I dare not affirm, Dr. Crosby will
know. But I dare affirm that the American mother, who
to day being pressed on every side by the aggression of
King Alcohol, confronts American men, the infant in her
arm her only sceptre, the motherhood upon her brow her
only crown, and cries to them for protection of her kingdom—the home—carries in her cry an argument. And I
dare affirm, for, thank God, it is a spectacle all may witness, that stalwart warriors pulling from their scabbards
trusty swords admit that cry to be an argument, by their
answering shout, 'We will fight for our king!' For
we all have a king, even doctors. There is a majesty of
right, a royalty of truth, which in manifold forms claims
our allegiance, and argues its claim. God sees in the tear-
ful cry of the bruised and baffled mother, sister, wife,
His own argument for the utter extinction of intoxicating beverages, the suppression, root and branch, of the
liquor traffic. And in that cry He makes his argument
to men.

" A chancellor's philosophy, grasping in its mighty sapi-
ence cults and sciences which we poor women cannot even
name, has as yet failed to apprehend that chemistry of
Heaven which distils from a Christian mother's tear the
first drop of that mighty gathering storm, whose full and
final outbreak shall sweep away for ever all refuges of
lies which, sincere or insincere, bulwark the liquor traffic.

"And the children of Israel sighed by reason of bond-
age, and they came up unto God, and God heard their
groaning, and God remembered His covenant ; and God
looked upon the children of Israel, and had respect unto
them."

*      *      *      *      *      *

Dear reader, the above came into my hands, and I was
so impressed with it that I thought it ought to be read

by thousands, and may it strike all with the force it struck me.   The above is a reply argument to Mrs. Ellen J. Foster, of Iowa, and Rev. Howard Crosby, D.D., by Elizabeth Cleveland, of New York.   May it have the effect upon the women and thoughtful fathers throughout our American land that it is destined to have.

"Be ye strong in the Lord."

# CHAPTER XXIII.

Temperance campaign in Toronto—Enters the work with many
doubts—Reception by officers Canadian Temperance League—
Preaches in Carlton-street Methodist Church —The opening
meeting in the Pavilion—Afternoon Bible readings—Witnesses
some sad scenes—Wedding anniversary and presentation—At
H. C. Dixon's free breakfast—The Lombard-street Mission—
A captivating chapter.


' The light of the body is the eye ; if therefore thine eye be single, thy
whole body shall be full of light."

THROUGH acts of the body we make known to the
world that the eye is single, hence the body is full
of light, and becomes a light to those who are in darkness.

Feb. 9th, 1890.—I was to open a week's campaign in
the city of Toronto, under the now well-known and vigorous organization known as the Canadian Temperance
League.

I had a great many misgivings about going there. It
was in Toronto that I led one of the most reckless lives
that a man can lead. Through drink, I was led into all
sorts of vices. There it was that my family nearly starved
to death, while I was away living a shiftless life. There
was no light of singleness in my eye, hence there could
not be any light in my body, debauching and drinking all
night, then come home and curse and fight the family.
Every time when I think of this my hate for the demon
rum grows stronger and more fierce.

After a consultation with my wife, it was decided I
should go back to the city from which I came away a degraded man, and so I wrote to Brother J. S. Robertson
that I would leave home for Toronto on Saturday, the
8th February.

I have not words to express my feelings on the train going towards the city of Toronto. At Hamilton I wanted to turn back, but something compelled me to go on. I cannot tell you what it was. At last we steamed into the Union Station, and as I alighted from the train Mr. H. M. Graham and J. S. Robertson grasped my hand and gave it a shake that shook me up so that even now, though it is over six months since, I am not yet settled down.

That kind of shaking does a man untold good. I was conducted to the carriage, and then driven to the beautiful residence of H. M. Graham, No. 4 North-street, where I was given a warm welcome by Mrs. Graham, who was now to be mine hostess for a time to come; how long at that time I did not know. I was conducted to my room. While preparing my toilet, before making my appearance for dinner, I sat down in the chair and pinched my legs to see whether I was awake or whether all this was a dream. I soon stopped pinching, and I found it was a reality. I was awake and in the house of a Christian gentleman.

The bell rang, and I quickly threw the hair brush on one side of the bed, the comb on the other side, pulled down my vest, straightened out my coat, and away I went. At the foot of the stairway I was conducted by mine hostess into the drawing room, and presented to one of Toronto's witty Irishmen, Mr. J. N. McKendry, a leading dry goods merchant. I was presented to Mr. G. B. Sweetnam, representing the Toronto Post Office Department. After dinner it was suggested to take a visit to the newly-established coffee house of the League. This place is located in St. John's Ward, in a locality where the downtrodden assemble. Here we were treated to coffee, which we took as a sample, and which was pronounced fit for a king or queen's table. We next paid a visit to the Y. M. C. A. building, which is an honour to the city. Promenading for another hour, we arrived again at the residence of Mr. Graham.

I was informed that I was to speak the next morning at Carlton-street Methodist Church. This completely upset me, as I had not come prepared to do anything of the kind. I prayed over it, went to sleep, and next morning I was wide awake. After talking with God for a time I made my toilet, then prepared to think what it was I should talk about. I knew that this church was composed mostly of fine people, highly educated, and this knowledge in itself was enough to upset me.

At ten o'clock Brother Graham started with me for church, where I was presented to Rev. Dr. Hunter, the pastor of the church. I asked him to let me off, but he would not, so what could I do but talk. As we mounted the pulpit, strange thoughts coursed through my head. Years before I acted as coachman for the leading man in this church, Mr. R. Walker, of the "Golden Lion," the same whose carriage was destroyed during one of my debauches, but he was now dead. I cast my eyes round the audience; there directly in front of me sat the son of Mr. Walker, Joseph Walker, there to my right was Robert Cheyne and wife, the nephew of R. Walker. All these persons knew me as Walker's coachman. What a change had taken place in so few years. Once the coachman being talked to, now the coachman talking to the people to better their ways. But the knowledge of all this almost drove me wild, and while sitting awaiting the time to speak, I was deaf to the singing or music. Not until I heard my name mentioned did I comprehend where I was. When I did arise, everything seemed to me one face. I spoke from the words " Come unto Me all ye that are weak and heavy laden, and I will give you rest," and when I had read these words every fear vanished. and I opened my mouth and the Lord filled it. At the close of the meeting most of those that knew me came and bade me God-speed in my work. After dinner I started for the place of conquest, where the battle was to begin for right against wrong.

The *Canada Citizen* had the following report on Feb. 15th, 1890 : " The Canadian Temperance League have inaugurated a series of temperance revival meetings. The first of these was held in the Horticultural Pavilion on Sunday last at 3 p.m.  At the opening meeting on Sunday the Pavilion was crowded to the doors.  The chair was occupied by Mr. J. N. McKendry, and a special service of song was conducted by the choir of Emanuel Baptist Church, led by Mr. R. J. Hall.  The speaker from the commencement of his address gained the sympathy and interest of his audience.  He referred to the splendid reception that had been given to him on his return to the city where he had spent years in dissipation.  He had been advertised as a prize-fighter ; it is true that this was his former profession, for every man who goes around the saloon  has got to be at some time or other a prize-fighter or a rough-and-tumble fighter.  An aggressive warfare against the liquor traffic has to be carried on, and the speaker as a prize-fighter said he would punch the devil rum right between the eyes every time. He had entered the ring to fight it out, as General Grant had said, on this line to a finish until the battle was won.  Lots of people never cease to pray for the temperance cause, but do little work."

The Pavilion was packed. I am told it will seat 2,000. I rose from my chair, my knees were weak, and I did not know how to open my mouth.  As I looked over the sea of faces, then back to the years when I left the city, a miserable vagabond caused by rum, dear reader you can yourself see the contrast.  At the close of my meeting, all who knew me in my former life, boys with whom I used to get on drunks—these welcomed me back, and all were glad to see me.  Over 100 signed the pledge on the first afternoon.  The ice was broken, and the first bombardment had begun.  Walking back to the residence of Brother Graham, a sharp wind prevailed, and I contracted a severe cold, which was a great drawback to me all through my meetings. After supper, amidst a severe snow storm, I was again conducted to Shaftesbury Hall, Queen-st., and on our way down I remarked that I did not think there would be many out, on account of the storm, but on arriving hundreds were leaving the place, as the hall was crowded all the way down the stairway. It took fifteen minutes to crowd my way to the stage, so densely was the hall packed.

Again I will make reference to the article that the *Citizen* had published: "On Sunday evening he preached in Shaftesbury Hall, in connection with the Rev. Mr. Wilkinson's, "The People's Tabernacle.' The place was packed to the doors. Mr. Hess gave a powerful gospel address from the words in 6th Galatians, ' Be not deceived, God is not mocked, whatsoever a man soweth that shall he also reap.' " Over one hundred signed at the evening meeting. Every night the hall was packed to the doors, and oh ! after the talking was done, and the pledge-signing was begun, then the work of rum could be seen, as both men and women came forward upon whom the rum master had tried his damnable work. Oh, the faces that came forward haunt me to this day. Yet there was still more of the terrible work to be seen at the *Citizen* parlors every afternoon, where I held Bible meetings. There some men came in, from whose back rum had often taken the shirt. Think, dear reader, if your body was to be found in such a condition, would you then take a decided stand ? Answer yes. One afternoon there came to the rooms a poor forlorn creature, who had no socks, no shoes, nothing but a pair of rubbers, which stuck to his feet. Oh what a sight ! At this opportune moment I wished there had come some legislator who had signed or voted for a higher revenue from this curse  The higher revenue takes the clothes of the men as well as the low revenue. These Bible meetings were a great help to many. One afternoon a young man about 24 years of age, well dressed, came into the meeting hanging on the arm of another young man.  When the request was made that those who wished to lead a better life and desired the prayers of the people, should make it known by raising the hand, this young man was the first to raise his, and 17 more followed.  Oh, how I wished that the preachers had been present and seen this pleasing sight.  But no, they were absent.  After the meeting I requested that all who had made a start should remain, as I wanted to enquire into their condition.  What was my surprise to find that this well dressed young man was blind, the cause I learned from his own lips was strong drink.  He was a reckless youth, the poison acted upon the nerve in the eye, which caused him to lose his sight.  Think twice young man before you raise the poison to your lips.

I turned my attention to some of the rest, and soon learned that the first kind of religion I must talk to these men and women would be a very practical kind.  I must see that their inner man was provided for, second that the body should receive the necessary clothing.  I appealed to the people at my evening meeting,and the next day many a bundle of clothing came in, and many hearts were made glad because of the warm covering over their body, many a " God bless you " came to my ears.  Oh, man's glory is his labor, but how great that glory if the labor is performed in the Lord's services.

The next Sunday I was to hold another mass meeting at the Pavilion when Mrs. Hess and the children were to be present.  Yes, she was to return to her old place where she had suffered so much, and receive her reward by seeing how the Lord was prospering her husband.

The League sent for the family, and when the hour came Sunday afternoon for the doors to be opened, hundreds of people were covering the gardens waiting for the doors to open.  When they were opened the great hall was packed in less than half an hour, 500 men actually climbed on the roof of the building and sliding the large windows back they peered down. The children captured the audience with their delightful singing. As Mamie, who was born in Toronto, and during her childhood as a baby had been robbed of her papa's love, finished reciting " Only a drunkard's child," there was hardly a dry eye in that vast audience.

The meetings were again continued during the week at Shaftesbury Hall with crowds and new faces, increasing until Thursday night, when I could scarcely speak because of the cold I had contracted. The next day was Saturday, and in the evening we were detained by Mr. James, at his residence, where we had supper, and in talking the time had passed away so quickly that when I looked at my watch I discovered that it was eight o'clock and two miles or nearly that away from the hall. All haste was now made, and arriving at the hall I found it packed to suffocation, and for reasons then unknown to me it was beautifully decorated. Cheers greeted our entrance. After some music and singing I began my speech. I referred to the fact that the date marked the 20th Anniversary of our wedding, which remark brought forth long applause. At the close of my address Mr. J. S. Robertson stepped to the front and said, " Mr. Hess, before you take your seat I want a word with you," whereupon he read the following address.

Toronto, 22nd February, 1890.

Joseph F. Hess, Esq.

Dear Brother,—On this the 20th Anniversary of your wedding-day, the members of the Canadian Temperance League, under whose auspices you are now laboring in this city, take this opportunity of expressing their appreciation of your services in the noble cause of total abstinence, to which you are now devoting your time, talents, and energies.

Those who have met you in personal intercourse have learned to love and esteem you for your many sterling qualities of head and heart. As an organization we have been delighted with the success that has attended your efforts, whilst laboring under our auspices, the result of a two weeks' campaign showing fifteen hundred signatures to the total abstinence pledge.

It has been a matter of gratification to those who have been laboring with you to know that many have been so impressed with your presentation of Gospel Temperance that they have not only signed the pledge of total abstinence from intoxicating liquors, but have been led to start on a christian life.

We have also been pleased to meet with your dear wife and children, and on behalf of the members of the League and their friends we would ask Mrs. Hess to accept this purse (here Bro. C. E. Smith, Treasurer, handed her the purse), and contents as a small token of their appreciation and esteem, and also as a testimony of their confidence in your prohibition principles and christian integrity.

Wishing you both many happy returns of the day, we beg to subscribe ourselves on behalf of the Canadian Temperance League, J. S. Robertson, Chairman Gospel Temperance Platform Work ; J. M. Depew, Chairman Temperance Service of Song; G. S. Youle, Chairman Temperance Missionary Work ; H. M. Graham, Chairman Temperance Education among the members of the League ; J. N. McKendry, Chairman Coffee Houses and Coffee Stands ; Thomas Bengough, Chairman Temperance Literature ; S. J. Coombes, Secretary; C. E. Smith, Treasurer.

It was impossible for me to make any reply at this time. This was a bright Saturday night ; how different it was from my former annual wedding days.

Sunday afternoon the Pavilion was again crowded. This time we had with us on the platform Walter Thomas Mills, the little giant Prohibition orator and editor of the

JOSEPH F. HESS AND FAMILY.

*Chicago Statesman,* and a number of delegates to the National Law and Order League, then meeting. It was requested that I repeat the story of my "Three Chums."

During all the time of the series of meetings there was a young man who attended every meeting and who claimed to be an infidel; I reasoned with him on every point, but to no purpose. After I had left Toronto he was haunted night and day, and at last gave up his heart to God.

The meetings during part of my stay in Toronto were held in the different churches. The most costly and refined opened their doors to these meetings ; but had they stood by at the beginning of the war against whiskey, more effective work could have been accomplished. I would like to give the names of the many people who took part in my meetings during the week, but I confess that my memory is too short at this point, so will say, may God bless all the workers.

During my stay I spoke at the free breakfast conducted under the supervision of H. C. Dixon, Esq. My readers may not be familiar with this phase of Christ's work. Here is practical Christianity. Every Sunday morning, scores of men made in the image of God, who have been destroyed by Satan, are given a free breakfast at Richmond-street West. From two hundred to four hundred, men, women, and children, come there on Sunday morning, and get their meals, because the Devil's strong drink has taken from them the money they should use in buying bread.

The first time I stood before these men, degraded and debased, with bloated faces, bleared and sunken eyes, ragged and dirty clothes, I the more fully realized the work of Alcohol. The condition of these people was beyond description. All these were some father's and mother's boys and girls at one time, who when young made the homes resound with their merry laughter; but now, oh! oh! Fathers, you have the power to save, not only your boy, but some one else's boy, from such a condition in the future by taking a firm stand against the rotten political machines who bow low at the feet of the liquor oligarchy, and sell their birthright for a drink of poison.

When I began my talk with these men I knew I would accomplish more by using the phrases and terms that they used in their ranks. I told them that when I was working for the devil, during the week, on Sunday I had to go and get a "hand-out," but which was not always so cheerfully given as was theirs on this morning; instead of the "hand-out" often I would get the "kick-out." At this they all had a good laugh, and at once they came closer to me. Many at the close promised to do better, and lead different lives.

Have also spoken on Stanley Street, now called Lombard Street, in a basement there. Some of the young people of the Metropolitan Methodist Church were holding and conducting a mission every Thursday and Sunday night, under the superintendence of Mr. B. G. Bull, a prominent barrister. I have spoken to many low and degraded people, but at this place I found them worse. The first time I appeared to these human wrecks a young man came up, and pulling a flask from his pocket, half-filled with whiskey, faced the people and said, he had drank his last drink, and at the same time smashed his bottle on the floor into a thousand pieces, then turned and signed the pledge. What a victory! and when I last heard from the young man he was still a sober, upright man.

I also spoke, by request, at Christie's Biscuit Factory, where prayer meetings among the employés are held at the dinner hour. The employés sat on boxes and barrels, and some on the floor, and listened very attentively.

I spoke one night in connection with Massey's extensive Agricultural Works. It was here that I met one of my old companions whom I had known when a boy, but drink had done its work with him as well as with me. Misery and shame are left behind in the trail where strong drink marches.

The newspapers of the city one morning had a heading on one of their pages: "He paid the penalty; Kane hung." This man, Kane, came home one night during January drunk, and getting into a quarrel with his wife, he became so enraged that he killed her. Then lying down on the lounge he fell asleep. Waking in the morning he saw what he had done. There lay his wife on the floor with her head in the wash basin, the basin half-full of blood. Going out he called in a neighbour, and showing him the corpse, said he: " See what whiskey will do." For this crime he paid his life. Who was responsible; the saloon keeper or Kane? Both; but the greater responsibility belongs to the city or nation that permits the establishment of this infernal institution known as the Brewery, Distillery, Saloon, for the sake of the revenue they derive from them. Let us legislate so as not to make people commit crime.

As a result of a little over three weeks' work in the city, some 2,700 signed the pledge, and about 200 that I know gave their hearts to God. True, some have gone back to their cups, but if only one has been saved, it has paid to hold the meetings. Glory be to God for all the work that was done.

A little about the city of Toronto. It is the Queen City of the Dominion. It is built more on the American plan than any other city in the Dominion. Its people are more Americanized; its population is about 190,000. It has many large factories and shops. It is now building a costly Parliament buildings for the Province. Many very fine buildings have been erected within the past few years, and others are in course of erection. But what makes Toronto a beautiful city? It is the only large city in America that can stand up and say it has but 150 legalized saloons existing in its midst. From Saturday, at 7 p.m., until Monday, 7 a.m., no rum shop is open. True, there may be some that keep the back doors open, but these are few. No street cars run on the Sabbath day; no hacks on the stand; no newspapers published on Sundays. It is truly a day of rest for all. This kind of thing exists in every town throughout the Province. Here is an example. Let the large cities do right, and the small ones will follow suit. Let the fathers of our country take a right stand upon all great moral questions, and the boys will follow. We are the models after which our posterity will be modelled. God give us more Torontos in the United States.

### " RIMES FOR THE TIMES."

There is a little public-house
  Which every one may close ;
It is the little public-house
  Just underneath the nose.
    *        *        *        *
The price each day of a single beer
  Will pay insurance through the year;
And one cigar a day less
  Insures your life and happiness.

# CHAPTER XXIV.

At home for a few days—Talks at Niagara Falls—Origin of the
famous " Palace " illustration—At West Toronto Junction—
Wonderful record at Peterboro'—The Dun-Hess slander suit
—A week at Bowmanville—The town badly shaken up—Incidents of the work—Goes to London—" Yes, that's John
Brooks "—Pays his old debts—1,000 pledge-signers—Sunday
spent in Toronto.

" For me to live is Christ, and to die is gain."—Phill. 1st chap., 21st
verse.

THESE are precious words.  To clearly know and understand them means to have Christ in you.  These
words were mine on the day of my departure from the
city of Toronto to a new field of labour.

March 3rd.—I started for home for one week's rest.
March 4th, I held forth at Rochester, N.Y.; the 6th at
Buffalo and Niagara Falls.  My friend, P. A. Burdick,
was holding a campaign at the latter place, and I had the
opportunity of speaking at one of his meetings.  As I
was going to the meeting I passed saloon after saloon.
Among others there was one which had a brilliant sign
in the shape of gas-lighted letters, and I read the word
" Palace."  I used this word at the meeting that night,
while the proprietor was in the hall ; there it was I first
used the word that has brought me into trouble.

March 7th.—I came back to Toronto and learned that I
was to speak that night at West Toronto Junction, which I
did to a large and interested audience.  Brother, J. N.
McKendry, was with me and also spoke.  Seventy-six
signed the pledge.

Saturday, March 8th.—I started for Peterboro', little
dreaming what the result would be of that week's work.
I went over the C. P. R., and was met by a delegation of

the Royal Templars, under whose management the meetings were conducted. My first place to visit was the Y. M. C. A., which is under the efficient secretaryship of Brother Colville. I spoke briefly here to a meeting of young men. About nine o'clock I was conducted to the residence of Mr. Bradburn, one of the finest homes in town. I was made heartily welcome by Mrs. Bradburn, who is a member of the W. C. T. U.

Sunday morning, March 9th.—I attended morning service at the Methodist Church, Rev. Mr. Pierson was in the pulpit and gave us an excellent sermon. At 2.30 p.m. I began battle at Bradburn's Opera House, which was densely packed. I had the best attention of any meeting I had had in Canada up to that time. Rev. Mr. Pierson acted as chairman. The writer spoke for about one hour. At the close the invitation was given to come and sign the pledge; many came forward. One tall young man, who had the appearance of an educated man, came upon the platform. He was well dressed, but I soon discovered what was the matter. I saw that he was under the influence of rum. I spoke to him, and gently took him by the hand, when he burst into tears and said, "Oh, the curse rum." Said he, " Mr. Hess, is there any help for me ? " I pointed him to the one who said, " Whosoever will come to me I will in no wise cast out." From his own lips I learned of his first step to ruin. As a young man of eighteen, he went to college, graduated, but like thousands of other young men who have gone the road before, he, too, learned to think that to be a boy he must be one of the boys; the road from total abstinence to that of the first glass was soon travelled, and the downward road was commenced. He afterwards entered a law office and read law five years, but through drink he lost his position; then he married, and to-day is the owner of a lovely home, and beautiful wife and three children. But even this did not keep him straight; the appetite had possession of him. I prayed with him, he signed the pledge, and began to lead a sober life. He is worth considerable money. There was rejoicing in his home, as the following letter, written by him some months after, will show:—

PETERBORO,' May 17th, 1890.

MY DEAR HESS,—Yours of the 14th instant is just to hand, and the fact of its being penned from within the hallowed precincts of your own home made its perusal doubly gratifying to me. I am penning this also from my own fireside. Oh, "There's no place like home," a clean, neat Christian home is there. I look forward to it from the time I go out on the road, Monday morning, until I return, Saturday night, and that, too, with constant longing. And only a few short months ago I would wonder if there were any clocks in the world as fast as the bar-room timepieces, when maybe their hands pointed to the midnight hour. Then home was the last place to go to. Now, thank God, it is the first consideration.

*     *     *     *     *     *

The writer was the young man who thought there was no help for him.

The Opera House was packed every night for four nights. The last night I had a ten-cent admission. This did not decrease but increased the audience. On this night Brother J. S. Robertson, of Toronto, was present, and made the opening speech. The writer talked of temperance from a business standpoint. The saloon keepers were invited, as they are business men. During the time of speaking I made reference to the word " Palace " that I had noticed as I was walking along the street, and it seems that the owner of the word was present. Soon after the meeting the streets were alive with the talk that " Tom Dun was going to make it hot for me."

The Toronto papers published a despatch stating that an action for $5,000 for slander had been entered against Joe Hess by saloon-keeper Dun, of Peterboro'. Over 500 signed the pledge during the meetings in Peterboro'. On my return from Peterboro', I again went back to West Toronto Junction for two days more, and spoke to two large audiences.

March 15th.—I started for Bowmanville, where Charles Jewell greeted me at the depot, and conducted me to Mr. Sam Mason's residence, where I was entertained during my stay in the town. On the train I learned that another great revivalist was to hold forth at the Methodist Church during the week of my stay, that the Salvation Army was holding extra meetings, and on Sunday the Presbyterian Church was to have the powerful boy-preacher. As Bowmanville is but a place of about 4,000 population, I feared that my audience would be small, but " trust in God, and thou shalt prosper."

After supper Brother Jewell was on hand ready to take me round the town and show me the sights by electric light. First we went to the Methodist Church, where the Rev. J. McD. Kerr, of Toronto, was holding revival meetings. The lecture-room of the church was packed, and the brethren were discussing the " holiness " problem. On invitation of the chair, I took a position on the platform and spoke for a short time.

I visited the Salvation Army's Barracks the same evening. Here, too, I was called on to speak. I knew that this denomination believed in a laugh, so I told 'em some funny things. The next day, Sunday, I opened my work at 3.30 p.m.. The Town Hall was packed; the meeting was presided over by the Mayor of the town. On the platform were seated some of the best people of the town, including a member of the Local Legislature.

I spoke vigorously against the traffic ; many signed the pledge after the meeting. Some of the politicians hung their heads and said that " Joe Hess is a bad Sunday man." Some of the worst drunkards signed during the week. Among them, a tailor by trade, Sam Mitchell by name. The next day he received a leather medal through the post, with a hole punched through it, in which was a blue ribbon, to which was attached a postal card. This was sent for an insult, with the hope that it might drive Sam back into the ranks of the bummer; but in this the devil failed; it made Sam more determined. During the week Revivalist Kerr left for some other appointment, and I was requested to speak in the church on Wednesday, Thursday, and Friday afternoons, which I did. The Salvation Army closed their extra meetings on the Tuesday night, which left the entire field for me during the balance of the week. At the meetings we had excellent singing. We were assisted by Brother W. Daly, from Peterboro', and on the last night we closed by charging a ten-cent admission. Some of the committee thought this would keep people away, but this is not my experience. We had an excellent programme. Brother J. S. Robertson was down from Toronto, so was Brother Charlie Johnson; besides, an excellent programme was furnished in the line of music by some of the people whose names I cannot remember. We closed with over 700 names to the pledge. Many homes were made happy as the result of the meeting, and the Royal Templars have greatly swelled their numbers.

Bowmanville has a population of 4,000, and is situated north of Lake Ontario, about two and a-half miles. The Grand Trunk runs to the south of the place, about one mile from the town. The various religious denominations are well represented. An organ factory, and several other factories besides, find an existence here. There is a very fertile country around it. It had only four drinking places at the time I write.

March 22.—I started for London, Ont., again, with a trembling heart. Before I had engaged with Bowmanville, I told the manager not to send me to London, because it was so dead; but no, I must go to the Forest City, so I took courage and went. When I was there in the early part of the winter I stayed but a day, and I

Q

was very glad to get out. It was in London where, in 1884, I had contracted some liabilities, and spending my money at the saloons, I had none to pay my other bills. This was the reason I did not like to go there, but go I did. When I had entered the car, sitting alone in one of the seats, I noticed a little dried-up fellow walking up and down the platform, and looking at me very closely. As the conductor shouted all aboard, the train commenced to move out of the Union Depot. This "two-by-nine" fellow stepped aboard and, almost breathless, said "Is this Mr. Hess?" I answered, "That's what they call me." Said he, "Here is a paper which might be of interest to you while on your way," and away he went like a whirlwind. It was what I expected every day, a writ in the celebrated Dun slander case of Peterboro'. I put the precious document in my pocket for safe keeping.

At London I was greeted with a welcome by Rev. Brother A. C. Courtice, pastor of the Dundas Centre Methodist Church. Brother Courtice is a small man, but in the pulpit he is a big man. On the car I told him right out what I had formerly been in London, and what I might expect. He thanked me for being so frank, and laying his hand on my shoulder said, "Brother Hess, we will stand by you."

Sunday, at 3.30 p.m., the first meeting took place, under the auspices of the W. C. T. U., at the City Hall, which was packed to suffocation. As I mounted the platform I could hear all over, "That's John Brooks," and when I looked up I saw so many of the old boys before me that it really gave me courage. At the close of the meeting many came forward and shook my hand, amongst them, none so hearty as Tom Tracey, the barber. The evening meeting was held in the Dundas-street Methodist Church, which seats about 1,400 people, and it was packed by 7 p.m., though the meeting was not to begin until 7.30. Many were the tears shed that night. There was no such fever in London on the temperance line in the history of the Forest City for many a year. It was verily a mixed crowd in the church that night. The rich along with the poor, the drunkard along with the sober. Gamblers, negroes, and all sorts of society were there  It was decided after the meeting to see if the Opera House could be secured. This was done, and on Monday night, and every night during the week, it was packed from pit to gallery, and hundreds could not get in. On Monday night I told the people that some years ago I was there under an assumed name, and I left behind some bills un paid, and that if they would call at 484 Dundas-street I would settle all legitimate accounts. This had such an effect upon the people that by one accord they cheered for five minutes. Though these bills had been outlawed, yet I knew I owed them. It was amusing to see the people come with accounts, some of one dollar, others of five dollars, and some of larger amounts. Some I refused to pay, because I did not owe them.. There was one case where certain men of reputed good standing in the city went to one McDonald, a saloon keeper, and got him to unearth old and musty records, and fix up an account against me. It was not the money they wanted, but they hoped to compromise me in the eyes of the public. They counted without their host. All accounts were paid, and in this way the devil was fooled.

Nearly 1,000 signed the pledge. Now that I had faced the enemy, and the combat was over, and victory mine, I was happy, but through it all my noble Brother Courtice was at my side, and when the time came to close the case it was laid before the W. C. T. U., and they allowed me $33 on what I had paid. God will look out for His own every time.

March 29th.—I returned to Toronto to speak at the closing Sunday afternoon meeting of the League in the Pavilion. This great building was crowded. At the close of the meeting three ragged boys came forward and signed the pledge. I took them by the hand and asked them

where were their parents ? One of them could not restrain the tears. Said he : " Father is in jail, charged with
the murder of my mother, he killed her one night when
he was drunk." After this meeting the first plea for
money was made by the committee, and in five minutes
nearly $200 was raised. That is what I call business.

March 31.—I started for Goderich, Ont. A carriage
awaited my arrival at the station. and I was immediately
driven to the hall. It was packed to the doors. The
meetings were under the auspices of the Y. W. C. T. U.,
who had secured an excellent orchestra. On the platform
were the local ministers, the editors of the newspapers,
and the principal of the High School. The meetings
continued for three days, and were a great success in
every way. The third morning a little man came in to
see me. He said he was one of the hotel keepers, that his
name was Wright. " Well," said I, " strange that you are
not in a right business." He said that though he had sold
rum for thirty years, never until last night had he realized what an infernal business he was engaged in. Said
he : " I will sell no more rum, and ' Point Farm ' shall be
a temperance resort as long as I (Wright) own it."

The lady with whom I stopped was nearly seventy
years old, and had never taken a trip on the cars in
her life. This was corroborated by her husband and
daughters.

April 3rd.—I left Goderich for home, Clarendon, N.Y.,
for a week's rest.

Drunken travellers — Meetings in Forest—Second campaign in Peterboro'—" Hold on Joe, I am Coming "—A grateful letter —A great work in Belleville—Visits the Deaf and Dumb Institute—At Picton—Young men who refused to sign the pledge—Work at Port Perry—With Lou J. Beauchamp—Sketchy account of the campaign in Cobourg, Brantford and Gananoque.

"Owe no man a farthing."

THE first of April I went home to make a payment on my property at Clarendon, N. Y. The family were delighted to see me. I returned promptly again to Ontario, travelling over the Buffalo and Goderich line to Stratford, then to the pretty town of Forest. At one of the stations on the way, several drunken men and one drunken young woman boarded the train, and the sight was appalling ; but what will whisky not do ?

At Forest I was greeted with a welcome by the Rev. W. Johnson, Rector of Trinity church, that I shall long remember. He conducted me to my place of entertainment, and at 7:30 Rev. Mr. Harris, the Methodist minister, came and took me to the town hall. The hall was well filled, and good music was furnished by the best talent of the town. These meetings were continued for three nights, and over 300 signed the pledge. The churches stood nobly by the work. Forest is located on the main line of the Grand Trunk Railway, west of Stratford. It is a very pleasant place.

April 12th.—I started back to Peterboro' for another week's work under the auspices of the Royal Templars of Temperance, and, as on my first appearance, the opera house was packed every night. Many who refused to sign the pledge the time before, now came up and placed

themselves against rum.  There are numbers of cases
that I might give an account of, but I will mention but
one.  Every night there came to the meeting a low sized
man, accompanied by his faithful wife.  But all the plead-
ing and talking had no effect; and saving my breath in
arguments with him, I went to the Lord with him and
pleaded that if it were the Lord's will to add this one
soul to my record, to do so.  I had hopes until the last
meeting was held and the lights put out, but no, he did
not come, and so I bid him good-bye, and along with the
workers I went to the Y. W. C. T. U. rooms, where a
little lunch was prepared.  On looking round I saw my
man in the corner, his wife in another part of the building.  After lunch several speeches were made, and a short
address by myself, when I again pleaded for the erring.
At this moment the little man shouted out, "Hold on
Joe, I am coming," and over the benches he flew, and
taking my hand he said, "I want to be a man."  I said
"God bless you;" he laid his head on my shoulder and
wept, then signed the pledge, and all the company sang
"Praise God."  This man's name I will not reveal, but he
is to-day a happy Christian man.  From a letter by his
wife to me, I will make an extract:     .

"Dear friend,—The Doctor read your letter to me yesterday at dinner.  We were so glad to hear from you.
What a weight has been lifted from me. I am so glad
that I insisted in going to the Y. W. C. T. U. rooms that
night.  The Lord led us.  We did not realize it at the
time.  We came home and the Doctor took the Bible and
read, and we prayed.  We have had family prayer ever
since.  He has many temptations, but he has overcome
them all, and stands to-day a monument of the power of
God to save to the uttermost."

During my stay, the saloon keeper who had a suit
against me for $5,000, sent for me and said he thought
that this trouble might be settled easily, if I would
retract what I had said.  I told him I had nothing to

retract, so the suit is still pending. Many homes were made happy during my second visit at Peterboro'.

April 19th.—I was called to Toronto by my solicitors, in reference to the Dun-Hess libel suit. One of the men who signed the pledge during the work in Toronto, had the misfortune to fall and injure himself, and he was obliged to take up his abode in the hospital, and on the 19th he was released. Knowing the dangers he would be exposed to, I took him with me to Belleville, arriving there at 12:30 Sunday morning. We were made welcome at W. W. Chown's home, and a right royal welcome did we receive from Mrs. Chown. Sunday morning after break-fast, we were sitting in the room, when in a moment this poor fellow gave a groan and commenced to reel from his chair. I was afraid he was gone over Jordan, but after a while he revived and I was thankful. Sunday afternoon at 3:30 p.m., we went to the opera house, which was crowded, and from the start the meetings proved a success, under the able leadership of Brother Chown. The last night we charged an admission of 10 cents, and yet the hall was packed. During the meetings several things occurred. One night the fire bells sent forth their peals of alarm ; after the meeting we learned with regret that the fire was at the river end of the city, and that a small house had been consumed, and a woman burned to ashes, only her feet were recovered. The woman was about 60 years old ; she and her husband had been drink-ing during the day, so report had it, and having a little set-to, it is surmised that they knocked over the lamp, which set the house on fire, and being drunk they were helpless.

One other incident. A young man who was under bail for murder, came and signed the pledge. Much good was the result of the meetings. Belleville has a good harbor, an excellent river, some factories, and many excellent buildings. Of these, I name only one, the institution for the education of the deaf and dumb. This institution is presided over by Mr. R. Mathison, as super-intendent. Mr. Chown presented the writer to him, and after a little conversation, I expressed the desire of visiting the several departments. I was wonderfully astonished at the great talents displayed by these deaf and dumb people. I found that their instruction is thorough, especially in industrial and domestic work, this kind of work being the most important when they leave the school. A record is kept of the inmates' behaviour during the year. I was informed that the pupils were all willing and very orderly. When the Superintendent made known to them what my former life was, they all had sad faces, but when he told them that now I was lecturing on temperance all rejoiced, and smiles lit up their faces. Truly this institution is an honour to the City of Belleville, and to Ontario.

April 26th.—I took the steamer Armenia, with Sam Anderson as captain and Mr. W. Power as purser. She runs between Trenton and Picton. Here Mrs. J. E. Lent, was waiting to conduct me to the only temperance hotel in the town. This town has a population of about 3,000, with sixteen rum holes. The first meeting was in the church, on Sunday afternoon, but on account of a mis-pronounced word the church was closed against me, and the Town Hall was engaged. This was packed every night during the progress of the meetings. I asked some young men to sign the pledge; they laughed. The same night they became drunk and knocked down a young man, and nearly bit his finger off. This caused warrants to be issued. At the closing meeting the mayor of the town signed the pledge. This caused a number of influential people to do the same. The meetings closed with a big boom.

May 2nd.—I left Picton in a hack at twelve o'clock at night, to drive to Trenton, twenty-seven miles away, to catch the 4.12 a.m. train for Port Perry. This was not the most pleasant drive I ever had in my life,

At Port Perry I had another success beyond my expectation. This place has a wonderful active Union, composed of the leading women of the place. Within six years I understand Port Perry has had two big fires, but to-day it is one of the most thriving towns in the Province.

I left Port Perry on Tuesday morning for Hamilton, Ohio. I was greeted there with a God bless you from Lou J. Beauchamp and his wife, and Dr. Julia Goodman. I was made the guest of Brother Lou, who has a neat home. The hall was crowded nightly. At the close of my five days' campaign, I was presented with $108 and a set of silver knives and forks and spoons, and in return I presented to them the pledge-roll of 400. So the work went on. I met here Jack Smith, the coloured prize-fighter, whose acquaintance I had made years before.

From here I went home for a few days, and returned to Canada May 15th, and began my work at Cobourg under the leadership of A. A. Barber. Cobourg is situated on Lake Ontario. It has great schools which teach both ways—one teaches up, the other down. Over 450 signed. Amongst the foremost workers was a young business-man, a jeweller by trade, W. H. Hopper; these people were ardent workers. I next went to the City of Brantford; Bro. W. F. Chapman, Secretary of the Y. M. C. A. was in waiting at the dépot. The meetings in this place, so far as numbers were concerned, was a failure. I spoke in the Harris shops to the working men. Brantford is a neat city, and has a population of 14,000. It has one of the best systems of water works that it has ever been my pleasure to behold. Its people are enterprising. It has influential citizens such as the Hon. Judge Jones, a thorough temperance man, and his wife is one of the leading lights of the W.C.T.U. H. Brethour is one of the leading business men of the city. It was also a pleasure to meet with Mr. M. H. Smith, Mrs. E. C. Gillespie, and others. Brantford has one of the most successful Y. M.

C. A. in the Province, with a membership of over 550. It has some drunkard manufacturers as well.

May 31st.—I was to go to Bowmanville but did not because of some misunderstanding, and went instead to Gananoque, a manufacturing town of about 7,000 inhabitants, situated on the banks of the St. Lawrence; a beautiful town, but also a rum-cursed place. The meetings were under the auspices of the W. C. T. U., but on account of the mistake as to date there was nothing arranged. I arrived in town at 2:30 a.m., and was compelled to stay in a whisky hotel over night. Next morning I looked round for Mrs. E. A. Byers (her husband is Mayor of the town). She is an earnest worker. She greeted me heartily, and after a consultation she proposed to have a meeting that night and make it known at the churches. After the church meetings numbers of people came to the rink, but to our horror we found that no light of any consequence was provided. The speaker was in the dark and so were the audience; well, to make a long story short, the meetings were a failure from lack of attendance. Numbers signed during my stay. I was invited to take a trip on the St. Lawrence with Captain J. H. Davies, who commanded the steamer *Antelope.* In our trip we passed Freemont Park, which is just opposite Gananoque, and many other places of interest. It being calm, the captain said that it was a regular white ash breeze. Asking what he meant by the term white ash breeze, he said to pull the oars for exercise. The Thousand Islands must be seen to realise what they are.

One of the most enthusiastic workers in the temperance cause is Dr. Atkinson. He is a royal man, so is his lady a royal woman. I closed my meetings at this place on the 6th of June.

# CHAPTER XXVI.

The last Chapter—Bobcaygeon—A notable campaign here—Rum-cursed Fenelon Falls—A week at Seaforth—Its noble workers —Free Methodist camp meeting at Uxbridge—"How they jumped and hollered"—Enterprising Aylmer—Only 20 houses and grand meetings at Enniskillen—Review of the work in Canada—Closing words.

"Delight thyself in the Lord."

THIS is my last chapter, and I think the text an appropriate one for closing words. Ever since I began to delight myself in the Lord, I have had success. So it is with all who serve Him faithfully.

I left Toronto June 7th by way of Lindsay, and there took the boat for Bobcaygeon. It was a cloudy, uninviting day, especially so on the water—cold and chilly. Such a condition of things would naturally make one feel blue and drowsy. Prior to my going to Bobcaygeon, I was told fifty times over what a terrible place it was, so I naturally concluded from what I saw, that the people had spoken the truth, and I looked forward to a tough time. We arrived at Bobcaygeon about 2.30 p.m. A delegation bid me welcome. I was conducted to Miss M. H. Orr's residence to be entertained there during my entire stay in the town. About one of the first questions I had to answer was this: Mr. Hess are you in this work for money? That was a kind of funny way of touching a fellow. I smiled and said to my enquirer, I will answer that by asking another. Does any man work for amusement or fun? I said, yes, I am working for money, because the money is in the world, and for money we make exchanges. I need money to support the family, and if I could not get it in the temperance work I will have to

275

quit it, and work at something else.    This kind of settled the matter.  The next question was :  Do you believe in holiness ?   I answered, yes, in the holiness of Christ, but as to my being holy I did not know.  I know some times when I hit the nail on the head (my finger nail), I want to say some very funny things ; that alone is proof that I am not an angel, my wings have not yet commenced to crop out.

The meetings were conducted by the W. C. T. U., of which Miss Orr was the mainstay.  She is a God-fearing young woman.  The large rink was secured.  Seats had been placed in the building ; and a stage, erected by the ladies, was beautifully decorated ; this was occupied with about 50 voices.  Along with this there was the ladies cornet band, which rendered several splendid selections, which were heartily applauded.  The audience numbered about 800 to 1000 people.  Where all came from was a mystery to me.  Sunday evening the Orangemen had special services in the M. E. church, after which they adjourned in a body to the rink,  The building was packed, and each meeting brought more people ; though only here three days over 350 signed the pledge. A Loyal Legion was organized ; among the signers were some of the prominent men and women who had never taken an active stand in the temperance cause, but who now resolved to become active.   I found here many true loyal hearts, and instead of the place being as tough a place as had been pictured to me, I found it was just the opposite. Bobcaygeon is a wonderful lumber country, its business is all lumber ; miles of stacks of lumber can be seen ; it is not a country of soil, but every thing is rock.   It has locks which connect a chain of lakes for miles round ; four liquor places ;  splendid water power ;  several churches.   Mr. Orr, deceased, kept a temperance hotel in days when this work was very unpopular, but a fearless man was he, and one who did delight himself in the Lord, and the Lord prospered him ; and now his daughter Miss Orr carries on his business, that of a general country store. I met a great many whose names I would be pleased to record in this book, but for lack of memory I cannot.

June 11th.—I was brought to Fenelon Falls, a place about seventeen miles from Bobcaygeon. The road led us through a wild district, here and there dotted with houses, which were occupied with tillers of the soil. Some very good farms were to be seen, and some very poor ones. After a drive of four hours we landed in the city of the Falls. I had looked forward to this place with great expectation, as I was informed that it was settled with some live people, and I would have a good time. But with a glance around, I knew that this was a hard place to work. The first meeting was held in the M. E. Church, half-way out in the country. This was filled with empty seats, only about seventy-five people were present. The next day the meetings were moved to the Salvation Army barracks. This was moderately filled ; altogether I had three meetings in the place; results very poor. I was entertained by the President of the Union, Mrs. M. H. Dickson, a very pleasant lady, and her husband a very genial man. Fenelon Falls has a great water power that ought to be utilized, and which can be done with very little expense. The fall is about 100 feet ; its current is very swift. There is a chance for capitalists. It has a rail-road ; its rivers are also navigable for steamers and packets, and the place is cursed with rum.

June 14th.—I secured a driver to bring me to Lindsay, from thence back to Seaforth. I laboured here under the auspices of the I.O.G.T., and was greeted with a welcome by J. W. Beattie, a fine young man, who conducted me to his father's residence, one of the finest in the town. Seaforth has a population of 5,000 people. Some excellent meetings were held, but it being so very hot, they were not as well attended as they might have been. Yet numbers of drinking men signed the pledge, and good work was done in the place. I left many warm friends in this place. Mrs. Beattie senr., knew how to welcome a stranger. Her husband, Mr. John Beattie, has lived in the town nearly forty years, is clerk of the court, and many were the persecutions he had to suffer because of his firm convictions on the temperance line, but, said he, "Brother Hess, I know that I am right, and that is enough for me."

June 21st.—I started for Uxbridge. I was greeted with a shake of the hand by A. D. Weeks, who conducted me to my place of entertainment. Now I learned that the advertising had been neglected, and that a free Methodist camp meeting was in progress. On learning this I said our meeting will not amount to anything. On Saturday evening I, with the rest of the people, went to the ground, and it was marvellous to behold how the people were seized with the spirit to jump up and down. Some hollered, some rolled on the ground, others danced. Well, Uxbridge meetings were not a success. During the time that I was here I was privileged to be at the W.C. T.U. Convention, which organized a County W.C.T.U.

My next place was Aylmer, a town of 3,000, one of the neatest little towns that I ever saw. Its streets are clean, its people enterprising, and many earnest temperance people are here. The meetings were held in the Town Hall, under the auspices of the R. T. of T. Brother O. W. Kennedy gave me a fine reception. We had grand meetings in this place. With every meeting the interest grew, and had it been so that the meetings could have been continued for another ten days, I know a great work might have been accomplished.

June 28th.—I had to be brought over to St. Thomas, a distance of twelve miles. When we left the town at four o'clock, everything looked bright, but before we reached the city rain poured down in a blinding sheet—no umbrella, no oil cloth ; you may know with a spanking team a-head, the mud flew. Soon I felt something cool under my seat. Raising, I saw that it was water. Never in all my life did I see it rain as it did that morning, but in due time we reached the city and took train for a place called Enniskillen, Ont. This place has only about twelve to fourteen houses, and was the first place that I met in Canada that did not have a licensed hotel. During my stay I was entertained by J. J. Virtue, a prominent farmer. I learned to know and respect in this town such men as Dr. J. C. Mitchell and F. Rogers, a general merchant. The population of this place is about 150. It has two fine churches. The meetings in this place were grand. Many signed the pledge.

July 2nd.—In the morning I was driven to Bowmanville, where brother Jewell made room for me, and I took an early train for Toronto. As I now look over the past six months of labor in Canada, I can see many rounding, cheery faces of children who are happy because papa has changed his way of living. The temperance cause is destined to make great strides in the next ten years in Canada.

Looking upon the many people who I see assembled from night to night, eager for information regarding this evil of strong drink, I know the temperance cause is moving on, and it is only a matter of time when the demon of rum will have to move back out of the way, and give to the sturdy soldiers of temperance fame the ground that was occupied for so many years by King Alcohol. Then there will be a blessing prayed upon the men who wrought such changes, and the true ladies who were ever by their side to assist them. May the glad day soon come when our children shall not be in danger of this mighty foe any longer. Where there is a will there is a way.

In conclusion, let me say to the readers of this book, that I have not tried to be a great author, nor have I tried to paint or exaggerate things, but instead, have told a plain and simple story, trusting it may do good wherever read. And, as my last words, I have a petition, if you are a Christian, bear me to the throne of grace, that I may be ever kept faithful until the end shall come. May we then reign together in the Kingdom of God.

Your most humble servant,

JOSEPH F. HESS.

# ADDENDA.

## SPEECHES AND NEWSPAPER CONTRIBUTIONS.

BY JOSEPH F. HESS.

### AN EARLY SPEECH.

LET us take the fact that the direct expenditure of our
nation (the reference is to the United States) for intoxicating drinks is reckoned at the astonishing amount
of $900,000,000 per annum. Is it any wonder when our
nation spends $400,000,000 more for liquor than it does
for bread, that we hear the cry of *hard times* on every
hand? When we consider these figures we must confess
that the liquor traffic is the greatest curse with which
the American people have to deal at the present time.
In years gone by alcohol was looked upon as a harmless
luxury; even if this were so, you will all agree with me
that it is not necessary for our natural demands. We
know of whole races who have not used alcohol, and are
stronger and healthier in consequence. We also know
that the 40,000 prisoners in the United States, as a rule,
improve in health as a result of strong drink being refused them from the day of their imprisonment. From
my own experience as an athlete, I know that the
greatest feats of physical strength are performed without
any alcoholic stimulants whatever.

I ask you seriously, my friends, can we bear this exhaustion which arises from this terrible drain on our national resources ?  If we will only stop and consider we will find that we are living in anxious times; the pressure of life, closeness of competition, both in the nation itself and with other nations, is very severe.  We have of late ample proof of these things when we look at the state of affairs in the *prairie* city.  I refer to the city of Chicago.  Look at the thousands who are starving as a result of strong drink.  Learn the terrible story of their hapless and grinding poverty, occasioned by the same cause.  Take the agonies of thousands of parents who contemplate the difficulty of starting their boys in the crowded race of life.  Can there be a shadow of doubt but that the nation would be better prepared for the vast growth of its population, and would not the conditions of average life be less burdensome were we to abandon this needless and worthless expenditure ?  I say, would not the position of the United States be more secure if that river of $900,000,000 of wasted gold were diverted into more fruitful channels ?—if the millions upon millions of bushels of grain which is now being made into soul-robbing drink were turned into useful food ?—if our country were relieved from supporting the great amount of misery, crime, pauperism and madness which drunkenness entails ?  It is high time we should rise against this traffic, which makes sober men support these different institutions for fallen men and women, made such by strong drink.

Looking at the matter from grounds simply economical, and considering that the laboring classes spend as much for drink as rent, and further that there is hardly a pauper in this land but who has spent for drink what would have furnished him a comfortable home ; I say if this curse were abolished, it would rain gold and silver among our laboring classes not for one but for many years.

Why this poverty in our own city of Rochester ?  Look at the vast amount spent daily for strong drink.  According to the statistics of P. A. Burdick, Rochester's drink bill is about $8,600 per day, or $3,140,000 per annum. Then is it any wonder we are heavily taxed to support poverty and pauperism ? Banish the saloons of this city, and the cry of *hard times* will go with them. Why so many thousands of little waifs in our streets and throughout the entire land ? Why so many heartbroken wives and mothers ? Why the many tears of anxious and almost despairing parents over wayward sons and daughters ? We emphatically answer *strong drink*. On almost every corner this terrible tempter stares our young and old in the face ; then shall we sit idly by and allow this state of things to exist longer ?

Among the many scientific discoveries of late, I am happy to say, the poisonous effect of alcohol on the system is among the rest. Yes, the voice of science has laid it down unconditionally that all who are in perfect health do not need alcohol and are far better without it ; and, furthermore, that even a moderate use of alcohol is the cause of many painful disorders and premature deaths. Among the middle class of Americans the use of two wines is almost universal. I refer to claret and sherry, and of late it has been decided that the strange concoctions of which these are composed are the cause of gout, and all sorts of gastric diseases.

Among the German middle class we find lager beer to be the prevailing beverage, and even in every low dive or brothel we find this *slush* of beer to predominate. My experience as a saloon-keeper has proved to me that what I have said is the fact, and if we are to judge the morals of Germany from what we see of its people here, they are certainly below par. To see these German women, young and old, publicly drinking their beer, has somewhat shocked our American women, but I am sorry to say many of the latter are gradually becoming *Germanized* in this particular.

Alcohol is a poison that first creates a craving, then an appetite that finally becomes a disease, and which binds its victim down in the strongest bands of slavery. As we find the drunkard here and there, he tells us he did not mean to become a drunkard, wrecked in body and mind, and yet our young men will not take warning when they know that every year one hundred thousand drunkards go to their graves in the United States alone. What more does drunkenness involve? To thousands life becomes a burden and a disease. What does Solomon say? " Who hath woe? Who hath sorrow? Who hath contentions? Who hath babbling? Who hath wounds without cause? Who hath redness of eyes?"

" They that tarry long at the wine; they that go to seek mixed wine."

" Look not thou upon the wine when it is red, when it giveth its color in the cup, when it moveth itself aright."

" At last it biteth like a serpent and stingeth like an adder."

*Delirium tremens,* that awful illness, is one of thé many punishments God will send upon those who destroy their bodies with strong drink.

As a general thing we find during an epidemic that drinkers of alcoholic beverages are the first victims. I denounce all makers and vendors of this terrible poison, for they not only destroy the bodies of their fellow-men but also their immortal souls. When those who are engaged in this nefarious traffic shall be called upon to give an account before the judgment bar of Christ, I fail to see how they will be able to explain away that *stumbling block* over which they have caused their brother to fall. Oh ! think of the abject servitude, spiritual catastrophy, of the man who has given himself over to this drink curse. When a man recovers from degradation lower than the animal, it is then he can somewhat appreciate the anguish of a lost soul.

Strong drink not only crowds our jails with felons, our asylums with lunatics, our workhouses with paupers, our hospitals with all sorts of diseased specimens of humanity ; more than this, it swells that awful appalling death roll of suicides, sending the poor drunkard unprepared, into the presence of his Lord and Master.  His mind bereft of reason, he seeks a deliverance from temporal sufferings, but only, methinks, to enter upon those eternal.  How men of good understanding in many ways can remain in a business that is sending their weaker brothers to everlasting damnation is beyond my comprehension.

To get a further idea of this rapidly spreading evil, let us look into our saloons on a Saturday night, between the hours of nine and twelve o'clock ; there you will find our laboring men, with those somewhat more prosperous in life, pouring their weekly earnings into the till of a man who is so depraved as to take, without the least hesitation, that money which he must know belongs to the poor wives and little ones of the men who are spending it, and who, in consequence thereof, will return to their comfortless homes empty handed.  I know whereof I speak when referring to a drunkard's home.  The very air within it is laden with the sound of blows and curses.  The children brought up under such influences are soon to go out into the world and recruit the ranks of crime and degradation.  In our large cities we have whole streets of poverty, crime and wickedness, and the cause of their existence is that curse of our nation, *strong drink.*

We have one day of the week commonly called payday, but which, I think, should more properly be called *crime*-day.  I firmly believe that the wives and mothers of our land shed more tears on Saturday nights than upon all other evenings in the week.  And why is it so ? Simply because that bread-winner, who receives his weekly wages upon that day, yields to the terrible temptation that surrounds him at every step.  Then, my Christian friends, let us remove these places of temptation and thereby dry up these rivers of bitter, bitter tears. In our own city, how many young men are to-day languishing in prisons, as a result of a crime committed while under the cup of intoxication, and that cup partaken of on this so called *pay-day*. When the young man enters a saloon with a few extra dollars in his pocket, meeting some friends, then this damnable treating curse is indulged in so freely, that our young man does not come from that place in a few moments, as he had anticipated, but remains ; is finally induced to take part in some game of chance, over which a dispute arises, resulting in perhaps that terrible crime of murder. This is no imaginary picture, but a terrible reality.

Then again, how many young men take perhaps their first glass, thereby laying the foundation for a ruined life, on that most holy day—the Lord's day—and all because our Sunday laws are almost entirely ignored. I appeal to the Christians, to the ministers of the Gospel, to all good citizens, is it not a disgrace upon us that we, in mortal laziness and cowardice, allow this terrible and most flagrant violation of the law to be carried on ? Let us no longer pray and *wait*, but rather pray and *work*. Oh ! my friends, how long will we allow our innocent sons and daughters to recruit the ranks of the drunkards ? Can we afford to do this ? I know you will agree with me that we cannot ; then, let us by our example, by our influence, and best of all, by our ballots, do with our might what our hands find to do, and drive this monster, this curse of our nation, forever out of the land. These are things I have felt it my duty to bring before you, and which I sincerely hope and trust you will prayerfully consider.

MODERATION.

*Delivered at Portageville, N.Y., June, 8, 1886.*

I had selected for the chairman to read the parable of the good Samaritan, because I think it suitable for everyone in this room to-night. We see a man lying in the gutter, who fell among thieves ; he lies there full of bruises and sores, but no one does anything to help him. As he lies there a priest comes along; at this time every man was called a priest who was a minister of God. I do not want you to mistake me in this matter; I have not been to college; I am simply Joe Hess. As the wounded man saw the priest coming along, he thought he was going to have a helping hand; but, lo, he passes him by, and he wonders how it is that he passes him by. By and by, he sees another man coming along, and he said: Why it is the priest's servant. How can I expect anything from the servant?" But the servant simply looks at him, and then passes away without any other interest in the matter. Next, comes a Samaritan. How could he expect any help from the Samaritan? Well, he does not expect it. But, what does he, the Samaritan, do? Why, he goes up to the wounded man, binds up his wounds, gives him every help in his power; then he puts him on his own beast and takes him to an inn, and gives orders that every care should be taken of him, and whatever had to be paid he promised to see it paid. But this is what I want you to notice. We are, as Christians, too indifferent in this great cause. We are like the priest and his servant; we just cast a wayside glance at the men robbed and made naked by the monster drink, and never stretch out a hand to save them. Instead of taking these men by the hand, as the Samaritan did, we pass them by. We ought not to hesitate in our duty; we should go right on and do it. If we do not do our Christian duty, how can we expect that others will do that duty which we, as Christians, should set an example of doing. This is the cause why so many pass by our churches; we are indifferent. It is for this reason that men never come to our churches. It is for this reason so many of our churches are never properly filled. If we will only do this (set an example by casting off indifference and crying Temperance), we shall have such full churches as we never had before. We are living in an advanced age. We are living in an age when they find silver in rock, and all kinds of wealth in the very soil on which we tread ; when the discoveries of all kinds of machinery are abounding to save labor and to make toil lighter for man. We have machinery of every description. But, with all these scientific discoveries, we have not time to stop and think what is the cause of so much of the dragging down of our fellow-men, and how to prevent it. But, when we do, what do we find out ? Why, scientific men find out, in their scientific advancements, that it is the liquor traffic that drags our boys and girls down to destruction, in our country. I dare say I am right in saying, that there is scarcely a family anywhere that is not a sufferer, in some degree, by strong drink.

I would like to give you a little illustration to-night how some men are made abstainers. A gentleman came to me and said : " Would you like to know why I am a temperance man and a Christian to-night ?" Yes, I would like to know how it all came about. Well, I have a vine-yard over there and have a winery, but I have not made a drop of drink for the sake of trade. I do not sell any-thing that would intoxicate. Well, I had a hired man, and I said to him : ' Take the offal of those grapes' (he took the grapes down to the mill), a kind of waste which had been lying exposed to the air a few days ; take the offal down to the pig-sty. He did so ; by-and-by my little boy came, breathless, almost, and said to me : ' Pa ! come and see what is the matter with the pigs.' I went and found that the pigs were all squealing and making the strangest noises imaginable ; some were on their back kicking im-mensely, and some were staggering from side to side. I said to the man, ' Why did you not give those pigs the grape offal that I told you ?' He said he had done so. I soon found out what it was ailed the pigs ; they were drunk. The next day I tried them again, and I found that they would not do what some of our two-legged pigs will do , they would not be made drunk, they would

not eat the stuff that made them drunk; they ran away
from it, they would not touch it." They had crossed
the bounds of moderation. And so with man; if he
would only look at the thing properly, he, too, would
exercise the same good sense and never touch a drop of
drink any more. Oh, I wish I had had the same sense as
those good pigs. I remember to-day how my first drink
affected me. There are a great many who say: "I am a
moderate drinker," because the Bible says so. It says,
" Be temperate in all things." Yes; but it says to be
total abstainers from all evil. It tells you to cast away
every thing that would do you or a fellow creature an
injury; and does not drink injure others? Is it not the
curse of many a home? Yes, my friends, it is the downfall of every man and woman who tastes it. You need
not go beyond your own door, beyond your own portal,
to see the effects of this evil. I saw one man to-day, and
it is plain he had suffered from the drink. And if that
man does not give up that drink it will drag him down
to ruin. Some will say, why, Christ made wine; He
turned the water into wine. Yes. Now, we know that
Christ never went about injuring men and causing them
suffering; it was not the character of His work. He went
about doing good to others and preventing misery. But
to put moderation against temperance, you will say
Christ turned the water into wine. I wish He was here
to-night to put you right on this matter. How can
men say this, that Christ made wine to give men a way
to hell? Why, it would be making Christ a liar. Would
He shed his blood for me, and then give me wine to ruin
my soul? I say drive that thought from you, drive it
away, because you are only deceived by it. It is the
devil getting hold of you and keeping you in chains. I
have got a little bill to-night, and if you will listen I
will read it, then you will see how man will spend his
money.

The moderate man's drink bill :
Per day, Whiskey,　　30 cts.　　Cigars, 15 cts.　$　0 45
Total for week,　-　-　-　-　-　-　-　-　-　3 15
　　"　month,　-　-　-　-　-　-　-　-　13 50
　　"　year,　-　-　-　-　-　-　-　-　-　162 00
　　"　ten years, -　-　-　-　-　-　-　1,620 00

Now, just see what a good sum you would have in ten years if this was deposited in a Bank at compound interest. And yet a young man will go into one of those places—he will go into one of those saloons night after night, and what does it do for him ? Why, it gets him into all sorts of trouble. Look at that father, look at that mother; she weeps for him. Oh, young man, beware of that demon, King Alcohol! At forty-five cents a day we find by the year that it amounts to one hundred and sixty-two dollars. Do you wonder ? can you wonder that these men are able to build fine houses—brick houses ? If a man was an honorable man he would give up such a cursed business. If any young man could see these figures he would stop and think with himself, how it is that the man across the road dresses in fine clothes, his wife dresses in silks and satins, while he has scarcely a shoe to put on ? Where will a man get to if he indulges in moderate drink with all that moral character, and all that love running soon to destruction ? Flee it ! give it up ! Look about you, and see what lots of young men are running to destruction, to endless ruin. I used to drink gin. I do not drink it any more. I drink this now (holding up a glass of water). It will never damn your soul. If you never touch or taste anything stronger than that you shall always be prosperous, you shall never have any headaches. When I used to drink I used to put my hand down here (stomach), I had pain there ; I had to hold my head ; I pained everywhere ; but now I have a pain of twenty dollars here (points to pocket). I want to say to-night, without contradiction, that our country is ruined to-night and it is the result of moderation. I say that our nation's depraved, debased and drunken condition is the result of moderation. As I said a while ago, there is no use of me putting my head in a noose, and falling out of a cart and breaking my neck when I have the power to hinder it.

There was a man, he was the foreman in the Penitentiary; I can tell you about his last drink. This man was a foreman. He walked out one night into one of these saloons, and he got something to drink, some of this poison. He was not in the habit of getting drunk, and did not intend it this night. It was a cold night and he thought a drop would warm him; well, he drank some of this poison; on his way home he fell and hurt himself, at least we supposed he did. Early in the morning a milk-man, going from his dairy, found him lying in the street at four o'clock, and he was dead, frozen to death. The milk-man looked at him; it was his neighbor. This poor man was a moderate drinker; he felt a little cold, and thought he would take a little to warm himself. What was the end of all this? His wife is in an asylum; his little children are waiting for him, but he will never come to them again. And what was the cause of all this? Why, he was a moderate drinker. And if you will not yield to this cause (temperance) you will be like that poor man. If you will indulge in moderate drinking, you will become accursed before all men.

Look at that man. I saw you drinking to-day; I can point you out. You are bringing ruin on yourself. You are a drunkard. Look at those children of yours. If you should die a drunkard, the finger of scorn will be pointed at them, and it will be said the father of that child died a drunkard's death; and my child must not attach herself to such company. It does not stop there; it follows on for ages after. I know one thing; let any minister of the gospel advocate moderation, and he will be made much of in every saloon; but let him advocate

total abstinence, and the saloon keepers will say : What
is he doing, to interfere with our business ? How dare
he do it ? But, let him preach moderation, and the
saloon keeper will admire him for it; from the most
gilded saloon palace to the lowest brothel. There is a
friend, a brother of mine, in New York, Rev Dr. Crosby.
He will advocate moderation; it is wrong, and if any man
will advocate such a doctrine, he deserves horse-whipping.
I want to ask who makes the drunkard ? It is you, the
moderate drinker. I was not always a drunkard. No ; I
became one from the moderate drinker's ranks. You
dare not say that I, that my wife, that that husband
will never be a drunkard, if moderate drinking is indulged
in. How can you say that ? If your men want to get
sick of drunkenness, I will give you a receipt. I did the
same thing yesterday. What, was I drunk ? Yes, and
so will any one be, if he rides long on that valley railroad.
You go down to Rochester on that railroad, and before you
get to the end you will experience what it is to be drunk.
And, by the way, this will only cost you a little over a
dollar. That is an awful road to travel on. I knew a
man, a barber, he had a hired man who was a barber, and
he knew another barber who told a tale about another
barber. They met in the barber's store, and one said to
the other, " Where are you going ? I am going to get a
drink of beer. I went into the saloon," he said, " and
spent one dollar or about one dollar and fifty cents, and
when I had drink enough I went into the butcher shop. I
stood a few seconds to look around me, when in comes
the saloon keeper. He would not look at me, the butcher
took no notice of me, either." He said to the saloon
keeper, with smiles all over his face : " What can I serve
you with ?" The saloon keeper very pompously enquired
the names of several pieces of meat, and finally bought a
piece of the best the butcher had. When the saloon
keeper had gone, the butcher turned round to me and
asked gruffly : " Well, what do you want ?" I said, sheep-

ishly, " twopennyworth of liver." " Here it is, where's your money ?" I would not stand that, that was too much for me. I went home with a resolve that such a thing should not happen again to me. I kept from the saloon all that week, and on Saturday, after labor, I went again to buy my meat at the same butcher shop. The butcher looked at me, but said nothing, At last I said : " What's that, and that, and that, and that ?" " That's the best end, too much for you." " Weigh it," I said. He weighed it and I paid him. It was very different from the twopenny-worth of liver. And I want to tell you young men who go to the saloon, playing billiards and drinking, when you grow old you will think of the liver story. Just think ; save all that you spend in drink, and you will find that you will have a goodly sum saved. There is not a saloon keeper who will tolerate the man who is not one of his supporters. There is not a saloon keeper anywhere who has a bone for anything but a man who has a thousand dollars.

I went in at the front door of a saloon, one day, but was glad to get out at the back. One saloon keeper once told me how to get sober. " Go," said he, " and throw a brick through a window if you have no money." Is not this so, boys ? Is it not so, men ? (here a man said, *no*, it is a lie ; a dispute arose for a few seconds, which ended by the disturber leaving the room) I guess some of you have been there to-day. I want to tell you something more about my life, but I have taken a long time in my address. Can you tell me where I left off ? I left off where I got married. I don't want to keep you too long. I wanted to regain my mind. My father said to me : " Joe, will you try and reform if I will help you ?" I said, " yes, I will." Well, my father said to me : " Here is some money—go to Canada." I went, and while there rented a farm. I planted and made my farm all nice. I had nothing to do but to wait for my crops growing. I said to my wife, I am going down to the jail, and will try and sell some of that stone on my way. I met my friend, George L——. I call him my friend because he has a soul. He asked me to go in and have a drink; I refused to have a drink. He then asked me to have a cigar. I had a smoke and a drink of soda water. While we were there, in came George P——. I got drunk and went to Toronto. I did not leave that saloon until I was drunk. I went to Toronto, took steamer and went to Buffalo to see my parents. My father sat at the door. "Why, Joe," said he, "are you drunk again?" I was ashamed. I left and went to Chicago. On the cars, I fell asleep, and when I awoke I found myself in a sleeping car. I went into a saloon at Chicago, got a drink, and then wrote to my wife, and getting no answer, I began to feel that I was cast off. From Chicago I went to Europe and to Australia. I got that low I wished I was dead. I liked drink so well that you might have thought that you were feeding a rat hole. I went back to Indiana. I had a prize match; he threw me over with a side lock; perhaps some of you know what a side lock is. I was so hard up at this time it made me desperate, and so I was determined to win. I did so in two more rounds. After the match, I received my two hundred dollars; I travelled at this time in the name of Brooks. I had been drinking a little bit. A man came up to me and said: "Is not your name Hess?" I said, "yes." Then he said he knew my brother, and told me what he (my brother) was doing. I got a message sent to my brother, who answered he did not know me. He said he had had a brother, but had not seen or heard of him for some time. I was asked to send some proof by which my mother might know me. I did so. My mother wired for me to come home; they had not seen me for years (7½ years). I went home and my mother met me at the door. "Is that you, Joe?" "Yes." "Then come in." I found a comfortable home. My mother was strangely altered. I looked around some time before I dare speak, then I asked where my father was. "Oh, son Joseph he is dead; he died four years ago."

When I think of all this grief, of this sad condition which I had brought upon others, I would plead with you to leave off all evil habits, to give up evil companions. and to cast away from your lips that accursed drink which works so much misery. Oh! that I could see my father come into this room to-night and behold the change God and temperance have made in me. How proud he would be (speaker wept and apologized for this show of feeling). Excuse my tears, I cannot help it. When I think of my father, when I think of the young men who despise these warnings, I feel ashamed ; when I look at my mother, so strangely altered (the speaker again burst into tears and abruptly said). I cannot tell you any more to-night, my heart is too full. I do not come to tell you these things for boasting's sake, but to rescue young men from that destruction into which drink is leading them. Young men, I stand before you to-night, to lead you away from that path which is leading so many to destruction. Come, fathers and mothers, come to-night and show by your actions that you are ready to help us in this grand cause for the sake of your sons and your daughters.

---

## OBJECTIONS TO LIQUOR LICENSE LAWS.

*(Written for the Canada Citizen.)*

All laws are supposed to be made for a certain object. I do not wish to assume that any legislature would pass laws simply to be able to say, "We are legislating."

But as a Christian, I am disposed to be charitable ; therefore I will concede that all laws are made to accomplish some object, good or bad.

Here again I must concede that in this enlightened age no legislature would pass any law simply to gain a bad end.  Then let us conclude that all laws are passed for a worthy object.  Taking this position, let us enquire into the necessity of liquor laws.

I will concede that at first this license law was meant to regulate the liquor traffic.  But we know that laws do not always accomplish the purpose for which they were intended,—indeed, in many cases they prove an utter failure.  The question is,—Have the license laws been a failure ?  To my mind the men best qualified to answer correctly, and to give clear testimony are the judges of the criminal courts, Why ?  Because they hold a position which gives them every opportunity to observe the workings of this accursed law.

What is their testimony ?  Judge Robt. C. Pitman, of the Superior Court of Massachussetts, in a book entitled, ' Alcohol and the State,' says : " License laws have not only failed in the past, but it is certain that they cannot succeed in the future because of inherent weakness.  .  .  .  License has had its day.  It is a disgrace and failure."

What is the history of license laws in England ?  Dr. F. R. Lees, in his ' Condensed Argument,' say : " Britain has tried, other nations have tried, restriction and regulation.  The experiment has failed, miserably failed."  *The* (London) *Times,* of May 13, 1857, the organ of public sentiment in England, says : " The  licensing system has the double vice of not answering a public end, but a private one.  It has been tried and found wanting."

Allow me to add my testimony in having bought license to conduct saloons, and to-day I say as far as it was a law it was a failure, for no man can sell rum under a license law and not become a law-breaker.  As a preventative of drunkenness it is a failure.  As a promoter of drunkenness it is a success without a parallel.

I am convinced that a law licensing the sale of alcoholic liquors is wrong, contrary to reason and righteousness.

The license system is founded upon a false assumption. To say we must have license for this curse, is the same

as saying there is a necessary demand for these destruc-
tive poisons.  Permit me, to say that the traffic in ardent
spirits is wholly unnecessary to the public good.  If this is
a fact, then its further continuance, in view of the numerous evils is high crime against both God and humanity.
It is certain to all who will give this matter one minute
reflection, that it is wrong to uphold a traffic which
undermines the principles of Government.  Back of the
question of revenue, and private gain, lies the base assumption that there is a public demand for these destruc-
tive poisons.  The supply is really the creator of the
demand.  Cut off the supply and you will not have the
demand.

J. F. HESS.

## TRUE AIMS OF LEGISLATION.

NOT A RIGHT TO DO WRONG.—THE SUBJECT INTELLIGENTLY
DISCUSSED.

*( Written for the Canada Citizen.)*

" Law grinds the poor, and rich men rule the law."—[Goldsmith.
" Law is a bottomless pit ; it is a cormorant, a harpy that devours
everything."—[Arbuthnot.
" Nothing is law that is not reason."—[Parnell.

According to the mind and idea of the wise Frederick
Powell, the science of government is divided into two departments—1st, To find what is right and just, and then
enforce it ; 2nd, To find what is beneficial, and then promote it.  The former he calls the science of politics, the
latter he calls the science of political economy.  These
two, then, must complete the system of political philosophy.
Upon philosophy, good governments are founded.

The ends of government are virtue and justice.  To
protect these ends should be the aim of legislation.  The
fruits of justice, along with virtue, are happiness and
peace.  Where happiness and peace exist you find a free

s

government. A government that cannot provide these ends for its people is not worthy of respect or loyalty. A government that promotes vice, and by such vice demoralizes and pauperizes its people, has a poor foundation. Men are not all depraved ; therefore men are not made happy by the cultivation of vice but by the cultivation of virtue

Legislation is a power delegated to certain men who are elected by the people, but such men have no right to do whatever they please in legislating, without respect to principle, and regardless of consequences. The power which is delegated to men elected does not give, then, a right to do wrong, but, rather, the right to make laws which will help the units or individuals to do right. What are legislators ? Purely and simply, they are the hired servants of the people, in the whole—not of the few and favored ones. What are their duties ? So to legislate as to promote "the greatest good of the greatest number." Legislators are not to create rights, but simply give protection and enforcement of rights. From a Divine law we get the right for protection to both person and property,which is bestowed upon all human kind, irrespective of race or sex. The duty of legislators is to protect, and not to create principle. Then laws should be made for the people, and not simply for the protection of a few mercenaries. They have no right to make laws to exalt one class and humble others, or to make one poor and the other rich. Then to carry out the legitimate end of pure legislation, we must have both positive and negative laws —laws which will prohibit, and laws to permit. These are the principles to which legislation is restricted. Therefore legislators should be the servants of the people, and not tools of political machines. Legislators should express, in a legal way, the wishes of the majority, and not give a listening ear to the corrupt minority. Let us use plain words. Legislators should at all times make laws which will insure and promote justice for the general welfare of all the people. If legislation is used for any other purpose than to direct the affairs of the people in the proper channel, it means to bring confusion in the body politic. With this idea as to how legislation shall be used, let us look into liquor legislation. The liquor traffic, from a law stand-point is a legitimate business. Legislation has put around it the arms of protection. By the act of a license law it has been made respectable, and to-day this vile traffic boasts of the money it pays towards the sustaining of the Government, and for this it demands that the people shall pay it homage and respect. The liquor-traffic to-day is securely protected behind the law. We wonder that its strength increases from day to day, and that it is now making threats toward the life of our country. This would not be so, were it not for the wicked law that makes it respectable. It is to-day before us as the one great mistake of legislation. Let us take from under it the pillows or props of legislation, and it will fall into a pit of shame. In examining this traffic, we find that it is not a public benefit or a blessing. Then for what reason should we make it such a special object of legislation? We know from the past that this traffic champions such vices as anarchy, brings confusion and produces poverty, and fills the prisons and almshouses with outcasts. Therefore instead of a permit for its life, let us have legislation to prohibit it, and use the legislative power to kill it.

Are tax-rates made any lighter because of its existence? Careful statisticians say that fully one half of the taxes are due to the liquor traffic. Take, for instance, the late murder trial in Toronto—how much did it cost the honest taxpayers to hang one man? Let every man enquire into this, and put the income of the Revenue on one side. Then the trial, conviction, wife and soul of the murderer on the other side—figure it out, and see who is the loser.

Is it right that the honest toiler should be compelled to support the victims of this unholy traffic. Again, can the legitimate manufacturers of this country point to the benefit that it is to their trade? It has always interfered

with the prospects of the manufacturers, because it produces idleness.   In large manufactures of the Dominion,
where hundreds of human beings are hutched together,
their safety depends upon the steady hand and clear
head of the engineer.   In most of the large manufacturing
establishments, the employees must be sober men, and
the drink of intoxicating liquor is prohibited.   Should
not this be a hint to the legislators to forever prohibit its
manufacture and sale.   Does it not prove that the
manufacturing establishments do not approve of the
liquor laws, in other words they prohibit that which the
legislature permits.   Now, which is wrong?   Where are
the benefits to the drinker?   Does it build fine houses
for him?   Does it put fine furniture into his home?   Does
it dress his wife and children?   Does it educate humanity
for God?   There can be only one answer to all these
questions—it does not.   Saloons are the seminaries of
vice and crime—saloons and free schools are open enemies.
Think that by legislation two kinds of schools are founded, one to educate up, the other to educate down.   In
this article we have shown that the traffic in liquor is an
injury to ratepayers, manufacturers, drinkers, church and
school   What is the gain to the man who sells rum?
On one side we have a few dollars, on the other he has
the loss of principle and the curses of the broken-hearted
mothers and starving children.   Woe unto him that
"putteth the bottle to his neighbor's lip, and maketh
him drunken also."   I have read much of late about the
amending of the present liquor laws.   The safest amendment for the good of all is—make liquor selling a crime,
put it on the calendar along with murder.   Instead of
protecting the man that sells, protect him that drinks
the cup of damning legislation; hold not the drinker of
rum responsible for the crimes he may commit under the
influence of drink, but hold those who legislate and make
laws responsible for the crimes that may follow from
their wrong legislation.

J. F. HESS.

# INDEX.

### CHAPTER I.


PAGE.

Birth—Parents—School-days—At work—First use of tobacco
—Running away from home—Return home—Father's advice
—Evil companions—First glass of Liquor—Losing employ-
er's confidence—Shipwrecked—Learns the "manly art"—
In prison—Delirium tremens.................................

### CHAPTER II.

Marriage—Housekeeping—Sixty days in Jail—A free fight—A
Father—A contractor—Mobbed—Attempted suicide—Refused admission to see my family—On the Mississippi—
—Gambling room—A perilous position—A sailor—Meeting
my family—Locates at St. Catharines—Next at Hamilton
—Residence in Toronto—Working for Gurney & Co.—Brakeman, Toronto to Belleville—First prize-fight—Father's death   17

### CHAPTER III.

Lost in the Michigan forests—Prize-fight—Returns to Toronto
—Sad condition of the family—Becomes coachman to Robert
Walker—Drunken spree and a smash-up—Goes to Whitby—
Work as a farmer—Forsakes his family—Life as bartender
and gambler—Assumes the name John Brooks—A bartender
—Meeting Frances E. Willard—Inebriate Asylum—The Far
West—Salt Lake City—City of Tents—A Stage trip through
Utah valley—Black Rock cañon—Great Sand Desert—Sil-
ver Reef—Tender feet—Row in a dance hall.....  .......   27

### CHAPTER IV.

Roaring Thunderbolt—Among the cowboys—Catching the Arizona mining fever—Some exciting experiences—Meeting a
hermit—A roll down the mountain side—The Mountain
Meadow massacre—Stage robbers—Sevier River—Bubbling
springs—*Pete* Nolan—A fight for a whiskey bottle—Prize

PAGE

fight with Nolan—Ninety-nine rounds with Trevelyn—Takes
passage for Australia—Returns from Europe—A varied experience as a saloon-keeper—Fight in a gambling-room—
Champion walker of Nebraska—Sparring *Billy* Madden—Forming a sparring troupe...................................... 39


## CHAPTER V.

Arrival in Milwaukee—Opens a sporting saloon—A chapter of
fights—Ryan & Sullivan's first appearance—Spar with Ryan
—Fight with Zowsta—Fight with Ward—Meeting "Jim"
Elliott—Wrestle with Primrose, Champion of Michigan—
Discovered to be *Joe Hess*—Returns to his family at Buffalo
—Opens the East Buffalo Gymnasium—Again comes to
Canada............................................................ 54


## CHAPTER VI.

Training "Billy" Baker—The process of training—The Baker-
Slattery prize-fight—The spectators—Arrest of the principals
—Bailed out—Description of the fight—Arrested as a participator—Taken to Rochester—Out on bail—At work in Bartholomay's brewery—Sending for my family—Starting a
gambling and boxing room—Roping in a *Sucker*—My last
glass—At P. A. Burdick's temperance meetings—Convicted
—Resolve to drink no more—First tempter, NO SIR—O
God ! help me —At church—Signing the pledge............. 64


## CHAPTER VII.

Now I love Papa—Joe Hess the temperance man—Let us Pray
—An errand boy—Funny experiences as a book agent—
Two baskets of provisions—My children at school—*Brother
Hess*—On the avenue—I will trust him—Moving—Wife,
this is our *new home*—A dinner party—Because I am a tem-
perance man.................. ..................... ......... 83


## CHAPTER VIII.

First attempt at speech-making—A failure—Rehearsing—A
call—An Audience of Five People—Large Audiences—Persecutions—Killed on the Railway—" I Signed the Pledge"—
" A Member of the M. E. Church"—Curious Introductions
—Fifty-seven cents.......................................... 95

## CHAPTER IX.

PAGE

"Taking up my pen "—Early lecture experiences -Story of a
tobacco pouch—A copper collection—Speech at P. A. Burdick's meeting—Attempt to murder Hess—Street insults—
"Shoot the orator"—Reformation of Drunkard "Bill"—
Opens a mission on Water street—Some lively incidents ... 103

## CHAPTER X.

Dissensions among the workers—Break up of the Water-st.
Mission—Difficulties in the pathway—Out of work—An overruling Providence--God takes care of His own—A remarkable experience—Some soul-stirring incidents in the work—
Influences that work against Temperance—What one saloon
did—A newspaper criticised .............................. 113

## CHAPTER XI.

Incidents of travel—Downfall of a promising young man—
Hess's politics—Slandered by a clergyman—A vigorous reply
"Making money out of temperance "—Some plain talk—A
happy Christmas and New Year—Buying coal by the ton,
not bushel— Confession of a drunkard.................... 123

## CHAPTER XII.

A three years' blank—A happy New Year's Day—Other New
Years—Cider and politics—No blood money for Joe—The
jealousy of singers—Joe and the school-teacher—Comes out
head—Encouraging words—Not all smooth sailing—The
Christian's prayer..................................... 130

## CHAPTER XIII.

An important point in Hess' history—Buys a home—The pleasantries of house-moving—Description of the new home—
Speaks for P. A. Burdick at Syracuse, N.Y.—Downfall of a
prosperous business man—Work among the children—A telling story of one man's reformation—The saloon in poetry.. 140

## CHAPTER XIV.

Half-hearted Christians—An interesting campaign in Lockport
—Talking temperance for money—First and last experience
as an orator—Syracuse by gas-light—Experience as a camp

PAGE

manager—Telling incidents—Hess' secret of success—First appearance at Graud Lodge I. O. G. T.— The high-license agitation in New York State ............................. 151


## CHAPTER XV.


" Consistency, thou art a jewel "—Injurious influences of inconsistent christians—Fighting for a woman's ballot—A lively scene—Sad stories of those who have suffered—The Evangelist, the confidant of the sorrowing—Hess visits Auburn State Prison—" What I saw behind prison walls "—Various lecturing trips—Au outline of the Brook's High License Law ......................................... 167


## CHAPTER XVI.


At Wellsboro', Pa.—Taken from the gutter—The Saloon Clock vs. The Home Clock—Campaign at Elbridge, N.Y.—Niagara Falls in Winter—How the iceberg struck Joe Hess—Eight days' meeting at Mohawk—Delegates to the Prohibition Convention—Something about tent work...................... 182


## CHAPTER XVII.


A chapter of tent work—Working for the Prohibition Party— Attempts to break up the meetings—The " Hoodlum " element of the old parties to the front—Letter of a Republican Prohibitionist—Delegate to the Prohibition Convention at Syracuse, N.Y.—An apt quotation from John Wesley— " Hess, Hess, Hess, come down quick "—Tent work in Pennsylvania ................................................... 191


## CHAPTER XVIII.


At Freemansburg, Pa.—Melodies of the Camp Ground—Home once more—Mamie a silver medalist—A great address by Hess—Meets Col. R. S. Cheves and Sam Small—Big country Meeting—Taken suddenly ill............................. 202


## CHAPTER XIX.


A continuation of tent campaign work—The start made at Apalachin, N.Y.—Chasing a slander—Attitude of the party press—A great meeting at Hickstown—Some appropriate quotations—Big success at Lockwood, N.Y.—A notable letter from Hon. Martin Jones of Rochester, N.Y............. 210

## CHAPTER XX.

PAGE

The idol of to-day—Work in Jersey City—Some cheering results—Speaks in Chickering Hall, New York—Visits the old
Washingtonian Home—Once an inmate himself—A graphic
description of 21 days' campaign in Evanston, Ill.—The home
of Miss Willard, as seen by Hess............. . ........ 218

## CHAPTER XXI.

A contrast—Joe " now " and " then "—Work in Peoria, Ill.—
Dick Corbett's fall—Hess and St. John—Voluntary and valuable testimony—Paying for the Home—In the Pennsylvania
amendment fight................................. ..... 228

## CHAPTER XXII.

An invitation to take Canada—Starts for London—Feeble
hands and weak knees—Clifton and Niagara Falls—A hod-
carrier in St. Catharines—Work in London—Testimony for
anti-Scott Act men—Chased home with boils and grippe—
Miss Cleveland's eloquent reply to Dr. Howard Crosby..... 238

## CHAPTER XXIII.

Temperance campaign in Toronto—Enters the work with many
doubts—Reception by officers Canadian Temperance League
—Preaches in Carlton-street Methodist Church—The opening meeting in the Pavilion—Afternoon Bible readings—
Witnesses some sad scenes—Wedding anniversary and presentation— At H. C. Dixon's free breakfast—The Lombard-
street Mission—A captivating chapter.................... 249

## CHAPTER XXIV.

At home for a few days—Talks at Niagara Falls—Origin of the
famous " Palace " illustration—At West Toronto Junction—
Wonderful record at Peterboro'—The Dan-Hess slander suit
—A week at Bowmanville—The town badly shaken up—Incidents of the work—Goes to London—" Yes, that's John
Brooks "—Pays his old debts—1,000 pledge signers—Sunday
spent in Toronto......................................... 261

## CHAPTER XXV.

Drunken travellers—Meetings in Forest—Second campaign in
Peterboro'—"Hold on Joe, I am coming "—A grateful letter

PAGE

— A great work in Belleville—Visits the Deaf and Dumb Institute—At Picton—Young men who refused to sign the
pledge—Work at Port Perry—With Lou J. Beauchamp—
Sketchy account of the campaign in Cobourg, Brantford and
Gananoque.................................................... 269

## CHAPTER XXVI.

The last Chapter—Bobcaygeon—A notable campaign here—
Rum-cursed Fenelon Falls—A week at Seaforth—Its noble
workers— Free Methodist camp meeting at Uxbridge—"How
they jumped and hollered "—Enterprising Aylmer—Only 20
houses and grand meetings at Enniskillen—Review of the
work in Canada—Closing words.......................... 275

## ADDENDA.

Speeches and newspaper contributions..................... 281

www.ingramcontent.com/pod-product-compliance
Lightning Source LLC
Chambersburg PA
CBHW031025120726
47905CB00007B/2039